ORTHOGONAL : BOOK ONE

THE CLOCKWORK ROCKET

Other books by Greg Egan:

ORTHOGONAL : BOOK ONE

THE CLOCKWORK ROCKET

WITHDRAWN

GREG EGAN

NIGHT SHADE BOOKS
San Francisco

First Edition

ISBN: 978-1-59780-227-7

Night Shade Books
Please visit us on the web at
http://www.nightshadebooks.com

CONTENTS

BOOK ONE:
THE CLOCKWORK ROCKET

1

When Yalda was almost three years old, she was entrusted with the task of bearing her grandfather into the forest to convalesce.

Dario had been weak and listless for days, refusing to move from the flower bed where the family slept. Yalda had seen him this way before, but it had never lasted so long. Her father had sent word to the village, and when Doctor Livia came to the farm to examine Dario Yalda and two of her cousins, Claudia and Claudio, stayed close to watch the proceedings.

After squeezing and prodding the old man all over with more hands than most people used in a day, Doctor Livia announced her diagnosis. "You're suffering from a serious light deficiency. The crops here are virtually monochromatic; your body needs a broader spectrum of illumination."

"Ever heard of sunlight?" Dario replied caustically.

"Sunlight is far too blue," Doctor Livia countered, "too fast for the body to catch. And the light from the fields is all sluggish red. What you're lacking lies between those extremes; a man of your age needs umber and gamboge, saffron and goldenrod, jade and viridian."

"We have all those hues right here! Have you ever seen such glorious specimens?" Dario, who'd taken to resting limbless, budded a lone finger from the middle of his chest to gesture at the garden around them. Yalda, whose job it was to tend the flower bed, warmed with pride, though the blossoms he was praising were closed for the day, their luminescent petals furled and dormant.

"Those plants are merely decorative," Doctor Livia replied dismissively. "You need a full range of natural light, at much greater intensity. You need to spend four or five nights in the forest."

When the doctor had left, Yalda's father, Vito, and her uncle, Giusto, talked the matter over with her grandfather.

"It sounds like quackery to me," Dario declared, snuggling deeper into

1

his indentation in the soil. "'Umber and gamboge'! I've survived for two dozen and seven years with sunlight, wheatlight and a few floral adornments. There's nothing healthier than farm life."

"Everyone's body changes," Vito said cautiously. "There must be a reason you're so tired."

"Years of hard work?" Dario suggested. "Or don't you think I've earned a rest?"

Giusto said, "I've seen you shining yellow at night. If you're losing that hue, what's putting it back?"

"Yalda should have planted more goldenrod!" Claudio blurted out accusingly. Giusto shushed him, but Claudia and Claudio exchanged knowing glances, as if they were the doctors now and they'd finally exposed the root of the problem. Yalda told herself that it was only an adult's admonition that meant anything, but her older cousins' smug delight in her supposed failure still stung.

Vito said, "I'll go with you to the forest. If the doctor's right, it will give you back your health. And if she's wrong, what harm can it do?"

"What harm?" Dario was incredulous. "I don't have the strength for a twelfth of that journey, and I doubt you could carry me even halfway. It would finish us both off!"

Vito's tympanum became rigid with annoyance, but Yalda suspected that her grandfather was right. Her father was strong, but Dario had always been the heavier of the two and his illness hadn't changed that. Yalda had never even glimpsed the forest, but she knew it was farther than the village, farther than anywhere she'd been. If there had been a chance of hitching a ride on a truck then someone would have raised the possibility, but the route must have been so rarely traveled as to make that an unlikely prospect.

In the awkward silence that followed, Giusto's rear gaze fell on Yalda. For a moment she thought he was merely acknowledging her presence with a friendly glance, but then she understood why she was suddenly worthy of attention in the midst of this serious, adult debate.

"I know who could carry you, Father!" Giusto announced happily. "There and back, with no trouble at all."

The next day, the whole family woke before dawn to help the three travelers prepare. By the soft red light of the fields around them, Lucia and Lucio, Yalda's brother and sister, darted back and forth from the store-holes, packing provisions for the journey into the generous pouches that their father had formed along his sides. Claudia and Claudio tended to Dario, helping him rise and eat breakfast then taking him by the shoulders and walking him around the clearing to prepare his body for the long ride.

Yalda's other cousins, Aurelia and Aurelio, acted as stand-ins for Yalda's passenger as Uncle Giusto coached her on her quadrupedal posture. "Make your front legs a bit longer," he suggested. "Your grandfather will need somewhere to rest his head, so it would be good if your back sloped higher." Yalda extruded more flesh into her two front limbs; for a moment her legs wobbled beneath her cousins' weight, but she managed to stiffen them before she lost her balance. She waited until she felt the central shafts harden and the old joints ossify, then she cracked a new pair of knees higher up and re-organized the surrounding muscles. The last part was the most mysterious to her; all she was conscious of was a sense of pressure moving down her limbs and imposing order, as if her flesh were a bundle of reeds being passed through a comb to rid it of tangles. But her muscles weren't merely straightening themselves out; they were making sense of their new surroundings and preparing for the new tasks that would be demanded of them.

Giusto said, "Try a few steps now."

Yalda moved forward tentatively, then broke into a slow trot. Aurelia kicked her sides and shouted, "Yah! Yah!"

"Stop it, or I'll throw you!" Yalda warned her.

Aurelio joined her in rebuking his co. "Yeah, stop it! *I'm* the driver."

"No you're not," Aurelia retorted. "I'm in front!"

"Then I should be in front." He grabbed Aurelia and tried to swap places with her. Yalda quashed her irritation at her squirming cousins and decided to treat it all as good practice; if she could keep her footing while these idiots sprouted arms just to wrestle with each other, she ought to be able to manage anything her ailing grandfather did.

"You're doing well, Yalda," Giusto called to her encouragingly.

"For a giant lump," whispered Aurelia.

"Don't be cruel!" Aurelio said, pinching her on the neck.

Yalda said nothing. Perhaps she was graceless compared to Aurelia, two years her senior—or even compared to her own brother and sister—but she was stronger than anyone else in the family, and the only one who could carry Dario into the forest.

She trotted to the edge of the clearing, where the wheat-flowers were starting to close. She couldn't see the sun itself yet, but brightness was spreading across the eastern sky. Dawn brought so many changes at once that Yalda had had to watch the flowers furling several times before she'd convinced herself that their petals really did grow dimmer, and weren't just being outshone as they curled in on themselves for the day.

"How do they know that they should stop making light?" she wondered.

Aurelia buzzed with amusement. "Because the sun's coming up?"

"But how do they *know that*?" Yalda persisted. "Plants don't have eyes, do they?"

"They probably feel the heat," Aurelio suggested.

Yalda didn't think the temperature had risen all that sharply. Yet the whole field had grown dim as they were speaking, the night's glorious red blossoms reduced to pale gray sacs hanging limply from their stalks.

She walked back toward Giusto, still pondering the question, remembering too late that she'd meant to race all the way to demonstrate her confidence in her new anatomy. Her father approached, on four legs too, Lucia and Lucio fussing at his pouches as they tried to even out the load.

"I think we're ready," Vito said. "Scram, you two!" Aurelio leaped off Yalda's back, rolling into a tight ball as he hit the ground; his co followed, shouting triumphantly as she landed on top of him.

Dario was still not walking unaided, and he was muttering to his helpers about everyone crawling back into the ground and declaring a day of rest. Yalda was untroubled by this; if he didn't believe she could carry him safely he wouldn't even have risen, let alone cooperated as much as he had. Claudia and Claudio brought him over to her, and she knelt down on her rear legs to enable him to climb onto her back. He hadn't bothered with arms before, but now he extruded three pairs, his chubby torso growing visibly thinner as the six ropy limbs stretched out to encircle her. Yalda was fascinated by the texture of his skin; the bulk of it appeared as elastic as her own, but scattered across the smooth expanse were countless small patches that had grown hard and unyielding. The skin around them was wrinkled and puckered, unable to spread out evenly.

"Are you comfortable?" Vito asked him. Dario emitted a brief, drab hum suggesting a burden borne without complaint. Vito turned to Yalda. "And you?"

"This is easy!" she proclaimed. She rose up and began promenading around her assembled family. Dario was heavier than the two of his grandchildren combined, but Yalda was untroubled by the load, and increasingly sure-footed in her new form. Giusto had chosen her shape well; as she peered down at Dario he lowered his head and rested it between her shoulders. Even if his grip loosened he could probably doze off without falling, but she would watch over him every step of the way.

Lucia called out to her, "Well done, Yalda!"

After a moment Lucio added, "Yeah, well done!"

A strange, sweet thrill ran through Yalda's body. She was not the useless lump anymore, eating as much as any two children, clumsy as an infant half her age. If she could do this simple thing for her grandfather, she would finally have earned her place in the family.

With the sun clearing the horizon and a cool breeze blowing from the east, Yalda followed her father down the narrow path that ran south between the fields. Though the wheat had lost its nocturnal splendor, the fat yellow seed cases near the tops of the stalks always attracted more interest from adults than the delicate hues of the crop's floral light—and when they came across two of their neighbors, Massima and Massimo, out baiting vole burrows, the talk was of nothing else. Yalda stood patiently, motionless save for the quivering required to send alighting insects on their way, ignored by everyone as they voiced their hopes for the coming harvest.

When the three of them had moved on, Dario noted disapprovingly, "Still no children! What's happening with them?"

"That's none of our business," Vito replied.

"It's unnatural!"

Vito was silent for a while. Then he said, "Perhaps his thoughts are still of her."

"A man should think of his children," Dario replied.

"And a woman?"

"A woman should think of them too." Dario noticed Yalda's rear gaze on him. "You concentrate on the road!" he commanded, as if that were sufficient to render the conversation private.

Yalda obeyed him, shifting her gaze to make him less self-conscious, then waited for the gossip to continue.

But Vito said firmly, "Enough! It's not our concern."

The path ended at a junction. To the right, the road led straight to the village, but they took the opposite turn. Yalda had set out this way many times before—playing, exploring, visiting friends—but she had never gone far. When she went west, it didn't take long to notice the changes: soon the crossroads were spaced closer together, other people were passing her, and she could hear trucks chugging between the fields even if she couldn't see them. The welcoming bustle of the village reached out and made itself felt long before you actually arrived. Traveling east was different: the same quiet and solitude with which you began the journey promised to stretch on forever. Had she been alone, the prospect of spending an entire day walking away from every familiar sign of life would have terrified her. As it was, she felt a desolate ache at the sight of the rising sun ahead of her, with the realization that even when it set she would still be heading in the same direction.

Yalda looked toward her father. He said nothing, but he met her gaze reassuringly, quelling her fears. She glanced down at Dario, but his eyes were closed; he'd drifted back to sleep already.

They passed the morning trudging through farmland, surrounded by fields so similar that Yalda was driven to hunt for patterns in the pebbles by the roadside just to prove to herself that they really were making progress. The idea that they might have lost their way and circled back was fanciful—the road was straight, and they'd been following the sun—but spotting these private signposts made a welcome diversion.

Around noon, Vito roused Dario. They turned off the road and sat in the straw at the edge of a stranger's field. Yalda could hear nothing but the wind moving through the crop and the faint hum of insects. Vito produced three loaves and Yalda offered one to Dario, who remained on her back; for a moment he appeared to be preparing to make a new limb for the occasion, but then the tentative bud on his shoulder disappeared and he used an existing hand to take the food.

"Have you ever been in the forest before?" Yalda asked him.

"A long time ago."

"Why were you there? Was someone sick?"

"No!" Dario was scornful; he might be willing to play along with Doctor Livia's ideas just to keep his family happy, but no one would have countenanced such nonsense in the past. "The forest was closer then."

"Closer?" Yalda didn't understand.

"Bigger," Dario explained. "Some of these fields weren't fields back then. When we weren't busy with our own work, we used to help clear new fields, at the forest's edge."

Yalda turned to Vito. "Did you go too?"

"No," he replied.

Dario said, "Your father wasn't around then. This was in your grandmother's time."

"Oh." Yalda tried to imagine Dario as a vigorous young man, plucking trees right out of the ground, her grandmother working beside him. "So the forest reached out to where we are now?"

"At least," Dario said. "The trip only took us half a morning. But then, we weren't carrying anyone on our backs."

They finished their loaves. The sun had passed its highest point; Yalda could see their shadows slanting to the east. Vito said, "We should get moving again."

As they set off down the road, Yalda kept her rear eyes on Dario to be sure that his grip didn't falter. She could always wrap him in arms of her own, if necessary. But though he appeared a little drowsy from the meal, his eyes remained open.

"The forest was different in the old days," he said. "Wilder. More dangerous."

Yalda was intrigued. "Dangerous?"

Vito said, "Don't frighten her."

Dario buzzed dismissively. "There's nothing to be frightened of now; nobody's seen an arborine for years."

"What's an arborine?" Yalda asked.

Dario said, "Remember the story of Amata and Amato?"

"I never heard that one," she replied. "You never told it to me."

"I didn't? It must have been your cousins."

Yalda wasn't sure whether Dario was teasing her or if he was genuinely confused. She waited until he asked innocently, "So would you like to hear it?"

"Of course!"

Vito interjected a hum of disapproval, but Yalda gazed at him pleadingly until it decayed into a reluctant murmur of acquiescence. How could she be too young to hear a story that her cousins had been told, when she was the one carrying its teller to the forest on her back, not them?

"At the end of the seventh age," Dario began, "the world was gripped by a terrible famine. The crops were withering in the ground, and food was so scarce that instead of four children, every family had just two.

"Amata and Amato were two such children, and doubly precious to their father, Azelio, because of it. Whatever food he could scrounge went first to his children, and he would only eat when they swore that they were satisfied.

"Azelio was a good man, but he paid a high price for it: one morning he woke to find that he'd gone blind. He had sacrificed his sight to feed his children, so how could he find food for them now?

"When his daughter Amata saw what had happened, she told Azelio to rest. She said, 'I will go with my co into the forest, and bring back enough seeds for all of us.' The children were young and Azelio didn't want to be parted from them, but he had no choice.

"The forest wasn't far, but the plants closest to the edge had been stripped bare long ago. Amata and Amato kept going deeper, hunting for the food that no one else had reached.

"After six days, they came to a place where no man or woman had been before. The branches of the trees were so close together that it was impossible to see the sun, and the flowers shone without rest, day and night. The wild mother of wheat still grew there, and Amata and Amato filled pouches with its seeds, eating enough to keep up their strength, but determined to bring back sufficient food to restore their father's sight.

"Above them, in the trees, the arborine was watching. He had never seen creatures like this before, and it filled him with rage to see them come into his garden and steal his food.

"Amata and Amato gathered all the seeds they could hope to carry, but they were weak from their journey so they decided to rest before setting back for the farm. They hollowed out spaces in the soil and lay down to sleep.

"Like the flowers around him, the arborine never slept, so for a long time he didn't understand the intruders' condition. But when he finally realized that they were blind to the world, he crawled onto a branch above them and reached down to wrap his arms around Amata.

"In his anger, though, he'd misjudged his strength; lifting her up wasn't easy. Amata was halfway into the trees when she woke, and the arborine's grip faltered. She fought him and broke free, falling to the ground.

"When she hit the ground she was too stunned to move, but she called out to her co to flee. He rose to his feet and began to run, but the arborine was faster, darting from branch to branch above him. When Amato tripped on the root of a tree, the arborine reached down and took him. Unlike Amata, the boy was light enough to lift... and small enough to swallow."

Dario hesitated. "It's not too frightening for you?" he asked.

Yalda was squirming inside at the scene he'd described, but she suspected that Dario was merely making fun of Vito's qualms. She gazed down at him as calmly as she could and replied, "Not at all. Please go on."

"Amata was mad with grief," Dario continued, "but there was nothing she could do. She ran through the forest, trying to imagine what she would tell her father. He had lost his sight to save their lives; this news would kill him.

"Then Amata's way was blocked by a fallen branch, and an idea came to her. She smashed two rocks together until she had a shard sharp enough to cut the wood. And she carved the branch into the shape of Amato.

"When she reached the farm, she dropped all the seeds she'd gathered on the ground in front of her father, and he rejoiced at the sound. Then she told him, 'Amato is sick from his travels; as you lost your sight, he has lost the power of speech. But in time, with rest and food, you will both recover.'

"Azelio was filled with sadness, but when he touched his son's shoulders the boy still felt strong, so he tried to stay hopeful.

"In the days that followed, they feasted on half the seed, and Azelio took Amata's word that both his children were sated before he ate. Amata planted the rest of the seed in their fields, and it began to grow. With her strength restored, she managed to gather more food from the edge of the forest, and the two of them saw out the famine.

"Azelio's sight did not return, but he was reconciled to that. What he could not accept was Amato's unbroken silence.

"The years passed, and finally Azelio said, 'It's time I had grandchildren.' In the hope of provoking a response from his son he added, 'Do you have the power to make that happen, Amato, or will your co have to do everything herself?'

"Of course there was no reply, and Amata didn't know how she could keep hiding the truth from her father.

"For twelve days, Amata worked hard to fill every store-hole with food, until there was enough put away for her father to survive for a year. Then, while he was sleeping, she walked away from the farm. She had decided to live in the forest, alone, and only return in secret to replenish the stores."

Yalda couldn't help herself now; her whole body shivered with anguish. It wasn't Amata's fault that her co had died. What was happening to her was so unfair.

"One night in the forest," Dario continued, "Amata looked up into the trees and saw the arborine darting from branch to branch. She had grown into a powerful woman, and the fearsome creature that had taken her co looked much more weak and vulnerable now.

"Day and night she watched the arborine, studying its ways. The arborine watched her too, but when it saw that she was doing nothing to take revenge, it grew complacent.

"After a while, Amata made a plan. She dug a nest in the ground, and filled it with four small, carved wooden figures. Then she hid beside the nest and waited.

"When the arborine saw the nest and what it thought were Amata's children, it couldn't help itself: it reached down to grab one and take it up into the trees. But Amata had bound the figures to heavy rocks beneath the soil, and covered them with sticky resin. The arborine was trapped, pinned against a branch of the tree by its own two arms that stretched down to the ground.

"Amata climbed up into the tree, and with the shard of stone she'd used to carve the wood, she sliced the arborine's arms off. As it tried to grow more limbs to fight her, she leaped on it, spread her mouth wide, and swallowed it whole, just as it had swallowed her co.

"When she jumped back to the ground, Amata felt sick, but she forced herself to keep the arborine inside her. She lay down and tried to sleep, but her body was racked by fevers and trembling. After a time, she lost control of her shape: flesh was flowing this way and that, with strange new limbs growing and retreating before her eyes. Amata was sure that the arborine was fighting her from within, so she found the shard again and prepared to cut off its head as soon as it showed itself.

"Sure enough, a head budded from her chest, and its four eyes opened. Amata raised the shard and began to bring it down, but then a voice said, 'Don't you recognize me?' The head was Amato's; he had survived inside the arborine all this time, waiting to grow strong enough to fight his way out.

"Amata calmed herself, gathered all her strength, and pushed the flesh of her co to one side of her body until nothing joined them but a narrow tube of skin, thinner than a finger. Then she brought down the shard and severed it, setting Amato free.

"They walked out of the forest and back to the farm, where they told Azelio the truth of what had happened. He rejoiced at the sound of his son's voice, and forgave his daughter for deceiving him.

"In time, Azelio was blessed with four grandchildren, and though he never regained his sight he did all he could to help raise them, and in turn they gave him ease and comfort in his old age."

As Dario fell silent, Yalda struggled to compose herself. She couldn't stop her passenger feeling the unsteadiness in her gait, but she still had a chance to appear impassive to her father, to show him that she could take this gut-wrenching tale in her stride.

The story hadn't left her fearful of their destination; she was prepared to be vigilant in the forest, but even if there were arborines still living there a creature that struggled to lift an ordinary girl would have no hope of abducting the giant lump.

What unsettled her more was the question: *What if Amato hadn't been rescued? What if Amata had remained alone?* In the story there'd been a magical way to fix everything, but Yalda couldn't help wondering: how would Amata have lived her life, if her co had been truly, irrevocably dead?

Late in the afternoon they came across two young farmers, Bruna and Bruno, heading into the village. Though no one in the family had met them before, after chatting for a while Dario discovered that he'd known their grandfather's brother. Yalda didn't envy them their long trip; it was one thing to walk this far as an occasional adventure, but to fetch routine supplies it would soon become tedious. If there'd been a truck running the length of the road every few days, from the village to the forest and back, everyone's life would have been simpler. But the trucks only came out here to collect the harvest.

They stopped to eat again just before sunset. The wheat fields still stretched out around them as far as Yalda could see, but the road they'd been following since the start of their journey had begun to meander slightly, and its surface had grown uneven. It was enough to puncture the numbing sense of repetition Yalda had felt when they'd first set out, but it was as hard as ever to believe that the fields would come to an end, and that they really were heading out into the wilderness.

"It's not too much farther," Vito promised. "We could stop and sleep here, but that would cost us a night in the forest." Yalda understood: the whole point was to give Dario the benefit of the wild plants' light, so delaying their arrival until morning would be a terrible waste.

When they took to the road again Dario soon dozed off. Once Yalda had convinced herself that he was holding onto her securely, she lifted her rear gaze to watch the stars come out. The trails of light that emerged were like multicolored worms struggling across the deepening blackness—though they appeared to be struggling in vain, swept across the sky in a slow whirl but coming no closer to their destinations.

"If the stars are so far away," she said, "that the red light reaches us after the violet… why do their trails all point in different directions?"

"Because they're moving in different directions," Vito replied.

"But they're not!" Yalda protested. "They're all rising in the east and setting in the west."

"Ah." Vito managed to sound both amused and pleased—as if her question was foolish, but welcome nonetheless. "When the stars rise and set, that's the world turning, not the motion of the stars themselves."

"I know." He had explained the turning of the world to her before, and Yalda hadn't forgotten. "But what's the difference? If the violet light reaches us first… and the world turns while we're waiting for the red light to catch up… shouldn't *that* spread the colors across the sky?"

Vito said, "I think you've answered your own question. You can see that the trails aren't lined up east to west."

"Then I don't understood anything," Yalda declared forlornly.

Vito buzzed gentle mockery at her melodramatic verdict. "You understand a lot," he said. "You just have to think things through a bit more carefully."

Encouraged, Yalda searched the sky for more clues, but instead of receiving any revelatory insight she merely recalled another source of puzzlement. "The sun has no trail," she complained.

"Exactly!" Vito replied. "It can't be the turning of the world that makes the trails, or the sun would have one too."

Yalda closed her rear eyes and tried to picture what was happening. Never mind the stars; if red light was so sluggish, how could the sun cross the sky *without* leaving a smudge of red in its wake, forever lagging behind the swifter greens and blues? "Doctor Livia said sunlight is too blue. So does it have no red or green in it at all?"

"No, it has them," Vito insisted. "Blue is strongest in sunlight, but it has about as much of the other colors as the stars do."

"Hmm." Yalda imagined the sun as a blazing blue-white disk, and the world as a cool, gray circle off to one side, slowly turning. "Light flies out from the sun, with two colors, red and violet, starting the journey side by side. But as surely as Lucia will beat Lucio in a race, the violet light will strike home first—and then the world will turn a little, moving the sun across the sky before the red light arrives. *So why aren't the colors spread out?*"

Vito said, "You just described a single flash of light leaving the sun. But the sun doesn't flash, does it? It's always shining."

Yalda was bursting out of her skin with frustration. "Then how does it work? How does it make sense?"

Vito said, "Pick a star trail, and tell me exactly what you see."

Yalda opened her rear eyes and complied, forcing herself to speak calmly. "I see a faint line of light. It's violet at one end, then along its length it changes to blue, then green, then yellow, then red."

"And are you seeing these colors at different times," Vito pressed her, "or are you seeing them all at once?"

"All at once. *Oh!*" Her father's simple question had thrown her old mental image into disarray. She'd been picturing red and violet light arriving at different times, but apart from reasoning that the sun would move across the sky in the interim, she'd ignored the timing completely, blurring the two events into something she expected to see in the same instant. "I have to think about what I *see* at one moment," she said, "not about the light that leaves the sun at one moment."

"Yes," Vito said. "Go on."

"But how does that change things?" Yalda wondered. "If I see red light and violet light at the same time… then the slower, red light must have left the sun earlier."

"Right. So how does that affect what you see?"

Yalda struggled to picture it. "Where the sun is in the sky depends on which way the world is facing *when the light arrives*, not when it left. The red light left earlier, but that makes no difference—we just see whatever reaches us at the time we're looking. So we see all the sun's colors in the same place, not spread out in a trail."

Vito's rear eyes widened with approval. "That wasn't too difficult, was it?"

Yalda was encouraged, but still far from confident that everything made sense. "And the stars? Why are they so different?"

"The stars are really moving," Vito reminded her. "Not just rising and setting with the turning of the world. Between the time when *the red light we're seeing now* left a star, and the time when *the violet light we're seeing now* followed it, the star will have moved far enough for us to see the different colors coming from different directions. When we look at the sun, the violet light and the red light follow the same road, even though the red light begins the journey earlier. When we look at a star, the violet light's coming to us from a different place, along a different path than the red."

Yalda turned this over in her mind. "If the stars are really moving," she said, "then why don't we see them move?" The colored worms were all pinned to the rigid black sky, sharing, but never exceeding, the illusory motion that came from the world's shifting gaze. Why didn't they advance along their own trails, wriggling out of their constellations into fresh new patterns every night?

Vito said, "The stars are moving quickly, but they're very far away. Even with a keen eye and a perfect memory, it would take us a lifetime to notice any change. But we're lucky, we don't have to wait that long. Some light trails show us in a single glance what happened over many generations."

The red light from the fields around them lit the way now. The familiar glow made Yalda sleepy, though the strength in her limbs was holding out well enough. If Dario could cling to her as he dozed, lost to the world but still disciplined enough not to slacken his grip, maybe she could close her own eyes and sleepwalk down the road. If only Vito had brought a rope to put around her shoulders and guide her steps, it might not have been a bad idea.

When she saw the lavish jumble of colors ahead, Yalda wondered if she was fully awake. Vito's body was partly blocking her view, and the strange apparition jittered around him, revealed and hidden in turn by the rhythm of their steps and the undulations of the road.

The road came to an end. They walked across scrubland strewn with the kind of weeds and low bushes that Yalda spent most of her days uprooting. The plants' tiny flowers shone up at her from around her feet, but the browns and yellows that, back on the farm, marked tiresome blemishes spoiling the wheat's pure light struck her very differently now. She stepped around them gingerly, no more willing to crush them than she would have dared trample a neighbor's crop.

The nearest trees weren't tall, and though it was hard to be sure in the unfamiliar setting Yalda thought she'd seen their like in uncultivated corners of the farm, or lining the streets of the village. They might have been sisters to the scrub plants; their muted colors were much the same. Behind them, though, exotic giants loomed, strewn with blossoms of every hue.

Dario stirred and opened his eyes. Yalda expected him to mutter some complaint about the lengths to which they'd gone for the sake of quackery, but instead he gazed up at the lights in thoughtful silence. Perhaps he was lost in reverie, drawn back to memories of his youthful adventures with Daria.

Yalda followed Vito into the forest. The undergrowth soon became too thick for her to avoid treading on the smaller plants, and she had no choice but to keep her soles as hard as she'd made them for the pebble-strewn road; if she'd softened her feet, as she did when she worked in the flower bed, the sharper stems would have lacerated her skin in no time.

She kept her front gaze locked to the ground, measuring every step, but after a while she grew confident enough to lift her rear eyes from her passenger toward the festooned branches above. Flowers wider than her shoulders shone up into the darkness, their violet petals draped across a network of supporting vines; she could not see their light directly, but the glow seeping through each petal's underside was bright enough to cast shadows. Around these monsters, smaller blooms in shades of orange, green and yellow crowded every branch and twig.

When they passed through a swarm of mites, Dario shuddered and cursed; Yalda could shake off the insects herself with barely a thought, but her grandfather's skin was not so fast to unseat them. He unwrapped two of his arms from around her torso and began to flail at the creatures, stretching the stubby fingers that had locked his hands together into broad fans better suited to sweeping the nuisance away.

As they threaded their way between the trees, the violet behemoths overhead gave way to a kind of cousin, slightly smaller, with intense green flowers sprouting from the vines that had previously been bare. Some of these faced down into the undergrowth, dazzling the travelers; others were turned toward the sky. Yalda tried to picture how the forest would appear from high above the trees, a giant's flower bed beside the staid red wheat fields.

Vito stopped and looked around. They'd reached a small clearing where the flowers were as bright and varied as Doctor Livia could have wished, while the trees were not too closely spaced nor the undergrowth too tangled. If the forest held a better place to spend the night they could have searched until dawn before finding it.

Vito addressed his father. "What do you think?"

"This will do." Dario turned to Yalda. "No arborines here, I promise."

"They don't frighten me," she said.

When Dario had climbed down, Yalda began resorbing the top halves of her long front legs. She was too tired to think carefully about her shape, but all it really took to regain her old posture was a forceful renunciation of the wariness she'd cultivated during the trip, when relaxing back to normality would have sent her grandfather sprawling onto the road.

Vito emptied his pouches onto the ground and made himself bipedal too, then he and Yalda worked together to dig spaces for the three of them to sleep. The roots of the plants ran deep, and Yalda's fingers had to bifurcate three or four times to slip into the soil alongside them and prise the whole mass loose; still, with her father helping the whole task was not too daunting. The worms whose homes she was wrecking were fatter and feistier than those she was used to, and after realizing that they weren't simply going to flee from her touch she started flinging them away across the clearing.

By the time the three indentations were ready, Yalda was almost asleep on her feet. As Dario waddled toward his bed on two short legs—the only limbs he was now sporting—he turned to Yalda. "Thanks for bringing me here, Vita. You did a good job."

Yalda didn't correct him; whatever was going through his mind, he'd managed to make the compliment sound sincere. Vito shared a glance with her that she took to express amused concurrence with Dario's sentiment, then he bid her goodnight.

Yalda was exhausted, but she stood for a while beside her grandfather, gazing down at his sleeping form. Giusto had claimed that he'd seen Dario glowing yellow at night. If they wanted to judge the efficacy of Doctor Livia's cure, shouldn't they check for this symptom, both now and when they returned? Yalda had noticed that she cast a multitude of shadows, so she'd hoped to see how Dario appeared from within them—but alas, none was deep enough to reveal what light, if any, was emerging from his skin. Wherever she stood, she couldn't shield him from every flower at once and observe the luminosity of his body alone.

It was frustrating, but as she gave up and crawled into bed, Yalda thought of the bright side. If any light emerging from Dario's skin was so faint that it was hidden by the forest's glare, surely that meant that whatever hue he'd been losing back on the farm was now being replenished faster than it was leaking away.

She wriggled deeper into the cool soil, squashing a few worms who'd escaped her earlier evictions, and gazed up into the violet backlight. She thought about the arborine—skulking along the branches somewhere, angrier than the worms—but if he came for her in the night she'd been forewarned. And if he snatched the men, smaller morsels that they were, she'd forego Amata's tortuous history of guilt and redemption and just cut them free first thing in the morning.

To Yalda's delight, the forest by day did show some fidelity to Dario's story: many of the smaller flowers in the undergrowth, shielded from sunlight by the canopy of branches, really did retain their radiance.

Most of the clearing, though, was not entirely sheltered from the sky. With the violet flowers curled up into crumpled sacs, sunlight spilled through the net of vines that had supported their outstretched petals, mottling the ground with brightness.

After breakfast, Yalda dug storage holes for the loaves they'd brought, and Vito used some of the groundflower petals in which they'd been wrapped as lining. Yalda didn't trust the worms here to obey the usual rules, but her father assured her that the pungent scent of the petals would keep any vermin away.

Once that job was finished, Yalda had nothing left to do but gaze into the forest. It was a strange situation; if she'd been moping around on the farm Vito would have quickly found her a task, and if there'd been no work at all her cousins and siblings would have dragged her into some game or other with their usual boisterous energy.

At noon, Vito brought out three more loaves. Dario remained half-buried as he ate, emitting unselfconscious chirps of pleasure. Yalda stood watching the slight movements of the branches around her, trying to unravel their causes. Over the course of the morning, she had learned to tell the difference between the swaying motion brought on by the wind, which was shared by many branches at once, and the trembling of a single branch when a small lizard ran along it. Sometimes she could even spot the successive rebounds when a lizard launched itself from one branch and landed on another.

"What do lizards eat?" Yalda asked Vito.

"Insects, maybe," he replied. "I'm not sure."

Yalda contemplated the second part of his reply. How could he not be sure? Were there things about the world that adults didn't know? Dario offered no verdict on the lizards' diet, and though he might just have been too preoccupied to bother, Yalda was beginning to wonder if she'd misunderstood something important. She'd thought that every adult's role was to instruct their children and answer their questions, until the children knew all there was to know—by which time they were adults too. But if some answers weren't passed down from generation to generation, where did they come from?

Judging that it would be impolite to probe the extent of Dario's knowledge in his hearing, Yalda waited until he had dozed off again.

"Who taught you about the stars?" she asked Vito. "All those things you were telling me last night?" She had never heard Dario speak about the origin of the color trails.

Vito said, "I learned that from your mother."

"Oh!" Yalda was astonished; how could you learn anything from someone your own age? "But who taught it to her?"

"She had a friend, a girl named Clara." Vito spoke slowly, as if the subject required some special effort to address. "Clara went to school. She'd tell your mother about the things she'd learned, and then your mother would explain them to me."

Yalda knew there was a school in the village, but she'd always thought its purpose was to train people for unfamiliar jobs, not to answer their questions about the stars.

"I wish I could have met her," she said.

"Clara?"

"My mother."

Vito said wryly, "That's like wishing you could fly."

Yalda had heard the phrase before, but now it struck her as an odd choice for the epitome of unattainability. "What if we stretched our arms wide, like a mite's wings—"

"People have tried that," Vito assured her. "We're too heavy, and too weak; it just doesn't work."

"Oh." Yalda returned to the subject of her mother. "What else did she teach you?"

Vito had to think about that. "A little bit of writing. But I'm not sure I remember much."

"Show me! Please!" Yalda wasn't sure what the point of writing was, but the prospect of seeing her own father perform the elaborate trick was irresistible.

Vito did resist, but not for long. "I'll try," he said. "But you'll need to be patient with me."

He stood for a while, silent and motionless. Then the skin of his chest began to tremble, as if he were shooing off insects, and Yalda noticed some strange, curved ridges starting to appear. They weren't holding still, though; they were slipping away across his body. Yalda could see him struggling to keep them in place, but he wasn't succeeding.

Vito relaxed, smoothing out his skin. Then he tried again. This time, a single, short ridge formed near the center of his chest, and though it quivered a bit, it more or less stayed put. Then as Yalda watched, it bent in on itself until it formed a crude circle.

"The sun!" she said.

"Let's see if I can do the next one." Vito's tympanum grew taut with concentration as the ridge spread out and reformed, winding itself into five wide loops.

"A flower!"

"One more." The flower split apart and the lines that had formed the petals softened, but then the fragments came together in a new configuration and the ridges grew sharp and clear again.

"An eye!"

"All right, three symbols, that's enough!" Vito's shoulders sagged.

"Teach me how to do it!" Yalda pleaded.

"It's not easy," Vito said. "It takes a lot of practice."

"There's nothing else to do here," Yalda pointed out. She would have happily gone exploring in the forest instead, chasing the lizards to find out what they ate, but they couldn't leave Dario behind.

"I suppose we could try one symbol," Vito said reluctantly.

He beckoned to her, and Yalda knelt down so she was closer to her father's height. He sharpened a finger and began scratching gently on her chest, never moving from the same small spot. Soon his touch was as irritating as the attentions of any insect.

Yalda squirmed; her skin was quivering, but that was giving her no respite. A mite would be swiftly unseated, but this prodding finger was far too heavy to dislodge.

"Don't move your shoulders!" Vito reprimanded her. "Just use your skin. It's something you're doing dozens of times a day already, but you have to learn to control it more precisely."

"I don't see any shapes yet," Yalda complained.

Vito said, "Be patient! The first thing is to make yourself aware of what's going on under your skin. Then you can try to shift the point where it's happening."

It was harder than changing her posture, harder than reshaping her hands, harder than anything Yalda had tried to do with her body before. Most transformations took some effort, but once she pushed herself her instincts took over. This was different; the only thing her instincts wanted her to do was stop wasting her time with this ineffectual shuddering and simply sweep away the nuisance with her hands.

But she persisted. Her mother had learned to do this, taught by her friend, then passed on the skill to her father. Impossible or not, *her mother's finger* was prodding her, urging her to keep on trying to tame the swarm of tiny muscles beneath her skin.

By the time the clearing fell into gloom and the violet flowers above them unfurled across their nets, Yalda had made her own sun, written on her skin. As she peered down at her chest the dark circle writhed like a worm chewing its tail, then broke apart.

Vito looked wearier from his efforts than she was. "Well done," he said.

"Can I show Dario?" He'd be amazed, Yalda thought. Not one day in school, and here she was writing!

Vito said, "Your grandfather's tired, let's not bother him with this."

Yalda woke, confused for a moment by the brightness of the clearing. It wasn't morning; she'd been roused from her sleep by the sound of Dario humming with distress.

She turned to look toward him, then rose to her feet for a clearer view. At first she'd thought that a strong wind must have blown through the forest, tearing petals from the trees and strewing them over his body as he slept. But the patches of luminous yellow belonged to his skin.

Yalda knelt by Dario's bed; his eyes were closed, but he was thrashing from side to side. She could feel mites coming and going all around him; she tried waving them away, but they were persistent.

She called out to Vito, "Father! Help me!"

As Vito stirred, the haze of sleep cleared from Yalda's vision and the throng of mites came into sharper focus. Those that were descending onto Dario's body appeared perfectly ordinary, but those rising up into the forest again, having bitten him, were imbued with their own small share of the strange yellow light. Yalda had never seen anything like it; when an insect fed on a flower it did not take on its glow.

She looked up to see Vito standing across the bed from her. "He's in pain," she said. "I think the insects are troubling him." She widened her hands and fanned more vigorously, hoping her father would join in.

"The heat!" Dario protested miserably. "Is this what childbirth is like? Is this my punishment?" His eyes remained firmly closed. Yalda doubted that he knew where he was or who was tending to him.

Vito said nothing, but he knelt and began swatting at the insects himself. Yalda peered down at Dario, hoping for a sign that their efforts were bringing him some respite from his suffering. A new patch of radiance had appeared, a shimmering yellow smudge that appeared to be leaking out from a tear in his skin. It was spreading at an alarming rate, as if it was made of some unimaginably soft resin. Yalda had never seen anything move so freely, other than the finest dust—but despite the steady breeze this wasn't scattering like dust.

"What is that?" she asked Vito.

"I don't know. Some kind of… *liquid*."

Vito spoke the last word with an air of dismay, but before Yalda could ask him what it meant the whole clearing lit up, brighter than day. She closed her eyes instinctively; when she opened them the light was gone, but everything looked darker, as if she'd been staring into the sun.

"We have to leave," Vito declared abruptly.

"*What?*"

"Your grandfather's dying. We can't help him anymore."

Yalda was stunned. "We can't abandon him!"

Vito said, "Listen to me: we can't help him, and it's not safe to stay with him."

Dario gave no indication that his son's terrible verdict had reached him through the thicket of his pain and confusion. As Yalda rose to her feet, forcing herself to obey Vito even though she couldn't bring herself to believe him, a speck of light hovering in the distance ahead of her erupted into painful, blinding brilliance. As she covered her front pair of eyes with her arm, she thought: *that was a mite*. The mites that had fed from Dario's skin and stolen his light were burning up, and each tiny blaze was brighter than the sun.

Still half-blind, she stumbled around Dario's bed toward her father. "We're leaving the forest?"

"Yes."

"Should I bring the food?"

"There's no time."

Vito leaned down and whispered something to his father, then he stood and led the way out of the clearing. Yalda stole a glance at Dario, then tore herself away. She would not accept that his fate was sealed; she would not say goodbye.

"Close your rear eyes," Vito told her sternly. "Stay close to me and don't look back."

Yalda obeyed. A third burst of light came from the clearing—behind her now, but even the glare reflected from the branches ahead was dazzling. Dark traces lingered on her vision, a second ghostly forest imprinted on the first, complicating everything.

"I don't understand!" she said. "I thought the light here would make him better!" If she forced her father to remember Doctor Livia's pronouncement, and tie what they were seeing to that, maybe he'd change his mind and turn back.

"We tried," Vito said, stricken. "But some things can't be healed."

Yalda pushed her way through the branches angrily, relying on touch more than sight; she was barely registering the ongoing flashes, but the afterimages kept building up until she was no longer sure which looming obstacles were real. Even in the depths of his illness, Dario had retained his gruff affection for her. How could she walk away from him?

They emerged from the forest and headed back toward the road. Maybe the mites were actually helping, drawing the poison out of Dario's body. *Dying in his stead.* If they stopped to rest, she'd sneak back while Vito was asleep. If Dario had survived, healed by the self-immolating insects, she could carry him out to rejoin his son.

The ground ahead of her brightened unbearably, then a rush of air knocked her flat. She tried to call out, but her tympanum had seized up, leaving her both mute and deaf. She crawled across the weeds; they looked like dead husks, but she couldn't tell if they'd really been transformed or whether it was her vision that had been stripped bare. She groped around, sure that Vito was close but afraid to lift her gaze to search for him. Then she felt him reach out to her and they held each other tightly.

They stayed there, huddled together on the ground. Her father's embrace was not enough to make her feel safe, but it was all there was.

Yalda woke to a brightening sky and the sound of insects. Vito was awake, crouched beside her, but he remained silent as she stood to survey the aftermath.

The forest was still standing but the closest part was visibly thinned and damaged, as if a giant had reached down and pummeled it. Some of the low bushes around them were dead. Yalda's skin was tender as she moved.

"He's gone," she said. Dario could not have survived at the center of this destruction—let alone survived being the cause of it.

"Yes." Vito rose to his feet and put an arm around her to comfort her. "It's sad that we've lost him, but remember that he had a long life. And most men go to the soil, to decay like straw. Only a few go to light."

"Is that a good thing?" Yalda had seen how much pain he'd been in at the end, but she had nothing with which to compare it.

"It's good that we left him in time," Vito said, avoiding her question. "It would not have made him happier to take us with him."

"No." Yalda felt her whole body shaking with an involuntary hum of grief. Vito held her until she was still again.

"We should start moving," he suggested gently. "It would be best if we reached the farm before night."

Yalda looked back toward the ruined edge of the forest.

"When I get old," she said, "what will happen to me?"

"Hush," Vito said. "That's the way of men. No daughter of mine is going to die."

2

In the spring following her grandfather's death, Yalda joined her cousins, her uncle and her father in the harvest for the first time. While Lucia and Lucio dashed around gathering up spills and wheeling the grain carts between the filling points—as Yalda had done the year before—the harvesters themselves marched steadily back and forth between the rows of wheat.

Working with two hands at once, Yalda plucked the seed cases from the stalks on either side of her, squeezed them until they popped, emptied them into the pouches she'd formed, then dropped the cases on the ground. It wasn't heavy work, like digging a store-hole, but the sheer repetitiveness of it took its toll. Though she'd toughened the wedge-shaped fingers she'd made to prise open the cases, after a while they started to yield to the pressure and she had to stop and re-form them. And when her arms and hands grew too sore to continue, she had no choice but to extrude a new pair and rest the muscles she'd been using. She was yet to acquire the endurance of a seasoned harvester, but her size alone had its advantages. While her male cousins cycled between two pairs of arms, and Claudia, Aurelia and the men three, by mid-afternoon Yalda was on her fifth pair, with the flesh that had formed the first still tucked away deep in her chest, recuperating.

At the end of each row she emptied her pouches into one of the grain carts that her brother and sister were nudging along the cross-paths, then she turned into the next row to start all over again. Giusto had told her that after the first day her body would refine her posture to make the work easier, but that there was no point in anyone instructing her on how to get there sooner; the adjustment was different for each person, and better achieved through instinct than imitation.

By dusk Yalda was exhausted, but it was satisfying to see how high the yellow grain was piled in the carts. She helped Lucio push one to the

23

central bin that the merchant's truck had left for them to fill.

"If I join the harvest next year," Lucio asked her, "who'll handle the carts?"

"We'll take turns," Yalda replied, trying her best to make the guess sound authoritative. Questions were for someone whose opinion was worth seeking: an older cousin, not a sibling. But apparently her size alone, having won her a place in the harvest, had come to mean more than her true age.

Everyone sat leaning against the huge bin as they ate the evening meal. Yalda gazed up at the darkening sky and listened to her father and uncle enthusing about the yield and the quality of the grain, while Aurelia teased Claudio by repeatedly punching him on the arm and then taking his retribution without flinching. Yalda felt peaceful; she still missed Dario, but she knew the good harvest would have pleased him.

Later, as the other children were scrambling into their beds, Yalda spotted one of the grain carts sitting at the end of its row, still full. She thought of calling Lucia to deal with it, but whatever the privileges of her newfound seniority-by-size, she didn't want to set herself above her own sister. She went to wheel the cart in herself.

When she had brought it to the foot of the ramp leading up to the top of the bin, she paused to straighten the wheels. "I just don't want to lose a good worker like that!" she heard Giusto complain. They were on opposite sides of the bin, but his voice was clear.

"She'll still be with us at harvest time," her father replied.

"A few days a year! And for how many years?"

Vito said, "I promised her mother: if any of the children showed signs that they'd benefit from an education, I'd do my best to send them to school."

"She never saw this one in the field!" Giusto retorted. "If she'd known what she'd be asking us to give up, I doubt she would have been so insistent."

Vito was unmoved. "She'd have wanted every one of her children to have the best life they could."

"I'll teach her to recite the sagas," Giusto promised. "That will keep her mind busy." Yalda recoiled; Dario's stories had been entertaining, but Giusto could ramble on for half the night, listing the unlikely deeds of a dozen tedious heroes.

"It's not just about her getting bored with farm work," Vito said. "She's never going to find a co-stead hanging around here."

"Does that matter?" Giusto replied, bemused. "She works as hard as any four children. And it's not as if she's your only chance at grandchildren."

Yalda clomped noisily up the ramp and emptied the cart into the bin; when the sound of falling grain had died away the conversation had come to an end.

By the time Yalda climbed into bed even Aurelia was asleep, too tired for their usual exchange of whispered jokes and taunts before the adults joined them. Yalda lay watching the stars in flight—trailing histories unadorned by bombast and braggadocio, just waiting for her to learn how to decipher them.

The possibility of school was thrilling: it meant walking right into the storehouse of knowledge, the source of all the answers to the questions she struggled with. At school, she could find out how the stars shone, how her flesh changed its shape, how plants knew night from day.

But nobody went to school merely to satisfy their curiosity; they went to learn new skills that their own families couldn't give them. A farmer's child who studied did not stay on the farm. They went out into the world and left their old life behind.

On the evening of the last day of the harvest, the merchant's truck returned to carry away the grain. Yalda stood and watched while Vito, Giusto, and the truck's driver, Silvana, maneuvered the ramp the harvesters had used to fill the bin into position for a new purpose: to slide the bin itself up onto the back of the truck.

Chains were unwound from the truck's winch and hooked to the edge of the bin. As the engine clattered and the winch began to turn, a swarm of sparks rose from the truck's chimney and drifted away into the gloom, like the mites in the forest ascending from Dario's skin.

The bin was jutting over the top of the ramp, poised ready to tip down and sit flat on the truck's bed, when the engine suddenly cut out. Silvana leaped from the cab and tugged open a hatch at the side of the vehicle.

Yalda gazed into the labyrinth of machinery, entranced. Silvana saw her, and with a friendly gesture invited her to come closer. "This is the fuel," she said, taking the lid off a hopper full of orange powder. "And this is the liberator." A second, smaller hopper fed a fine gray dust in from the front. "The fuel wants to become light, but it can't do it alone. Mix it with the liberator, though…" Silvana brought her hands together, then rapidly drew them apart. "Both of them turn to light and hot gas. The gas forces up the piston, which turns the crankshaft. Then the gears connect that motion either to the wheels at the front, or the winch."

Yalda had been told not to pester strangers with her questions, but this woman's generosity and enthusiasm emboldened her. "Why did it stop working?"

"Just a blockage, I think." Silvana opened a smaller access hatch below the two hoppers and started tapping along the length of a pipe. "You can hear it, when they get clogged up. Ah, yes." She tapped the same point repeatedly to demonstrate the dulled sound, then she fetched a hammer from the cab and whacked the pipe with alarming force. There was a spasm deep in the truck's body, and sparks rose from the chimney again, but the engine did not start up in earnest; this was just the fuel that had been trapped finally meeting its fate.

"What are the sparks?" Yalda asked.

"When the mixture's not quite right," Silvana replied, "some of the fuel's still burning as it comes out with the gas." She nudged a knob below the fuel hopper, turning it a barely perceptible amount. "That controls the outlet from the tank. As the pipes get encrusted you need to make adjustments."

Silvana returned to the cab and started the engine, hauling the bin up into place, then Giusto helped her secure it for the journey.

As the truck drove off, Giusto approached his brother. "What a waste, training a woman to do that," he declared. "In a few years they'll just need someone new."

Vito didn't reply. Yalda thought of Doctor Livia; the news in the village was that she'd given birth, and her father was seeing all her old patients. Yalda had returned from the forest convinced that Doctor Livia's advice to Dario had been worthless, but then she'd started wondering if the true reason for proposing the journey had been to lessen the risk to a dying man's family, when the honest prognosis might have been impossible for them to accept.

Lucio and Lucia fetched the loaves for the evening meal. It was late, and everyone was tired; they ate sprawled on the flattened ground where the bin had sat. Tomorrow the whole family would go into the village to celebrate, spending some of the money the harvest had brought them. Yalda was proud of the part she'd played, but she felt an odd pang of regret that it was over; the work had come to an end just as her body was growing used to it.

Without warning, a line of light streaked across the sky. Long and slender, dazzlingly bright and richly colored, it disappeared beyond the horizon before Yalda could let out a chirp of astonishment.

It was Claudia who spoke first. "What was that?"

"A shooting star," Giusto replied. "A shooting star, fast and low!"

Yalda waited for her father to correct him; Vito had pointed out shooting stars to her many times, and they had never looked like that. She closed her eyes to try to bring back the apparition. The streak of light had come and gone in an instant, but she was sure it had contained a clear progression of colors—a trail like a star's, but vastly longer. Shooting stars were lumps of rock falling through the air, having drifted by chance into the path of the world; they did not move so rapidly that the colors of their light were separated. Their trails were nothing but a fire in the air that kept burning for a moment or two as they passed.

When Vito remained silent, Yalda could not contain herself. "That wasn't a shooting star," she said. "It was too fast."

"How do you know that?" Giusto demanded. "What if it was traveling just above us?" He was trying to sound amused, but Yalda could tell he was affronted that any child would presume to correct him. He stood up and took a few steps toward her, then swiped his arm along a wide arc, almost slapping her. "Even my hand can cross the sky for you before you flinch, if it's close enough."

Yalda wanted to say something about the color trail, but the strange object had vanished so quickly. What if no one else had noticed the pattern she'd seen?

"And if it wasn't a shooting star," her uncle concluded triumphantly, "*what was it?*"

Yalda had no reply. She could not name or describe anything that could race from horizon to horizon in an instant, spilling its colors across a third of the sky.

Silvana, who made light in her engine every day, might have known the answer. Clara would surely have known, and would have told her friend Vita. But if her mother had chosen to keep a few of the secrets of light from Vito, Yalda couldn't blame her.

She lowered her gaze and let Giusto believe that she had deferred to his wisdom and accepted his claim. She had to be patient. In school, she would discover everything.

On the first day of class, Vito walked with Yalda into the village. He'd told her he had business to conduct, but she suspected that he would have accompanied her anyway.

"In the old days," Vito mused as a truck rattled past them, "they used to say there was no point in educating boys. They believed that a mother's knowledge shaped her children from birth, while anything their father tried to pass on to them only went skin deep. To educate a girl was to invest in every future generation; to educate a boy was to turn your wealth into straw."

Yalda had never heard of such ideas before; they had to come from older days than Dario's youth. "Do you think that's true?"

Vito said, "I don't believe an education's wasted on anyone who takes it seriously, boy or girl."

"But do you think a mother's knowledge is passed on to her children?"

Vito said, "Clever as you are, I've never heard you speak a word of your mother's that didn't reach you through me."

They entered the village from the south-east corner and detoured around the crowded markets in favor of the quieter tree-lined avenues. The small parks they crossed were mostly empty of people, but Yalda's gaze kept turning to the trees; since her trip into the forest she found herself noticing far more easily than before the lizards scuttling along their branches.

The school was enclosed by a thick hedge of matted twigs that Yalda had no trouble peering over; the broad square of bare ground within was twice divided by similar barriers. There were four classes, Vito explained; he led Yalda to the corner where the youngest students were gathering.

"Don't let anyone discourage you," he said.

Yalda had heard enough of Giusto's comments to know what her father meant. "I won't," she assured him.

Vito left her, and Yalda walked through the gap in the hedge.

There were almost four dozen children assembled in this part of the square; maybe half were lone boys, while the rest looked like paired cos. Yalda searched hopefully for another unaccompanied girl, but then she forced herself to stop fretting. She tried meeting the gaze of some of the students who were chatting in a small group in front of her, but nobody acknowledged her and she was too shy to intrude into their conversation.

The teacher arrived, calling to the children for silence then introducing himself as Angelo. He herded them into a tight cluster away from the hedge, then instructed them to sit and watch him carefully.

Yalda glanced at her neighbors; they were both boys, about half her size. "I'm Fulvio," whispered the boy on her right.

"I'm Yalda."

"Today," Angelo began, "we'll learn the symbols and their names." Chatter from the other classes, still teacherless, filled the air, but Yalda forced herself to concentrate.

Angelo formed a circle on his chest, as quickly and sharply as if it had been stamped there by a wheel pressed against his body. "This is called 'the sun,'" he said. Yalda was expecting him to ask them to try to reproduce the symbol on their own skin, but after repeating the name several times he moved straight on to the flower; this lesson was to be about committing the shapes and names to memory, not about writing anything themselves.

Yalda listened dutifully as he worked his way through ten dozen symbols; she had never known that there were so many. By the time he'd finished it was close to noon, and he asked some of the children to fetch loaves from a store-hole and hand them out.

As they ate, Angelo walked among them asking for their names and the names of their fathers. Yalda felt an odd sense of trepidation when he approached her, as if her right to join the class might be in doubt, but when she gave her reply he moved on without another word. Whatever the shifting beliefs of the wider world as to who was worth educating, Vito must have paid this man some of the money from the harvest, and that was all it took to be permitted to attend.

"Where's your co?" Fulvio asked her, the crumbs spilling from his mouth bouncing off his tympanum as he spoke.

"Where's yours?" Yalda retorted.

"Working," Fulvio replied.

"She ate her co," the boy on her left said; Yalda had heard him give his name as Roberto. "How else does anyone get so bloated?"

"That's right, I ate him," Yalda agreed. "But sometimes he still wants to come out and play." She raised a hint of a head-shaped lump in the middle of her chest, like Amato in the story; Roberto quailed, then leaped to his feet and fled to the far side of the class.

Fulvio reached out and prodded the lump with one finger, then chirped with delight. "Can you teach me to do that?"

"Why? No one will believe you ate your brother."

"What about a younger cousin?"

"Perhaps," Yalda conceded.

"So you're a solo?"

"What do you think?" Yalda resorbed the fake head; other children had started staring.

"I don't know, I never met a solo before," Fulvio confessed. "You've really got no brothers or sisters?"

Yalda tried to be patient with him; her neighbors had all simply known about her, she hadn't had to spell things out for them. "I've got a brother and a sister, Lucio and Lucia. My mother had three children."

"Oh." Fulvio's eyes widened with relief. "That's not so bad. It would be lonely if she'd had just one."

Yalda was on the verge of irritably declaring that it was impossible for a woman to have *just one child*, but then it struck her that she wasn't entirely sure that that was true. "I live with four cousins too," she said. "I promise you it's not lonely at all."

Angelo called the class to order and began working his way through the symbols again, this time inviting his students to shout out the names as the shapes appeared on his skin. Yalda had forgotten half of them already; some of the symbols looked like nothing in the world, and their names were equally baffling. But even when the responses dropped from deafening choruses to shy whispers, there were always three or four children who knew the answers.

When Angelo announced that they'd finished for the day, Yalda was frustrated; she knew she had to learn to read and write before anything else, and she hadn't even managed to complete the first step of that journey.

"Where do you live?" Fulvio asked her as they left the schoolyard.

"On our farm, east of the village. You?"

"On the west side," he replied. "My father has a refinery, so we live right next to it."

"What kind of refinery?"

"Truck fuel."

Yalda was intrigued, but she kept her curiosity in check; the courteous thing was to ask about people's family. "What about your cousins?"

"They're close by. My uncle's family is in the same business."

Yalda didn't want to part from her new friend immediately by retracing the route she'd taken with her father, so she steered a middle way and walked due south as they chatted, until they ended up near the center of the village.

"Should we cut through the markets?" she asked. She had no money, but she was happy just to wander around the stalls, trying to guess the ingredients in the fancier foods or the origins of the strange trinkets.

"Of course," Fulvio replied.

No sooner had they plunged into the crowd than Yalda spied a stall full of artificial flowers, made from some kind of polished, translucent stone. They wouldn't look like much at night, she guessed, but the way they caught the afternoon sun really did mimic a petal's glow. How could anyone have fashioned such a thing, so delicate and precise? As she walked past the stall her rear gaze lingered on the sparkling curios, but then she spotted a dye wheel up ahead, the pits arranged around its wooden disk filled with vivid powders of various hues. The stallholder was demonstrating their quality for a customer, raising a series of decorative patterns on the palm of her hand then sprinkling a different dye over each design before pressing it onto a square of paper.

"What about some groundnuts?" Fulvio asked.

"What about them?" By the time Yalda had turned to him he had already concluded the transaction, and he passed her a conically wrapped petal full of the expensive delicacies.

"But—"

"It's all right, I got two." Fulvio showed her his other hand.

"Thank you." Yalda was embarrassed by his profligacy, but she didn't want to be rude. She tried the nuts. The flavor was strong, and strange to her, but after a moment she decided that she liked it.

She said, "I don't think they grow around here."

Fulvio buzzed amusement. "They bring them from the Shining Valley, three severances away; that's practically on the other side of the world."

"Oh."

"By train from Mount Respite to Jade City and Red Towers, then by truck to Shattered Hill and Sunstone and then here." Fulvio spoke as confidently as if he'd ridden alongside a consignment himself. Yalda's astonishment must have shown in her eyes, because he added by way of explanation, "I hear the truck drivers talking all the time, when they're buying fuel."

"I'd like to be a truck driver," Yalda said.

"Really?" Fulvio sounded surprised by her choice, but his tone wasn't dismissive.

"What are you studying for?" she asked.

"To work in my father's business."

"Can't he teach you that himself?"

"He can teach me what he knows," Fulvio said, "but he wants me to be able to change the business, to do something different if I have to."

"Like what?"

"Who knows?" he replied. "Maybe something no one's even heard of yet."

When they parted, Yalda stared uneasily at the cone of groundnuts Fulvio had given her. It was still half full, and she wondered if she should share what was left with the rest of her family. But with so many people there would barely be a taste for each one, and she felt uncomfortable about showing them the lavish gift. As she cut across the park toward the eastern road, she hastily stuffed the remainder into her mouth and dropped the empty petal onto the ground.

It was still light when Yalda arrived home. Aurelia was in the clearing, milling grain and making loaves. "Can I help?" Yalda asked her.

Aurelia said sharply, "I didn't think you worked here anymore."

Yalda knelt beside her and took the mill. The resistance as she cranked the handle sent a welcome surge of vitality through the muscles in her arms, which had grown sluggish after a day spent sitting motionless.

"You smell peculiar," Aurelia complained.

"They gave us something strange for lunch," Yalda said. "I think there were worms in it." She handed the mill back to Aurelia, who squeezed a thumb-sized piece of resin from the sweetbush branch she'd cut and started mixing it into the flour.

That night, as they lay in their beds, Yalda told Aurelia about the lesson she'd received. Every child knew the twelve basic symbols, but it was a revelation to learn that there were ten times more. And just as Clara had shared her lessons with Vita, Yalda had decided that she would pass on everything she learned to Aurelia.

But after Yalda had described just three of the new symbols, Aurelia said irritably, "Go to sleep. I'm not interested."

The next day, Angelo began teaching his class how to write. The students formed pairs and used the same trick that Vito had shown Yalda in the forest: prodding their partners with sharpened fingers to goad them into taking control of the instinctive twitching of their skin. Yalda's brief introduction to the technique helped a little, but it still took a few days' practice before she and Fulvio could form even the simplest symbols accurately, and hold them for as long as they wished. Yalda walked to school with shapes flickering over her skin, imagining a time when she'd have something written on her chest worth sprinkling with dye and committing to paper.

As the class was gathering for what should have been the last day of their third stint, one of the other teachers came to them with a message: Angelo was sick. His illness wasn't serious and he expected to be back soon, but for today his students should return to their families.

Yalda was disappointed; she'd grown used to the routine of eleven days of school then one day off, and the prospect of two days' farm work in a row felt tedious now. As she slouched despondently out of the schoolyard, Fulvio said, "Why don't you come and see the refinery?"

Yalda thought it over, and could find no reason to refuse the invitation.

As they crossed the village to the west, the market stalls, parks and gardens gave way to warehouses and factories. Trucks were coming and going constantly; Yalda had never seen so many at once.

"How do you sleep?" she asked Fulvio. He looked at her blankly. "Or does the noise stop at night?" It wasn't just the trucks; most of the factories were emitting some kind of clattering or thumping.

"It doesn't stop," he said. "But I like it. It's soothing. If there's silence I wake up; silence means something's broken."

All around them, buildings made from timber or stone rose to twice Yalda's height or more. Some were sleek, some were shoddy, but apart from the roads there was scarcely a stride of land left bare. Yalda understood that some kinds of manufacturing needed shelter from the dust and the wind, but she would have been hard-pressed to name half a dozen. How little she knew of her own village, she thought, let alone the wider world.

"There's the refinery." Fulvio pointed out a broad stone building ahead of them. A truck was parked some distance away, its winch attached to a complicated system of pulleys that was raising a bin full of brown ore toward a long chute leading into the building.

"Why make it so complicated?" Yalda wondered. "Why don't the trucks just tip their load in where it's needed?" She gestured at the point where the chute entered the refinery.

"The trucks need to keep their distance," Fulvio explained. "The liberator they use has to be ground very fine, which means it leaks out of everything. That's bad enough for the trucks themselves, but if it gets into our production line people can die."

"Oh." Yalda had been striding forward eagerly; now she slowed her pace.

"Don't worry, we're careful," Fulvio assured her. "And the liberator factory is a long, long way away."

As they approached, a rhythmless cacophony rose up over the sounds of traffic and the noises from the other factories. Fulvio led her to an entrance on the other side of the building from the ore chute. Yalda stepped through, peering into the gloom ahead; the air was thick with dust, shimmering in pale columns slanting down from the grubby skylights.

As her eyes adapted, she made out a long line of shallow trays, joined to each other in a sequence that zigzagged across the cavernous space. People were standing beside the trays, bashing lumps of ore with hammers, scraping smaller rocks over elaborate toothed sieves, sorting fuel from clods of dirt with practiced darting fingers. There must have been four dozen workers in all, laboring amid the noise and dust.

Yalda let out a faint hum of distress. The harvest wasn't easy, but it only lasted six days. The work here looked like a kind of never-ending torture.

Fulvio must have noticed her discomfort. "There are three shifts," he said, "so it's really not so bad. I used to help out myself, before I started school. And my brother, my sister and my co all still work here."

Yalda waited for him to introduce her to them, but then she realized that he wasn't prepared to do anything that might interrupt the flow of ore from tray to tray, as it grew ever finer and lost its troublesome impurities.

"Your co works here?" she asked. "Fulvia?"

He gestured toward a girl bent over a sieve. "And there's my brother, Benigno." The slender boy was sweeping orange dust across the floor into a grate, carefully separating spilt traces of fuel from the general muck; if he knew Fulvio was watching, he gave no sign of it. "Benigna works a later shift; so do my cousins."

"Where's your father?"

"He's in the office with my uncle. We shouldn't disturb them."

Yalda retreated into the sunlight. Fulvio followed her. "I don't know why you're so upset!" he said. "Your brother and sister still work on the farm, don't they?"

"Yes."

"Everyone has to do something," Fulvio declared. "Or they'll starve."

"I know," Yalda conceded. "But you and I, our lives are so easy now—"

"You and I are learning to do other kinds of work. Why should we feel bad about that?"

Yalda didn't know how to reply. After a while, she said, "Couldn't they use an engine to smash the rock?"

"They use engines at the mine," Fulvio said. "But once the pieces of ore are smaller than a certain size, having any liberator around is too dangerous."

"There has to be a better way than people with hammers."

Fulvio spread his arms. "Maybe there is. And maybe when I'm educated, I'll find it."

Yalda said, "I should probably get home now."

"I'll walk with you back to the village," he insisted. "I don't want you getting lost."

Yalda didn't object. As they walked, she wondered what she'd expected to see in the refinery, if not toiling children. Some dazzling secret of light, revealed? Fulvio and his family didn't know how fuel turned into light, any more than she knew why wheat-flowers glowed. Half the things that happened right in front of their eyes remained as mysterious as the most distant stars.

As they approached the village, Fulvio turned to her.

"Do you have a plan yet?" he said. "For your children?"

"What?" Yalda stared at him.

"A plan for them. Who'll raise them, who'll feed them?"

Yalda felt her skin writhing, as if it could sweep his words away like troublesome mites. "That's a long way into the future," she said.

"Of course," Fulvio agreed. "I just wondered if you had something in mind."

Yalda said, "Thank you for the visit. I'll see you in school."

When she reached the empty eastern road, she started humming quietly to herself. She'd thought she was turning into Clara, that mysterious paragon of knowledge and friendship from her father's stories of her mother's time. But what exactly had become of Clara? Yalda had never dared ask.

Giusto had wanted to harness her strength for the farm until she went the way of men—but what kind of escape from that fate was it, to step into a world where would-be co-steads were already sizing up her children as factory fodder?

When she came to the turn-off leading back to the farm, Yalda kept walking. She found a quiet corner of a neighbor's field where she knew no one would disturb her.

She knelt low on the ground beside a sweetbush and let a sharp twig press into her skin, until the muscles all around the point of impingement were sweeping back and forth, desperately trying to dislodge it.

The third symbol of the third dozen was one of the hardest: a full figure of a person, bipedal, four-armed, standing alone. Composed, self-contained, holding no tools. Maybe the four arms were for balance, or beauty.

Yalda stayed kneeling against the bush, shouting with frustration at all her stupid failed scrawls. A teacher and a writing partner made it easier; rest and guidance and encouragement made it easier.

But when the sun had crossed half the sky, the figure from her memory was there on her chest, imperfect but legible, hers to command.

3

On the day after her twelfth birthday, Yalda woke before dawn and forced herself to open her eyes before the cool soil lured her back to sleep. The vines that crisscrossed the low ceiling above her were studded with tiny yellow blossoms; thumps and scraping sounds filtered through from the floor of the markets as the stallholders made their preparations.

Zeugma's public beds were much in demand, and Yalda preferred to be gone before the night shift workers came down grumbling and prodding for spaces of their own. She rose and threaded her way between her sleeping neighbors, aware of other shapes moving softly nearby. The slender vines gave out just enough light to let her see where she was going, but it took care and practice not to step on a sleeper, or collide with someone else on the way to the exits.

She bounded up the stairs and ducked into the markets to buy a loaf, then made it out onto the street in time to see the stars before the pale sky extinguished them completely. In Zeugma, only the wealthiest inhabitants with their private, walled gardens had the choice of sleeping in the open air; if you dug an indentation beside the flowers in the parks you were beaten for damaging city property. But Yalda preferred to spend her nights beneath the markets rather than waste money on an apartment in the towers, where your bed was cooled by a thermal conduit of calmstone columns, buried in the ground but stretching up to drain the heat from the highest of those dreary cages.

She still had five chimes before her appointment with Eusebio, but she wanted to be thoroughly prepared in order to ensure that the session didn't run over time; there was a mid-morning lecture by a visiting scientist on new developments in optics that she didn't want to miss. So she paced the grimy streets between the markets and the university, planning her lesson in detail, composing diagrams as she walked. There weren't many pedestrians about, and in any case the people she passed showed no surprise at the strange shapes forming and shifting on her skin. Some academics went to great pains to conceal their priceless musings, learning to make purely mental sketches or to ensure that anything showing on their body was at least writ small on the palms of their hands, but Yalda had never felt the need to cultivate those furtive habits.

She had timed her peregrinations perfectly; the university clock made its doleful noise just as she entered the stone tower where Eusebio lived. Yalda took the stairs quickly; to arrive right on the chimes would have been ill-mannered, but a sprint to the fourth floor would be enough to take the edge off her punctuality.

When she reached the apartment the curtained entrance was already parted to welcome her; she called out "It's Yalda!" and stepped through. The room smelled of dye and paper; there were dozens of textbooks stacked against the walls, and Eusebio's own notes rivaled them in bulk. A merchant's son hoping to break into the railway business, he took his engineering studies seriously. Even the three small clockwork figurines, marching back and forth beside one pile of books, were evidence of a diversion equally concerned with the subject of what a machine could or could not be made to do.

"Good morning, welcome!" Eusebio was sitting on the floor in the corner, loose pages spread out in front of him. He was bulky for a man, but no less agile for it; Yalda suspected that he'd strived from childhood to match the deftness of smaller peers, much as she had.

She sat facing him, cross-legged, and got straight to the point. She knew exactly what he would have been told in the lecture he'd had the day before; not one word had changed in the introductory physics course since she'd taken it herself, four years previously.

"Conservation of energy and momentum," she said. "How much did you understand?"

"Maybe half," he confessed. But Eusebio didn't claim understanding lightly; Yalda suspected that he'd followed the whole lecture, but longed for a deeper grasp of the subject.

"Let's start with something simple," she suggested. "Suppose an object is free to move, without friction. It starts out at rest, and you apply a constant force to it. After some time has passed, tell me how the force, the time, and the object's velocity are related."

Eusebio said, "Force equals mass times acceleration; acceleration by time gives velocity. So, the product of *force* and *time* equals the product of the object's mass and its velocity—also known as its 'momentum.'"

Yalda widened her eyes approvingly. "And in the general situation, where the object need not start from rest? The product of the force and the time for which it's applied gives…?"

"The *change* in the object's momentum." Eusebio lifted a sheet of calculations. "I confirmed that."

"Good. So, if two objects interact—if a child throws a stone at an approaching train, and it bounces off the front carriage—what happens to their momenta?"

"The force of the train on the stone is equal and opposite to the force of the stone on the train," Eusebio replied. "And since both forces act for the same amount of time, they cause equal and opposite changes of momenta: as much as the stone's momentum rises—measured in the direction of the train's motion—the train's will fall."

Yalda said, "So the total, the sum of the two, is unchanged. What could be simpler?"

"Momentum is simple enough," Eusebio agreed. "But energy—"

"Energy is almost the same!" Yalda assured him. "It's just that instead of the product of force and time, you use the product of force and distance traveled. What's an easy way to turn the first into the second?"

Eusebio thought for a moment. "Multiply it by distance over time, which is the *average velocity*. For an object that started from rest and accelerated smoothly, that's half the final velocity it's reached. So the product of the force and the distance traveled is the product of momentum and half the velocity… or half the mass times the velocity squared. The kinetic energy."

"Exactly," Yalda said.

Eusebio understood these calculations well enough, but he was less happy with the bigger picture. "Energy is where the 'conservation laws' start to sound more like a long list of exceptions," he complained.

"Maybe. Tell me about the exceptions."

"Gravity! Drop a book from my window; its kinetic energy certainly won't stay the same. And the fact that the book pulls the world up toward it with as much force as the world pulls it down doesn't help; that keeps momentum balanced, but not kinetic energy."

"Sure." Yalda brought one of the diagrams she'd rehearsed onto her chest.

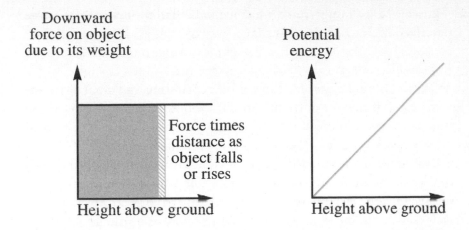

"If you plot the downward force on the book against its height above the ground," she said, "it's a constant, a flat, straight line. Now think about *the area under that line*, up to the point representing the book's current height. When the book falls, the reduction in the area—the little rectangle that gets chopped off—will equal the *force* on the book times the *distance* it travels—which is precisely the amount by which its kinetic energy increases: force times distance."

Eusebio examined the diagram. "All right."

"Alternatively, if the book is tossed upward and gravity starts to slow its fall, it will be losing kinetic energy… but the area under the line will *increase* in a way that precisely balances the loss. So, we call this area 'potential energy', and the sum of the two kinds of energy, kinetic and potential, will be conserved.

"This works for other simple forces, too—like the force on an object attached to a stretched spring."

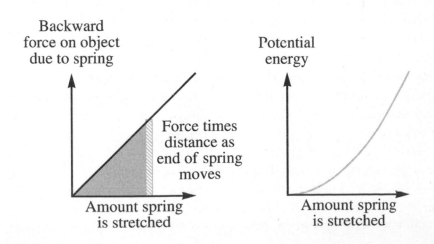

Eusebio said, "I understand why the mathematics works out as you've described it. But isn't this just a fancy way of saying: kinetic energy isn't conserved, it changes… and in a few simple cases we understand the forces responsible, well enough to be able to keep track of the changes?"

"Well, yes," Yalda agreed. "It's a kind of accounting. But don't disparage accounting; it can be a powerful tool. Elastic potential energy can tell you how fast a projectile will fly out of a slingshot; gravitational potential energy can tell you how high that projectile will rise."

Eusebio wasn't persuaded. He gestured at his marching figurines; two of them had wound down and come to a halt, while the third had ended up on its back, kicking its legs ineffectually. "In the real world, energy isn't conserved," he said. "It comes out of food, or burning fuel, and it vanishes as friction."

"That might sound like the best explanation," Yalda said, "but those processes are just more complex examples of the very things we've been discussing. Friction turns motion into thermal energy, which is the kinetic energy of the constituents of matter. And chemical energy is believed to be a form of potential energy."

"I understand that heat is a kind of invisible motion," Eusebio said, "but how does *burning fuel* fit into this scheme?"

Yalda said, "The way to make sense of a particle of fuel is to imagine a ball of springs all knotted together tightly, then tied up with string. The action of the liberator is like cutting the string: the whole thing flies apart. But instead of a tearing sound and springs flying everywhere, from fuel you get light and hot gas."

Eusebio was bemused. "That's a charming image, but I don't see how it helps in any practical way."

"Ah, but it does!" Yalda insisted. "By reacting various chemicals together in sealed vessels—which trap all the products, and turn all the light into heat—people have built up tables showing how much potential energy different substances have, relative to each other. Fuel and liberator are like something on the tenth floor of this tower, while the gases they produce are on the ground floor. The difference in chemical energy manifests itself as pressure and heat, just as the difference in gravitational energy, if you dropped a book from that height, would manifest itself in the book's velocity."

Eusebio was growing interested now. "And it all works out? Chemical energy is like a kind of accounting, it's as simple as that?"

Yalda realized that she might have oversold the idea, just slightly. "In principle it should work, but in practice it's hard to get accurate data. Think of it as a work in progress. But if you ever go out to the chemistry department—"

Eusebio buzzed amusement. "I'm not suicidal!"

"You can always watch their experiments from behind the safety walls."

"You mean the 'safety walls' that need to be rebuilt three or four times a year?"

The truth was, Yalda had only visited Amputation Alley once herself. She said, "All right… be content to reap the benefits from a distance."

"You say it's a work in progress," Eusebio mused. "Fatal explosions aside, what's the hitch?"

"I'm no expert in their methodology," Yalda admitted. "I suppose there's room for errors to creep in when they measure temperature and pressure, and I expect it's also hard to trap all the light. We can measure the energy in heat, but if there's light emitted we don't know how to account for that."

"So how exactly do you know that they've made mistakes?" Eusebio pressed her. "What is it that tells you that their data is wrong?"

"Ah." Yalda hated to disillusion him, but she had to be honest about the magnitude of the problem. "Someone showed that the values in the last table they published could be used, indirectly, to derive the result that pure, powdered firestone and its liberator contained only slightly more chemical energy than the gases they produce—nowhere near enough to explain the high temperature of the gases. But that extra thermal energy can't just fall out of the sky; it has to come from a change in chemical energy. And that's before you even start worrying about the energy carried off by the light."

"I see," Eusebio announced cynically. "So 'chemical energy' is a beautiful theory… but after all that risk and toil, the results show that it's actually nonsense?"

Yalda preferred a different interpretation. "Suppose I told you that a friend of a friend of mine had seen a pebble drop from a third floor window, but you knew that the pebble in question had hit the ground with a deafening crash, and made a crater two strides deep. Would you throw out the whole idea of conservation of energy… or would you doubt my third-hand account of the height from which the pebble had fallen?"

Yalda squeezed into the lecture theater just as the guest speaker, Nereo, began ascending to the stage. There were only about four dozen people in the audience, but the venue had been chosen for its facilities, not its capacity, and the optics classes that were given here usually attracted just a couple of dozen students. Her late entry brought some resentful glares, but at least her height gave her the advantage of not needing to jostle for position—and when she realized that she was blocking the view of the young man behind her, she quickly changed places with him.

"My thanks to the scientists of Zeugma for their generous invitation to speak here today," Nereo began. "I am delighted to have this opportunity to discuss my recent work." Nereo lived in Red Towers, where his research was supported by a wealthy patron. With no university there, he had no colleagues around him to challenge or encourage him, though perhaps the whims of a rich industrialist were less onerous to deal with than Zeugma's academic politics.

"I am confident," Nereo continued, "that this learned audience is intimately familiar with the competing doctrines regarding the nature of light, so I will not spend time recapitulating their strengths and weaknesses. The wave doctrine rose to favor over the particle doctrine more than a year ago, when our colleague Giorgio showed that two narrow slits in an opaque barrier, illuminated with light of a single color, cast a pattern of alternating bright and dark regions—as if waves emerging from the two slits were slipping in and out of agreement with each other. The geometry of this pattern provided a means of estimating the light's wavelength—and the measurements suggested a wavelength for red light about twice that for violet."

Yalda looked around for Giorgio, her supervisor; he was standing near the front of the audience. She'd found his experiments persuasive, though many long-time proponents of the particle doctrine were unmoved. Why invoke some fanciful notion of "wavelength", they argued, when every child who'd ever glanced up at the stars could see that what distinguished one color of light from another was simply its speed of travel?

"With all respect to my colleague, though," Nereo said, "the double-slit pattern has often proved difficult to work with. The pattern is faint and the features that we wish to locate precisely can be indistinct, leading to considerable uncertainty in the measurements. In the hope of remedying these problems, I have investigated a natural extension of Giorgio's idea.

"Suppose we obtained a large number of identical sources of any vibration, and arranged them in a line in a regular fashion, with a spacing roughly comparable to, but exceeding, the wavelength of the vibration itself."

An image appeared on Nereo's chest.

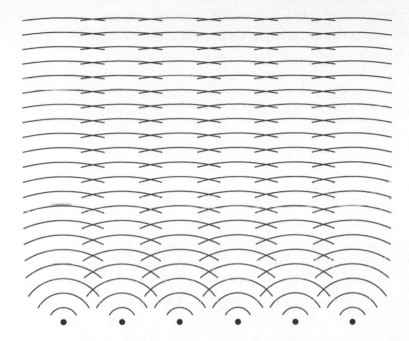

"If we ask *in what direction* the wavefronts from all these sources will come into agreement," he said, "the answer is that, firstly, they will agree if you move orthogonally away from the line on which they lie. However, that's not the only case. They will also agree at another angle, at a particular inclination to the central direction on either side."

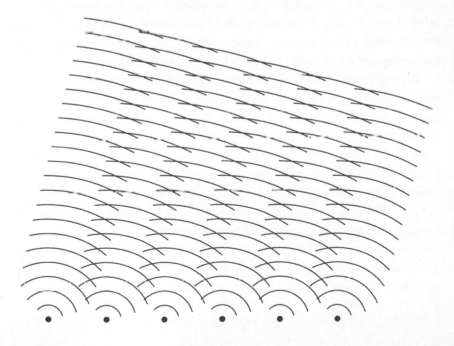

"Unlike the first direction, though, this one will depend on the wavelength of the vibration: as the wavelength grows, the angle from the center grows too."

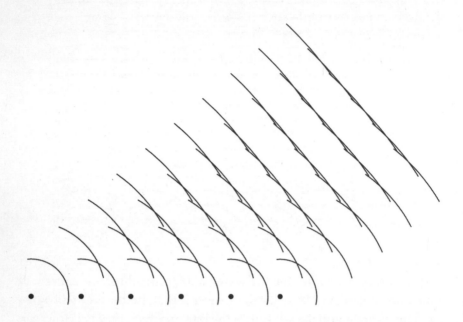

"The precise relationship between *wavelength* and *angle* is a simple trigonometric formula that will be familiar to all of you from Giorgio's work; he dealt with two sources, and I am merely extending that idea. But increasing the number of sources does yield a powerful advantage: the passage of more light delivers a brighter, clearer pattern."

Nereo gestured to an assistant, who pulled on a control rod for the blinds covering the skylight, plunging the theater into darkness. Before Yalda's eyes had time to adjust, three brilliant patches of light appeared on a screen behind the now-invisible speaker. She recognized the central one as an almost unmodified image of the sun, captured by the heliostat on the theater's roof. On either side of it were two dazzling streaks of color, distorted echoes of the primary image. Their inner rims, closest to the center of the screen, were deep violet, and they progressed in a rich, clear spectrum all the way to red. They were like star trails for the sun.

Nereo spoke from the darkness. "With the aid of my benefactor's best machinists, I constructed a system of pantographs to etch precisely-spaced apertures in a sliver of calmstone: more than two dozen gross per scant. My measurements imply that vibrations of violet light come six dozen gross to the scant; the reddest light about three and a half dozen." This was broadly in agreement with Giorgio's results: a refinement, not a contradiction.

Yalda had seen a similar spectacle produced many times before, with clearstone prisms, but beyond the sheer beauty of Nereo's crisper version she understood its significance. No one could give a detailed account of the underlying process by which a prism split light into its individual colors, so the angles at which different hues emerged from the slab of clearstone revealed nothing about the light itself. But Nereo's barrier was not mysterious; every aperture's location was known to him, every microscopic detail was there by his design. That light could be a vibration at all defied common sense—what was there to *vibrate*, in the void between the stars?—yet here was not only compelling evidence for that doctrine, but also a clear, unambiguous way to attach a wavelength to every hue.

The blinds were opened again. Yalda barely listened to the audience's questions; the only thing she wanted to ask Nereo was how soon he could make another of these marvels. While Ludovico droned on about the "obvious" possibilities for reconciling Nereo's experiment with the doctrine of luminous corpuscles, Yalda fantasized about pantographs. If Nereo could not supply them with a light comb, perhaps the university could make its own?

When the session ended, she moved quickly to the front of the theater; as one of Giorgio's students it was her responsibility to help provide hospitality to his guest. Rufino and Zosimo were already hovering nearby, ready to escort Nereo to the food hall. But as the two great experimentalists chatted, Nereo's rear gaze fell on Yalda. Her size made it hard for anyone to ignore her, and when their eyes met she seized the opportunity.

"Excuse me, sir, but I neglected to ask a question of you earlier," she said.

Giorgio did not look pleased, but Nereo indulged her. "Go ahead."

"The position of light within a star trail depends on its velocity," she began. "If you fed successive slices from a star trail through your device, might that not allow you to build up a detailed picture of how the wavelength and velocity are related?" When Nereo did not reply straight away, Yalda added helpfully, "The university has an excellent observatory on Mount Peerless. A collaboration, combining the two instruments—"

Nereo cut her off. "If you took a sliver of a star trail narrow enough to characterize the light's velocity, it would not make a bright enough source. The diffracted image with the wavelength information would be so dim as to be invisible."

He turned back to Giorgio. Yalda cursed herself silently; she hadn't thought through the practicalities.

As the five of them left the lecture theater and crossed the cobbled grounds, she struggled to find a way to salvage her proposal. The chemists were forever promising to devise a light-sensitive coating for paper that could record a telescopic image of the stars if subjected to a sufficiently long exposure. But their best offerings to date only responded to a narrow band of colors, and were prone to spontaneous combustion.

When they reached the food hall, Ludovico was waiting just inside the entrance. Zosimo bravely split off and approached him, improvising some diversionary nonsense about an administrative issue with his fees. Everyone welcomed debate about the merits of the wave and corpuscular doctrines, but Ludovico had crossed the line into monomania.

Yalda and Rufino went to fetch food from the pantry. "You must have sensitive eyes, Yalda," Rufino teased her, "to aspire to measure the wavelength of a wisp of starlight."

"There must be a way," she retorted, extruding an extra pair of arms to deal with the choice of six seasoned loaves it was customary in Zeugma to offer to a guest.

The food hall wasn't crowded; most people took lunch later, at the third bell. As Nereo and Giorgio sat eating, Yalda and Rufino stood by attentively; Zosimo was nowhere to be seen, but he must have stuck to his story and goaded Ludovico, as the department's treasurer, into dragging him back to his office to check the payment records.

Contemplating the effort and skill that must have gone into the construction of Nereo's marvel, Yalda realized that it would take the university years to develop the facilities to make their own light combs; the precision required was far beyond their present capabilities. If Nereo departed without an agreement to collaborate with them, they'd be left with nothing but the tables he'd doubtless publish in due course, assigning wavelengths to various subjectively judged hues. Being told how many vibrations of "red", "yellow" or "green" light there were to a scant wasn't utterly useless, but compared to being able to quantify the wavelength of an actual beam of light on an optical workbench it was a miserable second best. And to have any hope at all of making sense of light, they needed good numbers. Mathematics had been used to understand the vibrations of sound, the vibrations of solids, the vibrations of plucked strings—linking the properties of those diverse kinds of wave with the properties of the media that supported them. The medium that supported light was the most elusive of all, but if they could wrap the waves themselves in numbers, even this strange substance might yet be brought into the realm of comprehension.

Nereo stood and addressed the students. "The food was delicious;

thank you."

Desperate, Yalda blurted out an idea that had been lurking unvoiced in the back of her mind. "Sir, forgive me, but… what if you fed *an entire star trail* into your device? Properly focused, wouldn't the spread of colors be recombined into an image that was bright enough to see?"

Giorgio said, "Please! Our guest is tired!"

Nereo raised a hand, requesting his forbearance, and responded to Yalda. "By the principle of reversibility, yes—but only if the way the colors were distributed by the two methods were in precise agreement, which I doubt would be the case."

Yalda's skin tingled with excitement. If the recombination of the colors was sensitive to the detailed way the light was brought together, *all the better*.

"What if the star trail was focused by means of a flexible mirror?" she suggested. "A band that could be adjusted to vary the angles at which the colors were delivered, all along its length. By changing the shape of that mirror until the combined system yielded a single, sharp image for the star… wouldn't the final, successful shape embody information about the relationship between wavelength and velocity?"

Nereo fell into a thoughtful silence. Rufino stared at the floor, embarrassed. Giorgio stared directly at Yalda; she could tell that he was actually quite taken by the sheer audacity of her suggestion, if not by the clumsy way she'd raised it.

Nereo said, "It just might work. And if you blocked the center of the star's image—the brightest part—your eyes would adapt to the lesser brightness of the remaining halo, allowing you more easily to judge when your adjustments had diminished it as much as possible."

Yalda was momentarily lost for words. If Nereo was offering her ways to improve her methodology, that meant he was taking the whole thing seriously.

"So you think it's a worthwhile experiment?" she asked.

"Absolutely," Nereo assured her. "And better you than me on Mount Peerless! I've grown used to the presence of certain decadent comforts, such as air."

Giorgio buzzed amusement.

Yalda had never been to the observatory, but she didn't care what hardships it entailed. "You'll let us borrow the light comb, sir?" The glittering key to the secrets of wavelength, bought with his patron's incomparable wealth, would be borne up the mountain's slope to meet the starlight… *in her hands*?

"I'll let you borrow it for eight chimes," Nereo replied, "before I have to leave to catch my train. That should be long enough for you to calibrate your best prism against it."

"Prism? But—"

Nereo said, "Everything in your methodology should work just as well with a prism used to recombine the star trails; all you need in order to make that worthwhile is a conversion table that translates between the angles at which the same hue emerges from the different devices. Do you think you can manage that, before I depart?"

In the optics workshop a young student was using the heliostat for an experiment in polarization, but when Yalda asked if he could take an early lunch he obliged without a moment's hesitation.

From the storage room, she chose a prism that she'd used before; the sides had been polished to near-perfect flatness, and were unblemished by chips or scratches. Equally, the clearstone from which it had been cut appeared to contain no internal flaws. She knew that it would separate the colors smoothly, however mysterious its method.

With the prism in place in the beam of sunlight that was brought down from the clockwork-driven mirror on the roof, Yalda locked Nereo's comb onto a platform that could swivel through the emerging fan of colors, along with a slit for selecting a narrow range of the prism's light. The slit could not be set too fine, though, or it would itself diffract the beam.

She placed a white screen half a stride beyond the comb, and set about recording the pairs of angles for a succession of hues: the angle at which the light had been bent by the prism, and the angle at which it was subsequently bent by the comb.

Yalda worked with scrupulous care, but after a while the process became mechanical, automatic. She glanced at the polarisers she'd taken off the bench: slabs of an exotic form of clearstone from Shattered Hill. Place one of them in a beam of light, and the beam's brightness was diminished by one third. A second polariser aligned identically with the first had no effect, but if the two were "crossed"—their axes arranged at right angles to each other—the original brightness was diminished by a further third.

Giorgio had sought to explain this in terms of the wave doctrine. An elastic solid could experience *shear waves*, in which the medium suffered distortions perpendicular to the direction of the wave's motion. A polariser, he argued, must somehow be inhibiting light's equivalent of such waves when they lined up with the stone's special axis. A horizontal polariser could rid a beam of sunlight of its left-to-right vibrations; a second, aligned vertically, would rid it of all waves that vibrated up and down.

A mystery remained, though. Along with shear waves, every solid carried *pressure waves*, which were much like the sound waves in air. The velocities of the two kinds of wave were due to distinct properties of the material, and pressure waves always traveled faster than shear waves. It would require both a truly bizarre material *and* an absurd coincidence to force the two to share the same speed.

When two crossed polarisers were held up to a star trail, if the light that emerged had traveled from the star at a different speed than the light that was blocked, some portion of the trail's spread of velocities should have been favored over the rest. But in fact what was seen was a perfectly uniform dimming of the entire trail. Light waves that lacked polarity—supposedly the equivalent of a solid's pressure waves—were no faster or slower than the rest.

Yalda could not believe that this was a coincidence—a perfect conspiracy of elastic moduli. Rather, what it suggested was that the whole analogy was flawed. Whatever carried light between the stars wasn't actually being squeezed and stretched and sheared. Nereo had pinned down light's wavelength, the distance at which each cycle repeated, but the truth was that no one yet had an answer to the question: *cycles of what?*

When Yalda had a full range of measurements, she sprinkled dye onto her chest and made three copies of the figures on paper: one for Giorgio, one for Nereo—not much use to him, since the numbers were tied to a particular slab of clearstone, but an appropriate gesture nonetheless—and one to keep in the workshop alongside the prism.

Nereo was waiting at the university's southern gate, an ornate stone archway encircled by violet-flowered vines that had been bred to open their blossoms even in daylight. Yalda thanked him profusely, and almost offered to carry his luggage to the station, but Rufino and Zosimo were already grappling with the cases, and she'd learned not to wound their pride with gratuitous displays of physical prowess.

When they'd left, Giorgio upbraided her sternly before finally conceding, "I suppose it was worth it in the end. You're not much of a diplomat, but this could yield interesting results."

The understatement was insulting, but Yalda didn't push her luck. "I hope so," she said.

Giorgio regarded her with weary affection. "And I hope you're ready to try displaying a bit more tact."

"Of course!" Yalda said, genuinely chastened now. "The next visitor, I promise—"

Giorgio hummed, annoyed. "Forget about the next visitor! You want to use the telescope, don't you?"

"Yes." Yalda was bewildered; did he mean that she'd probably be up on the mountain, unable to cause any more embarrassment when his next guest came to speak?

Then she understood.

"The next unallocated slot at the observatory begins in seven stints," Giorgio said. "If you want that slot for your wavelength measurements, you know who you're going to have to deal with."

A motif of two entwined helices was carved into the wall outside Ludovico's office. The curves represented the motion of Gemma and Gemmo, co-planets that circled a common center every eleven days, five bells, nine chimes and seven lapses. Of course, they also traveled around the sun, and their distance from the world rose and fell substantially during each six-year orbit. Before Yalda had even been born, Ludovico had noticed that as Gemma and Gemmo drew farther away, the precise clockwork of their mutual circling seemed to slow, very slightly: the observed times when one planet crossed in front of the other slipped behind the predictions of celestial mechanics. But Ludovico had realized that the laws of gravity were not at fault; the light was just taking a little longer to arrive. With this insight, his observations had allowed him to compute the first reliable figures for the speed of light, averaged across the colors.

By the time Ludovico called Yalda into his office, the sun had set. He'd lit a firestone lamp, which sat sputtering and sizzling on a corner of his grand, paper-strewn desk. Standing before him, eyes respectfully downcast, Yalda summarised her proposal quickly. Her aim, she declared, was to correlate the angles of separation in a star trail with the angles of deflection produced by a clearstone prism; there was no need to mention Nereo's device at all. "If I can find the formula that links the prism's effect with the light's velocity, that might lead to some insight into the mechanism of chromatic deflection." In fact the data she gathered would be perfectly suited to that purpose; she was not really being dishonest.

When she'd finished speaking, Ludovico emitted a muted hum, the tone signifying gratitude that a tedious ordeal had finally ended.

"I've never had much time for you, Yalda," he said. "Not because you hail from the benighted eastern provinces, with your quaint dialect and bizarre customs; that can be endearing, and even correctible. And not because you're a woman—or almost a woman, or something that might have been a woman if nature had taken its proper course."

Yalda looked up, startled. She hadn't been insulted in quite such an infantile fashion since she'd left the village school.

"No, what I find objectionable is your arrogance and your utter inconstancy. You hear of an experiment, you read of some research, and whatever ideas you've supported in the past fly out the window. You simply trust in your own infallible powers of reasoning to guide you to the truth, as you swerve this way and that." Ludovico held up a hand and made a zigzagging motion. "Well, I've heard of all the same experiments, I've read all the same research. I suppose I must not share your hubris, though—because I'm not driven to the same undignified series of self-contradictory declarations and endless changes of allegiance."

Yalda said nothing, but she struggled to recall what she might have done to earn this tirade. At her admission interview, where Ludovico had sat on the panel, she'd professed some sympathy for the particle doctrine; that had been before Giorgio's double-slit experiment. But at a debate half a year ago, she'd taken the side of the wave doctrine, and expressed the flaws in the opposing view quite forcefully. Why not? The evidence had mounted up, and she'd found it increasingly compelling. But apparently it was a kind of arrogance, to trust her feeble powers of reasoning to bring her to that conclusion.

Ludovico reached down to a shelf below his desk and lifted up a bulky stack of paper. In fact it was a book, Yalda realized, though the binding was in a terrible state.

"Have you ever read Meconio on the theory of luminous corpuscles?" he demanded.

"No sir," Yalda admitted. Meconio had been a philosopher in the ninth age; she'd heard that he'd made some minor contributions to the study of rhetoric, but his grasp of natural phenomena had been less than impressive.

"*If* you can produce a halfway perceptive, three-dozen-page essay on Meconio within the next two stints, I'll allow you to use the observatory." Ludovico held out the tattered book; Yalda reached across and took it carefully. "A little exposure to a truly great mind might finally endow you with a trace of humility."

"Thank you, sir. I'll do my best."

Ludovico hummed irritably. "If you can't manage a commentary that's worthy of my attention, leave the book with my assistant and don't ever waste my time again."

Yalda left his office and trudged down the dark hallway toward the exit. Two bells ago, she'd been euphoric; now she just felt hopeless. This man had set her an impossible task; even if Meconio's tome was strewn with dazzling insights worth praising to the sky, she would never be able to plow through so much fusty ninth-age language in time to write anything sensible about his ideas.

"Are you all right?"

Yalda turned, startled; someone had just emerged from one of the unlit rooms opening into the hallway. The voice had come from nearby, but all she could see was a faint outline in the darkness.

"I was measuring floral spectra," the woman explained—work best done at night, without a lamp, the better to observe the plant's luminescence. "My name's Tullia."

"I'm Yalda. Pleased to meet you." Yalda couldn't keep the despondency from her voice, but Tullia's solicitousness had come before she'd said a word. "Why did you ask me—?"

"I could tell you'd had one of those Ludo moments," Tullia confessed. Her outline was growing sharper as Yalda's eyes adjusted to the gloom. "There's actually a distinctive effect on people's gait as they come down the hall. Sadistic belittlement is his specialty, so I know exactly how that sounds. But if he starts to get you down, just remember: everything he says comes from halfway up his anus."

Yalda struggled to stifle her response, lest the sound echo all the way back to his office. "That's remarkably flexible for someone his age," she observed.

"Flexibility is *not* a quality I associate with Ludikins," Tullia replied. "I expect his tympanum's been stuck there for the last dozen years. Let me get my things."

Tullia ducked back into the workshop, then they walked together out into the night. As they crossed the starlit courtyard, she said, "I see he's given you his favorite reading material."

"I have to write an essay on it in the next two stints," Yalda lamented.

"Ah, Meconio!" Tullia chirped sardonically. "Proof that it *is* possible to fill five gross pages with scholarific assertions about the world, without bothering to test even one of them. Don't worry, though, we've all had to do the essay. I'll give you an old one, with enough tweaks to disguise it."

Yalda didn't know whether to be scandalized or grateful. "You'd do that?"

"Of course. Why wouldn't I?" Tullia was mocking her; she'd picked up the undertone of disapproval. "It's not as if I'm helping you cheat in some serious assessment; this is just Ludi's ludicrous self-indulgence. Well... octofurcate him at every opportunity, that's my policy. What's the favor you needed from him, anyway?"

Yalda explained her wavelength-velocity project.

"That's an elegant idea," Tullia declared. "It's tough up on the mountain, though, so remind me to give you a few tips before you go. It's easy to overheat there."

"You've been to the observatory?"

"Six times."

Yalda was impressed—and not only by the woman's physical stamina. "What are you working on?"

"I'm looking for life on other worlds." Tullia's tone made this endeavor sound entirely practical, as if it were no different from looking for weeds in a wheat field.

"You think we could see signs in the spectra?" Yalda was skeptical, but the notion was delightful.

"Of course," Tullia replied. "If someone observed our world from a distance, its light trail would be very different from any star's. Plants create a wide variety of colors, but they come in discrete hues. When rock burns, the fuel itself has a distinctive color in its emissions, but the spectrum from the hot gas is continuous."

"But how can you know what the plants on other worlds will be like?"

"The detailed photochemistry might be different," Tullia conceded, "but I bet life would still show up as discrete bands of color. I mean, do you know of any method for getting energy out of rocks without producing light along the way? And if it's *not* staged and controlled, if it's not confined to specific channels the way plants do it… that's a world on fire. That's a star."

Yalda had become so caught up in the conversation that she'd barely noticed them leaving the campus. She looked around to get her bearings.

Tullia said, "I'm going to meet some friends in the south quarter. You're welcome to come along if you like."

"Are you sure?"

"Absolutely."

They turned into the avenue that led south toward the Great Bridge. Yalda liked the evenings in Zeugma; light spilt from the windows of restaurants and apartments to reflect off the cobblestones, but you could see the star trails clearly too. Families and couples were out walking, lost in their own concerns; no one looked twice at her bulky form. If she hadn't run into Tullia she would have been pacing through the city alone now, waiting for the beauty of the streets and the sky to overcome her anger at Ludovico's patronizing diatribe. Belatedly, she formed a pocket and slipped Meconio's treatise into it for safe-keeping; if she lost the book itself, not even the most ingratiating tribute to his genius would be enough to save her.

Halfway across the Great Bridge, they stopped to stare down into the blackness of the crevasse that divided the city. Several ages ago the ground here had been full of firestone; the first settlements had grown up around shallow mines. Later an elaborate system of tunnels had been built, plunging deep into the stone. But early in the eleventh age there'd been an accident in the mines and the whole deposit had been ignited. Half the city had been destroyed, and every trace of fuel had been burned away. All that remained was this jagged abyss, a taunting geochemical map in reverse: *here's what you could have had, now that it's gone.*

"I think every world probably started out with much the same mixture of minerals," Tullia said. "Maybe they were all part of a single, primal world, eons ago. But I suspect that, whatever its origin, there are only three things that can happen to a world: it remains dark, like Gemma and Gemmo; it catches fire, like the sun and the stars; or life comes along to perform the same kind of chemistry in a more controlled way."

Yalda gazed into the hole left behind by the Great Ignition. "This place makes me think that those possibilities need not be mutually exclusive."

"True enough," Tullia replied. "In fact, for all we know that might be a universal truth. Maybe the stars didn't just burst into light; maybe they started out covered in plants, which grew too productive for their own good. All the liberators we've discovered so far are plant extracts, after all. And maybe it's just a matter of time before the same thing happens here—either the plants do it, or the honor goes to someone in the chemistry department."

"Now I'm worried," Yalda said, only half-joking. "If anyone can set calmstone on fire, it's a chemist."

They continued across the bridge into the south quarter. "I used to work in that restaurant," Tullia said, pointing to a brightly lit building on a crowded side street. "When I was a student."

"Is that where we're going?"

"Only if you want to drop in for a spot of arson."

"You sound nostalgic."

"The clientele were mostly Councilors' sons and their entourages," Tullia said. "How could I not have fond memories?"

She led the way to another restaurant, one that Yalda had passed many times before, but instead of taking the front entrance they slipped into a winding alley that ran behind the kitchen. Tullia exchanged shouted greetings with a woman Yalda glimpsed working inside, but they continued down the alley until they reached an unlit flight of stairs. It took Yalda a moment to orient herself; the stairs led back to a second story over the restaurant.

"Your friends aren't eating with everyone else?" Yalda was growing puzzled, and a little anxious; why were they creeping around in the dark like this?

Tullia paused on the stairs. "This is a place to talk freely, without worrying who's listening," she explained. "We call it the Solo Club—though there are only a few genuine solos among us. Some of us had cos who died, some of us are runaways, some of us are just thinking about breaking the tie."

Yalda had heard of runaways—and thoroughly approved, in principle—but it was something else to be told that there was a whole cabal of radicals huddled a few strides away at the top of these stairs.

She said, "If the city police—"

"The police won't come here," Tullia assured her. "We make it worth their while to stay away."

Yalda steadied herself. One reason she'd rarely befriended the women she'd encountered in Zeugma was the disparity between their expectations and her own. Here, finally, was a chance to meet a few whose lives did not revolve around the imminent certainty of childbirth. What kind of coward would she be to forego that, just because some of them were on the wrong side of the law?

She said, "I'd like to meet your friends."

Though the stairway was dark, the curtain at the top parted to reveal a room as brightly lit as the restaurant below. No one was huddled behind partitions, whispering seditiously; they were seated on the floor in small groups, clustered around lamps and dishes, talking and buzzing and chirping just like students in the university food hall.

One woman in a group of three turned toward them and called to Tullia. They approached, and Tullia made introductions.

"Daria, Antonia, Lidia: this is Yalda. We only met a few chimes ago, but she's into the glorious mysteries of optics, so she must be worth knowing."

"Please join us," said Daria. There was a diagram of some kind displayed on her chest, though Yalda could make no immediate sense of it.

As they sat, Tullia asked about the picture.

"I was just talking about the western shrub vole," Daria explained. "The young need care for half a year after birth, but they have no sterile caregivers; instead, one of each brood delays reproduction for a season. Children whose mother was an early reproducer are cared for by their late-reproducing aunt; those whose mother was a late reproducer—making *their aunt* the early reproducer—are cared for by that aunt's late-reproducing child."

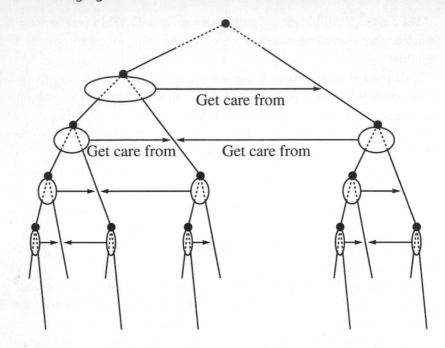

Yalda could interpret the diagram, now; the lines sloping down across Daria's chest represented the life of each vole, with dashed lines when they were so young as to need care, and annotations showing which relative provided it. "Some late reproducers look after two young, some four," she noticed. "They all look after their sister's children, but if their mother was an early reproducer they're stuck with their aunt's children as well. That's hardly fair."

Daria was amused. "And the early reproducers live half as long as the others—of course it's not fair! But it's worth learning about the full range of possibilities nature has invented, in the hope that one day we can steal the useful parts and assemble them into something better."

Before Yalda could ask how anyone might *steal a useful part* of another species' biology, Lidia said, "How about a drug that lets men reproduce? That would make a nice addition to holin!"

"I doubt that a drug alone could do that," Daria replied. "Men aren't likely to possess any kind of dormant capacity for childbirth, given that all our close relatives have sterile caregivers. Even when the young need more physical protection than education—so the caregivers tend to be quite large—the pattern is the same: reproduction or care, never both. The voles are an interesting exception, but they're on a distant branch of the family tree."

Daria smoothed the picture away, and the conversation turned to more mundane matters. As the women recounted the day's tribulations,

Yalda picked up a little more about Tullia's circle of friends. Daria taught medicine at the university, while Lidia worked in a dye factory and Antonia sold lamps in the markets.

"Anyone for six-dice?" Lidia suggested.

"Sure," said Daria. The others agreed.

"I don't know the rules," Yalda confessed.

Lidia pulled a handful of small cubical dice from a pocket. "We each start with six of these; the sides are numbered one to three in red and in blue." She gave one to Yalda to inspect. "You roll your dice, and your total is the sum of the blue faces minus the sum of the red. There are some simple rules which decide how many dice you *should* have, according to your total; if it's not correct, you either have to get rid of some dice, or collect some from the bank. When you collect, you always take pairs and set them down with the same number showing, one red one blue, so your total is unchanged.

"Then, we take turns playing. The player can make any change to one of their own dice that they can balance with a corresponding change to another person's. For example, I can turn my *red three* into a *blue two* by turning your *blue three* into a *red two*. Then both of us adjust our numbers of dice to fit our new totals, and on it goes."

"How does someone win?" Yalda asked.

"Their total hits a gross, or they have the highest total after everyone has made six dozen moves."

"Those rules about the numbers of dice—?"

"You'll pick them up easily," Lidia promised.

In fact, it took Yalda three games before she really knew what she was doing. Lidia won the first two, Daria the third.

After the fourth game, a win to Lidia again, Antonia made her apologies and rose to leave.

"My co thinks I'm taking a delivery," she said. "But he knows they never come much later than this, so I'd better not push my luck."

When Antonia had left, Yalda asked glumly, "How does anyone put up with that?" Whatever taunts and humiliations she'd suffered herself, at least she was nobody's prisoner.

"Things are going to change," Lidia said. "Once we get a few women on the City Council, we can start to work toward banning forced returns."

"Women on the Council?" The idea struck Yalda as utterly fanciful. "Are there any women with that kind of money?"

Tullia pointed out a woman seated on the far side of the room. "*She* owns the company that distributes grain throughout the city. She could easily afford to pay for a seat; the real issue is wearing down the men who are refusing to let her buy in."

"We'll live to see it happen," Lidia declared confidently. "There are a dozen wealthy women in this city who are working toward the same agenda. First, legalize runaways. Second, legalize holin."

"What's holin?" This was the second time Lidia had mentioned it, but Yalda had never heard the word used anywhere else.

For a moment the whole group was silent, then Daria said, "I know you only met her tonight, Tullia, so I don't blame you at all. But if an educated woman in Zeugma doesn't know what holin is, what hope has anyone got out in the sticks?"

Yalda was bemused. "Lidia said it was a drug, but what does it treat? I've actually been quite healthy ever since I came to Zeugma; maybe that's why I haven't heard of it."

"Holin inhibits reproduction," Daria explained. "How old are you?"

"Twelve. I just turned twelve."

"Then you need to be taking it."

"But…" Yalda preferred to keep these matters private, but in the circumstances there was no point being coy. "I have no co," she said. "I'm a solo. I'm not looking for a co-stead. And I'm strong enough to take care of myself, so I really don't think I'm going to be abducted by some poor, deserted rich boy who's desperate for heirs. So why would I need a drug that inhibits reproduction?"

Tullia said, "None of us have cos around—and holin gives very poor protection against triggering anyway. What it inhibits most effectively is spontaneous reproduction. The chance of that is quite small at your age, but it's not zero. I'm two years shy of two dozen, myself; without holin I wouldn't last another year."

Yalda had never heard any of this before. She said, "My father always told me that if I didn't find a co-stead, I'd go the way of men."

"There's no reason he would have known the truth," Lidia said. "It's not as if he would have been acquainted with any great number of women of Tullia's age."

"That's true." Yalda doubted there'd been a woman in her village more than four years past a dozen.

Daria added, "I've also heard claims that spontaneous reproduction is more likely in concentrated population centers. If you'd stayed at home then your father's prediction might have come true, but in a city like Zeugma the odds are skewed against it."

Yalda was beginning to feel disoriented. She had always imagined that she would eventually ease her father into accepting her belief that a solo was born to a different kind of destiny—and then that would be the end of the matter. He might still nag her occasionally, but she knew he would never have forced a co-stead on her. Now she had to think about ways of getting her hands on a drug that Zeugma's Council deemed illegal—and taking that drug for the rest of her life.

Daria could see that this was making her anxious. "I can get you some holin," she said. "It's probably better that we don't meet at the university, though. I'm giving a public lecture in the Variety Hall three nights from tonight; if you want to come along we can meet afterward."

"Thank you."

"The young lady's had a shock," Tullia said, "and I'm tutoring the laziest of my merchants' sons tomorrow, so we should probably call it a night."

They left Lidia and Daria still talking. Tullia walked with Yalda to the edge of the markets. "You really sleep down there? You should get an apartment."

"I like sleeping in the ground," Yalda replied. "And I don't care about privacy; no one ever bothers me."

"Fair enough," Tullia conceded. "But you have something new to consider now."

"What's that?"

"Where exactly are you going to hide your holin?"

4

Yalda met Tullia outside the Variety Hall. Daria's lecture, entitled "The Anatomy of the Beast", was advertised with garishly colored posters showing a fearsome creature standing on a tree branch, one hand clasped around a hapless lizard, another outstretched toward a second, unsuccessfully fleeing meal. Infant care of the western shrub vole might not have been quite so enticing a subject to Zeugma's moneyed classes.

Tullia harangued the ticket-seller into checking for a list of free admissions, and both their names turned out to be on it. "I should hope so!" she told Yalda as they moved from the ticket queue to the equally crowded one leading to the entrance. "I've paid for enough of Daria's meals at the Solo to keep her in scalpels for the rest of her life."

Once they'd entered the hall, Yalda saw that the stage had been decorated with a number of small but authentic-looking trees, augmented with a scaffolding of branches and twigs that served to heighten the impression of a dense forest canopy. As stagehands moved through the hall extinguishing the wall lamps, the crowd buzzed with anticipation, as if they expected a whole menagerie of nocturnal wildlife to reveal itself in this motley imitation jungle.

A few sickly buds on the trees did open in the gloom, but they soon closed again as brighter lights were trained on the stage from above. Yalda looked up and caught a glimpse of a girl perched on a narrow railing, struggling to maneuver an unwieldy contraption of burning sunstone behind a clearstone lens.

The impresario walked onto the stage and delivered a spiel about the perilous expedition that had been mounted to the Shining Valley to capture the subject of the night's demonstration. "In its natural state, this creature is too ferocious to be allowed into the city at all; the Council would never permit it! However—after feeding the beast stupefying drugs for six days, in a holding pen a safe distance beyond the city limits, we are able to present, for the first time ever in Zeugma, our wild, uncultured cousin: the arborine!"

A cart was wheeled on, bearing a thick branch suspended between two supports. The arborine's hands and feet were bound to the branch with ropes; it was in no state to grip anything itself. Its head hung limply, and though its eyes were open they were dull and fixed. Yalda thought it was a male, but she wasn't sure; she'd only ever seen sketches of the animal before. Certainly it was smaller than she was.

"I hope it's already dead," she whispered.

Tullia said, "Ah, a sentimentalist."

"Why should it feel pain for our entertainment?"

"Do you think it lived a life of comfort in the trees?"

Yalda was annoyed. "No, but that's beside the point. Nature wants to split *your* body in four and pulp your brain. We should be aiming higher."

A man in front of them turned and hushed her.

"Only a woman," the impresario was saying, "could possess the physical strength to handle such a beast. But we are lucky to have found a woman with both the strength *and* the expert knowledge to be our guide into this dangerous territory. From Zeugma University, I give you: Doctor Daria!"

As the crowd erupted with the sound of acclaim, Tullia whispered, "Don't worry, fashions change. One day we'll be up there with our prisms and lenses, raking in just as much cash."

Yalda said, "Only if there are other-worldly arborines in your forests in the sky."

Daria strode into a waiting spotlight, a third arm sprouting from the middle of her chest. She was carrying a circular saw connected to a long tube that stretched all the way back into the wings.

"Rest assured," she said, "we will all be safe tonight." She held up the saw for their inspection. "This instrument is powered by compressed air, and makes a dozen gross revolutions every flicker. Should the arborine somehow escape from its stupor, I can sever its head in an instant." She squeezed a trigger and the blade became a blur of screeching stone.

"Now, though, it's time to feed our wild cousin his very last meal." An assistant brought a bucket onto the stage; Daria took it and approached the arborine. With a scoop that was sitting in the bucket, she lifted out some of its contents—which resembled coarsely milled grain, but had somehow been rendered a startlingly vivid red—and poured it into the arborine's slack mouth.

Yalda watched with revolted fascination as the muscles around the arborine's throat began to move. It was alive, and, drugged or not, still able to swallow.

"You might be wondering at the unusual hue of our unfortunate guest's repast," Daria noted. "In fact, over the past six days his food has been mixed with a different dye for every meal." As she spoke, the arborine kept gulping mechanically at the trickle of grain.

When the creature would take no more food, Daria put the bucket aside and set her blade spinning. With the audience cheering her on, she stepped up to the arborine and began carving into its flank.

If her victim made a sound, the machine was more than loud enough to conceal it. Yalda could see the arborine twitching pitifully for a while, but by the time Daria stood aside to reveal her handiwork its convulsions had ceased.

The saw had removed a wide rectangular slab of skin and muscle that stretched almost the full length of the arborine's body. Yalda was sickened by the needless cruelty of the methodology, but she did not look away.

The red-dyed food had penetrated a surprising distance already—perhaps four or five spans from the creature's throat—but it was the evidence of past meals that was truly revelatory. The six bands of color painted a veritable history of digestion and excretion: the previous day's orange meal had been squeezed from the esophagus into dozens of smaller tubes that branched out from that central passage, while the yellow had progressed into a multitude of vastly finer tubules. The green dye occupied a convoluted surface that curled around within the arborine's flesh, like some huge tarpaulin that had been folded and re-folded on several different scales in order to pack it down to the smallest possible volume; Yalda suspected that it, too, had been carried by a system of tubes that were simply too fine for her to resolve from this distance. The green layer, Daria explained, was food that had finally come within reach of virtually every muscle in the body.

For the still-earlier meals, a similar process could be seen in reverse: fine vessels gathered up the unused portions of the food, along with a cargo of metabolic wastes, and brought them together in ever-larger conduits. At the far end of the gruesome window, a cluster of violet faeces could be seen, waiting to be expelled.

"Six days—half a stint—from mouth to anus," Daria marveled. "So long to cross such a short distance. But then, most foods need to be milled finely by the body—crushed and re-crushed by the muscles at every junction—and every scrag of nutrition needs to be extracted along the way.

"One question might occur to you, though: if it takes so very long for our vital sustenance to travel through the body, how does *the will to move* pass from the brain to the limbs in an instant? While it's true that the passage of food is deliberately sluggish, no chemical we know of can diffuse through a solid or a resin in the requisite time, nor can muscular contractions convey any cargo through a tube with sufficient rapidity."

The stage dimmed, and an assistant wheeled on a new prop: a small sunstone lamp, burning fiercely but covered with a hood that allowed only a narrow beam of light to escape. Daria directed the beam onto the arborine's exposed flesh, taking some time to aim it carefully; perhaps she wished to highlight a particular feature, but she offered no explanation for her choice.

Next, she took a knife and cut the rope that bound one of the arborine's arms to the branch from which it was suspended. A murmur of disquiet spread through the crowd, but once freed the limb simply hung from the creature's shoulder like a long sack of meat.

Daria said, "Some philosophers and anatomists have conjectured that a gas, not unlike air itself, might be spread or squeezed throughout the body in order to convey our will to move. On the contrary, my research has shown that the answer is both simpler and more wondrous: what informs the muscles is... *this*." She took a pinch of fine powder from a dish beside the lamp and flicked it into the flame. There was a flash of intense yellow light as the substance was consumed—and the arborine's arm swung up from its position of rest, twitched, then fell back down again.

The audience yelled and stamped their feet in approval. Tullia leaned toward Yalda and whispered, "If only she'd got it to do summersaults; we could have had a full-blown riot."

Daria acknowledged the acclaim graciously, but then gestured for silence; the demonstration was not yet complete. "Light of the correct hue can excite the muscles into action. But is that its only role in the body? I think not."

The stage dimmed further, finally becoming completely black. The decorative trees unfurled their wan blooms once more, but the petals were just barely visible. From the darkness came the whine of Daria's spinning blade; when it stopped Yalda heard her take a few steps across the stage.

As Daria moved aside, a patch of shimmering yellow light was revealed behind her. The light throbbed and shifted in waves; Yalda was unpleasantly reminded of the swarm of mites that had feasted on her dying grandfather. But these specks of radiance didn't flee into the air; no flock of hapless insects was feeding on the arborine. Daria had opened up the creature's skull, and its last thoughts were playing out in front of them: a sad dance of fading luminescence, like a gust of wind rustling through a dying garden.

When the glow from the arborine's brain had flickered out completely, the lights came up and Daria spread her arms in a gesture of finality. The crowd made its approval known. Yalda had to admire the woman's stagecraft, but the whole performance had left her disquieted.

It took even Tullia a while to talk her way backstage, with Yalda in tow. They found Daria relaxing in a luxurious bed of white sand.

"Did you like the show?" she asked them.

"Yalda thinks you should have killed the beast before you cut it," Tullia volunteered.

"The brain's light would have been invisible, then, by the time I opened the skull," Daria replied. "Honestly, we drugged it very heavily. The swallowing is a reflex; I don't believe it was conscious at all."

Yalda was not convinced, but she let the matter drop; she had no real evidence either way.

"I promised you some holin," Daria recalled. She climbed out of her bed and rummaged in a cupboard in a corner of the room, emerging with a small clearstone vial. "Take two scrags with breakfast, daily." She handed Yalda the vial; the green flaky substance had been prepared in small cubical lumps. "You'll need to increase the dose in a year or so."

"How much do I owe you?" Yalda asked.

"Forget it," Daria replied, slipping back into her sand bed. "Pay me when you're wealthy." She turned to Tullia. "Are you off to the Solo?"

"Not tonight."

"Well, I'm sure I'll see you both around."

Yalda thanked her and began to leave. Daria said, "Keep it safe, and never miss a dose. I know you're still young, but that only means you have all the more to lose."

"I'll follow your advice," Yalda assured her. She slipped the vial into a pocket before they left the room.

On the street, she asked Tullia, "Would you be able to give me that essay on Meconio that you mentioned? I should probably spend some time rewriting it in my own style."

"Good idea," Tullia said. "I think I have a version in my apartment."

As they crossed the Great Bridge, suspended over the city's deep lesion, Yalda's thoughts kept returning to the night of her grandfather's death. Every living thing needed to make light, but like all chemistry it was a dangerous business. There was always a risk that it would go too far.

When Tullia remarked on how distracted she was, Yalda told her the story of the trip into the forest, and how it had ended.

"That's hard," Tullia said. "No one so young should have to witness a death."

"Have you seen people die?"

"Two friends, in the last few years, but I never saw anyone go to light." Tullia hesitated. "My co died when I was a few stints old, but I don't remember that at all."

"That's terrible."

Tullia spread her arms; there was no call for sympathy. "I never knew him. Most of the time I might as well have been a solo."

"Is your family still pushing you to find a co-stead?"

"My father's dead," Tullia replied. "My brother and cousins would nag me if they could, but they don't even know where I'm living now."

"Oh." Yalda found it hard to imagine Aurelio or Claudio, let alone little Lucio, taking it upon themselves to tell her how to live. But people changed; once they were adults with children of their own and the neighbors were asking them, "What happened to Yalda?", perhaps they'd start to see it as their duty to have an acceptable answer.

They reached the tower where Tullia lived. Her apartment was on the eleventh floor—the cheapest location in the building, she explained. Most people didn't want to climb so many stairs, though they made an exception for the very top floor, which was more expensive thanks to the skylights. Yalda could understand that; she would have loved to sleep beneath the stars again.

Tullia had no lamps in her apartment, just a long shelf of small potted plants, arranged by color. Between the glow of the flowers and the starlight that came through the windows, she could see well enough to search through her stacks of paper.

After a while she said, "It's not here. I must have given it to someone else then neglected to make a new copy."

Yalda said, "What would you have copied it from?"

"Oh, I still have it *here*." Tullia thumped her chest. "Once I write something, I never forget it. But I don't have any dye right now, or enough blank paper for that matter. How's your touch memory?"

"My what?"

Tullia reached over and took her right hand. "Try to remember this without thinking about it. Don't read it, don't describe it to yourself, just try to keep the feeling of the shape."

"All right."

Tullia pressed her palm against Yalda's and wrote a short passage *on both of their skins*. Yalda let her own muscles conform to the pattern of pressure from the curved ridges jutting against them; in a curious reversal of cause and effect, it soon felt as if she'd shaped every line herself. A few symbols drifted into her mind, but she blocked them out, forcing them to remain uninterpreted.

"Now give it back to me." Tullia released Yalda's right hand and took the left one. "Don't think about the details, just bring back the memory of how it felt."

Yalda summoned the shape, sharply tactile but still unvisualised, and pushed it onto her left palm. Tullia offered a congratulatory chirp. "Perfect!"

Yalda drew her hand back. "Can I read it now?"

"Certainly."

She didn't need to examine her palm; she could sense the disposition of every muscle directly. "Meconio," Yalda read, "was undoubtedly one of the greatest minds of the ninth age." The text, she realized, was mirror-form compared to her own usual skin style.

"Isn't it amazing what people can write when they don't have to think about it?" Tullia marveled. "Let alone believe it."

"Am I being dishonest?" Yalda wondered. "I know Ludovico is abusing his power, but there's still a principle at stake. Maybe we should try to get someone else put in charge of the observatory schedules?"

Tullia sagged against the wall, exasperated. "In an ideal world: of course! But you know how long that would take. If you're serious about gathering your wavelength data before you drop dead—or worse—you're just going to have to humor Ludo. Life is too short to make everything perfect."

"I suppose so."

"Do you want the whole essay?"

Reluctantly, Yalda gave her assent.

"Come closer."

Tullia took her by the waist and spun her around so that her back was against the wall. Then she moved toward Yalda, the whole length of her body drawing near. Instinctively, Yalda put up a hand to stop her.

"Palm by palm would take us all night," Tullia said. "This is faster. What are you afraid of? I can't hurt you; I'm not a man."

"It feels strange, that's all." And was it true that only a man could trigger her? If a woman could give birth at any time—entirely unaided, against her will—Yalda didn't know what to believe anymore. Maybe every awful children's story, every cautionary tale, every rumor of magical comeuppance was really grounded in cold, hard fact. Maybe you could trip on the stairs or fall off a truck and find you'd been traded-in four for one.

"It's up to you," Tullia said. "I can get some dye tomorrow and write the whole thing on paper, then you can spend the afternoon reading it."

Yalda considered this, but then she fought down her unease. Surely Tullia wouldn't do anything that risked their lives?

"No, you're right," she said. "This way is easier."

She lowered her hand, and Tullia pressed her skin against Yalda's. Her head barely reached halfway up Yalda's chest, and there were gaps where they weren't quite making contact; Yalda put a hand in the middle of Tullia's back and drew her gently forward. Behind her, the row of shining flowers stretched across the room like the trail of some impossibly fast star.

Tullia began writing. Two bodies, one skin. Yalda left the words unread; she could entertain herself later with the awfulness of the essay. Now, she simply let the shapes flow from skin to memory, feeling a sense of rightness to them on a different level: each symbol on its own was elegantly constructed, each page was beautifully composed. Let the words give Ludovico the empty flattery he craved, while she and Tullia smuggled the true meaning right past him.

Tullia stepped back.

"That's it?" Yalda was surprised.

"Three dozen pages: that's what he always asks for."

"It went so quickly."

Tullia was amused. "If you still have an itch, I can give you my whole dissertation on plant spectra."

Yalda looked away, confused. She didn't care that this pleasure was so strange that she'd never even been warned against it, but she had no sense of what it meant, what obligations it entailed.

"You should give up the basement," Tullia suggested. "Come and stay here with me."

"I don't know." Yalda wasn't looking for a co-stead, male or female. "I like the basement. Honestly."

"Think about it."

Someone shook the chimes by the entrance. Tullia walked across the room and opened the curtain; in the dim light, Yalda didn't recognize the visitor as Antonia until she spoke.

Tullia invited her in. Antonia was flustered. "I'm sorry, I didn't know where else to go."

"It's all right," Tullia said. "Sit down, tell us what happened." The three of them sat on the cool stone floor.

"My co closed the business," Antonia began, calmly enough. But then she stopped talking and began to shiver.

"Your business?" Yalda pressed her. "In the markets? He canceled your stall?"

"Yes." Antonia struggled to recover her composure. "He told them I wouldn't be coming anymore. Then I heard him talking with our father, making arrangements: the times that each of them would spend looking after the children."

Now Yalda's own skin crawled.

"He never even asked me if I was ready," Antonia said. "If I'd done everything I wanted to do, if I'd completed my own plans."

Tullia said firmly, "So now he's blown it, he's lost you for good. If he wants children, let him carve them out of stone."

Antonia wasn't so sure. "If I leave him, what then? Who'll look after my children?"

Tullia said, "So what do you want to do?"

"I don't know," Antonia admitted. "But I need to get away from him for a while, while I think things through. And maybe then he'll understand that he has to change his own thinking."

"It's up to you," Tullia said. "You're welcome to stay here, if you like."

"Thank you."

Yalda was relieved; Tullia's needier guest would save her from having to find excuses not to move in herself.

"I *want* children!" Antonia declared passionately. "And I want good lives for them. I was working for *them*, saving money for *them*. All I wanted was to choose the time. Shouldn't that be my decision?"

"Of course," Yalda said gently. She tried to recall Lidia's optimistic arguments, tried to think of a way that politics and holin could put this mess right.

The three of them sat talking for half a bell, then Yalda realized that they were all absurdly tired; they'd long ago stopped making sense.

She bid her friends good night and made her way back to the basement. Antonia's plight haunted her, but no one could fix the world overnight.

5

Yalda wasn't sure whether Mount Peerless had been named with honest innocence in an age of limited travel, or whether the label was a vain boast intended to dismiss the claims of any rival. Either way, reputable surveyors had long since established that Mount Magnificent stretched five strolls and eleven saunters from base to peak, while Peerless was a mere five strolls and five.

A few commentators still contended that the top of Mount Peerless might nonetheless be *higher*, in the sense of being farther from the center of the world. But geodesy remained too imprecise an art to settle the question definitively, while the effects of local climate on air pressure rendered that criterion equally unhelpful. Nobody could say which of the two mountaintops was closer to the stars.

What Yalda knew for certain now was that a *stroll* deserved an entirely new and less frivolous name when it was directed vertically. On Zeugma's flat roads, she could easily walk seven strolls in a bell—but the truck carrying her along the winding road that edged up the slopes of Mount Peerless had only managed to ascend half that distance after laboring for more than a day. At which point, the road became too narrow for the vehicle to proceed at all.

Fosco, the driver, helped her pack a small cart with supplies; even Yalda couldn't fit everything she'd need into pouches and pockets. The plan was for him to wait to give Renato, the observer Yalda was replacing, a ride back to Zeugma.

"Are you going to be all right here?" Yalda asked. The long wait struck her as a lonelier, more stressful task than her own purposeful ascent.

"I've done the changeover dozens of times," Fosco assured her. "You should be thinking about your own health. The moment you start to feel uncomfortably warm—"

"Lie down in the loosest soil I can find," Yalda replied. "And don't get up until my temperature's normal." Tullia had rammed that point home. Air played an important role in cooling the body, and by the time she reached the summit it would be carrying heat away much more slowly than usual. Only a direct, solid connection to the ancient, chilly depths of the world could rid her of the thermal energy that built up from her body's metabolism.

The morning sun was still low when Yalda bid Fosco farewell and set off up the narrow trail. Once he was out of sight, she took Daria's vial from her pocket and swallowed two of the holin cubes. She relished the bitter taste; after all, if she'd been the descendant of generations of women who'd considered goldenrod petals to be a tasty delicacy, that wouldn't bode too well for the efficacy of an anti-divisive derived from the plant.

Yalda surveyed the route ahead. Slender trees lined the path and shrubs sprouted from every crack in the rocks. Plants appeared untroubled by the thin air, though she'd been warned against trying to grow anything inside, in pots, at the summit. As she resumed her ascent, Yalda scanned the trees for lizards. Each twitching branch was an encouraging sign that animals could thrive here, too.

The path veered closer to the edge of the slope; Yalda could catch glimpses between the trees of the plain they'd crossed on their way from Zeugma. From this height, she could see the dust haze they'd ridden through as a puny, finite thing, thinning out to nothing far below her. The flat brown land, sparsely studded with shrubs, was adorned with a network of shallow, wind-carved channels. There was no doubt that, over the ages, the plain had been scoured ever flatter and lower by wind and dust, while a favorable combination of tougher rock and protective vegetation had spared the mountain from the same fate. What Yalda had trouble imagining was the starting point for the whole process. Had the world been born smooth, or craggy? Had Mount Peerless been carved into existence, like a figure sculpted from a featureless slab, or had it been there from the start, towering over its ancient surroundings, and then retained or improved upon that initial advantage?

Tullia believed that there had once been a giant, primal world, with every planet, every star, a fragment left behind by its destruction. Yalda wasn't so sure; the gravitational pull of so much concentrated matter would have been stupendous. It was hard to believe that even a wildfire in some massive seam of sunstone piercing the depths of that ur-planet could have fractured it into rubble and scattered the resulting worlds across the void. Then again, maybe sunstone was nothing compared to the rocks that had blazed in the past. To expect the scatterer of worlds to be stable enough to persist to this day, to be recognized and studied, might be as naïve as hoping to meet your own mother.

By mid-afternoon Yalda was growing weary. When she'd first set out, the path's steep gradient had felt like a promise of rapid progress: the faster she was ascending toward her destination, the better. Now the lack of respite from the endless climb simply made her angry.

Only stubbornness kept her going, and it kept her going too long. When she was forced to stop, retching and shaking, she finally understood what she'd done to herself. She'd brushed the symptoms aside, treating them as ordinary signs of fatigue and telling herself that she could overcome them with sufficient resolve.

Cursing her stupidity, she lay on the path, trying to cool herself against the uneven slabs of fractured rock, too weak and queasy to go looking for a proper bed of soil. She could feel the heat moving through her flesh, a stinging presence probing for an exit like a swarm of trapped parasites. The thought of dying here embarrassed her; she'd been told what to do, she had no excuses. Triumphantly pointing to her dissected corpse, Ludovico would ban all women from using the observatory. "Look at the size of this bloated creature! With a ratio of surface area to mass *less than half* that of a man, how could she be expected to survive the rigors of altitude?"

When night fell, Yalda tried climbing to her feet; on the third attempt she succeeded. She was still nauseous and trembling. She took a trowel from the cart and stepped off the path; there was no bare soil, but there was a patch of shrubs that she believed she could uproot. In good health she could have done it with her fingers alone, but the flesh she extruded now to follow the roots down was too weak to dislodge them. She hacked at the plants with the trowel, severing enough of the woody cores to free a shallow layer of soil. She lay in it and rolled back and forth, crushing worms and scraping her skin on broken roots, trying to maximize her area of contact.

Some time later she found herself lucid again, gazing up at the stars through a gap in the trees. Fragments of hallucinations lingered; she remembered thinking that she was already in the observatory, adjusting her equipment and wondering why the colors in the star trails were refusing to merge. She'd thought the glowing blossoms above her were flaws in the optics, surfaces chipped in the bumpy truck ride scattering stray light everywhere.

Contemplating the flowers' cool radiance, Yalda wondered why nature hadn't stumbled on some easier way to rid her body of its heat. Why couldn't thermal energy simply be converted into light and tossed into the sky? Plants were believed to turn the chemical energy they extracted from the soil into light, a small amount of heat, and a new, more accessible store of chemical energy in their seeds and other structures. Animals, burning that secondary fuel, used the energy to move their muscles and repair their bodies, and to make a little light for internal signaling—but the rest became a wasteful, burdensome dose of heat. Why couldn't they shift more of it into light, instead? Why had her grandfather's glowing skin signified a fatal pathology, when every living thing would surely have had an easier time if it could shine like a flower?

Yalda clambered to her feet and returned to the path. Her mind was still a little askew; she found it odd that the cart had sat there for so long, undisturbed. By now, shouldn't someone have chanced upon it and come looking for its owner—or failing that, ransacked it for valuables?

Well, no.

She took a loaf from the cart, sat on the ground, and ate half of it; at that point her body indicated abruptly that it had had enough. She rested for a lapse or two to make peace with the meal, then she set out again, moving slowly, vigilant for warning signs.

The sun was setting over the plains below, complicating the dusty brown channels with shadows, as Yalda approached the observatory. Renato was sitting outside; he'd not known exactly who'd be coming to replace him, but he'd known the schedule, and Yalda was late.

She couldn't help calling out a greeting to him, though even to her the words sounded muffled and distorted, and she'd been told that her speech would be inaudible to any intended recipient. As she drew nearer, she saw the words on his chest: **What took you so long?**

Too much stopping to admire the view, she replied.

I'll need to show you everything tonight. Renato waited for her to acknowledge that she'd read this, then he replaced it with: **I have to leave in the morning.** Yalda doubted that Fosco would abandon Renato if he didn't show up precisely when he was expected, but the delay was her fault, and it would be unfair to put any pressure on Renato to rush his descent.

Renato showed her the living quarters first. There was a pantry, which she'd replenish from the cart, an inside bed—which she had to admit would be easier to keep free of weeds—and a storeroom with lamps, fuel, and an assortment of tools. **No toilet**, Renato wrote. **Sorry.**

I'm a farm girl, Yalda replied.

The office was still well-stocked with paper and dye; Yalda had brought a little of both. She was used to doing all her scribbling and jotting and rough calculations on her skin, saving paper for the final, polished results.

The telescope itself was not housed; the ten-stride-long box that held the heavy clearstone lens in place, its sides built of struts and crossbeams, had only a few skinny, strategically placed boards to block scattered light from entering the optics. The machinery that drove the mount, and the observer's station, sat inside a kind of swiveling hut at the instrument's base.

They entered the hut. In the dwindling light, Renato pointed out a printed maintenance schedule; Yalda replied that she'd read a copy back in Zeugma. Tullia had already told her most of what she'd need to know, though it was something else to have the tracking drive right in front of her, with its terrifying plethora of mirrorstone cogs and springs. The prospect of having to repair it if it broke seemed about as daunting as trying to bring one of Daria's mutilated arborines back to life.

There were no lamps in the hut, but Renato moved about confidently, and apparently he could still read Yalda's skin; maybe all astronomers ended up with eyesight like Tullia's. When an indistinct gray smudge appeared on his chest, Yalda tentatively gestured that she'd need to touch him, and he spread his arms, granting permission. She moved her palm quickly over his body. **Let's see you line up a star and follow it**, he'd written. **I'll feel better about leaving if you know what you're doing.**

Yalda had used a much smaller telescope at the university, but the principles were the same. Standing by the observer's bench, she checked the clock by touch. Sitha would be high above the horizon; she had memorized its celestial coordinates, and she scribbled the conversion to altitude and azimuth for two separate times: the coming chime, and the one after. She cranked the telescope to point to the first location; it was well balanced and surprisingly easy to move, but there was something surreal about the walls of the hut turning on their rails as she labored against the azimuth wheel. Then she calculated the changes in the two angles that the star's location would undergo between the successive chimes, and set them into the tracking drive.

She wound the drive's spring, lowered the bench to make more room for herself, then lay down beneath the telescope. A selection of eyepieces sat in a rack beside her; she picked one with a modest magnification that would allow her to view Sitha's trail all at once, and inserted it into the holder.

With three eyes closed, she peered through the telescope, adjusting the focus. So soon after sunset, most of the sky would just look gray, but she'd expected a little of Sitha's trail to be showing in her field already. She checked the time again, and did a few calculations; she should have been seeing something. She reached over and put her hand on the azimuth wheel; there was some play in it, rendering the narrow engraved markings she'd carefully aligned nothing more than rough landmarks. Painstakingly, she nudged the wheel back and forth, until a wisp of red and orange appeared in the corner of the field. The time was getting closer; she kept making adjustments until the whole trail was visible.

The clock chimed; Yalda released the brake on the tracking drive. The mechanism was not sophisticated enough to follow the star for an indefinite period as it circled the celestial pole, but the telescope's steady movement from the current location to the predicted one would take most of the burden off the observer for one chime, allowing her to keep the trail centered with just a few corrective nudges.

With the hard work done, Yalda finally relaxed and let herself marvel at the telescope's power. Even in the gray twilight, Sitha's trail was already brilliant and clear. Most bright stars were bright because of their proximity, and that in turn usually meant that their trails were short; a close neighbor of the sun was rarely rushing by with great haste. But Sitha was an exception, a brilliant oddity fast enough to spread its colors wide. When she made her measurements, it would be her first choice.

Yalda squeezed out of the way and let Renato check the result of her efforts; he needed to prop himself up on the bench to reach the eyepiece. He remained there, perfectly still, for what must have been a full lapse. Then he climbed out and put a hand on Yalda's shoulder.

On his palm he'd written, **Well done. You'll be fine.**

Renato insisted on sleeping outside and giving Yalda the debris-free bed in the living quarters; she would have had no qualms about sharing it with him, but she decided it would be presumptuous to expect him to feel the same way. The clean white sand had a peculiar, slippery texture, but the stone base certainly kept it cool, and Yalda surrendered to her weariness with luxurious rapidity.

She woke before dawn and unpacked the cart so Renato could use it to take his own notes and equipment back down the mountain. When he had departed, the muffled sound of her footsteps in the thin air took on an eerie, distant quality; she could not expect to see another person for the next three stints. She'd asked Ludovico for four stints, assuming that he'd grant her two at the most, but he must have mistaken the curious familiarity of her Meconio essay for some kind of genuine resonance with his own views. Either that, or he was wise to the whole scam and simply enjoyed watching people scrambling about trying to satisfy his whims.

Yalda set up her equipment in the observing hut, and spent the morning testing and aligning it; there were parts of the task that were actually easier in daylight. In the afternoon she forced herself to sleep; she needed to nudge herself into a cycle of nocturnal wakefulness, but it was hard to relax when her first observations were just a few bells away.

She woke around sunset, ate half a loaf, then went to the hut while it was still light. In time, she hoped to be able to operate the telescope's machinery by touch and memory alone, but for now she was better off starting each session with a clear view of her surroundings, giving her a chance to get oriented.

With her own bulky contraption clamped over the telescope's eyepiece holder there was no longer room for the observing bench; she'd taken it out and put it in the office. She cued up Sitha and checked the image by flipping down a mirror that diverted the light into an ordinary eyepiece; it didn't take long to center the trail, as she'd done the previous night. Then she raised the mirror and let the same light pass into her purpose-built optics. Sliding her body around on the floor, she peered into the second eyepiece. In this view, the trail was replaced by a broad elliptical blur—more compact than the long streak she'd started with, but still multicolored and not remotely point-like.

She reached into the side of the device and began adjusting the distance between two lenses. The principle was simple enough: if a clearstone prism spread a narrow shaft of white light into a fan of colors, the very same fan fed back through the prism would have to emerge as a single, sharp beam. Sitha's trail provided a ready-made fan, albeit a far from perfect match. A system of lenses could magnify the overall angular width of the star trail, and then a flexible mirror could tweak the detailed progression across the colors. Yalda's first task was to get the width right: to shrink the blurred ellipse as much as possible by changing the magnification alone. Then she could tinker with the shape of the mirror to perfect the transformation.

That had been the plan; the reality wasn't so simple. Once she started moving the pegs that deformed the mirror, she realized that she was still altering the overall size of the color trail. In theory, it might have been possible to make the two kinds of adjustment independently, but with nothing actually enforcing that the idealization was irrelevant.

Yalda spent a few pauses cursing her stupidity, then reached back to adjust the lenses again. The ellipse became a little less broad, but also grew thicker in the other direction. The clock chimed; it was time to change the tracking parameters.

Improvements came painfully slowly. When Sitha drew too close to the horizon to be followed—more than a bell before dawn—Yalda was still not happy with the results. Rather than choose another star and start again from scratch, she decided to call it a night; this way she could preserve all the Sitha-specific adjustments she'd made, ready for a further round of refinements.

Trudging back toward the living quarters, she stopped to look up at the sky, at all the burning worlds rushing by. Sitha was just one transient neighbor among this staggering multitude. How could anyone hope to wrap the stars in mathematics and draw them into their mind? She was a child fumbling with a clumsy toy, pretending that it granted her magical powers, while this vast, magnificent procession continued on its way, entirely oblivious to her fantasies.

Yalda slept until mid-afternoon, then she sat in the office planning a new strategy. If she disciplined herself when she reshaped the mirror—always making changes in pairs that largely canceled each other's effects on the overall spread of the color fan—it might save her some unnecessary adjustment of the lenses.

Two bells later, lying on the floor of the hut with her skin chafing and her fingers cramped, she allowed herself a chirp of celebration, unperturbed by its distorted tones. Sitha's trail had finally shrunk to an almost circular patch of light, only slightly bluer on one side than the other.

It was time to make use of Nereo's trick. Yalda slipped a mask into the light path that blocked the center of the image, leaving only the faint halo that surrounded the bright core. As her eyes accommodated to the much dimmer partial image, it became easier to see the changes caused by each slight movement of the mirror's pegs.

Half a chime later, a single, fine adjustment plunged the view into total darkness. Yalda was ecstatic; Sitha's image was now smaller than the mask that was blocking it!

She slid the mask away, expecting to see a tiny, perfect disk of light, but the whole field remained black. She'd bumped the telescope, and it was no longer pointed at Sitha at all.

Yalda found the star again, but it was hard to keep it centered for long without losing some of her dark adaptation. She tried switching to her left eye each time she had to pull away the mask to correct the tracking, then switching back to the right to resume shrinking the halo, but the two eyes were in cahoots, their pupils contracting in tandem even when only one of them was dazzled. Finally, she tried flipping onto her chest and letting one of her rear eyes take the glare. Amazingly, it worked: her front eyes retained their sensitivity.

When Sitha dropped out of reach once more, Yalda realized that for the last three chimes she'd been unable to make any improvements; she'd simply been trying out small adjustments and then undoing them. But the halo was very faint now, and it was unreasonable to expect it to vanish completely. She had gone as far as she could with Sitha.

And she had collected her first set of data.

Yalda woke early and set about translating the positions of the two dozen mirror pegs into a set of wavelength and velocity values. It was a complex calculation; it took her until late afternoon to complete it, double-checking every step. She plotted the points on a sheet of paper that she'd prepared with a grid; there were some tasks that were just too difficult to perform on her own skin.

The data curved down across the upper right corner of the plot: with increasing velocity, the wavelength fell. That general trend wasn't news, but here at last was a hint at the detailed shape. Yalda contemplated some possibilities for the precise form of the mathematical relationship, but she knew that was premature. She needed to see if other stars gave her the same curve.

Tharak was next, almost as bright as Sitha, though its trail was less than half as long. Zento was faster, more distant. Yalda was learning what worked and what didn't, acquiring an instinctive sense of the adjustments she needed to make to shrink the colored ellipses down to sharp white disks. On her sixth night of observations, she managed to peg two different stars, Julila and Mira, before dawn.

Laboriously, she added each star's points to the plot. That the light velocities she was sampling were clustered together was no great achievement; that simply reflected the fixed positions of the holes in which the adjustment pegs sat. But the corresponding wavelengths weren't scattered too widely, either. Her method was yielding the same pattern, star after star.

As she ran out of bright targets, the observations became more difficult. After three nights of increasing frustration, Yalda gave up on Thero, unable to distinguish any change in its image despite wildly different settings for the pegs. She wondered if she'd grown sick from exhaustion: if she'd lost Thero's trail, and was simply hallucinating blotches of light to fill the darkness.

She rested for two days: doing nothing but eating, sleeping, and taking short walks along the access path. Tullia had warned her not to push herself; nobody was immune to heat shock. After her trouble with the ascent she should have been more careful.

She tried a different star, Lepato. It took her all night, but her mind was clear now, and by dawn she'd shaped the mirror to conform to Lepato's faint trail. Starlight was not as fragile or elusive as it seemed; with enough patience, you could even capture its likeness in stone and wood.

Yalda had been on Mount Peerless for a stint and seven days, and she had data for a dozen stars. It was time to try to make sense of what she'd gathered. Curled up on the observation bench that she'd moved into the office, she contemplated the sweep of the curve across her plot.

Wavelength

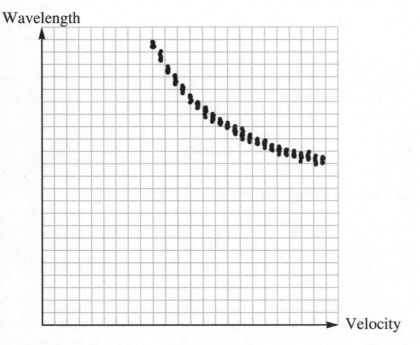

Velocity

The velocity of light rose as its wavelength fell. Each quantity, then, might merely be proportional to the inverse of the other. If so, multiplying the two of them together would always yield the same result.

Yalda tested this idea for a dozen points across the spectrum. The product varied—by too much to be nothing but the jitters expected from imperfect data.

Still, if the relationship was more complex than her first naïve guess implied, that guess could still take her in the right direction. She drew a second plot, this time setting wavelength against the inverse of the velocity.

Wavelength

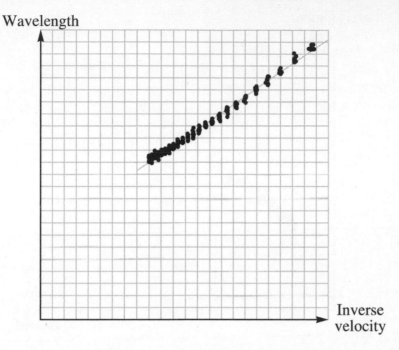

Inverse
velocity

Her naïve guess would have required a perfectly straight line here—and chance errors alone would not have seen the points weave so systematically from one side of the line of best fit to the other.

In fact the data looked like a segment of a parabola or hyperbola, a quadratic of some kind. Yalda tried squaring the velocity as well as taking its inverse, but the plot was still plainly curved. She tried squaring the wavelength instead; that was no better.

Then she tried squaring both.

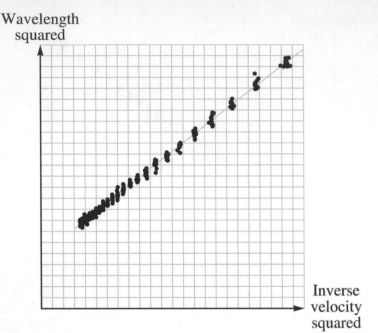

Wavelength squared

Inverse velocity squared

Yalda was too excited to remain still; she left the office and walked around the observatory grounds, wishing she had Tullia or Giorgio beside her to celebrate her discovery. A linear relationship between two squared quantities was neither too simple to believe, nor too messy and complex to be useful. Maybe it was just an approximation to the true relationship, but for now it would be enough of a challenge to take this result as given and see where it led.

Light was a very strange kind of wave. Under ordinary conditions, elastic waves in a string or pressure waves in a gas moved with a fixed velocity regardless of their wavelength. Exotic exceptions could be contrived—but with light, there was nothing exotic about it. The fact that its velocity varied wildly with its hue was the one thing everyone agreed upon: you only had to look up at the stars to be convinced of it.

One consequence of the varying velocity was that a pulse of light was not even expected to move in the same direction as the individual wavefronts within it. Bizarre as that sounded, it had been clear since Giorgio's first tentative wavelength estimates. Every pulse of light, however apparently pure its color, would contain at least a small spread of different wavelengths. But since the different wavelengths moved at different speeds, the points where they all agreed and reinforced each other wouldn't drift along merrily with the wavefronts themselves, as they did in a wave on a string. If the slippage in the velocity was great enough, they'd actually travel in the opposite direction.

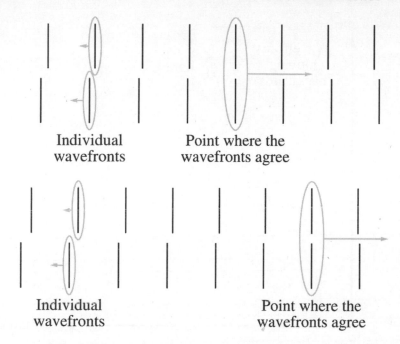

Individual wavefronts

Point where the wavefronts agree

Individual wavefronts

Point where the wavefronts agree

Yalda summoned onto her skin a sketch she'd made in one of Giorgio's lectures. With a few simple calculations, Giorgio had convinced her that if she could somehow watch a pulse of light in motion, she'd see the wavefronts within it *sliding backward*.

What did her own results add to that? She could now construct a more precise account of how these two different aspects of the light behaved. If she chose, say, a pulse of red light, she could plot its movement through space, along with the backsliding wavefronts from which it was built.

She returned to the office to consult her sheets of paper, then she sketched a new diagram on her chest.

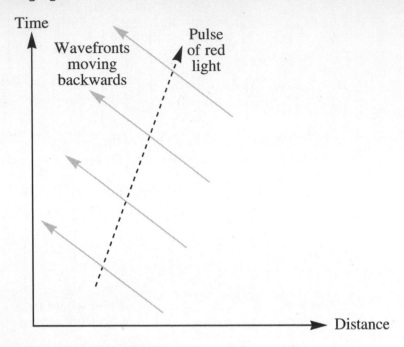

As Yalda contemplated the picture, it struck her just how reminiscent it was of a beam of light and its accompanying wavefronts, shown at a single moment in time. The main difference was the annoying tilt between the wavefronts and the "beam"—here, a line showing the history of the pulse.

But what did that skewed angle actually signify? By changing to different units of measurement, she could stretch or squeeze the diagram as much as she liked. Nature had no idea what a pause or a flicker was; nothing real could depend on adhering to that traditional system of units. So she chose units of time that forced the pulse and the wavefronts to trace out lines at right angles to each other.

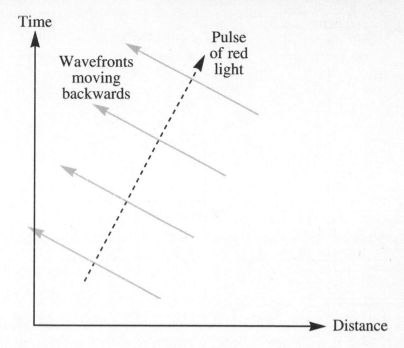

Where did that leave her? She had a right angle between some lines…
and a linear relationship between two quantities squared.

She played around with the diagram for a couple of chimes, changing
the units for distance as well as those for time in such a way that the
separation between the wavefronts was simply declared equal to one.
Well, why not? It wasn't just time whose units were completely artificial;
a *scant* had once been defined as the resting width of some self-important
monarch's thumb.

When she was done, a small right triangle sat inside a larger one in the
same proportions. The hypotenuse of the larger triangle was a horizontal
line that joined one wavefront to another, making its length simply equal
to the wavelength of the light. The small triangle's sides—corresponding to a distance the pulse traveled and a time in which it did so—had
a ratio of lengths equal to the light's velocity. The larger triangle shared
that ratio, in such a manner that the length of one of its sides was the
inverse velocity.

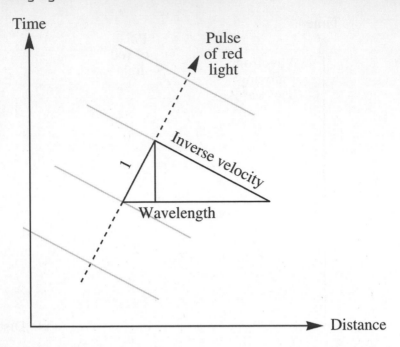

In her chosen units, then: the inverse velocity squared, plus one squared, was equal to the wavelength squared. That simple equation corresponded to the straight line that passed through the data she'd plotted. But now this relationship didn't need to emerge from any hypothetical properties of the hypothetical medium whose vibrations manifested as light. *The sum of the squares of the sides of a right triangle equaled the square of the hypotenuse.* That was it: the entire wavelength-velocity relationship that she'd extracted from all those nights of painstaking observations had turned out to be nothing but a theorem from elementary geometry in disguise.

Except… that was nonsense. Geometry was concerned with figures in space, not lines that stretched across time as well. However suggestive these results were of geometry, that could only be an analogy, at best.

Albeit a mathematically perfect one. If she pretended that she really was doing geometry in a plane, she could simply *rotate* the whole physical structure of the red pulse—rigidly preserving the spacing of the wavefronts—and transform it into a faster, violet pulse.

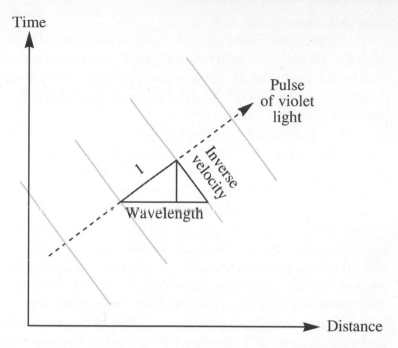

The wavelength and velocity changed, of course, but those things were just measurements that depended on the way the stack of wavefronts was disposed, relative to the person doing the measuring. The two pulses, red and violet, were no more different in essence than a pulse of light traveling north and another traveling north-east.

The message from the stars was: light is light, always the same on its own terms. Qualities such as *color*, *direction* and *speed* were only meaningful distinctions once the light bumped into something else, against which it could be measured. In the void, it was simply *light*.

Yalda was feeling disoriented; she walked in a daze to the living quarters and lay down in the bed's slippery white sand. None of her conclusions made sense; this was just heat shock talking. If she could hallucinate Thero for a whole night, she could lose her powers of reasoning for a day. She'd sleep off her sickness, and everything would be clear in the morning.

Yalda spent the next day re-checking her calculations. All the numbers she'd relied on were correct—and her geometrical constructions were so simple that a five-year-old could have confirmed that they were right.

The only thing she could still doubt was her interpretation. Her right triangle with its wavelength-long hypotenuse might actually be nothing but a useful mnemonic, an easy way of remembering the velocity-wavelength formula. Mathematics that echoed the rules of geometry could arise anywhere, with all the lines and angles that it implied really nothing more than abstractions.

So… light was a vibration in some exotic medium that just happened to possess qualities that *perfectly mimicked* all the would-be geometry she'd found in the equations? As well as contriving to support shear waves and pressure waves that traveled at exactly the same speed? Was there nothing this magical material couldn't do?

The three polarizations of light traveled at the same speed, as if they were all the same kind of thing. Yalda brought one of her diagrams of pulses and wavefronts back onto her chest. The picture projected the three dimensions of space down to just one, but in reality each wavefront was a plane, and it traced out a three-dimensional set over time. Within that set there would be three independent directions that were orthogonal to the path of the light pulse through the four dimensions that included time. The three polarizations could *all* be transverse waves—waves that pointed sideways, in that four-dimensional sense. There'd be no need for a miraculous coincidence to make all their velocities the same.

It was almost dusk. Yalda walked out of the building and sat at the top of the access path. Either she had lost her mind, or she had stumbled upon something that needed to be pursued much further.

She tinkered with the wavefront diagram on her chest. She'd been wondering about the significance of the inner triangle, the triangle whose hypotenuse was one. The ratio of its sides was the light's velocity, but what exactly did the individual side lengths represent?

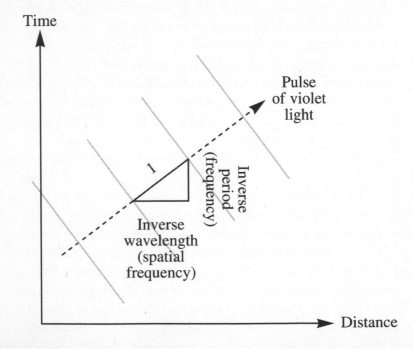

A simple argument with proportions established their values—which yielded a new triangular relationship, more elegant and symmetrical than the first: *the sum of the squares of light's frequencies in time and in space would equal one.* Well, only her special choice of units set the sum equal to *one*, but the fact remained that the equivalent in cycles per scant or stride or saunter would still be independent of the color of the light.

That was really no different from saying that the true distance between furrows ploughed by a given plow did not depend on whether someone happened to walk across them askew. The wavefronts of light were all furrows from the same plow; the light's speed, color, wavelength and frequency simply measured the angle at which you crossed the furrows.

But if light was going to play by these geometric rules, then everything it touched—every system that created or absorbed light, every substance that bent, scattered or distorted it—would have to function the same way. Ultimately, to keep the world consistent, *any kind of physics* that took place at one angle would have to work just as well if you picked it up and rotated it in four dimensions.

To accommodate light's simplicity, half of science would need to be rewritten.

Yalda looked up; Sitha was starting to show against the fading gray sky. The colors were still weak, but the trail's violet tip was as prominent as a skewer-worm's barb.

"What have you done to me?" she said.

Then she remembered that there was no air between them, and she wrote the words across her chest instead.

6

"If time is exactly the same as space," Giorgio asked Yalda, "why is it that I can walk to the Great Bridge, but I can't walk to tomorrow?"

Yalda was distracted by a hubbub of exuberant buzzing and chirping from the adjoining room. In her absence, Giorgio's co had given birth, and though the children were being cared for by their grandfather during the day, Giorgio couldn't bear to be separated from them. He'd set up a nursery in the room beside his office.

Yalda focused on his question. "You're already traveling toward tomorrow, along the most direct route possible. The shortest distance there is a straight line, and by standing still you're following that line; you can't do any better than that."

"That makes sense," Giorgio conceded. "But if I can't do better, why can't I do worse? Why can't I dawdle and delay, and reach tomorrow later than expected? I can certainly do *that* if I walk to the Great Bridge."

"And you can do it on your way to tomorrow," Yalda replied. "If you cease standing still, if you wander around Zeugma, you *will* add some time to your journey. But because you can't move very quickly, you can't really manage much of a detour. The distance to tomorrow is vastly greater than the distance across Zeugma; the proportion by which you can increase it with any plausible peregrinations is unmeasurably small."

Giorgio was amused, and she saw him slip out of his role for a moment to marvel openly at the sheer strangeness of these notions. Yalda knew she hadn't convinced him that her ideas were correct, but he believed nonetheless that it was worth presenting them to the whole school of natural sciences: physicists, mathematicians, chemists and biologists. Before she spoke before so many colleagues, though, Giorgio wanted to be sure that she could defend her ideas against the inevitable barrage of objections, and he was doing his best to prepare her by anticipating every possible question and complaint.

"Exactly how far away is tomorrow?" he asked.

"As far as blue light can travel in a day."

"*Blue* light? What's so special about blue?"

"Absolutely nothing," Yalda said firmly. "Violet is faster, and I believe there are even faster hues that we can't perceive. But just as there's a line in space that lies halfway between *right* and *forward*—marking equal progress in those two directions—there's a line halfway between *right* and *into the future*. We perceive the light that reaches us at such an angle to be blue, and if we follow that light for a day, its progress marks out the equivalent distance."

"I can't compete with blue light," Giorgio said, "so I can't noticeably delay tomorrow. But why can't I walk to yesterday?"

"For much the same reason," Yalda replied. "Bending your path around until it's turned backward would require an immense, sustained acceleration. In principle it ought to be possible, but it's not something you should expect to be easy. You're heading toward the future with a lot of inertia; you can nudge your trajectory a little with muscle power or a truck's engine—but as you said, blue light isn't easily outpaced."

"But even if we only *imagine it*," Giorgio persisted, "traveling toward the past would be very different from traveling toward the future. Traveling toward the future, we can shatter a stone into pieces with one blow; if we were traveling toward the past, the pieces would rise up and remake the whole before our eyes. Why is *that* distinction so clear… when directions in space such as *north* and *south* can barely be distinguished?"

"The same reason as we always suspected," Yalda countered. "In the distant past, our part of the cosmos had much lower entropy; whether or not there was a single, primal world, things were certainly more orderly. The direction of increasing entropy looks radically different from the direction in which entropy decreases—but that's not a fundamental property of space or time, it's a happenstance of history."

Giorgio wasn't satisfied. "Time in *either* direction looks utterly different from any direction in space."

"That's because we're surrounded by things that are moving almost entirely along that one axis," Yalda said. "Not because physics decrees that they *must* move that way, but because they share a common history that has set them on that course. All the histories of all the worlds we can see form an almost straight bundle of lines through the four dimensions. The fastest star we know of is moving at barely one part in a gross of the speed of blue light. Living in a bundle of lines that are all so close to being parallel to each other, we shouldn't be surprised that their common direction appears special to us."

Giorgio changed his attack. "You say physics itself doesn't decree that our histories are almost parallel. So according to your theory, an object could have a trajectory entirely orthogonal to our own?"

"Yes."

"It could move with an *infinite velocity*?"

Yalda didn't flinch. "Yes, that's how we'd describe it." It could cross what she and Giorgio thought of as a region of space in no time at all. "But that's no stranger than saying that a vertical pole has an 'infinite slope': unlike a mountain road, it gets where it's going vertically without bothering to go anywhere horizontally. An object that gets where it's going without bothering to move across what we call time isn't doing anything pathological; in reality, there's nothing 'infinite' about it."

"What about its kinetic energy?" Giorgio demanded. "Half its mass times its velocity squared?"

"That formula's merely an approximation," Yalda said. "You can't use it for anything but small velocities."

She summoned a diagram onto her skin. "If you want to know an object's energy and momentum, draw an arrow whose length is the object's mass, and point it along the line of its history. If you think the object is motionless, the arrow will point straight along the time axis; if you think it's moving, the arrow needs to be tilted accordingly."

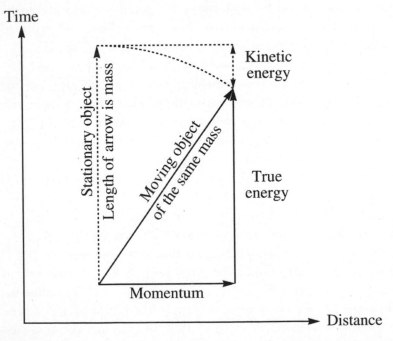

"The amount by which the height of the arrow is diminished—compared to the motionless version—is its kinetic energy. For small velocities that will match the old formula, but for higher velocities it will grow much more slowly. The object's momentum is the distance across space that the arrow spans; again, that agrees with the old formula if the object is moving slowly."

Giorgio pretended that he hadn't seen the picture before. "What's this 'true energy'?"

"The natural measure of energy is the height of the arrow in the time direction," Yalda explained. "That way, energy is related to time in the same way momentum is related to space. Kinetic energy is a derived, secondary quantity."

"But 'true energy' becomes less when you tip the arrow over," Giorgio noted. "So when something moves… you're now declaring that its energy is *decreased*?"

Yalda said, "Yes. Nothing else makes sense."

Giorgio's eyes widened in admiration at her effrontery. "So your theory turns the last three ages' worth of science on its head. I suppose you're also claiming that potential energy is upside-down in the same fashion?"

"Of course! We *defined it* to agree with kinetic energy, so it has the same relation to true energy." Yalda summoned a picture of two springs accompanied by appropriate mass-length arrows: their four-dimensional momenta. "When the springs are compressed and motionless, we say they have a high potential energy. Now release them, let them fly apart, and see how things add up."

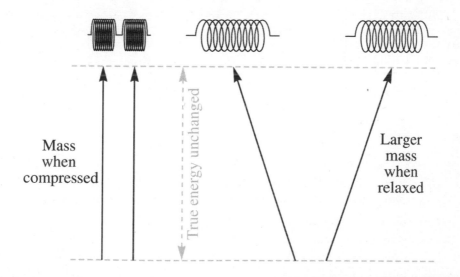

"For true energy to be conserved, the heights of the pairs of arrows have to be identical before and after the release. But the arrows after the release are tilted, because the springs are now in motion. So those later arrows need to be longer, in order to reach the same height. That means that each relaxed spring has a slightly larger mass than it had when it was compressed—and from the point of view of someone traveling alongside it, a larger true energy. Less potential energy means more true energy. Both the old energies are upside-down."

Giorgio let a hint of pained, Ludovico-esque weariness into his voice. "If kinetic and potential energy still agree, what can it actually *mean* to claim that they're 'upside-down'? *Upside-down compared to what?* When do we get to see any of this so-called true energy, to compare its direction with its alleged opposites?"

"In light," Yalda said. "We see the direction of true energy every time we create light."

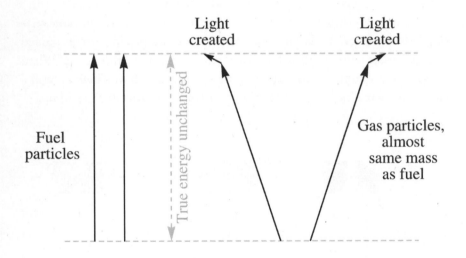

She drew a simple diagram, line by line. "The chemists," she said, "have been having a lot of trouble with their ladder of energies. If we're to believe their calculations, the difference in chemical energy between fuel and the gas it becomes after burning isn't anywhere near enough to account for the thermal energy of the gas. We kept telling them that they'd made a mistake, and that they should improve the accuracy of their measurements. But they were right, and we were wrong. The fuel itself doesn't *need* to provide the energy to heat the gas... because that energy comes from the creation of light.

"Light brings its own four-dimensional momentum into the equation. It's the need to balance *that* that forces the gas particles to be moving so fast. We thought that when fuel was burned, the light and the heat that was created both came from the release of chemical energy—but the truth is nothing like that! Light energy and thermal energy are *opposites*: creating one is what gives us the other.

"And we thought that when plants made food from soil, the light was merely an unintended by-product, a measure of inefficiency. But the energy in food isn't extracted from the soil, and the light shining from a flower's petals is not wasted energy escaping. Light energy and the chemical energy in food are opposites, too. If plants *didn't* make light, they'd have no energy source at all."

Yalda paused to give Giorgio a chance to respond, but he remained silent. Whatever radical notions she was proposing for the foundations of physics, these claims about food and fuel were the most shocking: the least abstract, the most tangible.

"Why can't we cool our bodies by emitting light?" Yalda continued. "That's what I asked myself on my way up Mount Peerless. But now it's obvious! Emitting light can only give you *more* thermal energy than you started with. The very act of emitting too much light can make a living body as hot as burning sunstone." Her grandfather's frail body had never held enough energy to flatten a forest; rather, it had lost control of its production of light.

Giorgio said, "If emitting light generates thermal energy... why can't we cool down by *absorbing* light instead? Why isn't sunlight as good as our beds for making us cooler?"

Yalda was prepared for that. "Entropy. Light carries a certain amount of entropy—so if you absorb light, your entropy must increase. But if we cool down, our entropy *decreases*. What I think happens when sunlight strikes our body is that we don't absorb it, we just scatter it. That way, we can simply take a share of its kinetic energy, and be warmed by it."

Giorgio stopped the interrogation to take stock. "Well, you'll certainly please the chemists," he said. "If you're right about this, they'll build a statue in your honor. And the biologists will be intrigued by your ideas on energetics, even if half of them think you're insane. There's even something to make Ludovico happy."

Yalda doubted that, though she knew what he meant. A wave traveling through any ordinary medium marked an increase in kinetic and potential energy, not true energy. If creating light required true energy, it could not be a ripple in some pre-existing medium; it had to be a whole new substance or entity that was created afresh in every flame. But if that brought the term "luminous corpuscles" to mind, in Yalda's scheme light still had a *wavelength*—so Ludovico would call this arrogance and hypocrisy, not a triumph for his beloved Meconio.

"Now a question from the mathematicians," Giorgio said. "You've shown us equations for the geometry of wavefronts, but what about an equation for the wave itself—something analogous to the wave equation on a string?"

"The geometry gives us that, easily," Yalda replied. "For a simple wave, the sum of the squares of the frequencies in all four dimensions equals a constant. But we also know that the wave's *second rate of change* in each direction will be the original wave multiplied by a negative factor proportional to the frequency squared."

She sketched some examples, showing how doubling the frequency of a wave *quadrupled* its second rate of change. The square of the frequency and the second rate of change were just two ways of talking about the same thing.

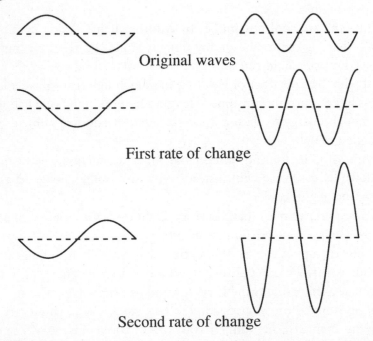

Original waves

First rate of change

Second rate of change

"So if you sum the second rates of change of the wave along each of the four dimensions, and negate that sum, then you've got the original wave multiplied by a constant times the sum of the squares of the frequencies—which itself is a constant. And that's the equation for a light wave: *the sum of its second rates of change, negated, must equal a constant times the original wave.*"

Giorgio contemplated this for a pause or two, then responded with a sketch of his own.

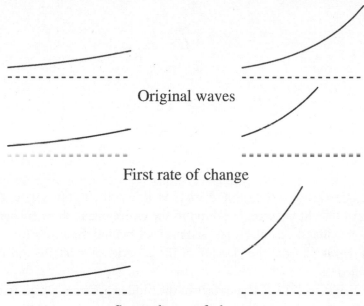

Original waves

First rate of change

Second rate of change

"An oscillation's second rate of change is proportional to the opposite of the original wave," he said. "But an exponential growth curve has a second rate of change proportional to the wave itself—there's no negation."

"That's true," Yalda said. "But—"

"If you construct a wave that oscillates rapidly as you move in one direction," Giorgio said, "what's to stop you from choosing a frequency in that direction so large that its square, alone, is greater than the number you're aiming for as the sum of all four?"

"But then you've overshot the total," Yalda protested. "So you won't be able to satisfy the equation."

"No? What if one of the other terms is negative?"

"Oh." Yalda knew where he was heading now. "If one of the oscillations has too large a frequency, you *can* still satisfy the equation—by replacing the oscillation in another direction with exponential growth." The negated second rate of change, in that case, would be a *negative* multiple of the original wave, allowing the sum of all four terms to be brought back down to the target.

Giorgio said, "So the question is: if light obeys the equation you've given us, how can it possibly be stable? Why doesn't every tiny wrinkle in the wave explode at an exponential rate?"

7

As the crowd spilled out of the Variety Hall into the starlit square, Yalda's feeling of delight lingered. She'd found the entire magic show enchanting, but the fact that she'd quickly guessed the trick behind the astonishing finale hadn't detracted from the pleasure of the experience at all; instead, it had intensified it.

She turned to Tullia. "That image of the hidden assistant, projected onto a curtain of smoke... if I ever get to teach the optics course, I'm going to steal that for my first demonstration!"

"That part wasn't bad," Tullia conceded. "The pyrotechnics before the intermission were awfully tame, but that's the new safety regulations for you. I suppose we should give the City Council its dues: letting off rockets inside the hall was never a good idea."

"Antonia should have come," Yalda said, turning sideways to squeeze through a gap in the throng. "It might have cheered her up."

"Antonia doesn't want to be cheered up," Tullia replied. "She's committed to sitting at home moping until she undergoes spontaneous fission."

"It must be hard for her to make a decision." Yalda had found it difficult enough trying to side-step her own family's expectations, but growing up with a co and then walking away from him would be something else entirely.

"We could get her safely to another city in a couple of days, if she agreed to it," Tullia said irritably. "But she's got herself caught up in negotiations with her co—some complicated business involving four or five interme-diaries. She thinks she can go back to him on her own terms."

"Maybe she can. Maybe she's arranging that."

"Ha."

"Is it so bad that she wants him to raise her children?"

"In principle, not at all," Tullia replied. "The trouble is, he's already

96

proved himself incapable of taking her wishes seriously. If Antonia wanted to, she could spend five or six years living the free life in Red Towers or Jade City, and then find a nice co-stead who'd be grateful for the heirs."

Yalda said, "You make it sound so easy, it's a wonder everyone isn't doing it."

A streak of brilliant violet light appeared in the sky above the eastern horizon, spreading out rapidly from a fixed central point. The center itself remained dark, but as Yalda watched, the two dazzling threads emerging from it turned blue, then green, the new colors chasing the old in both directions. It was as if someone were dragging a giant star trail out from behind the edge of a mirror, exposing ever more of it while creating a perfect duplicate that seemed to be rushing in the opposite direction.

Yalda was transfixed; Tullia was already counting out pauses as she threaded her way through the crowd, trying to sight the nearest clock tower and fix the time of the event precisely. The two of them had never actually made plans as to what they'd do if they witnessed a Hurtler, but they'd managed to get the division of labor exactly right without a single rehearsal. Motionless, Yalda could etch the position of everything she'd seen into her memory, holding on to an image of the line of light against the stars. Tullia wouldn't have those details, but she'd soon have the crucial timing information that would render comparisons with reports from other cities twice as valuable.

The center disgorged two red tails and faded to black; the pair of mirrored spectral worms, now fully birthed and separated, disappeared into opposite corners of the dusty haze that hung over Zeugma's towers. Yalda had only ever seen the final part of this spectacle before: all those years ago, after the harvest, when the center must have been below the horizon for her. To date, seven reports of the same phenomenon had reached the university; the one she'd witnessed as a child was the third in that list. History and legend were full of shooting stars—some of them accompanied by all manner of implausible flourishes—but neither ancient astronomers nor the authors of the sagas had ever claimed to have seen anything like the Hurtlers.

Yalda remained still, carefully gauging the angles between her memory of the Hurtler's trajectory and the nearest bright stars. In her rear gaze she could see the young man glaring at her, shouting, but even if she'd been wandering the square aimlessly she would have done her best to pay him no attention.

"Where's your co?" he yelled again. Yalda marveled at his sheer boorishness; the most extraordinary event ever seen in the sky—unknown to the ages, but glimpsed by the luckiest people now once or twice in a lifetime—had just unfolded before his eyes, and all he could think to do was taunt her for her size, or her lack of a partner.

The man bent down, picked up a broken piece of cobblestone, and flung it at her; it struck her on the side of the head. Yalda couldn't stop herself; she turned toward him.

He squealed triumphantly, "I said: *where's your co?*"

Yalda squatted and retrieved the stone from the ground, feeling the heft of it and the sharp edges. This made her far angrier than when it had collided with her skull, because she knew firsthand now what the thrower should have known, what should have dissuaded him. Unusually, the man was accompanied by his own co, as well as the expected group of delighted male friends.

"Where's your *mother?*" Yalda called back, and pitched the broken stone at him with all her strength.

If her choice of words stunned him, it was the impact that brought him to his knees. She'd hit him squarely in the tympanum, more by luck than intent. He cried out in agony—which could only have made the pain in his organ of speech more intense—and his hum began warbling up and down, as the need to express his suffering fought with his attempts to curtail it.

Some of his friends looked shocked; others were even more amused than before at this unexpected twist in the night's entertainment. The man's co bore an expression of horrified disbelief, as if she'd just seen a freight train run down an infant. Yalda felt a sudden pang of fear; she'd done the greater harm, and most potential witnesses around them were still paying more attention to the sky than the ground. Whatever they'd glimpsed in their own rear gaze, they might only be aware of half the story.

Yalda hurried away from the scene of her imprudent revenge, and caught up with Tullia on the other side of the square.

"You fixed the time?" Yalda asked her.

"Yes." Despite her presence of mind as the event had unfolded, Tullia now appeared a bit dazed. This was her first sighting, and it would have confirmed all the scarcely believable claims that until now she'd been free to doubt.

"I've got the bearings," Yalda said. "We should write up the observation now, and dispatch it tomorrow."

"Of course." Tullia shook herself out of her stupor. "That was, what, three and a half pauses from violet to red?"

"Sounds right."

"Which puts it far above the atmosphere, but still close; a fraction of the distance to the sun."

"A gross and a half severances or so," Yalda confirmed.

The people around them were still buzzing with excitement, but Yalda detected no real sense of how extraordinary the sight had been; it was as if they'd just witnessed an elegant fireworks display to cap off the magic show.

"What if it had been closer?" Tullia asked. "What if it had hit the ground?"

Yalda had never seriously considered the possibility of a collision; with barely more than half a dozen sightings in a generation, it struck her as a remote prospect. "I wouldn't like to be standing at the point of impact," she conceded.

Tullia said, "I wouldn't like to be on the same planet."

The current thinking about the Hurtlers was that *something* was colliding with the tenuous gas that wafted out from the sun to occupy the surrounding region. Just as an ordinary shooting star could burn up brightly in the atmosphere, even the sun's thin exhaust might be enough to ignite a sufficiently rapid interloper.

How rapid were the Hurtlers? If an object was moving so speedily that you might as well imagine its entire trajectory erupting with light all at once, then the closest part of that long straight line would appear to a watcher first in violet, the fastest color, with the other hues following. Each color would appear to fly out along two opposing, symmetrical trails, as the light arrived from pairs of equidistant locations ever farther from the watcher. Any measurable asymmetry in the color trails would imply a lower speed for the object itself—with light from earlier parts of the trajectory gaining a head start—but as yet nobody had observed such subtle effects with enough confidence even to be sure which way the Hurtlers were traveling.

"If you can salvage my geometrical theory of time," Yalda bargained, "the pay-off is that something so fast won't be carrying as much kinetic energy."

"If I salvage your theory," Tullia retorted, "nothing will even *need* kinetic energy to tear itself apart. Everything in the cosmos will be itching to turn into light and hot gas."

"Don't blame me if there are no happy endings; I didn't invent entropy. Darkness and cold dust… bright light and hot gas. Does it really matter which one we end up as?"

They began making their way toward Tullia's apartment, to put their observations onto paper.

Tullia said, "You do realize that according to your theory, someone traveling along with the Hurtler would think that half the light we just saw was *coming in toward them*, not going out?"

Yalda made a quick sketch on her chest.

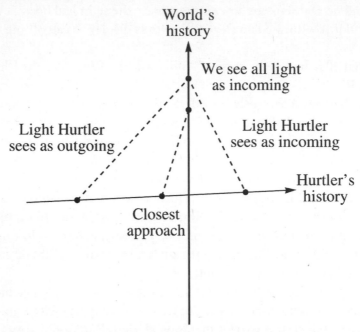

"You're right," she said. "That's eerie." The arrow of time shared by the world and the solar atmosphere was so different from the Hurtler's arrow of time that Tullia's hypothetical traveler would have seen a part of the light-burst converging on them—violating the law of increasing entropy as surely as if a roomful of smoke had shrunk in on itself and turned back into fuel. Obviously entropy *couldn't* increase along every direction in four-space at once, but it was unsettling to have an example of the bizarre disparity play out right in front of their eyes.

Yalda brushed the complication aside; she was having enough trouble trying to make the exponential blow-up in the light equation go away. She was scheduled to deliver a summary of her theory to the school of natural sciences in less than two stints, but if she couldn't offer Giorgio a plausible solution to the flaw he'd uncovered, he'd cancel the talk.

When they entered the apartment, Antonia was seated on the floor with dye and paper beside her. A firestone lamp was sputtering on the shelf above, casting a forlorn shadow. She'd probably been composing another letter to Antonio, but when Yalda and Tullia approached to greet her, her skin was blank. Yalda wished she could have offered her advice or comfort, but what did a solo have to say about the choices she faced?

"How was the magic show?" Antonia asked, forcedly cheerful.

"Upstaged," Tullia replied. She described the celestial mirror trick that had followed.

"I heard some commotion from the street," Antonia said. "I looked out the window, but it must have been over by then."

"Do you mind if we use the dye?" Yalda asked. She wanted to have the report on the Hurtler completed as soon as possible, ready for the couriers who'd be leaving at dawn.

"Of course not." Antonia put the lid back on the pot and slid it toward her. "I was still gathering my thoughts; it can wait until morning."

Yalda saw the curtain part at the entrance to the apartment. As she spun around to face the intruders one of them screamed, "Lie on the floor! *All of you!*" By now, four men had filed into the room, and there were more behind them. They wore police belts, and they'd unsheathed their knives.

Antonia began wailing. "I'm sorry! Tullia, I'm sorry! Someone must have—"

Tullia said, "Be quiet, you don't know—" One of the officers stepped up to her, knife outstretched.

"Lie down, or I'll split you open!"

Tullia knelt then lay on her chest. Yalda met her rear gaze, hoping for advice, but if there was a message she couldn't read it.

Yalda said, "Antonia, get behind me." She moved toward the officer who'd threatened Tullia. He was tiny; if not for the knife she could have done what she liked with him. "You want to go out the window?" she taunted him. "You've got no business here. Go harass someone else."

The man raised the knife confidently, no doubt accustomed to its power to induce obedience. Yalda advanced on him, undeterred. She wouldn't even need to extrude extra limbs for the encounter; if she seized him with both hands it wouldn't matter if she lost an arm in the process, she could still fling him down to the street with the remaining one.

"Please, Yalda, don't!" Antonia implored her, distraught. "I'll go back! Don't make trouble for yourself!"

Yalda was unmoved; what gave these buffoons the right to interfere in anyone's life? If one of them spilled his brains on the cobblestones, the others might rethink their priorities.

Tullia addressed her calmly. "Yalda, if you resist, we'll all get a beating. If you harm even one of them, we'll all be killed."

Yalda stared at the man in front of her, then forced herself to look past his triumphant sneer to the long line of colleagues waiting behind him, knives at the ready. She might be able to deal with three or four of them before she was overpowered—but if Tullia was right, it would not be worth the price.

She knelt down, then lay on the floor, subduing her rage. Her physical strength meant nothing. The rightness of her cause meant nothing. The Council had given these men the authority to capture and return runaways; Antonia's plans for her life were irrelevant.

The officer she'd confronted put a foot on her back and held her arms behind her while someone passed him a length of hardstone chain. He slipped the loop at the end of the chain around one of her arms, then took a vial from his belt and shook a few beads of bright red resin onto her palm. It stung fiercely, but Yalda forced herself not to lash out. Then he pressed both of her palms together. Skin stuck tightly to skin, in itself no great hardship, but the resin made her body act as if these ordinary surfaces comprised a kind of internal partition, a pathological mistake that needed to be broken down.

Yalda closed her eyes for a moment, fighting not to lose consciousness. She had no right to be surprised by any of this; how many prisoners had she seen shuffling through Zeugma with their arms melded? She'd looked away, like everyone else. Murderers and thieves got what they deserved.

The officer ran the tip of his knife over her skin methodically, until he found the telltale crease of a pocket.

"Do you want me to cut it open?" he asked.

Yalda opened the pocket. He reached in and took out a handful of coins and her vial of holin.

In the corner of the room, Antonia was pleading with her own captor. Her hands had been bound with rope, but she and Tullia had been spared the melding resin, no doubt as a reward for their swift compliance. Once they were down on the street, Yalda thought, Antonia could easily slip out of those unreliable bonds and make a run for it.

Yalda's tormentor walked over to Antonia. "You're a runaway?"

"Yes, sir."

"And you're willing to return to your co?"

"Yes, sir. But my friends didn't know; I told them he was dead. I'll go back to him willingly, but you have to release them."

This attempt at a bargain amused the officer. "This patrol wasn't looking for you," he said, "but it's kind of you to volunteer the truth. We only came here for the fat one, the solo. She assaulted a Councilor's son."

He walked back to Yalda and began kicking her in the tympanum.

The room fractured, the walls collapsed into rubble. Yalda writhed and screamed, buried in shards of noise and pain.

8

"When you come before the sergeant," Tullia whispered, "don't argue about anything. Agree to the fine, agree to the conditions, and you'll be out of here in a few more days."

Yalda was bound to the wall of her cell, her own flesh the last link in the chain. She'd threaded her body through the loop of her melded arms so they were in front of her now, a minor improvement. The cell was bare and windowless, equally dark by night and by day. Twice, someone had entered unseen; the first time to beat her, the second to strew rotten grain on the floor. The loudest sounds that reached her were the thwack of wood against flesh and the hums of misery from other cells.

They'd granted her two unintended mercies, though. The floor was real soil, her favorite kind of bed; the worms that might have revolted a more fastidious guest just made her feel at home. And they'd put her next to Tullia, allowing them to whisper to each other through the wall's porous stone. Without that, she would have lost her mind.

"I'll be charged with sheltering a runaway, and for the holin in my room if they found it," Tullia explained. Apparently she'd been through all of this before. "They'll fine me a few dozen pieces, and make me swear an oath not to repeat my crimes. Your fine will probably be larger, but don't worry: they'll give you a chance to contact people who can help you pay it. I expect I'll be out before you, so I'll talk to Daria and the others at the Solo. Whatever you need, we'll raise it."

"*He* threw the stone at me!" Yalda complained. "Don't pay them anything! Let them charge that shit-head with assault as well."

"Can you produce a dozen witnesses against him?" Tullia asked.

"Probably not."

"Then it doesn't matter what he did. Stop telling yourself that it matters, or you're going to make everything harder."

Yalda could not accept this advice. She knew she should have restrained herself: she should have resisted lobbing back the cobblestone, sharp and heavy as she'd known it to be. But she still ached to see her assailant locked up beside her, beaten beside her, fined and humiliated and forced to promise to reform his own violent ways.

She knew that her actions had cost Antonia her life. Maybe a few years of it, maybe a few stints, but Antonia's chance to bargain with her co had been lost the instant Yalda had brought the police into Tullia's apartment. *That* was the worst of what she'd done, and she'd willingly confess her recklessness to anyone accusing her on Antonia's behalf. But her own culpability excused no one else. Let Antonio, who was merely eager for children, let the Councilor's son, who was only teasing a solo, let the police, who were simply doing their jobs, all line up and take their punishment beside her.

Otherwise, octofurcate them all.

Tullia grew weary of the subject, and after making her advice clear she steered their conversation elsewhere.

"Come out of this stinking prison with me for a couple of bells," she begged Yalda. "Why live the life of the mind at all, if you're not going to live it now?"

"I'll lie here and hallucinate Hurtlers, shall I? That will be a real comfort."

"Last time I checked, you had a more urgent problem," Tullia reminded her.

"You want us to solve the exponential blow-up, *here?*"

"How would you rather spend your time? Plotting the dismemberment of Councilors' sons?"

In truth, Yalda longed for a distraction, and she wished she shared Tullia's discipline and resolve. But the problem itself seemed as intractable as their incarceration. "Giorgio was right," she said. "The equation I found has exponential solutions. And if I try to damp them down—if I try to get rid of them by adding new terms to the equation—I just lose the original solutions."

"It's a strange equation for a wave," Tullia conceded. "The nice thing about the wave equation on a string is that you can set the initial conditions and just watch them unfold: you can pluck the string into any shape you like, and give it any kind of movement, and from that the equation lets you find the shape of the string at any time in the future. What's more, if you make a small mistake measuring the initial setup, it's not a calamity; the errors in your prediction are equally small.

"But your light equation is more like the equation for the temperature distribution in a solid. If you have, say… a thin slab of stone and you want to know its temperature at every point, to get reliable solutions you need to specify the temperature all the way around the border of the slab. If you tried to start with the temperature along a single edge and its inward gradient, any tiny error in the data there would blow up exponentially as you moved across the slab. Your equation acts the same way."

Yalda pondered this in the darkness. "So by analogy, to calculate the behavior of light in a certain place, over a period of time… I'd really need to know what it does on the entire border of that four-dimensional region? Not only what it's doing at the start, but everything that happens at the boundary, *and* how it all ends up?"

"Precisely," Tullia said. "The equation you've come up with might be said to *govern* the behavior of light, but practically speaking it's no good for making predictions. Everything it tells you could be tested in retrospect, but you'd always need to know how the story ends before you can start reliably 'predicting' the middle."

Yalda said, "Waves on a string can only have one velocity. We know that violet light can travel much faster than red light—and it's not implausible that there are even faster hues, beyond our ability to detect. So why should we expect that knowing the state of the light in just one place should ever be enough to say what happens next? Some other wave we haven't accounted for—just beyond the edge of the region we know about—could always be on the verge of crashing in and spoiling our prediction."

"Good point," Tullia replied. "So let's accept the possibility of light that travels as fast as you wish… but then to compensate, I let you know about every wave that presently exists *as far away* as you wish. That way, you get as much warning as you could hope for; you can't complain that some fast wave came hurtling in from a place beyond the reach of your data. And if the cosmos goes on forever, you get to know about the entire, infinite present: for one moment in time, there are no secrets from you anywhere."

"Go ahead and grant me that!" Yalda urged her. "Wouldn't that eliminate the problem?"

"No!" Tullia sounded both exasperated and amused that Yalda had taken the bait so readily, without thinking it through. "Your equation still has solutions that can blow up exponentially out of the tiniest mismeasurement. You *still* wouldn't be able to predict what happens right in front of your eyes over the next few pauses. Does that really accord with your instincts about the way the physics of light should work?"

"No," Yalda admitted. She adjusted her position, then cursed softly and braced herself for the sound of tearing flesh. She'd been trying to keep her arms a few scants apart within their shared sleeve of skin, hoping to make her eventual liberation less traumatic. But her body thought it knew best. Every time she dozed, or her attention wandered, she had to rip apart a fresh bundle of muscle fibers that had formed between the ends of her limbs.

When she was done, she thought back over the steps in Tullia's argument. "What if the cosmos didn't go on forever?" she said. "In space, or in time?"

"Then you'd still need to know what happens at its boundary," Tullia replied. "Like the slab of stone: you need to know what's going on at all the edges."

Yalda considered the possibilities this offered. By declaring that the boundary of the cosmos was subject to some special rule—perhaps that the wave simply had to be zero there—she could probably keep it from blowing up in the interior. But that was an ugly resolution, an arbitrary constraint that came from nowhere and offered no deeper understanding.

"What if there *are no edges?*" she suggested. "What if the cosmos is like the surface of the world—finite, but borderless?"

Tullia lapsed into silence for so long that Yalda grew worried. She extruded a new, free arm and thumped the wall. "Are you all right?"

"Yes! *I'm thinking!*" Tullia almost sounded happy, as if Yalda had finally suggested something novel enough to be truly diverting.

Eventually Tullia declared, "I'm fairly sure that that would solve the exponential blow-up. You can wrap an oscillation around a sphere so that it joins up with itself smoothly—but you can't do that with an exponential growth curve, which never revisits its earlier values."

Yalda chirped with delight. "So if the cosmos is a four-dimensional version of the surface of a sphere—"

"Things would still be very strange," Tullia warned her. "The prediction problem jumps from one extreme to the other."

"What do you mean?"

"Think about the two-dimensional version," Tullia said. "If you draw a circle around Zeugma, the data lying on that circle—combined with your equation—tells you everything that happens in the city. Information about the border gives you information about the interior."

"But that's nothing new. Where's the problem?"

"A circle around Zeugma," Tullia replied, "is also a circle around *everything else in the world*. The border of the city is also the border of everything that lies beyond. So from the data on that one circle, you can find the solution to your equation on the entire sphere."

"Oh."

Tullia drove the point home. "In the four-dimensional version, that's like claiming that you can measure the light in a patch a few scants across, for a couple of pauses… and learn everything there is to know about light throughout the history of the cosmos. Because the border of your tiny region is also the border of everything else."

Yalda buzzed wryly. "I can't say that *that* accords with my instincts about the physics of light."

"Nor mine." Tullia's surge of enthusiasm was gone, but she was doing her best not to sound despondent.

"We tried," Yalda said. "And it was worth trying."

They had managed to leave the prison for a while, but nothing was easy, even in freedom.

When it was quiet in the cells, Yalda could hear the bells from one of the city's clock towers; she missed a few from noise, or sleep, or inattentiveness, but never so many as to lose track of time. So she knew it was the middle of the morning on their third day when the guards came and took Tullia.

This had to be her hearing with the sergeant. Yalda waited, trying to be patient. Tullia had told her that there was usually a large group of prisoners to be dealt with in each session, and the whole thing could last a bell or two.

By evening, Tullia had not returned. Either they'd set her free, or they'd moved her to a different cell while she arranged the payment of her fine.

Yalda chose to believe that she'd been freed. Tullia hadn't resisted arrest, and she knew the system well enough to say the right things at her hearing. If the fine had been small enough she might have been released on a promissory note, rather than forced to wait until actual coins had been delivered to the sergeant. Tullia would be at the Solo Club, celebrating her freedom and looking for ways to help her friend.

Yalda blocked out the sad humming of her neighbors; she felt for them, but she didn't have the strength to involve herself in their plights. She would have her turn before the sergeant soon; she needed to decide what she would say.

When the guards came the next morning, the light of their lamp almost blinded her. She'd planned to sneak a look at the tool they used to disconnect her chain from its place on the wall, but everything was veiled in painful brightness. As they tugged on the chain to draw her out of the cell, she quickly lengthened one of her arms and shortened the other, allowing the force to be borne by solid flesh instead of the loose tube of skin between them that she'd fought to keep empty.

She stumbled up the broad staircase into a corridor filled with searing daylight, then hurried along with slitted eyes, not wishing to drag the chain and provoke her captors. In a room full of prisoners, she was secured to the wall again. Yalda raised her gaze cautiously; there were more than a dozen men and women chained up beside her, most of them with melded limbs. Everyone looked as wretched and afraid as she was.

She felt herself shivering. No friends were permitted here to offer support. Nobody could advise her now, or speak in her defense. All she had to guide her was Tullia's counsel, which she'd been so vehement in opposing.

The sergeant entered the room—wearing a belt much like his subordinates', but adorned with no less than four knives—and took his place behind an impressive calmstone desk. An assistant brought in a stack of paper, smelling of fresh dye; for an instant the scent was almost comforting.

As the first case was heard, Yalda tried to concentrate on the procedure and learn what she could. A young man had stolen a loaf from the markets, and then fled from the police. He did not deny the charge.

The sergeant fined him a dozen pieces. "How will you pay this?" he asked.

"My brother might help me," the man said, his voice soft with shame.

"Give his details to the messenger; you can wait in your cell." A guard took the man's chain and led him away.

The next prisoner, another young man, had trespassed in a private garden; he was not accused of stealing anything, but his fine was three times as much as the thief's.

Everything about the process was humiliating, but Yalda prepared herself to swallow her pride. Tullia had offered to help her find the money for her fine; Daria would probably be willing to loan her a few dozen pieces. She could be out of this place by nightfall if she was suitably humble and penitent. And whatever blame fell upon her for Antonia's fate, there was nothing to be gained by making trouble for herself. No one was going to rise up against the Council to overthrow the law on runaways because one fat solo argued with the police about an unrelated assault.

When her turn came, a guard unclamped her chain from the wall and ushered her in front of the sergeant's desk.

"Are you Yalda, daughter of Vito?"

"Yes, sir." The sound of her father's name stung; Yalda had no wish to imagine him witnessing any of this.

The sergeant scanned the paper in front of him. "You are charged, firstly, with possession of a substance contrary to the order of nature and the public good. Do you dispute the charge?"

"No, sir." In the darkness of her cell she'd rehearsed speeches on the insanity of banning a drug that spared the world fatherless children, fantasizing about the power of her impeccable logic to sway even the most hostile audience.

"On that charge, I fine you a dozen pieces."

"Thank you, sir."

The sergeant glanced up at her, irritated, as if her anxious tic might actually be taken to imply that the fine was lenient. "Secondly, you are charged with a grievous assault against the person of Acilio, son of Acilio, four nights ago in the square outside the Variety Hall. I have statements from six witnesses to the effect that you threw a sharpened stone that struck him and caused substantial injuries. Do you dispute the charge?"

"No, sir."

"Do you have anything to say in mitigation?"

Yalda hesitated. Surely an honest answer would not be treated as hostility or disputation? Why ask about mitigation if you had no wish to hear the truth?

"Sir, Acilio did throw the stone at me before I assaulted him with it. It only struck me lightly, but that's how I came to have it in my hand."

The sergeant re-examined the paper in front of him then slid it aside and gazed up at her coldly. "What witnesses do you name for this accusation?"

"None, sir," Yalda admitted. "Most people were looking at the sky," she explained, "and my friend was on the other side of the square."

"Then I fine you two dozen pieces for a gratuitous and cowardly libel," the sergeant said, "and a further dozen for wasting my time."

Yalda's skin quivered, as if her body believed it could rid her of this strange insect that kept taking bites out of her flesh.

"As for the assault," the sergeant continued, "the complainant has requested a payment of a dozen gross pieces in reparation, an amount with which I concur. Additionally, on behalf of the citizens of Zeugma, I fine you a further gross. Your total fine is a dozen-and-one gross and four dozen pieces. How will you pay this?"

Yalda couldn't speak. Even Daria, with the fees from her public dissections, wouldn't make that much in a year; for Tullia or Lidia it would be a lifetime's wages.

"How will you pay?" the sergeant repeated impatiently.

"I can't," Yalda said. "I don't have anything like that."

The sergeant hummed wearily. "I don't expect you to pluck that many coins from your pocket, you simpleton. Just give the messenger the name of someone who can organize the money for you."

"There's no one who can do that," Yalda insisted. *A dozen gross?* She couldn't burden Tullia with that surreal demand; she couldn't bury all her friends in impossible debts. "Can't you... reconsider the size of the reparation?" she pleaded.

"What I'll do," the sergeant said, his tone now sarcastically good-natured, "is return you to your cell for a stint, so *you* can reconsider the resources at your disposal." He gestured to the guard.

As she was led back down to the basement, Yalda kept tripping on the stairs. The guard waited for her to right herself; perhaps the sheer size of her fine had impressed him to the point where any further mistreatment was superfluous.

He said, "You should pick your fights more carefully."

Yalda said, "I didn't even know who he was."

The guard buzzed with mirth. "You do now."

At first, Yalda refused to believe that things were as they seemed. A dozen gross pieces? It had to be a kind of cruel joke, a punishment for her "cowardly libel". After a day or two she'd be hauled before the sergeant again and told what the true fine would be.

But as she heard the bells marking the end of her sixth day in prison— with the spoilt grain that she'd spurned at first, then scrabbled for blindly, now entirely gone—she experienced a moment of clarity. A part of her, she realized, had been laboring under a strange assumption: that people with the power to release her would be spending their days pondering her fate, agonizing over her hardship, questioning her punishment's severity. And since no one was entirely devoid of feeling... anything truly intolerable to her would, in the end, be intolerable to them. Any treatment so unjust that it threatened to crush her spirit would, in the end, wear down their resolve to impose it.

But it was not like that at all. The sergeant, the guards, the Council, her accuser, buttressed by each other's mutual approval, shared the burden of her imprisonment so equitably that it became no burden at all. *No one*, individually, was responsible for what they'd done to her in concert. She could die in this cell, and none of them would feel the faintest twinge of discomfort.

All she could do now was wait out the stint, then send an honest message to Tullia explaining her situation. She would not let her friends go into debt, but if they told her story to everyone at the Solo Club, perhaps some of the wealthier customers would be sympathetic to her plight. Perhaps over a year or two the money could be raised.

A narrow bridge of flesh had formed again between her sleeved arms. Yalda tugged at the fibers angrily, jerking and tearing them until the last one snapped. However long she stayed here, it wouldn't be the guards who set her free.

On the morning of her eighth day of imprisonment, Yalda woke to find something hard on the floor when she moved her feet. She picked up the grains one by one until she had a handful, then she tipped them carefully into her mouth.

Why did she need food at all? Why not just make light, and get the energy she needed for free? She wasn't growing, like a child; she didn't need to add new matter to her body.

But the matter she did have was growing disordered; the microscopic building blocks of her flesh were slipping into disarray. Soil for a plant, food for an animal, offered more than materials for growth and repair: it was a source of *low entropy*. The rock from which it came was highly ordered—and without order, energy was useless, as likely to push you one way as another. Life rode the arrow of time that came from the world's slow decay.

But now that she had a little order in her body, what was she going to do with it? Her captors wouldn't let her starve to death, but how would she stay sane?

"All right, Tullia," she whispered. "I'll show you the life of the mind."

Tullia had claimed that if the cosmos resembled the surface of a sphere, Yalda's equation would render everything absurdly predictable. Her argument had sounded plausible, but Yalda wanted a deeper understanding of the problem before she abandoned the whole idea.

On a sphere, she realized, the fundamental solutions of her equation would be *spherical harmonics*: a kind of waveform she'd encountered once before in a course on seismology. Whatever complicated solution held across the whole surface of the sphere, it could be written as a sum of these harmonics, each multiplied by a suitable factor measuring the size of its contribution.

Yalda worked through the calculations, raising equations on her skin in the dark. First, you fixed the physical parameters: the radius of the sphere and the wavefronts' separation. Then, as the wave's frequency with respect to longitude rose, its frequency with respect to latitude would fall. Since you always had to wrap whole numbers of waves around the equator and around any meridian, in the end there were only a finite number of possibilities—a finite number of relevant harmonics.

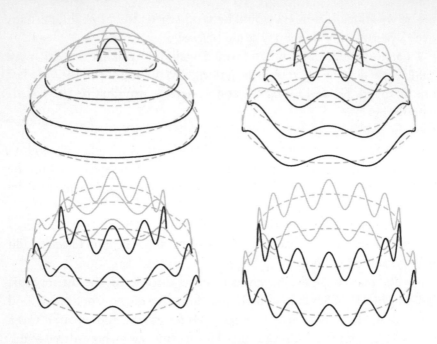

She sketched a few examples to make the calculations tangible. The north and south hemispheres were identical, so she only bothered with half the sphere, drawing the waves along the various circles of latitude where they were strongest.

Around any circle of latitude, though—however large or small—each particular harmonic would execute the same number of cycles, making each one as distinctive as the harmonics of a plucked string. So if you were given the values on *any* circle of latitude of *any* wave obeying the equation, you could separate out the harmonics and determine their respective strengths—which would give you the entire, global solution. What's more, the choice of where the "pole" lay in this scenario was completely arbitrary; in principle, you could perform the same analysis anywhere at all.

In practice, though? If the waves were already packed six dozen gross to the scant as they marched around the cosmic equator, how could you ever hope to observe their proportionately finer undulations around a circle that was just a stride or two across? And to make the problem even more acute, the higher the harmonic the faster its strength dropped as you approached the poles, so the wavefronts associated with it would be preposterously weak, as well as unmeasurably close.

Tullia's objection, then, was purely philosophical: the idea that the entire cosmic history of light was writ small in every last corner of the world was simply too shocking to countenance—however useless it would be for aspiring fortune-tellers. Yalda was prepared to set her unease aside and see where the rest of the theory took her, but other physicists might easily view this as a flaw as fatal as Giorgio's original complaint. What was the use in being half right, if she wasn't even half-believed? She needed other scientists to pursue these ideas; imprisoned or free, she couldn't begin to explore all of their ramifications herself.

Yalda slumped forward and rested her head against the aching circle of her arms. She wanted to drag the weary muscles in these limbs all the way back into her chest and replace them with rested flesh, but with no instinct or experience to guide her, she couldn't find a safe, painless sequence of movements that would fulfill this wish. For all the many postures she'd tried since childhood, she had never before suffered a change in the topology of her skin.

She butted the gap between her arms with the top of her head, allowing the limbs to relax for a while without touching. The sense of respite was glorious, but she knew it would only be a lapse or two before her arms started to slip together.

The loose skin in the gap was puckered into folds that brushed against the top of her skull. Yalda played with the wrinkles, sliding them back and forth to massage the top of her head. To her amusement, she realized that they'd naturally arranged themselves into a set of evenly spaced "waves", a few dozen oscillations circumnavigating the sleeve of skin. She was practically a spherical harmonic come to life—except that she was no longer even roughly spherical. She was more like a torus, now.

A torus, instead of a sphere.

What would that change?

A torus would still prevent the exponential blow-up—you couldn't wrap an exponential growth curve around a torus, any more than you could around a sphere—but its fundamental solutions would be different.

Yalda lifted her head and stared into the darkness. A torus didn't even need to be curved; mathematically, you could slice it open and lay it flat, turning it into a rectangle or a square. You simply had to guarantee that the wave at each edge of the square agreed with its value on the opposite edge, so the whole thing could be put back together smoothly.

The fundamental solutions would be waves that executed whole numbers of cycles as you moved across the square in either direction, bringing the wave back to its original value. The sum of the squares of those two whole numbers would have to equal a constant—fixing the relationship between the size of the cosmos and the wavefronts' separation.

She quickly sketched some examples, picking a constant small enough to be manageable, but large enough to be broken down into a sum of squares in a few different ways.

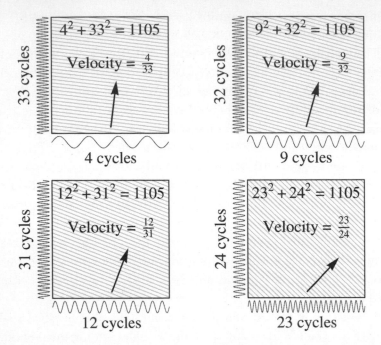

For the kind of waves she could draw on her body, completing a few dozen oscillations at most, there would only be a handful of solutions—which was tantamount to saying that light could only travel at a handful of different velocities, equal to the ratios between its frequencies in space and in time. But in the real, cosmic, four-dimensional case, the sum of squares would be so vast that it could be written in more ways than there were grains of sand in a prison cell, and the ratios would be so numerous and closely spaced that you'd never know they were not continuous.

For each choice of the number of waves spanning the square, you could also choose to have the wave in each direction either start at zero on the edge of the square, or start at a peak. With that additional flexibility, a completely general solution—whatever its complexities and quirks—could always be written as a sum of the fundamental solutions, multiplied by various factors.

What data would you need, in order to find those factors and reconstruct the whole wave—the whole history of light for a toroidal cosmos? Unlike the spherical harmonics, the imprint of these fundamental solutions didn't get funnelled down toward any poles. To measure their contributions you'd need to know what the wave was doing along one entire edge of the square—and not just its value, but also its rate of change in the orthogonal direction, in order to learn about the waves that had a value of zero along the chosen edge.

These requirements were almost exactly the same as those for the physicists' beloved plucked string: you set the initial shape of the string, and its initial motion, and the equation told you what followed. The only difference was that *this* equation allowed waves of any speed, so you needed to gather the same information from far away—potentially, across the whole width of the cosmos. This was the offer Tullia had made—"for one moment in time, there are no secrets from you anywhere"—no longer rendered useless by exponential growth.

In a toroidal cosmos, predictions became *reasonable*: by knowing about your immediate surroundings, you could predict what would happen with sufficiently slow waves in the immediate future. You'd be neither helpless nor absurdly omniscient. A wave faster than anything you'd prepared for could always come along and surprise you—like a Hurtler appearing out of nowhere—but if it didn't, things proceeded as expected.

Replace the torus with its four-dimensional equivalent, and light that followed these hypothetical rules started to behave just as it did in the real world.

Yalda lowered her head and tried to rest her arms again, but her shoulders were burning with fatigue. She couldn't replenish those muscles, either; all of the moves that would have achieved that required her to separate her arms completely.

At least she now knew how to word her message to Tullia. "If you can't help me pay this fine," she'd say, "I only ask you to think carefully about the shape my body is in."

On the eleventh day, two guards with lamps entered Yalda's cell and unclamped her chain from the wall. She didn't question what was happening; if the sergeant had rescheduled her appearance for a few days earlier, so much the better.

Upstairs, she was almost blinded by the glare. She didn't realize she'd been taken to a different room than before until one of the guards made her kneel and held something in front of her face. As he turned the object, her eyes were stabbed by a glimmer of reflected sunlight.

"Are you ready?" he demanded impatiently.

"For what?" she asked, alarmed and confused.

"Someone paid your fine," he said. "We're cutting you free."

Yalda tightened the skin between her arms, shrinking it down to a thumb-sized stub. She'd had fantasies about making the cut herself, or even using her teeth to tear through the skin, but at least there was still no flesh to be severed.

The guard had her place her arms on a wooden bench. The process was swift, and if it wasn't exactly painless it hurt far less than the original melding. When the guard slipped the chain off her arm, Yalda resorbed the abused limbs completely. She rose to her feet and took a step back, then rolled her shoulders and chirped with bliss as she rearranged half the flesh in her torso. Her two small wounds ended up at the sides of her back.

The guard said irritably, "Could you groom yourself outside?"

"With pleasure." Yalda didn't waste time asking him who'd paid her fine; Tullia would know which businesswoman from the Solo Club had taken pity on her, and would be able to advise her on the proper way to express her thanks.

Yalda moved slowly down the corridor toward the dazzling rectangle of light that marked the entrance to the barracks. She would never have lasted a year; she could admit that now. She would have been dead or insane in a dozen stints. She needed to visit the chemistry department at the first opportunity, and come back with something volatile enough to turn this whole abomination into rubble.

She stepped out beneath the sky, shivering, humming softly to herself. For a moment she was hurt that Tullia wasn't waiting on the street to welcome her back to freedom, but that was petty; the world hadn't come to a halt, Tullia still needed to earn a living. She extruded two fresh arms and shielded her eyes as she looked around, trying to orient herself.

"Yalda?" A male figure approached through the haze of brightness.

"Eusebio?" Yalda had lost count of all the lessons they'd missed. First her three stints on Mount Peerless, and now this unexplained absence. "I'm sorry, I couldn't get word to you—"

He was close enough now for Yalda to read the embarrassment on his face. Of course he would have heard exactly what had happened to her.

"May I walk with you?" he said.

"Of course." She let Eusebio lead the way; she had yet to recover her sense of direction, let alone decide where she wanted to go.

Eusebio remained silent for some time, his gaze directed at the ground. "If you choose to end our arrangement," he said finally, "I'll understand your decision. And I'll pay you for the lessons to the end of the year."

Yalda struggled to make sense of this strange invitation. Was he trying to tell her that he was so ashamed of her scandalous behavior that he no longer wished to be her student—but he expected *her* to act, sparing him the unpleasantness of having to dismiss her?

"Actually, I'd rather go on tutoring you," she said coolly. If he wanted to be rid of her, he'd have to find the courage to spell it out.

Eusebio shuddered, emitting a hum that sounded more like shame than disgust. "I can't believe you're not angrier," he said wonderingly. "It was my fault; I should have warned you."

Yalda stopped walking. "What should you have warned me about?"

"Acilio, of course. All of them—but Acilio's the worst."

Yalda was utterly lost now. "How could you have known that Acilio would decide to throw a rock at me?" Unless the cosmos was spherical after all, and Eusebio had sat in his apartment one night reading the harmonics for the entire future.

"I couldn't," he replied. "And that might well have been sheer coincidence. But once he found out who you were, that you were connected to me…"

Yalda struggled to absorb this. "You mean, he asked for that huge reparation as a way of getting at *you*?"

Eusebio said, "Yes. Of course you humiliated him, so he didn't care what harm he did to you, but the penalty was chosen for my edification."

It was Eusebio who'd paid the fine and set her free. But she'd only faced the prospect of a lifetime in the cells in the first place because of some childish dispute between him and Acilio.

And she had been the last to know about any of this. When the sergeant had urged her to *reconsider the resources at her disposal*, he'd been hinting that he expected her to beg her wealthy employer to come to her aid.

"So what now?" she said bitterly. "You've bought me, you own me?"

Eusebio recoiled, wounded. "I was remiss in not warning you about my enemies, but I've never treated you with anything but respect."

Yalda could not dispute that. "I'm sorry," she said.

"Acilio is nothing to me!" Eusebio declared. "I don't want to fight with him! But his grandfather and my grandfather are rivals. It's all so tedious it would merely be a tired old joke if it didn't damage other people's lives. All I want to do is get an education and make something of myself. But I should have warned you that I have adversaries who'll treat anyone close to me as fair game."

"It might have been helpful," Yalda agreed.

"I'll give you their names, I'll show you their portraits," Eusebio promised. "Everyone you should avoid."

"I probably shouldn't injure… anyone, really," Yalda decided.

Eusebio said, "These are people you don't even want to bump in a queue."

"I see." Yalda contemplated the situation. "Is this over now? Or will Acilio have something more in mind for me?" She wasn't keen on being shuttled in and out of prison until Eusebio was bankrupt. Couldn't these idiots learn to ruin each other in pointless games of chance, instead?

"I don't think he'll repeat himself," Eusebio said carefully. "And it's one thing to exploit an opportunity, but using you to bludgeon me repeatedly would be seen as rather crass."

"Well, that's a relief. I'm so glad there are standards to be upheld."

Eusebio met her gaze; he was still ashamed over what had happened, but he'd done all he could to make amends. "So what do you say about our lessons?"

"I want them to continue," Yalda said. "Draw up a guide for me, on surviving the whims of Zeugma's ruling class, and then we can get on with the things that matter."

The prison guards hadn't returned the coins the police had taken from her pocket, but Yalda still had some money in the bank. The clerk looked dubious when he compared the signature she made on her chest with a print of it on paper, and insisted on asking her three of her secret questions as well.

"Give the largest proper factor of the eighth power of a gross plus five gross squared plus eleven?" The clerk interrupted her before she could answer. "What kind of question is that?"

"Too easy?" Yalda wondered. "You might be right."

She bought a loaf in the markets, then walked past the place where Antonia's stall had been.

She couldn't face the university yet; she sat in a quiet park until evening, then went to Tullia's apartment.

Tullia greeted her with a look of pure astonishment. "What happened? I heard rumors of some preposterous fine, but they wouldn't tell me anything at the barracks. I was waiting for you to send me a message!" She ushered Yalda inside; the apartment was lit only by plants once more, but prison had given Yalda astronomer's eyes and every sheet of paper in the room stood out clearly.

She explained what Eusebio had told her. Tullia said, "Next time I complain about my own students, you now have permission to slap me in the head."

"Any news about Antonia?"

"I met her three days ago," Tullia replied. "In the markets, with her co. She insisted that she was with him voluntarily; he insisted that nothing was going to happen to her by force."

"Did you believe him?"

"Does it matter what I believe? There's nothing we can do now."

"I was so stupid," Yalda said angrily. "The police weren't even looking for her—"

"And what about Eusebio!"

"What about him?" Yalda wasn't going to blame him for her own carelessness. "Any fool could have picked a fight with me that night; even if Eusebio had warned me about Acilio, the same thing might have happened with someone else."

Tullia went over to one of her plants and dug into the soil with narrow fingers, finally plucking out a vial.

"Did the police find your holin?" Yalda asked her.

"Not a scrag. You should have some now; you've missed a lot of doses."

"I'm no older than Antonia," Yalda said. "And spontaneous reproduction was the least of her worries."

"Actually, Antonia took holin when she was staying here," Tullia replied. "I insisted. If there's one thing worse than living with an indecisive runaway, it's coming home to find that she's been replaced by four screaming brats." She handed Yalda two green cubes; Yalda didn't want to argue anymore, so she swallowed them.

She sat on the floor and put her face in her hands. "So now it's back to ordinary life?"

"We can't win every battle," Tullia said firmly. "If you want some good news, though… Rufino and Zosimo made their own observations of the Hurtler. And, strange to say, there was another one three days later."

"*Another one?*"

"Not visible from here, but they saw it in Red Towers."

Yalda was perplexed. "What does *that* tell us?"

"That they're random events?" Tullia suggested. "There isn't some cosmic slingshot out there that takes years to replenish its energy and spit the next one out. If the timing's completely random, there's no reason why they shouldn't come one after the other, occasionally."

"From exactly the same direction?" Inasmuch as the Hurtlers' trajectories had been pinned down by people's hasty observations, they had all been more or less parallel. "Why random in time, but not in space?"

Tullia considered this. "From the Hurtlers' point of view, they *are* random in space. What we see as the time between them, they see as distance."

"Now I'm getting a headache."

"You know, even when he heard you were in prison, Giorgio didn't cancel your talk?" Tullia marveled. "I wish I'd had a supervisor with that much faith in me. I was going to break the news to him that we never did solve the prediction problem—" She broke off, reading Yalda's expression. "You didn't?"

"No exponential blow-ups," Yalda announced proudly, "and no seeing the cosmos in every grain of sand."

"How?" Tullia pressed her, delighted.

Yalda shuddered, overwhelmed for a moment; she knew she wouldn't be able to recount the discovery without reliving her imprisonment and mutilation. And after eleven days abandoned in the dark, she wasn't ready to go and sleep beneath the markets again, surrounded by strangers who didn't care if she lived or died.

She said, "Come closer, and I'll write the answer on your skin."

9

The truck dropped Yalda off in the village, then she walked the rest of the way to the farm in the mid-morning heat. After three days of traveling she'd been expecting the last leg of the journey to pass quickly, but she soon realized that her memory of the walk was a heavily edited version, concentrating on a few distinguishing features—a hill, a tree, a crossroads—while excising all the monotonous stretches in between. Halfway to the farm, she began noticing shapes among the chance arrangements of pebbles by the roadside that she could have sworn had been there since she was a child.

As she walked north along the access path, a girl she'd never seen before approached her.

"Are you Yalda?" the girl asked.

"Yes. Who are you?"

"I'm Ada."

"Pleased to meet you," Yalda said.

They walked along the path together. Yalda had felt herself twitching at the mites ever since she'd left the village, but now that she had company she redoubled her efforts to stop random fragments of writing from surfacing on her skin each time she dislodged one of the insects.

"My father told me to see if you were coming," Ada explained.

"Who's your father?"

Ada was amused that anyone could need to ask this. "Aurelio!" she said.

Yalda shed the last of her lingering nostalgia. "Do you have any cousins?"

"Of course. Lorenza and Lorenzo and Ulfa and Ulfo." After reflecting on the depth of Yalda's ignorance for a moment, Ada added for completeness, "Their father is Claudio. And my sister's name is Flavia."

"And you both have cos?"

Ada buzzed with mirth. "Everyone has a co!"

"Really?"

"Yes," Ada confirmed. "I know your co lives in a city called Zeugma, but he wasn't born with you, that's why he isn't coming to visit us."

"You know a lot about me, considering we only just met."

"You're my father's cousin," Ada said, as if that were enough to make Yalda's life an open book to her.

Yalda said, "Tell me about my brother."

"Lucio? He and Lucia were going to move to their own farm. Vito was going with them. But now..." Ada stopped, unsure what she should say.

"I know about Vito," Yalda said gently. No one had bothered to tell her when Aurelia's life had ended, or Claudia's. Only Vito's demise counted as a death, worthy of mourning.

When they walked into the clearing, Yalda was overcome with sadness. Even eight exuberant new children could not make up for the three missing faces.

When she'd embraced everyone, Giusto said, "You should have brought your co-stead, he would have been welcome."

Yalda made a sound that she hoped expressed no more than gratitude at this proposition in the abstract. Although she had never tried to correct the assumption that she was in Zeugma to hunt for a co-stead as much as to pursue her education, she had never actually lied and said that she'd found one.

Giusto led her to the pit that had been dug in a corner of the clearing. Yalda looked down; the body was wrapped in petals, it could have been anyone. She sank to her knees, humming and shaking inconsolably.

When she'd recovered her composure she turned to Giusto. "He was a good man." Her father had done his best for her, always; she owed him her life and her sanity.

"Of course." Giusto squeezed her shoulder awkwardly.

"What happened?"

"He went quietly," Giusto said. "Sleeping. He'd been sick for a few days."

Mites were swarming around the grave. Yalda said, "Should I—?"

"Yes. Everyone else has been; everyone from the village."

Yalda shaped her hands into scoops; Giusto knelt and helped her shift the soil back into the pit. She wanted to ask him about Aurelia and Claudia, too—at least to learn how old the children were—but this wasn't the time. Childbirth was not to be lamented like death. Any hint of a comparison would be treated as a kind of derangement.

Yalda offered to help prepare the midday meal, but there were too many hands already, all accustomed to their own tasks. She watched Aurelio and Claudio affectionately guiding their boisterous children, intervening in the worst spats, making peace without taking sides or becoming angry. Who could condemn such able, loving fathers? But while she'd never know what the children's mothers had wanted, she could be sure that no one had allowed them the kind of choices she'd had herself.

When the meal was over, Giusto took her aside.

"I want to hear about your co-stead," he said. "What is it that he does? I should know what kind of business my great-nephews will inherit."

"There is no business," Yalda said. "I study at the university. I support myself with tutoring. That's my life: work and study. There is no co-stead."

Giusto's face betrayed no surprise. "So you're free? That's good news! I'm glad there's no one tying you down."

"You approve?" Yalda was confused.

Giusto said, "Without a co-stead to worry about, you can take your father's place on the new farm. Your brother can hardly work the farm alone, with young children."

"*Young children?*" Yalda gestured around the clearing. "There aren't enough children here already?"

"It's Lucio's time," Giusto said. "How long should he wait? We've bought the farm already. Only Vito's death has held things up."

Yalda said, "Here's a plan: rent out the second farm for a few years, then once your grandchildren are a little older, either Aurelio's family or Claudio's can take it over, along with Lucia and Lucio."

Giusto buzzed derisively. "You want to scramble the generations? You want your brother to be so old when his children are born that his *cousins' children* have to raise them for him?"

"What Lucio and Lucia do is up to them," Yalda replied. "But I'm not going to work on that farm."

Giusto was growing angry now. "So you've forgotten your own family?"

"My family doesn't need me," Yalda said calmly. "I've told you how you can make the second farm work."

"Your duty is to take your father's place there."

"I doubt that would have been his opinion."

"What is it that you think you're doing in Zeugma?" Giusto demanded. "I'd like to know what's so important that everything else in your life can be neglected."

"I'm studying light," Yalda said. "Star trails. The Hurtlers."

"Hurtlers?"

"They're a bit like shooting stars. We saw one, here, years ago—"

Giusto cut her off impatiently. "I taught Aurelio and Claudio to recite the sagas, and I'm willing to do the same for you. If you want a real education, start with six ages' worth of knowledge."

"All of it at least six ages out of date," Yalda retorted.

Giusto stared at her as if she'd lost her mind. As far as Yalda could tell, his whole idea of *knowledge* was as something static, perfected in the distant past by the great poets and philosophers. The only truth to be had was passed down from them; there was nothing new to be found.

"I'm not leaving Zeugma," she said. "No one understands light fully, yet, but people are working toward it—in Zeugma, in Red Towers, in the other cities. You can't ask me to walk away from that! It's the most exciting thing happening in the world right now. And I'm part of it."

Giusto looked away, disgusted. "That was your father's first mistake."

"What mistake?" Yalda demanded angrily.

"Flattering you," Giusto replied. "Letting you think that you were something special, as a compensation for having no co. That, and sending you to school."

Yalda hadn't expected to find it easy to sleep, but it felt perfectly normal to be lying in the clearing again, with the soil beneath her and the stars above. Ada had taken Aurelia's spot, but she was asleep long before Yalda settled into her own old indentation. The flowers arranged around the sleepers glowed softly in every hue, but if Yalda raised her head slightly she could see the wheatlight beyond them.

She woke well before dawn, confused for a moment to have heard no bells, but sure of the time regardless. She rose and walked over to Lucia's bed, then crouched down and touched her sister's shoulder.

Lucia opened her eyes; Yalda gestured for silence, holding a motionless hand in front of her tympanum. Lucia climbed to her feet and followed Yalda to the edge of the clearing.

"I'm going now," Yalda said. "The trucks leave the village early."

"Do you have to? I'd hoped you'd stay a few more days." Lucia sounded disappointed, but not greatly surprised.

"Why don't you come with me?" Yalda suggested.

"To Zeugma?"

"Why not?"

Lucia buzzed softly with mirth. "What would I do there?"

"Whatever you like," Yalda replied. "You can look around and decide what suits you. I'll take care of you until you find a job."

"But there's work for me here; I don't need a new job."

Yalda said, "Don't you want to see more of the world than this?"

"That might be nice," Lucia conceded. "But I'd miss everyone."

"You could come back and visit, any time," Yalda promised her.

Lucia thought for a while. "Let me wake Lucio." She took a few steps before Yalda grabbed her arm.

"No! You can't—"

"You're not inviting him too?"

"No."

"Are you crazy?" Lucia was baffled. "Why would I go to Zeugma without him?"

"That's the whole point of leaving!" Yalda said, exasperated. "If you go by yourself, you won't have to worry."

"Worry about what?"

"Children."

Lucia said, "We're not having children for at least four more years. If we went with you to Zeugma, it wouldn't be any different."

"Four years?"

"Yes."

Yalda sat on the ground, shivering, not knowing whether to believe her. "Aurelia didn't *wait*. Claudia didn't *wait*."

"Well, I'm not Aurelia."

"Don't you miss them?"

"Of course I do," Lucia replied. "If you missed them so much," she added pointedly, "you should have visited more often."

Yalda was ashamed. "I didn't think I'd lose the chance so soon." She searched her sister's face, determined to uncover the family's secrets. "What happened? Did Giusto force them?"

"He *nagged* them," Lucia said. "But they had their own ideas, it wasn't all down to him."

"And you think he'll let you wait four years?"

"It's not his decision, Yalda! Lucio and I have everything planned: we're going to work on the new farm together and save as much money as we can. Then when the time comes, he'll hire some people to help run the farm for a couple of years while he takes care of the children. If some of the young cousins want to do it, that's fine, but we're not going to rely on that."

Yalda said, "And what if you change your mind? What if you want to wait longer?"

"Then we'll wait," Lucia said mildly. "He's not going to force me."

"What makes you so sure of that?"

"He's my co! I've known him my whole life."

"Men are driven to have children," Yalda said. "It's in their nature, they can't help it." How had Daria put it? "It's what they were invented for. There are no male insects, no male lizards—because the young of those creatures can look after themselves from birth. The only reason men *exist* is so they can raise children."

Lucia said, "Women are driven to have children, too. Do you think I didn't feel the urge myself, when I saw Aurelia's? But if I can hold off, so can Lucio. Neither of us are helpless."

"But you're the only one who pays with your life."

"Yes," Lucia agreed. "But that's not Lucio's fault. It's not in his hands, or anyone's. However much he cares about me, he can't take my place—that's just impossible."

Yalda sat in silence for a while. The stars were beginning to fade; she'd need to leave soon.

"Do you want to wake Lucio, and ask him?" If she could show them both life in Zeugma—show them both some new possibilities—that would still be worthwhile.

Lucia said, "It's not the kind of thing we should decide in a hurry. We'll talk about it over the next few days; if we want to come, we'll follow you."

"All right."

Yalda stood and embraced her. "You won't let Giusto pressure you?" she pleaded.

"I won't," Lucia promised. "Do you think Vito taught his other children nothing?" A thin gray ridge appeared on her chest; at first it was barely visible, but then it strengthened and grew, looping across the skin until it spelt out a shaky sequence of symbols: *Safe journey, sister.*

"You could use that skill in Zeugma," Yalda enthused.

Lucia said, "Maybe. Go and catch your truck before someone else wakes and you have to explain why you're sneaking out on us."

"Write and let me know when you're coming," Yalda said.

"Of course."

Yalda turned and walked away. She watched Lucia in her rear gaze until they lost sight of each other behind the dying red light of the fields.

"I have a gift for you," Cornelio announced solemnly.

"A gift?" Yalda had accepted his invitation to the chemistry department as much out of courtesy as curiosity, but she'd hoped there'd be more to the visit than the bestowal of some token of gratitude. "Your success in your work is all the thanks I need." With her rear gaze, she eyed the glistening vials and bottles on the shelves that lined the workshop, trying to remember how long it had been since the building had last had its roof blown off.

"That's very gracious of you," Cornelio said. "But have you forgotten your request?"

Her host sounded more amused than offended, but Yalda searched her memory desperately. She'd spoken to Cornelio for a chime or two after her talk to the school of natural sciences, but they'd discussed so many things that it was impossible to recall the entire conversation, ten stints later.

"I asked you what the one thing was that you'd welcome the most," Cornelio reminded her, "if we were to repay you with something practical."

Yalda wasn't sure how seriously she'd taken the question, but she remembered now what her answer had been. "And you've made good on that offer already?"

"It's not perfect," Cornelio admitted. "But you might find it useful nonetheless—worth having, even short of perfection."

"Of course." Yalda set her anxieties aside. If Cornelio really had created what she'd asked him for, it was well worth the risk of being here.

"Let me show you." Cornelio led her to a bench at the side of the workshop. In lieu of a heliostat, he'd set up a pair of manually adjustable mirrors that brought sunlight into the room and directed it into a box three spans or so wide.

He opened the side of the box, revealing a prism mounted within that split the beam into a spectrum that fell on a white screen. "Note the locations of the various hues, if you will," he suggested to Yalda.

"Noted." After witnessing three Hurtlers over Zeugma, Yalda could memorize the position of a spread of colors against any backdrop in an instant.

Cornelio covered the aperture that admitted the sunlight into the box with a card pierced by a far smaller hole. The spectrum remained visible, but it was much dimmer now. Then he slid a second, entirely opaque card into another slot, parallel with the first one, blocking the light completely.

Next, he took what appeared to be a stiff sheet of paper from a cupboard below the bench, and fastened it in place over the screen where the spectrum had been seen. Then he produced a small vial that had been divided partly in two, with one half containing an orange powder, the other a green resin. He attached the vial to a loop of cord that dangled into the interior of the box through its top face.

Cornelio closed the side of the box, carefully checking that there were no gaps along the edges. "This needs to be entirely sealed against the light," he said. "Not a crack."

Yalda was surprised by his diligence, but it was a good sign. "I understand."

"First, you shake the vial," Cornelio explained, taking hold of the cord where it protruded from the top of the box and jiggling it slightly. "That lets the ingredients react, and the gas that's produced activates the paper."

"Activates?"

"Sensitizes it to light. But only for a few pauses, until the gas disperses, so I shouldn't delay—"

Cornelio pulled the opaque card most of the way out of its slot, then pushed it back in immediately.

"What's wrong?" Yalda asked.

"Nothing," he assured her. "That was the necessary exposure to the light: about a flicker."

The spectrum from the smaller aperture had barely been visible, yet *one flicker* was long enough to cause a reaction?

Cornelio said, "The gas should have dispersed of its own accord now, but I'm thinking of adding a bellows to ensure that it's expelled completely. Maybe we should wait a couple of pauses longer to be sure though, if you don't mind."

"Believe me, my patience has not been tested yet." Yalda had seen a demonstration of an earlier version of the same idea; it had required an exposure of at least *three bells* to capture even the brightest star trails—after which the paper had needed to be treated with a resin that, as often as not, caused it to burst into flames.

"I think..." Cornelio opened the box, fumbling with the clasps. He peered in, then stood aside and let Yalda take a look.

The paper had been darkened very visibly in three places; three narrow black strips marked the locations of—if Yalda's memory served her—shades of red, yellow and blue. It hadn't captured the whole spectrum, but the very fact that the reaction was *not* an indiscriminate, panchromatic response would make it all the more valuable. A smudge of black that covered the entire trail of a star or a Hurtler would have been useless. This system could capture the precise locations of three specific hues at one instant, finally making it possible to quantify details of the Hurtlers that were presently just the subject of fleeting impressions.

"This is wonderful!" she declared ecstatically.

"I'm glad it meets your approval," Cornelio said modestly.

"Does the paper ever...?"

"Start burning? No. This is a completely different reaction from the old one."

"Then it's perfect. I don't know what to say."

Cornelio had already assembled a box full of the treated paper and a rack of the activating vials. "These are yours. When you need more, just let me know."

"Thank you."

Yalda could already picture the device she'd build to capture data on the Hurtlers, but it would be rude to snatch up this generous gift and rush away.

She said, "I don't know if the light recorder has occupied all of your time, but I'd be interested to hear how any of your other research is progressing."

"I've been doing some theoretical work as well," Cornelio replied. "Rotational physics vindicated our earlier measurements of chemical energy differences, but the implications need to be developed much further. In fact, we're having to reinvent most of thermodynamics."

Yalda was surprised. "That sounds a bit extreme."

Cornelio said, "If I told you that your theory implies that everything in this room is *hotter than infinitely hot*, would that justify rewriting the textbooks?"

"Infinity is my least favorite temperature," Yalda confessed. "If you're serious, I might have to recant."

Cornelio buzzed softly. "Let's call them negative temperatures, then; that's formally correct, though the first way of speaking has its merits too."

Yalda found the second way much more agreeable. "True energy has the opposite sense to kinetic energy, so to be consistent I suppose you could just declare all temperatures to be negative. Since a hot gas has less true energy than a cold gas, its temperature should be less... no?"

Cornelio was regarding her with an exasperated expression, but he was too polite to articulate precisely what he was feeling.

"I'm a physicist, show some mercy!" Yalda pleaded. "Thermodynamics is your domain. All I ever studied was the ideal gas law."

"Temperature is *not* a synonym for energy," Cornelio said sternly. "It's about the proclivity of energy to pass from one system to another, not the quantity of energy that either one contains."

"I'm willing to believe that," Yalda said. "But how do you make such a 'proclivity' precise?"

"First," Cornelio said, "think about the range of different ways in which one system can possess the same energy. Start with a single particle of gas, under the old physics."

He summoned a diagram onto his chest. "The particle's kinetic energy is proportional to its momentum squared. Pick a few examples of the energy the particle might have, but don't pin it down precisely; just say that the energy lies in some small interval. From the plot on your left, you can read off a corresponding range for the momentum in each case."

Yalda examined the diagram. "So you follow the horizontal lines for energy across until they hit the curve, then drop them down to the momentum axis?"

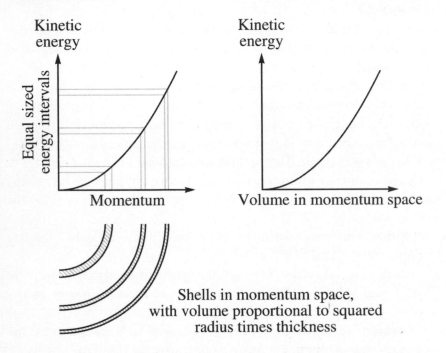

Shells in momentum space, with volume proportional to squared radius times thickness

"That's correct," Cornelio said. "But then, recall that momentum is a *vector*. The energy has given us a range of sizes for that vector, but no information at all about its direction. The particle might be traveling north, west, up, down; we don't know. So, take an arrow whose length you know, more or less, and swing it around freely, without any constraints. The tip of the arrow traces out a sphere—or rather, because the length isn't fixed exactly, a spherical shell. The volume of that shell in 'momentum space' represents all the possibilities open to the particle, while still having an energy that lies within the given range."

Yalda said, "So you've sketched parts of these shells, and plotted their volume against the kinetic energy… which turns out to be the same kind of curve as the momentum itself."

"In this case, yes," Cornelio said, "but that's not true in general! So forget the resemblance, and just concentrate on the right-hand curve on its own terms. What does it tell you?"

"The volume in momentum space gets larger as you increase the kinetic energy," Yalda said. "That makes sense. A faster particle has its momentum lying on a bigger sphere; the shells do get thinner as the momentum grows, but the larger surface area of the sphere more than compensates for that."

"So the volume grows," Cornelio agreed, "but when does it grow most rapidly?"

"At the start," Yalda said. "When the energy is low, the volume shoots up; after that, it grows ever more slowly."

"Precisely."

"But where does that get us?"

"Particles bounce around, collide, exchange energy," Cornelio said. "Give a particle a little more energy when its original energy is *low*, and the volume in momentum space accessible to it shoots up. And if it happens to get that energy by colliding with a particle that was moving faster, the volume for the faster particle goes down—*but not by as much*."

"So… you need to add the two volumes?" Yalda suggested. "And see how the sum changes when energy moves from one particle to the other?"

"Not quite," Cornelio said. "You *multiply them*. Each volume measures the possibilities that are available to one particle—and each possibility for one can be accompanied by any of the possibilities for the other. So it's the product that you need." He produced a new diagram.

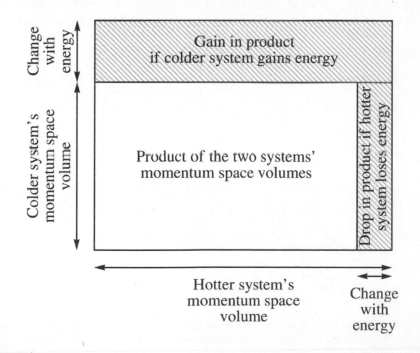

"If energy moves from one system to the other, the product of their momentum space volumes grows along one edge of this rectangle, and shrinks along the other edge. So whether there's an overall growth in the product depends on which of those changes is the larger."

Yalda said, "You describe one system as being hotter and one colder—but where does temperature appear in all this?"

Cornelio said, "For each system, take the volume in momentum space and divide it by its rate of change with respect to energy. That encodes all the relevant information in a single number: the temperature. Then if one system's temperature is greater than another's—so long as they're either both positive or both negative—that immediately tells you that if the first system gives energy to the second, it will increase the total number of possibilities. That's why energy flows from hot to cold: the result ends up encompassing more possibilities."

"Whew." Yalda summoned her own version of Cornelio's first diagram onto her chest and performed the final stage of the calculation. "So in our simplest possible example, temperature ends up being... proportional to kinetic energy! All that work, to get back to the naïve idea that they're really the same thing."

Cornelio resisted rebuking her further. "Of course the true definition doesn't contradict any of the results you were taught—for an ideal gas, under the old physics. But if you're still clinging to some notion that temperature and energy are the same, take a look at what your own work has given us."

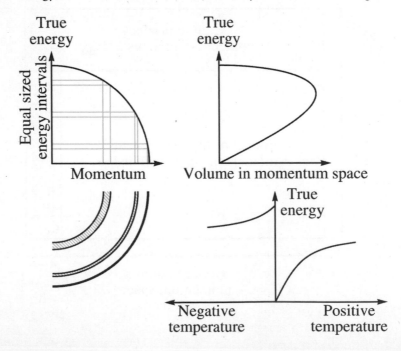

Yalda gazed at his finely ridged skin, feeling suitably chastened and bamboozled. Then she began following the steps he had described for the simpler case, and the whole strange construction took on an eerie inevitability.

The true energy and momentum were linked by a circle, each simply rotating into the other. As the particle's momentum grew from zero, its true energy began to fall—and at first, everything behaved very much like the earlier calculations, merely plotted upside-down.

But as the particle moved faster, its momentum could no longer increase without bounds. With the momentum levelling out, not only did the shells in momentum space cease growing so quickly, they became much thinner. At about two-thirds of the maximum total energy, the shells reached a peak in volume and began to shrink.

At that point, the effect of a change in energy on the number of possibilities open to the particle was reversed. A slow-moving particle could gain options by moving a bit faster... but a sufficiently fast-moving particle would *lose options* if it sped up. The ceiling on momentum made things cramped at the top.

The same thing showed up in the temperature, which switched sign when the shells' volume peaked. And while negative temperatures on their own might merely have been the result of an idiosyncratic choice of conventions, Cornelio's diagram made it clear that both negative and positive were real possibilities. You could always swap the labels for them by tinkering with the definitions, but you couldn't banish the distinction itself.

Yalda said, "If everything in this room has a negative temperature, where are the positive ones?"

"On the surface of the sun," Cornelio replied. "In our own burning stones."

"I see." A burning stone heated its surroundings, adding kinetic energy to them, so true energy would have to be flowing the other way, into the flame. Did that make sense? Cornelio had warned her that energy only flowed from the higher temperature to the lower if both had the same sign.

The mixed-sign case wasn't hard to understand, though. A system with a positive temperature would gain possibilities if it *gained* energy. A system with a negative temperature would gain possibilities if it *lost* energy. Putting the two together, there was no subtle trade-off anymore—this was a win-win situation. Both systems could gain volume in momentum space from the same transaction.

So, any system with a negative temperature would lose true energy to any system with a positive temperature. That was why Cornelio had seen merit in calling ordinary objects "hotter than infinitely hot"; however high the positive temperature of a blazing sunstone, a "hotter than infinitely hot" cool breeze could still heap true energy upon it.

Yalda said, "But how can you know for sure that something has a positive temperature—and not just a large negative one? How do you know when things aren't just 'hot' in the old-fashioned way?"

"Light," Cornelio replied. "Whenever a system freely creates light—not in the orderly way a flower does it, but in the chaos of a flame—it's turning true energy into something that didn't exist before, opening up new possibilities. That's the very definition of positive temperature."

"So once an ordinary system with a negative temperature starts creating light," Yalda ventured, "its temperature *must* change sign? Crossing infinity along the way?"

"Precisely," Cornelio said. "Once it's creating light, it's lost to the ordinary world."

Yalda couldn't help stealing another glance at the workshop's collection of energetically precarious concoctions. Above the shelves, the ceiling still showed signs of recent repairs.

"In the end," Cornelio declared, "everything becomes heat and light. It's not in our power to stop that. All we can do is slow it down a little and try to enjoy the ride."

Yalda ended up staying in the chemistry department until dusk, then she caught a lift in the department's truck back to the city campus, along with Cornelio and five of his students. As they drove across the dusty plain, Cornelio explained how the pressure of a gas could remain positive as its temperature changed sign, and finite as its temperature crossed infinity. The old ideal gas law—*pressure times volume is proportional to temperature times quantity*—was receding into the distance; it wasn't even true within the flames of an ordinary lamp.

The back of the truck was open to the sky, so Yalda saw the Hurtler's violet tip rushing toward them from the north, but then the driver panicked and slammed on the brakes, sending the vehicle lurching and skidding. When it came to a halt she could recall nothing but a whirl of color across a spinning bowl of stars.

Everyone clambered out, checking themselves for injuries, but it was soon clear that nobody had been hurt. Yalda was still clutching her light recording supplies; she examined the contents of the box in the starlight, but Cornelio had packed everything carefully and none of the vials appeared to have been damaged. She helped some of the students push the truck back onto the road, wasting no time fretting over the lost opportunity. At this rate, there'd be another Hurtler over Zeugma in a couple of stints.

"What do you think they are?" she asked Cornelio, as the truck lurched into motion again.

"Fragments from a big explosion," he replied. "Something so distant that even the smallest differences in the speed of the debris could spread out its arrival over many years. My hunch is that successively later fragments will prove to be moving more slowly."

"That's an interesting idea." Yalda tapped the box of goodies appreciatively. "Hopefully I'll be able to test it soon." A crisp image of a Hurtler's light trail, captured at a single moment, might enable her to measure its asymmetry and finally quantify the object's speed.

It was dark when they reached the city. At the university, Yalda bid farewell to Cornelio, stashed her new supplies in the optics workshop, then braved Ludovico's wing of the department to see if Tullia was still around. But the place was empty. Tullia might have caught some observations of the Hurtler, then, on her way to her apartment or the Solo Club.

At the Solo, Yalda found Daria and Lidia; they hadn't seen Tullia, but they persuaded Yalda to join them in a game of six-dice. To everyone's amazement, Yalda won, so she stayed for a second game. Lidia beat her this time, but it was close.

Yalda was tired now, but she decided it was worth stopping by at Tullia's apartment; it would be good to share the highlights of her trip to Amputation Alley. Tullia was planning to head up to Mount Peerless in a few stints; she could probably make use of Cornelio's invention there herself.

When she arrived at the apartment, Yalda found the entrance unbarred but the curtain closed. She called out softly a few times, but received no reply. Tullia didn't usually sleep so early, but if she'd dozed off after a hard day it would be unfair to wake her.

Yalda turned and started toward the stairs, but then she changed her mind; it wouldn't hurt to sneak in quietly and check that everything was all right. She walked back, parted the curtain and stepped into the apartment.

Tullia was lying on the floor near the window. Yalda called her name but there was no response. She approached and knelt to examine her; Tullia was limbless, and her skin displayed a strange sheen. For one panicked moment Yalda thought of her grandfather, but then she realized that the patches of light she was seeing were just distorted reflections of the flowers above.

Yalda took her friend by the shoulders and shook her gently; her skin felt strange—tight, almost rigid—and she did not react at all. There was a furrow down the middle of her chest: a deep, narrow fissure, the first line of a symbol that Tullia would never have written by choice.

"No," Yalda whispered. "That's not happening." She scrabbled in her pocket for her vial of holin. If Tullia had taken a weak dose, it might not be too late to augment it. Yalda tipped three of the small green cubes into her palm, then reached for Tullia's mouth.

But Tullia had no mouth. The darker pigmentation of her lips remained visible, but the skin that bore their color and shape was part of a smooth, seamless expanse. Yalda dropped the holin and moved her fingers over Tullia's face, gently probing one of her eyes; the eyelids were still discernible, but they'd fused together. Below her mouth, her tympanum was rigid. Her body was becoming as hard and featureless as a seed case.

Yalda was shaking now; she forced herself to be still. Who would know what to do? Daria, surely. Yalda leaned out the window and spotted a boy on the street; she threw him a coin to get his attention, then begged him to run to the restaurant under the Solo and ask the chef to "fetch Daria, urgently, for Yalda". Two more pieces and the promise of two more on his return did the trick.

As Yalda knelt down again, her shadow fell on Tullia and she saw that there *was* a faint glow from her body—though it was not on the surface, like her grandfather's affliction. This light came from deep within, and it flickered and shifted constantly: a frenzy of signaling so intense that it could now be seen through all the intervening flesh.

Yalda stroked Tullia's forehead. "We'll fix you up," she promised. "It will be all right." If Daria could get hold of some melding resin, they could glue together the sides of the furrow and let Tullia's own body attack the dividing wall. And if Daria sent for her sunstone lamp, the same kind of flash that had set the captive arborine's muscles twitching could disrupt the signals that were organizing Tullia's fission. There were so many things they could do. Tullia wasn't sick, or old, or frail. She wasn't enslaved to an impatient co. She was a free woman, in the care of her friends.

Having reached the top of her torso, the furrow now began to divide Tullia's tympanum. Yalda took hold of the edges and squeezed them together with all her strength. "No further," she said. "And when this hand grows tired, there are ten more waiting." But in fact there was no great force opposing Yalda's intervention, just the faintest springiness in the underlying flesh.

Tullia would survive; Yalda was sure of that now. Survive, and flourish. She would enlighten her students and delight her friends for a dozen more years. She would find the light of a forest on a distant world.

The furrow itself wasn't lengthening, but Yalda could see the walls of hard skin stretching beyond the point where she was pinching them together, growing up toward the place where Tullia's mouth had been. The slight convexity of her blind eyes had vanished now; the organs had been resorbed and their lids subsumed into the featureless skin around them.

Yalda heard footsteps, then the curtain parted. Daria hurried in, followed by Lidia.

"You promised some boy that I'd pay him four pieces?" Daria asked irritably. "This had better be—"

As Yalda moved aside to let Daria apprehend the reason she'd been summoned, she saw that a cross-furrow was forming now, threatening to divide each of Tullia's lateral halves. "Did you bring some melding resin?" she asked Daria. "Or should we stitch the gaps together? Clamping with my hands doesn't work."

Lidia approached. "There's nothing we can do," she told Yalda gently. "Any resin, any drug, any surgery—all that would do now is kill the children."

Yalda looked to Daria. "That can't be true."

Daria said, "Once division starts, it's irreversible."

Lidia put a hand on Yalda's shoulder. "Let her be."

Yalda turned to her. "What—just let her die?"

"It's not a choice anymore," Daria explained sadly. "You can hold her body as tightly as you like, but her brain is already in pieces."

"Her brain's destroyed?" Yalda stared down at Tullia's blank face. "It's her brain that's making this happen, isn't it? Sending out the signals. Don't tell me it's in pieces."

Daria walked up and knelt beside her. "Yalda, she's gone. She would have been gone long before you found her."

"No, no, no." No more lives cut short. Claudia and Aurelia had been far away, out of her hands, but not Tullia.

She turned back to Lidia and pleaded, "What do we do? Tell me!"

Lidia said, "All we can do now is remember her."

Yalda ran her hand over Tullia's wounds; the furrow now reached the top of her skull. "There must be something."

Daria spoke firmly now. "Yalda, this is beyond changing. She was our friend, and we loved her, but her mind is gone; she's as dead to us now as any man in his grave. Tonight we can only grieve for her."

Yalda felt herself shivering and humming. She didn't believe Daria's words, but some traitorous part of her had decided to behave as if they were true.

"And in the morning," Daria added, "we'll need to talk about the way we're going to raise her children."

10

As Yalda stood in the courtyard waiting for her guest to arrive, she counted two dozen pale streaks of color drifting in mirrored pairs across the afternoon sky. From their leisurely pace she could tell that these Hurtlers were not especially close—perhaps a little farther than the sun itself—but to be visible by day at such a distance they would have to have blazed far more brightly than the specks that only showed at night.

Brighter almost certainly meant *larger*.

She spotted Eusebio crossing the courtyard and held up a hand in greeting. "Hello, Councilor."

"It's good to see you again, Yalda," he said.

"You too."

He glanced up at the sky. "It seems almost normal now, doesn't it? People can get used to the strangest things."

"Sometimes that's a useful trait," Yalda said.

"But not this time," Eusebio suggested.

"Maybe not."

They left the courtyard and strolled across the campus; Yalda had offered to organize a meeting room, but Eusebio had wanted to avoid any suggestion that either of them were acting in an official role. Two old friends were getting together to reminisce, that was all.

"I've only heard third-hand versions of your theory about the Hurtlers," he said. "But they were enough to get me worried."

"The whole idea's extremely speculative," Yalda said. "I wouldn't go jumping off any bridges yet."

Eusebio was amused. "Yet? Believe me, that's not where I'm headed, prematurely or otherwise."

"But you say you're worried."

"Of course I'm worried. Wasn't that the point? Why else would you raise those possibilities?"

Yalda wasn't sure how to answer that. The truth was, when she'd first begun discussing the idea with a few colleagues, she hadn't taken it very seriously. It had been nothing more than an audacious stab in the dark—and far too esoteric, she'd thought, to pose any risk of sowing panic.

Eusebio said, "Maybe there's something you can clear up for me, to start with. Years ago, you gave a talk where you said the cosmos was a flat, four-dimensional torus. In which case... if you followed a bundle of histories through time, wouldn't they remain pretty much parallel? And when they met, wouldn't they just form a loop?" He drew a two-dimensional version, first as a square and then curled up to remove the artificial edges.

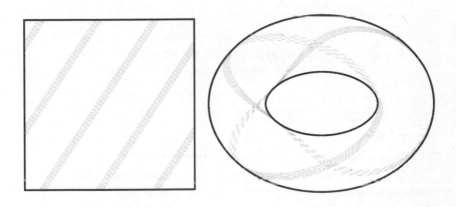

Yalda said, "The flat torus is just an idealization—the simplest case where the light equation can be solved nicely. The topology of the cosmos might be more complicated, or the geometry might not be flat. Or maybe the histories of the worlds haven't stayed together in a nice tight bundle, the way you've drawn them; it's true that everything has to join up in the end, but it doesn't have to do it *tidily*. If there was a primal world that fragmented in both directions—one we'd think of as the future, and one we'd think of as the past—and the fragments themselves then broke up, and so on... we could end up colliding with the past fragments at almost any angle."

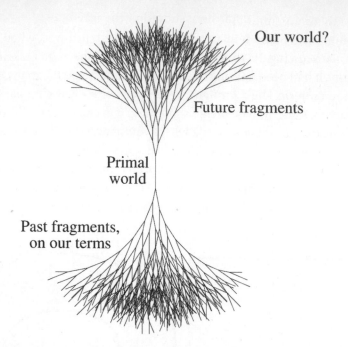

Yalda sketched a crude illustration of the idea. "I won't try to draw this wrapped around a torus, but you can imagine the possibilities if those two sets of fragments ever came to overlap."

"So the primal world gets to explode both backward and forward?" Eusebio gave a chirp of delight tinged with skepticism.

"I know it sounds strange," Yalda conceded, "but if the primal world is where entropy reaches its minimum value, it's just as reasonable for it to explode in one direction as the other. Imagine the cosmos filled with a vast tangle of unruly threads—the histories of all the particles of matter—and then demand that *somewhere* they're all packed together and perfectly aligned. I'm not sure why that has to occur at all, but unless there's some extra rule imposed on top of it, the threads are going to break free in the same way on both sides of the constriction—creating two localized arrows of time pointing in opposite directions."

"But whatever the fine details," Eusebio said, "so long as the cosmos is finite—and the light equation suggests that it must be—there's a potential for the Hurtlers to be the harbinger of something worse."

"*A potential.* Exactly." Yalda didn't want him losing sight of that. "Admitting that there could be places in the cosmos where two sets of worlds cross paths with each other doesn't mean that has to be what's happening here and now."

"Except that the alternative explanations for *here and now* aren't working out too well," Eusebio replied. "If the Hurtlers are just debris from a single monstrous explosion, shouldn't the fragments be arriving ever more slowly?"

Yalda said, "Yes—but whether we could measure the change in velocity over just a few years is another question. It's been tough enough quantifying the velocity at all."

Eusebio was unpersuaded. "Why should the change be so hard to spot, though? I can imagine an exploding world sending out a blast of high-speed dust, along with a slower-moving barrage of pebbles. But if that really does explain everything, shouldn't the difference in speed be as striking as the difference in size?"

"Perhaps," Yalda admitted

"My third-hand source implied that you'd more or less predicted this"—Eusebio gestured at the color trails crowding the sky—"almost two years ago. A cluster of worlds and stars, much like the one we seem to lie within ourselves, would be surrounded by a halo of fine dust. Then as you penetrated deeper into its environs you could expect to encounter larger objects."

"It's hard to know for sure what the structure would be," Yalda said. "We don't understand the breakup of worlds, let alone the long-term effects of gravity and collisions between the fragments."

"But it's not an *unreasonable position*," Eusebio persisted, "to posit rarefied dust at the edges and more substantial material closer in?"

"No." However much she wished to downplay the conclusions, Yalda couldn't retreat from the entire argument she'd made.

Eusebio said, "Then if our notion of *time* corresponded to one of this cluster's notions of *space*… we should expect to find ourselves encountering successively larger objects, all moving at similar speeds. Isn't that right?"

He offered an illustration.

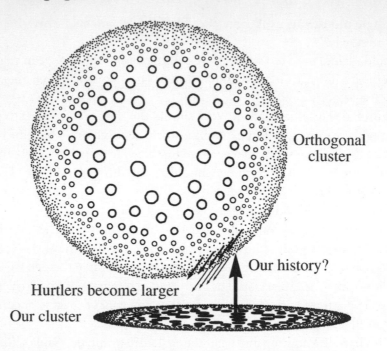

"Couldn't you at least have us glancing the edge?" Yalda pleaded. "We don't need to be heading in as deeply as you've drawn it."

Eusebio obliged. "I knew I should have been a physicist," he said. "If there's something you don't like about the world, you merely adjust a free parameter and everything's perfect."

"What would you have me do?" she said. "Give up hope for all of our grandchildren?"

"Not at all. I want you to imagine the worst, and then tell me how we can survive it."

Yalda emitted a bitter, truncated buzz. "*The worst?* The Hurtlers will keep coming, ever larger and in ever-greater numbers, until the odds that we're struck approach a certainty. If we survive that, we'll probably collide with an orthogonal clump of gas—turning the world itself into something like a giant Hurtler. Somewhere along the way, there will be gravitational disruption, maybe ripping us free from the sun completely—or maybe tossing us into it. And if none of these things sound sufficiently fearsome, the encounter might scramble our arrow of time completely, leaving us with no past and no future. The world will end as a lifeless mass of thermal fluctuations in a state of maximum entropy."

Eusebio heard her out without flinching, without disputing anything. Then he said, "So how can we survive that?"

"We can't," Yalda said bluntly. She pointed to his chest. "If it's more than a glancing blow—if you're going to deny me my choice of impact parameter—then we're all dead."

"Are you telling me that it's physically impossible to protect ourselves?"

"Physically impossible?" Yalda had never heard an engineer use that phrase before. "No, of course not. It's not *physically impossible* that we could shield ourselves from all of these collisions, or side-step them, or simply flee from the whole encounter. It would violate no fundamental law of physics if we built some kind of magnificent engine that carried the whole world off to a safer place. But we don't know how to do that. And we don't have the time to learn."

"How long would it take?" Eusebio asked calmly. "To learn what we need to know to make ourselves safe."

Yalda had to admire his persistence. "I can't honestly say. An era? An age? We still don't know the simplest things about matter! What are its basic constituents? How do they rearrange themselves in chemical reactions? What holds them together and keeps them apart? How does matter create light, or absorb it? And you want us to build a shield against collisions at infinite velocity, or an engine that can move an entire world."

Eusebio looked around at a group of students chatting happily near the food hall, as if they might have overheard this catalog of unsolved problems and decided to rise to the challenge.

"Suppose we'd need an age, then," he said. "A dozen gross years. How long do we actually have before the danger becomes acute?"

"I can only guess."

"Then guess," Eusebio insisted.

"A few dozen years," Yalda said. "The truth is, we're blind to whatever's coming; a whole world, *a whole blazing orthogonal star* might already be disposed to strike us tomorrow. But from the progression in the size of the Hurtlers that we've seen so far, unless we're especially unlucky..." She trailed off. What difference did it make? Six years, a dozen, a gross? All she could do was go on living day by day, averting her gaze from the unknowable future.

Eusebio said, "We need an age, and we don't have it."

"Exactly."

"That's what I thought," he said, "but I had to hear it from you to be sure."

His tone was solemn but far from despairing. Yalda stopped walking and turned to face him. "I'm sorry I had no good news for you," she said. "Perhaps I'm wrong about all of this. Perhaps our luck will be far better than—"

Eusebio raised a hand, cutting her off. "We need an age, and we don't have it," he repeated. "So we find the time elsewhere."

He wiped the colliding clusters from his chest. Then he drew two lines, one straight, one meandering, and added a few simple annotations.

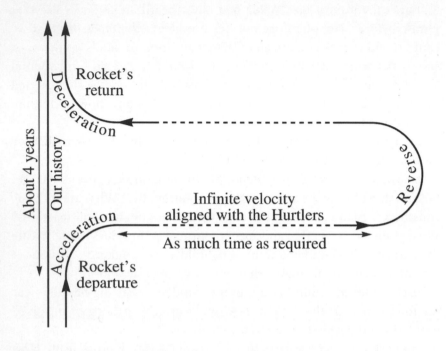

"We make a rocket," he said, "powerful enough to leave the world behind. We send it into the void and accelerate it until it matches the velocity of the Hurtlers. Once it's done that, there'll be very little chance that anything from the orthogonal cluster will strike it—but we might need to offset its position at the start, to keep it from colliding with gas and dust in our own cluster.

"The complete journey is as I've drawn it. The time that passes for the world will be the time it takes to rotate the rocket's history by a full turn: one quarter-turn to accelerate, one half-turn to reverse, one final quarter-turn to decelerate. If the rocket accelerates at one gravity—giving the passengers no more than their ordinary weight—the time back home for each quarter-turn will be about a year, making four years in all.

"The time that passes on the rocket for those stages of the journey won't be much greater: each curved segment is only longer than its height by a factor of pi on two. But when the rocket's history is orthogonal to the history of the world, *no time at all passes back home*. So for the travelers, the journey can last as long as it needs to. If they require more time to complete their task, they can prolong the flight for another era, another age; it won't delay their return by one flicker."

Yalda was speechless. Their roles really had been reversed: the physics Eusebio was presenting was so gloriously simple that she was ashamed she hadn't thought of it herself—if only in the same whimsical spirit as that in which she'd first thought of the Hurtlers as past-directed fragments of the primal world.

But when it came to practicalities, where did she begin?

"What kind of rocket can you hope to build," she said, "in which generations can survive for *an age*—let alone flourish to the point where they have any chance of fulfilling their purpose? The largest rocket I've seen with my own eyes was the size of my arm; the largest I've heard of was smaller than my body. If you can send my optics workshop into the void that would be the talk of Zeugma for a generation, but I don't know where we'd put the wheat fields."

Eusebio hesitated, considering his reply, but he did not appear the least bit discouraged by her response.

"I believe you've been on Mount Peerless," he said.

"Of course. The university has an observatory there."

"Then you'll know that it's far from any permanent habitation."

"Certainly." Yalda thought she knew where he was heading: an isolated, high-altitude site would be the perfect place to test new kinds of rockets.

Eusebio said, "The geologists tell me that the core of Mount Peerless is pure sunstone. I plan to tunnel into it and set it alight, and blast the whole mountain into the sky."

Yalda collected the children from school and took them back to the optics workshop. Amelia and Amelio were happy playing on the floor with a box of flawed lenses, lining them up to form impromptu telescopes and buzzing hysterically at the sight of each other's distorted images. Valeria and Valerio were going through a stage of drawing pictures of imaginary animals that they insisted had to be preserved; Yalda gave them some old student assignments that were blank on one side of the paper, and some pots of dye that Lidia had brought home from the factory.

Then she stood at her desk watching over them while she tried to decide what to make of Eusebio's plan.

Giorgio brought a group of students into the workshop to use the heliostat for an experiment in polarization. The children ran to greet him, and he accepted their embraces without a trace of annoyance or embarrassment before gently shooing them back to their activities. Yalda produced a stack of mechanics assignments and proceeded to mark them, marveling that she could feel guilty for taking a couple of chimes away from her conventional duties to ponder the correct means of averting the planet's annihilation. She'd shared her ideas about the Hurtlers with Giorgio—and he'd offered his usual perceptive comments and objections—but in the end he'd still treated the whole thing as if it were an exercise in metaphysics.

Yalda arrived home with the children just as Lidia returned from her shift.

"Did you bring some more dye?" Valeria nagged her. She and Valerio had used up the last of their supplies on a series of images of giant worms with six gaping mouths arrayed along the length of their bodies.

Lidia spread her arms and jokingly opened six empty pockets. "Not today. Every batch was perfect."

Valeria went into a sulk, which meant wrapping six arms around her co and trying to pull his head off. Yalda warned her three times, increasingly sharply, then stepped in and physically disentangled them.

"You always take his side!" Valeria screamed.

Yalda struggled to hold her still. "What side? What did Valerio do?"

At a loss for an answer, Valeria changed tactics. "We were just playing, but you had to spoil it."

"Are you going to be sensible now?"

"I'm always sensible, you fat freak."

Lidia made a reproving hum. "Don't talk to your Aunty Yalda that way."

"You're a bigger freak!" Valeria declared, turning on her. "At least it's not Yalda's fault she doesn't have a co. She might have swallowed hers by accident before she was born, but everyone knows you killed your co with a rock."

Yalda tried to draw on her reserves of patience by reminding herself how well Valeria had behaved in the workshop.

Daria had actually predicted that the third year of school would be the time when Tullia's children started lashing out at their adoptive parents, punishing them for the derision they received from their increasingly unsympathetic classmates. So before the school year began, Yalda had encouraged the four of them to talk about the ignorance and hostility they were facing, and tried to suggest strategies for dealing with it. At the time, the recipients of her advice had promised that nothing in the wicked world could stop them feeling the same love and loyalty for their Aunties as ever.

Amelio had been looking on impassively, but now he decided that this was the right time to announce in a tone of weary resignation, "Women are for making children, not raising them. You can't expect them to do a good job."

Yalda thought: *Bring on the Hurtlers.*

Lidia said, "Why don't we try making our own dye? We can go to the markets and look for the ingredients."

Valerio's face lit up with excitement. "Yes!"

"I want to come too," Amelia pleaded.

Valeria held out for a few pauses, then decided that the whole thing had been her idea. "I know where we should go first. I already made a list in my head."

Yalda exchanged a glance with Lidia, thanking her for halting the descent. "Why don't we all go," Lidia said. "Before it gets dark."

Yalda woke on the first bell after midnight. Daria still hadn't come home; some nights she went straight from the university to the Solo Club, then slept in her own apartment. That left Yalda or Lidia to get the children to school in the morning, depending on Lidia's shift, but it was hard to complain that Daria wasn't pulling her weight when she paid more than half the rent.

There was a patch of light on the floor beside the window, a hint of color in its diffuse edges. Yalda rose and walked quietly over to it. Through the window, four pairs of trails were visible, spreading slowly but still bright enough to bury most of the stars. In the early days every Hurtler reported had been fast and close, presumably because the more distant ones had been too dim to see with the naked eye. If anything in the current crop ever came that close, it would be spectacular. Maybe that would be enough to jolt her out of her stupor—assuming it didn't achieve something far worse.

If a part of her had trouble believing that the world could end in a barrage of rocks from the distant past, the part that *did* believe struggled even harder to imagine that such grand cosmic mayhem could be avoided. Maybe everyone was simply born predisposed to expect life to go on as normal—and whatever the benefits of her education, hoping to overturn that innate conviction with an argument that started with the right triangles she'd found hidden in her plots up on Mount Peerless was asking too much of her animal brain.

Yalda glanced over at the sleeping children. However much she resented them at times, she certainly wasn't indifferent to their fate—but she could summon no deep, visceral sense that their lives, and the lives of their own children, now lay in the hands of her earnest, enthusiastic, possibly deranged ex-student.

What would Tullia have done? Joked, reasoned, mocked, argued, probed all the competing theories for weaknesses, shone some light into other people's blind spots, then followed her own imperfect instincts like everyone else. Yalda had never stopped missing her, but she was confused enough already without resorting to begging ghosts for advice.

The light on the floor brightened; Yalda turned back to the window. A fresh, dazzling streak of violet had appeared; it spread out slowly, parallel to the older trails.

She needed to make some kind of decision, if only to let herself sleep. So... she would take an interest in Eusebio's plans and offer him whatever guidance she could, trying to help him spot the pitfalls in his strange endeavor. She could do that much without agreeing to be a passenger on his mad flying mountain—and without abandoning hope that the cosmic pyrotechnics that obsessed them both might yet turn out to be as harmless as a swarm of mites.

Eusebio led Yalda on foot for the last few saunters across the dusty brown plain. "Sorry to make you walk so far," he said. "But it's not a good idea to bring the trucks too close."

Yalda took a moment to understand what he meant. The liberator for truck fuel wasn't identical to that used with sunstone, but it could still cross-react. A pinch of gray powder spilt from a tank and carried the wrong way on the wind could heat things up very quickly.

"So how did you get the sunstone out here in the first place?" she asked.

"The way it's always transported: well wrapped, in small pieces."

They reached the test rocket: a cone of hardstone about Yalda's height. Apertures near the top revealed an intricate assembly of cogs and springs secured within. "Most of this is for attitude control," Eusebio explained. "If the sunstone burns unevenly, that puts a torque on the rocket and the whole thing will start to swerve. The mechanism needs to detect that and respond quickly, adjusting the flow of liberator between the combustion points."

"Detect it how?"

Eusebio took a crank from a box of tools that had been left beside the device, and began winding the main spring. "Gyroscopes. There are three wheels set spinning rapidly on gimbals; if their axes shift relative to the housing, that means the rocket is veering off a straight course."

When he'd finished winding the spring he squatted down and gestured with the crank at the bottom of the cone, which was held half a stride above the ground on six stubby legs. "There are four dozen tapered holes drilled into the sunstone, lined with calmstone most of the way. The conical plug of sunstone that was cut out to make each hole is also lined and put back in, but with grooves carved into it that leave a gap between the pieces. The liberator flows down through the gaps and ignites the unlined part at the bottom. As the sunstone burns, the lining's corroded, progressively exposing the fuel."

Yalda joined him and peered up at the orderly array of not-quite-plugged holes. Sunstone lamps used the tiniest sprinkling of liberator, diluted with some kind of inert grit, to keep them blazing for a night's performance in the Variety Hall—and they still killed a few careless operators every year. Deep inside this rocket, waiting to trickle down into the fuel, was a whole tank full of the stuff in its pure form.

"I remember when you were afraid to visit the chemistry department," Yalda said.

"I was never afraid!" Eusebio protested. "You told me not to waste my time with chemists, because they couldn't get their energy tables straight."

"Yes, of course, that's exactly what I would have said." Yalda straightened and stepped back from the rocket.

Eusebio tossed the crank into the toolbox, then looked back across the plain toward Amando, one of the three assistants who'd been working at the site when Yalda arrived. Eusebio waved broadly with two hands, and received the same gesture in reply. Then he reached into the cone and released a lever.

"What does that do?" Yalda asked.

"One chime to ignition."

"Thanks for the warning."

"One chime!" Eusebio scoffed, picking up the toolbox. "We'll be behind the barrier long before then."

Yalda was already ten strides ahead. "Did your father really let you design his trains?" she called back to him.

"Yes, but I just tweaked someone else's plans," Eusebio admitted. "Trains are complicated. I wouldn't want to have to invent them from scratch."

When Yalda reached the truck closest to the rocket she saw the other two assistants, Silvio and Frido, lying chest-down on the tray. A sturdy timber barrier some four strides high had been attached to the side of the vehicle; the two men were propped up on their elbows behind narrow slits in which theodolites had been fitted. The theory was that the rocket would ascend vertically, run out of fuel, rise a little farther from momentum alone, then plummet back to the ground to make a crater at more or less the point from which it had risen. Knowing the height it reached would allow the team to quantify the amount of energy produced that actually ended up doing something useful. It was one thing to measure the effects of a quarter of a scrag of sunstone incinerated in a workshop experiment, where the gases produced in a sealed chamber drove a piston against a load. Expecting the same yield when gas was spilling off the sides of the rocket and fragments of heat-cracked fuel were free to sprinkle down onto the desert might be a bit optimistic.

Eusebio caught up and joined Yalda and Amando behind the shield. Amando said, "One lapse to go"; he'd synchronized his own small clock with the one Eusebio had set ticking inside the rocket. Yalda stared anxiously at the clock's face. If the sunstone burned hotter and faster than expected, it wasn't inconceivable that the flame could rise up and eviscerate the tank full of liberator, bringing everything together in one mighty flash when the rocket was too high for the barrier to protect them.

"What am I doing here?" she muttered, trying to decide how low to squat for safety without completely obscuring her view.

"Watching history being made," Eusebio replied, not entirely seriously. Yalda glanced at Amando, but his face gave nothing away.

"Three, two, one," Eusebio counted.

The barrier concealed the flash of ignition, but by the time Yalda felt the ground tremble a dazzling line of white light had risen into view. A moment later a deafening hiss arrived through the air.

Yalda shielded her eyes and sought the rocket at the top of the afterimage, but something wasn't right; the line seared on her vision had been joined by an arc, a circle, a widening helix. Then the point of radiance that had been inscribing these curves dropped below the barrier, and the ground shuddered. She stiffened her tympanum protectively, deafening herself to the sound of the impact, then tensed for a larger explosion.

Nothing followed. Either the fuel had all been consumed, or the liberator had ended up scattered.

Yalda turned to Eusebio. He looked shaken, but he recovered his composure rapidly.

"It reached a good height," he said. "Maybe ten strolls."

It took them more than a bell riding around the desert before they found the remains of the rocket. If it had stayed in one piece it might have made a spectacular crater, but the fragments of hardstone casing and mirrorstone cogs strewn across the ground had barely gouged the surface, and some were already half-buried in the dust. If Yalda had stumbled upon them unawares, she would have called for an archaeologist.

"Attitude control," Eusebio said. "It just needs some refinement."

He left the others sorting through the debris and gave Yalda a ride back to the city.

"What does your family think about all this?" she asked him. Yalda had said nothing to Lidia and Daria, or any of her colleagues; Eusebio had asked her to hold off mentioning the project to anyone until he'd tied up various "administrative loose ends".

"I've managed to convince my father that it's worth risking the money," he said. "Even if the world's in no danger from the Hurtlers, anything that the travelers invent on their journey could easily double our fortune."

"What about your co?"

"She thinks I'm crazy. But I've told her—and my father—that I can't countenance bringing children into the world until this rocket's been launched to vouchsafe their future… which seems to have made both of them happy."

"Why?"

Eusebio buzzed amusement. "She's glad the day's so far away. He's glad it's going to be so soon."

Yalda said nothing. Eusebio turned to her and added, "Just to be clear, she can actually wait as long as she wishes."

Yalda fought down the urge to reply sarcastically: *How generous of you.* If Eusebio really was supporting his co against their father's nagging, it wasn't worth starting a fight with him just because he sounded smug about it.

"Are you sure this isn't going to *lose* you your fortune?" she asked. "What's the going price for a mountain these days?"

Eusebio said, "I've already bought mining licenses from all the Councils that claim jurisdiction. It wasn't cheap, but it didn't ruin me."

Mount Peerless was almost equidistant from five different cities; the only way to ensure an undisputed title would be to pay them all off. Yalda said, "Doesn't a mining license include some deal about a share of the profits?"

"Of course. And if I do make any money from the project, I'll give the Councils their cut."

"But they all think you're planning to dig out the sunstone and sell it?"

"I haven't disabused them of that assumption." The truck shuddered on the stony track. "But do you really want me to try lecturing my fellow Councilors on rotational physics? My father was willing to take my word for it—having paid so much for my education—but I can't see Acilio and his cronies patiently following the trail of evidence from the velocity-wavelength formula to the passage of time for fast-moving travelers."

"No." The mention of Acilio reminded Yalda of someone else she'd been trying not to think about. "How do things stand with the university?"

"I'm negotiating a payment for them to relocate the observatory," Eusebio said. "It's not finalized, but given the amount we've been discussing they'll be able to build a new telescope twice the size."

"But not at the same altitude."

"You can't have everything. Don't you think this is more important?"

"It's not me you'll have to convince," Yalda warned him. "Have you ever heard of a man called Meconio?"

"*Meconio?* I thought he was long dead."

"Not in spirit." Perhaps the university would take Eusebio's money and accept the deal before Ludovico discovered the connection between this "mining project" and the loathsome subject of the new physics.

"How much of the mountain do you think is sunstone?" she asked.

"Maybe two-thirds, by mass."

Yalda did some quick calculations on her back. "That might be enough for one quarter-turn in four-space, but there's no chance at all that it will cover the whole voyage."

Eusebio glanced at her, surprised. "You expect the yield to stay the same, after half an age working on improvements?"

"Maybe not, but if there's barely any sunstone left over from the acceleration stage… what kind of yield are you hoping for?"

"I don't expect the travelers to burn sunstone for the later stages," Eusebio replied.

Yalda was startled. "You want them to turn hardstone and calmstone into fuel?"

"Either that," he said, "or move beyond the need for fuel entirely."

Yalda waited for a sign that he was joking; none came. "So you're counting on this rocket riding the Eternal Flame? Is that what you told your father to expect?"

Eusebio hunched his shoulders defensively. "Just because Ninth Age charlatans wrote a lot of nonsense about a similar idea doesn't mean it's actually impossible."

"A flame that consumes no fuel?"

"Tell me why it can't exist!" he demanded. "Not the version the philosophers imagined: some magic stone that would sit on your shelf, creating light and nothing else—that would violate conservation of energy. But if light and kinetic energy are created together there's no reason they couldn't balance each other precisely, without any change in chemical energy to plug the gap. Fuel doesn't *need* to be consumed; that's just the way it works with the kinds of fuel we have right now."

Yalda had no argument about the energy balance, and while she couldn't calculate the relevant entropies on the spot, creating light generally meant an increase. In conventional flames the hot gas formed by the spent fuel also contributed to the rise in entropy, but there was no reason to think it was essential. On the face of it, then, a slab of rock could create a beam of light—balancing the energy and momentum of the beam by recoiling in the opposite direction, but suffering no other change—without violating any principle she could name.

Accepting that statement of theory was one thing. Being stranded in the void with an infinite velocity, exiled from your home until you conjured the Eternal Flame into existence, was a different proposition.

"I can't tell you it's impossible," Yalda conceded, "but you still need to ensure that there's a useful amount of sunstone left after the acceleration—even if you have to throw away half the rest of the mountain to eliminate some dead weight. Give them something they can make more efficient, not a choice between bringing a Ninth Age myth to life, or never coming back!"

"Let's see what the detailed surveys tell us," Eusebio said, trying to sound conciliatory. "Two thirds was just a conservative guess."

Yalda stared out across the desert. Who was going to volunteer to ride on this folly if it looked harder to survive than the Hurtlers?

She said, "Please tell me you're not expecting the travelers to invent their own means of dealing with waste heat."

"Of course not."

"So...?"

"I'm planning to divert some of the exhaust gas," Eusebio said. "Letting it expand and drive a piston while it's thermally isolated will cool it down and supply some useful energy—then decompressing it further while it's circulating around the habitation will draw in heat. Most of it will then be released into the void, but some will be used to maintain the pressure in the habitation, which would otherwise decline over time as the original atmosphere leaks out."

"So you'll be burning some sunstone for these purposes, even when the rocket isn't in use?"

"Yes—though compared to the amount used for propulsion it won't be much."

Yalda couldn't fault this scheme, or suggest any obvious refinements, but that wasn't good enough. "Now that you've proved that you have no fear of explosions," she said, "how about a detour to Amputation Alley?"

Eusebio regarded her suspiciously. "Why?"

"There's a man there called Cornelio who knows more about heat than either of us. You should ask his advice on this."

"Can he keep a confidence?"

"I have no idea," Yalda replied, irritated. Cornelio had always treated her honourably, but she wasn't going to vouch for his willingness to go along with Eusebio's whims.

"Never mind," Eusebio said. "I'll hire him as a consultant, have him sign a contract."

Yalda lost patience. "Do you honestly think you can send a whole mountain into the void *in secret?* Just you, and a few dozen advisers? Maybe you could get that much dead rock off the ground through sheer trial and error, but we're talking about risking lives! You need the best people in the world to know about this, to think about it—to criticize all your ideas, all your systems, all your strategies. And I do mean the *best* people, not the best you can afford to put on your payroll and subjugate to a vow of silence."

"I have enemies," Eusebio said pointedly. "People who, if they knew of these plans, would happily spend a good part of their own fortune just to see me fail."

"I don't care," Yalda replied coolly, resisting the urge to remind him that she'd suffered far more from his enemies' pique than he had. "If the travelers are to have any hope of surviving, you're going to need every biologist, agronomist, geologist, chemist, physicist and engineer on the planet as worried about their fate as you are."

"And why should they fret about the lives of a few strangers?" Eusebio retorted. "You didn't seem too eager to spread news of the catastrophe that this trip is intended to forestall."

"I was wrong," Yalda admitted. "First I didn't take my own reasoning seriously, and then I was vain enough to think that if I could see no remedy myself, there was none. You've shown me otherwise, and I'm grateful for that. But it can't end there."

Eusebio said nothing, his gaze fixed ahead.

"No more silence," Yalda declared. "I need to make the case for the problem, and you need to make the case for the solution. Let people argue, correct us, support us, tear us down. It's the only hope we have to get this right."

When Yalda arrived home Daria was in the apartment, helping Valeria and Valerio infuse some anatomical realism into their sketches of giant lizards laying waste to Zeugma.

"Lizards *can* rearrange their flesh almost any way they like," Daria explained, "but they have five favorite postures, which are used in different places for different tasks. If they were on the ground, smashing buildings like this, you can bet they'd have a lot of flesh in their rear legs and their tails. It's no good drawing them the way they'd look running along a slender twig."

The children were entranced. Yalda sat and listened, not saying too much, hoping that merely sharing their interest would be read as a sign of affection. When she tried too hard Valeria reacted with scorn, but if she kept her distance she was punished later with accusations of indifference. It was exhausting having to be so calculating about it, but whatever it was that could sometimes make the relationship between a child and their protector almost effortless, it rarely seemed in evidence with Tullia's children and the three friends who'd agreed to raise them. This was a labor of love, but that didn't stop it being the hardest thing Yalda had done in her life.

Lidia had taken Amelia and Amelio to the doctor, but they were expected back soon. When the children were asleep tonight, Yalda decided, she would tell Lidia and Daria everything.

They had a right to know the truth—but what if they simply doubted her sanity? Watching Valeria chirping happily as she and Valerio re-drew each other's lizards in a cascade of jokes and refinements, Yalda felt her own conviction about the peril of the Hurtlers faltering yet again. Whenever she immersed herself in domestic life, instead of apprehending the threat to the people around her more acutely she found herself growing numb and disbelieving. It wasn't hard to imagine a time when everyone in this household would be gone; with the passage of years that was inevitable. But picturing every woman and every girl that lived having *gone the way of men*, leaving not a single child to survive them, only made her mind rebel and doubt the entire chain of reasoning that could lead to such an absurd conclusion.

Daria disengaged from the anatomy lesson for a moment to speak to Yalda directly. "There's a letter for you on the sideboard."

"Thanks." Yalda judged the artists sufficiently engrossed not to care if she briefly left the audience.

The letter was from Lucia. Yalda had written to her several times since her last visit to the farm, but their correspondence had been intermittent.

She uncapped the wooden tube, tugged out the rolled-up sheets and smoothed them flat. Some of the symbols were a bit shaky, as if Lucia had been unable to keep the ridges still when she pressed the paper to her skin.

My dear sister Yalda

I'm sorry that it's been so long since I last wrote to you. I'm sorry, too, that you haven't been able to visit us yet and see the new farm, but I understand that you must be busy, taking care of your friend Tullia's children as well as continuing your work at the university. (You won't be surprised to hear that when I finally told Giusto about the children he denied that such a thing was possible, and said you needed to hunt down the derelict co or co-stead responsible!)

Claudio and his children joined us on the new farm a couple of stints ago. It's lovely to have so many people around after all these years on our own. We never stopped visiting the old place, of course, but since tradition demands that the two farms are more than a separation apart, it hasn't been too often.

The main reason I'm writing to you now is to tell you that this will be my last letter. I remember how hurt and saddened you were that you had no news or warning about Aurelia and Claudia, and I wanted it to be different for us. So: tomorrow I will become a mother.

I would be lying if I told you that I wasn't afraid, but I'm also filled with great hope and happiness, knowing that Lucio and I have done our best to prepare for the children's future. The farm is very well established, and we have plenty of money saved, so while the young cousins work under their father's watchful eye, Lucio will mostly be free to take care of the children. (And please don't be angry with him, this is my decision as much as it is his.)

Do you have the same beautiful shooting stars there in Zeugma that we have here? I know you're studying these things, so it must be an exciting time for you. I can't believe how glorious they look, even during the day, and it's rather strange and wonderful to think of my children growing up to take such sights for granted. They'll be amazed to hear from their father that there was once a time when the sky was so much emptier!

Your sister Lucia

11

The morning after her first appearance with Eusebio in the Variety Hall, Yalda woke early and went out to see what the papers had made of it.

A boy on a nearby corner was selling *City Skin*, so she bought a copy, but after flicking through the sheets three times it was clear that the end of the world didn't rate a mention here. She went back to ask the boy for *Talk*; he'd sold out, so she waited while he dusted his chest with dye and made a fresh one for her.

"I'll pay you the same for just the news and entertainment sections," she offered impatiently.

"We're not allowed to do that," he said, summoning the memory of another sheet onto his chest.

"Why not?"

"The advertisers don't like it."

When he'd finished, Yalda took the whole bundle from him and walked around the corner before discarding the financial advice, restaurant reviews and railway timetables. She had to search the remainder twice before she found what she was looking for.

Last night our spies were at the Variety Hall, where the preternaturally plump Professor Yalda regaled a non-paying (!) audience with news of civilization's impending demise. In a performance mixing the illusionist's art with the terrors of geometry, the bountifully bulky Professor attempted to tie fleet-footed Mother Time in knots, leaving many observers wondering at her motives.

If the audience was unpersuaded by her message of doom, the attempt that followed by Councilor Eusebio to attract supporters (or even volunteers!) for his Ride Beyond the Sky was greeted by a veritable uproar of disbelief and derision. To anyone willing to back this venture: we have a design for Mechanical Wings gathering dust in our cupboard, awaiting only the life-giving touch of a gullible investor.

In the interests of sanity, *Talk* consulted Professor Ludovico of Zeugma University, who explained that the Hurtlers bringing such angst to last night's double act are in fact nothing more than Spontaneous Excitations of the Solar Miasma. Despite its alarming appearance this phenomenon can do no harm to anyone, given that said Miasma is unable to interpenetrate our own plentiful atmosphere.

Ten more nights of this unprecedented madness remain. If the customers were paying then this cheerless and unscrupulous diversion would quickly close for want of funds, but *Talk* urges the next best outcome: an empty hall, to shame these charlatans into silence.

When Yalda reached the apartment Daria was awake, so she showed her the piece.

"I wouldn't pay too much attention to *Talk*," Daria said loftily. "Their idea of pushing the intellectual boundaries of journalism is to cover a literary salon."

"What's a literary salon?"

"An event where people who can't read or reason gather to reassure each other of their own importance."

Yalda said, "But anyone who reads this will think the whole thing's some kind of… investment scam!"

Daria was amused. "Anyone who'd take this uncomprehending babble seriously was already a lost cause: they were never going to help you improve the *Peerless*, let alone volunteer for the ride."

"Maybe not," Yalda conceded. "But—"

"But you want everyone in Zeugma to understand what's at stake?" Daria suggested.

"Of course. Don't you think they're owed that?"

Daria said, "I've been in the business for ten years, and I've had notices far worse than this. Believe me, the people who are truly curious will still come." She rolled the sheet deftly into a cylinder and launched it across the room. "Just forget about it."

Lidia had worked a late shift and was still asleep; Daria agreed to take the children to school. Yalda did her best to follow Daria's advice, but when she reached the university Giorgio had more bad news for her: the senior members of the department had voted to refuse Eusebio's offer to fund a new observatory. What's more, they were taking their title over the land to Zeugma's Council, seeking an order forbidding Eusebio from interfering with their present use.

Giorgio said, "If the telescope is raised entirely above the atmosphere it would actually improve the quality of observations. So if you can get the right wording on the order…"

Yalda was in no mood for jokes. "I thought you were going to persuade your friends to vote for this! Whatever they think of Eusebio's rocket, a bigger telescope would be a worthwhile trade-off, surely."

"I'm sorry," he said. "Ludovico had more favors to call in than I did."

Yalda didn't doubt that Giorgio had kept his word. But he was still trapped in the kind of anesthetized state from which she'd taken so long to emerge herself. When he argued the physics with her, he accepted that the orthogonal cluster theory of the Hurtlers was as plausible as any alternative—but he still couldn't bring himself to take the threat seriously, to look at his children and imagine their extinction.

Yalda had a lecture to deliver for the introductory optics course. As her students dutifully recorded her diagrams and equations for the laws of thin lenses, she felt like someone handing out useless trinkets at the edge of a raging wildfire. But she was forbidden from discussing Eusebio's project during her lessons, or holding recruitment meetings on the campus. If any of these bright young men and women wanted to know the truth about the matter, they'd have to make the effort to turn up for the night's unscrupulous diversion.

At lunchtime, as Yalda entered the food hall she saw Ludovico coming out of the pantry, his arms laden with loaves for a group of fellow diners. She hung back to avoid crossing his path, but he saw her and approached, calling out to her in a booming voice pitched to attract as much attention as possible.

"Professor Yalda! I'm surprised to see you here! I thought you'd left us for the entertainment business."

Yalda humored him with a desultory buzz, but couldn't help adding, "It seems everyone has two jobs these days; I see you've gone into journalism, yourself."

"I was *consulted* by journalists," Ludovico replied stiffly. "As a noted authority on the Hurtlers, not a paid employee."

Yalda said, "Forgive me, but I must have missed all your learned publications on 'Spontaneous Excitations in the Solar Miasma'. Perhaps you can rectify my ignorance on the topic by explaining precisely what that phrase means?" Everyone in the hall was watching them now, through rear eyes or front.

Ludovico said, "Gladly. One particle of the solar wind expels a fast luxite, which strikes another, prompting it to do the same. And so on. Other, slower light is emitted as well. That is what the Hurtlers are: long chains of activity arising within the gas itself, mediated by fast-moving particles of light."

Yalda bowed her head in a gesture of gratitude, then feigned deep contemplation for several pauses—contemplation that failed to dispel her puzzlement. "But why are these 'chains of activity' parallel to each other? Why are these 'spontaneous excitations', these random events, all lined up in exactly the same direction?"

Ludovico replied without hesitation, "A distant source of rapid luxites—not quite at the resonant energy that would trigger an excitation itself—illuminates the solar wind and nudges the particles into alignment. The gas spontaneously emits its own light, but it is not randomly oriented when it does so."

Yalda was speechless for a moment, marveling at the utter shamelessness of this absurd contrivance. "That's nonsense," she said cheerfully. "And you know it's nonsense."

Ludovico replied with calm hauteur, "Refute it, then. Show me your meticulous observations establishing my theory's falsehood." He began to walk away, but then he paused and turned back to face her. "Oh, I'm sorry, that was thoughtless of me! To make an observation, you might need an *observatory*… a facility that you'd prefer to see shattered into dust by your demented co-stead. Enjoy your meal, Professor Yalda."

On stage in the Variety Hall, Yalda tried to push the day's setbacks out of her mind and focus on the presentation. Even her bountifully bulky body was too small for people to read from the back row, so she'd worked with the Hall's set designers to create a contraption with a sunstone lamp and lenses that projected a series of printed images onto a large white screen behind her.

As she gazed out into the darkness that concealed the audience, she honed her message, stressing its simplicity. Time was just another direction in space: nothing else could make sense of light's behavior, or the ferocity of burning fuel. And to keep light tame, time needed to be finite—which meant that history would wrap around and meet itself, as surely as the system of roads and railway lines that wrapped itself around the planet. But while neighboring cities worked together to plan the railway lines between them, any intersections in the histories of worlds would be haphazard and ungoverned. Spectacular as they were, the Hurtlers were mere pedestrian tracks on this map; ahead, there would be busy freight lines.

Eusebio joined her, and the screen reprised the simple sketch he'd shown her: the detour, the long slow zigzag into the future that could buy them time, and with it fresh ideas and discoveries. It would be a risky journey, daunting for anyone to contemplate, but the *Peerless* needed whatever Zeugma's people could bring to it. Navigating the void was just the start; to keep the community of travelers alive and thriving would take a whole city's worth of inspiration and expertise.

Daria had advised them not to take questions from the floor; that only invited attention-seeking hecklers. Instead, they set up two desks in a corner of the foyer and invited people to come and speak with them after the performance, quietly, face-to-face.

Yalda had braced herself for a frenzy of disparagement spurred on by the negative coverage in *Talk*, but the audience as a whole had been no rowdier than the night before, and the individual interlocutors who approached them after the show were, if anything, more polite and encouraging. "I don't believe a word of your scaremongering," one young man told Yalda amiably, "but I do wish you luck."

"Why do you think it's scaremongering?"

"The world has survived for eons," he replied. "History might not mention shooting stars like these, but the world is far older than we are. Geologists say the planet has been bombarded many times before; a few more stones from the sky will hardly be a calamity. But if you can send a rocket through the void and bring it back safely, that will be something to admire."

"I can't interest you in being a passenger yourself?" Yalda wasn't taunting him; it might be worth having a thoughtful, good-natured skeptic among the travelers.

He said, "I think my children will stand a better chance of surviving with solid ground beneath their feet."

Eusebio had to leave for an appointment with a legal adviser about the observatory dispute. Yalda decided to stay on a little longer; the foyer wasn't empty yet, even if most of the dawdlers seemed to be talking among themselves rather than waiting for the right time to approach her.

When the clock struck two chimes before midnight, she started packing away her information pamphlets. She'd gathered five more names on top of the seven from the night before, and even if these volunteers were willing to do no more than plant crops in an artificial cave inside the mountain, that would be something.

As she stepped away from the desk, a young woman hurried across the foyer toward her.

"I'm sorry," the woman said. "I wasn't sure if I should speak to you, but…"

Yalda put down her box of pamphlets. "What did you want to say?"

"I was thinking about your rocket. One thing worries me—" She stopped and lowered her gaze, suddenly shy, as if her words might already have been too presumptuous.

"Go on," Yalda encouraged her. "If there's only one thing that worries you, you're a dozen times more confident than I am."

The woman said, "When the rocket turns around and comes back toward us… from the point of view of the travelers on the first half of the journey, isn't it now moving backward in time?"

"Yes it is," Yalda agreed. "That's exactly right."

"And from the point of view of the Hurtlers, and the worlds you think might collide with us… the same thing is true? In the second half of the journey, the rocket will be traveling into their past as well?"

"Yes." Yalda was impressed; though it was a simple enough observation, only Eusebio and Giorgio had raised it with her before.

The woman looked up, fidgeted anxiously. "Is that… *safe*?"

"We don't know," Yalda admitted. "To what degree the rocket will carry its own arrow of time, embodied in its passengers and cargo, and to what degree its surroundings will influence the arrow… we don't know."

"So you're hoping the travelers will learn enough on the outward voyage to protect themselves on the inward leg?" the woman suggested.

"I suppose it does come down to that." Yalda had berated Eusebio for relying on uninvented methods of propulsion, but the truth was they had no hope of preparing the travelers in advance for every hazard the journey would entail.

Gaining courage, the woman said, "I'd be satisfied if you could at least be sure that the rocket was heading into the Hurtlers' future at the start of the trip. If it takes half an age to prepare for the clash, so be it—but having to face that problem from the very beginning would be too much."

"Satisfied enough… to approve of the venture?"

"Satisfied enough to be a passenger myself."

Yalda said, "Can I ask your name?"

"Benedetta."

Yalda took her over to the desk and recorded her details, trying not to let slip that no one else had come close to making such a commitment—not even the recruiter herself.

"Have you studied somewhere?" Yalda asked her. The first passenger of the *Peerless* had described her profession as "factory worker".

"In Jade City," Benedetta admitted reluctantly, as if this were somehow shameful. "I studied engineering, but only for a year."

"It's not important, I was just curious." Yalda heard the forced joviality in her own voice, and struggled to bring the tone back to normal. Asking Benedetta if she were a runaway might frighten her off completely; it was an issue they'd need to deal with at some point—in order to protect both her and the project—but for now all that mattered was that she was keen, and a quick enough thinker to have spotted a genuine problem.

They were alone in the foyer now. Yalda said, "I'm supposed to be out of here before the cleaners come in at midnight, but we can talk for a bit outside if you're not busy."

"There's nowhere I need to be," Benedetta replied.

Outside, the city was quiet. A dozen slow Hurtlers were spreading their colors across the sky. As the two of them walked away from the hall across the cobblestones, Benedetta said, "Do you really believe that time loops around on itself?"

"I can't be certain," Yalda replied. "But I think the evidence is strong."

"So the future is no different from the past?"

"The real difference is a matter of what we know," Yalda said. "What information is easily accessible to us. We can know much more about the past than the future, at least if we don't try to look back too far. But that's a product of the vagaries of history; there's no absolute distinction."

"But then… everything that's yet to happen is fixed, just as much as everything in the past?"

"Yes."

"So why are you striving so hard to change the future?"

Yalda buzzed with delight; she should have seen that coming. "'Change' isn't quite the right word," she suggested. "You can strive to *change* a bad law—because the law can be different at different times. But either we survive this encounter or we don't. Whatever the outcome is, no one will change it."

Benedetta accepted this, but persisted. "What word should I use then? 'Influence'?"

"I can live with that," Yalda said. "I'll own up to striving to influence the future."

"But how can you influence the future if it's as fixed as the past? Do you try to influence what happened yesterday?"

"Not anymore," Yalda said, "but I certainly did the day before."

"*Why, though?* If you believe that what happened yesterday has *always* been fixed, wouldn't it have turned out the same, regardless?" Benedetta wasn't teasing her, or playing rhetorical games; she genuinely needed an answer.

"Ah." Yalda hadn't had a conversation like this since the long nights she'd spent talking with Tullia—and back then, the roles would have been reversed. "I don't believe in the kind of predestination that says our actions are irrelevant. So I don't accept that yesterday would have turned out the same, regardless of what I did."

"But if your actions *aren't* irrelevant, then you can't be choosing them freely, can you?" Benedetta argued. "If the future is fixed, and your actions affect the future… then your actions themselves must be fixed, otherwise they could lead to the wrong outcome. That means you have no real choice in what you do; you're just a puppet, steered by forces beyond your control."

Yalda thought for a while. "Raise your right hand."

"Why?"

"Go on, humor me."

Benedetta complied.

"Were you free to raise it or not, as you wished?" Yalda asked her.

"I believe so."

Yalda said, "Tell me why you should feel any differently about that, depending on whether or not time is a loop and the future is really the distant past."

Benedetta puzzled over the question. "If it was always going to happen—if in a sense it had *already happened*—then when I thought I was making the decision, that was just an illusion."

"An illusion compared to what?" Yalda pressed her. "Tell me how the world could work—how physics could function, how history could be arranged—in a way that would somehow make you 'more free'?"

"If the future is open," Benedetta replied. "If our actions are undetermined until we decide what to do."

"Suppose that really is the case," Yalda said. "Then what is it that finally determined whether you raised your arm or not?"

"I did. It was my choice."

"But why did you make that particular choice, and not refuse me?"

Benedetta didn't reply immediately. "The way you asked, I suppose," she said finally.

"So *I* determined your action?"

"No, not completely. My mood, my state of mind played their part as well."

Yalda said, "None of the things you've just referred to disappear from the world if the future is fixed rather than open. Both of us are still here. Our actions are still related in exactly the same way to our wishes, our wishes to our personal moods and histories, and so on."

Benedetta was not convinced. "If the future is *fixed*, how can this conversation even mean anything? If it's an unchangeable fact that I *will* say whatever I end up saying to you—as if we were just actors following a script—then how can we really be changing each other's minds? How can we be communicating anything?"

"Do I sound as if I'm making random noises for no particular reason?" Yalda joked.

"No."

"If there's a script," Yalda said, "then we're the playwrights as well as the actors; there's no one else who could write our lines. There's no puppet-master rushing around coordinating everything, forcing us to act against our will—or to make choices that go against our nature—just so history will reach its pre-ordained conclusion."

"Then how does it work?" Benedetta demanded. "How do things turn out the way they have to?"

Yalda said, "The trick is to stop thinking that it works like fate in the sagas: some tedious monarch overcomes the odds and wins a great battle, because all the bit-players are nothing but cogs whose every action is subservient to his destiny. The reality is the opposite of that: 'the way things have to be' is completely unspectacular, and it's fulfilled at the lowest possible level.

"We don't know the details for every kind of matter, but in the case of free light the basic building blocks are just cyclic waves. When you make a full circuit of the cosmos in any direction, these waves undergo a whole number of cycles, so they return smoothly to their starting values. That's it, that's destiny fulfilled already… because anything constructed from waves like that will automatically share the same property. However complex a pattern of light you build up, it can't contradict itself when it comes full circle. That's guaranteed by the lowest-level physics; it doesn't have to be orchestrated, or scripted, or contrived."

Benedetta considered this. "So where are *we* in this picture? If the matter we're made from works the same way, where are our choices?"

"In our biology," Yalda said. "I think there's a degree of consistency between our desires and our actions grounded in the structure of our brains and bodies. What you want, what you do, who you are… these things might not be in perfect harmony, but we're not prisoners trapped in our bodies while they follow some plan that has nothing to do with us." At least not until fission took over and split you in four, but Yalda didn't want to get into that.

Benedetta fell silent as they started across the Great Bridge. Yalda didn't expect to change her mind on this; the important thing was for her to understand that she could raise anything with her colleagues in the project. When you planned to send a mountain flying through the void at an infinite velocity, there was no such thing as too abstruse a concern.

Finally she said, "I'll have to think on this more deeply. I can certainly see some force in your arguments."

Yalda could hear the reservation in her voice. "But?"

Benedetta said, "It's one thing to argue an abstract case that the future being fixed changes nothing: that there's really no freedom lost, because our actions are determined in the same way, regardless. The fact remains, though, that we're *accustomed* to seeing the future as open. That's how our lives appear to us, that's how we usually feel."

Yalda stopped walking. They were halfway across the bridge, supported by a slender arch of stonework over the blackness of the crevasse. She felt a shudder pass through the skin of her back; she'd just had an eerie sense of knowing what her shy, intense new colleague would say next.

"When our descendants turn around and travel back in time," Benedetta wondered, "will they still have the luxury we have, of debating this in the abstract? Once past and future are no longer so clear, will they still have the choice to go on seeing things the old way?"

Eusebio counted, "Three. Two. One."

A distant line of light split the sky, wavering in the heat haze. A pause later the bunker trembled; as the timber boards holding back the sand flexed and rattled, the air filled with fine dust. Yalda and her companions were lying flat on their backs, a stride beneath the ground, but the tilted mirror above let them watch the ascending rocket as if they were upright in the desert, while the tinted clearstone pane protected them from the glare.

Yalda was prepared for the hiss when it came, but not the crack that abruptly bisected the pane along a jagged diagonal. She reached up to support the two pieces before they could slip from the frame and decapitate someone.

Amando cursed quietly and raised his own hands to help; Eusebio did the same, exchanging a glance with Yalda expressing relief that it hadn't been worse. They'd isolated both the mirror and the pane from ground vibrations, but the shock wave in the air had still been enough to do damage. Nereo didn't flinch; he was still tracking the rocket with his theodolite, and probably hadn't even noticed the crack.

Giulio, the journalist from Red Towers, turned to Eusebio chirping with excitement. "To be honest with you, I thought it would just explode on the ground. But it's really up there!" He was too overwhelmed by the spectacle of the launch to care that he'd narrowly avoided being sliced in two by a giant stone blade.

"That's what rockets do," Eusebio replied modestly. "Ascend."

"When does it fall down again?" Giulio asked.

"This one won't," Eusebio predicted.

Yalda wasn't so sure. Through the protective filter the rocket had almost dimmed to invisibility; Eusebio would have gauged its progress by eye, but it would take the precise measurements of their independent observer to confirm its ultimate destination.

Giulio raised his head so he could peer over the intervening bodies and see what Nereo was up to. Nereo was propped up on a special bench that Amando had constructed; this allowed him to watch a clock with his rear gaze at the same time as he followed the rocket through the theodolite. Yalda could see a list of pairs of times and angles written along the length of Nereo's right arm; as she watched, he added one more pair then looked away from the theodolite and began producing further columns of numbers. The rocket would still be burning fuel—so there was still a chance that it could lose stability and drive itself back toward the ground—but on the assumption that it would do no worse, now, than if it had simply cut off its engines at the last clear observation, Nereo could give a tentative verdict on its fate.

"It's escaped the world's gravity," Nereo declared. "I suspect it's heading for an eccentric orbit around the sun with a period of several dozen years."

"How can it have *escaped*?" Giulio asked. "Are you saying it's already reached a height where gravity's negligible?"

His tone of incredulity was appropriate, but he'd missed the point. Nereo said, "At the altitude it had reached on my last observation, gravity is barely diminished—but it was already moving rapidly enough to guarantee that it would never be brought to a halt. Not by the world—though the sun still had hold of it."

Yalda looked to Amando, and together they managed to slide the tinted pane aside without the pieces falling on them. The bunker's five occupants climbed to their feet and scrambled up onto the sand, slipping between the ground and the mirror.

Yalda searched the sky, high to the east. There weren't many Hurtlers today to confuse the view, and she could see a faint gray speck that could only be Eusebio's house-sized pillar of rock—engines still blazing, still gaining speed. The escape velocity for the sun itself was only three times greater than the world's. Given the results from earlier yield experiments, if the rocket burned all its fuel without mishap it could actually end up leaving the solar system.

Giulio addressed Eusebio. "You should come to Red Towers and talk about your plans. Nereo's already given public lectures on rotational physics, so the ideas aren't completely new to people, but I can run some articles in the *Report* beforehand to help your audiences prepare."

Yalda wondered what was in the crops around Red Towers that was missing from Zeugma's diet.

Eusebio said, "I'd be delighted."

Yalda thanked Nereo for his participation. "It's a pleasure," he said. "I don't know if your guess about the Hurtlers is right, but I'm glad someone's thinking about these possibilities."

"I can't interest you in a place on the rocket?"

Nereo buzzed with mirth. "I'd rather stay safe on the ground, and wait for your dozen-fold-great-grandchildren to tell me all the marvelous science they've discovered."

Yalda said, "I get that answer a lot."

She wished she could have spent longer with Nereo, but he and Giulio needed to get back to Red Towers. Amando brought one of the trucks out of the shed and sped off across the desert with their guests.

Eusebio turned to Yalda. "Will you come to Red Towers with me? Tour the show?"

"If I can get leave from the university." Yalda hesitated. "Do you think you could pay me a small fee for that?"

"Of course." Eusebio had invited her several times to become an employee, but so far she'd resisted; she'd wanted to retain her independence, in order to be able to speak her mind to him freely.

She added apologetically, "If I'm not teaching I won't get paid, and it's not fair on Lidia and Daria to be looking after the children with no help."

"Hmm." Eusebio had already made it clear that he disapproved of what the three of them were doing: women—however capable they could be in other spheres—had not been shaped by nature for the raising of children. There were plenty of widowers in Zeugma desperate for heirs, and prepared to treat them like the flesh of their own co.

But he had more important things to think about than the flaws in Yalda's domestic life. "Beyond spreading the news to the citizenry of Red Towers," he said, "I'm hoping your colleague Nereo can arrange a meeting for me with his patron."

"You can't get an introduction to Paolo yourself?" Yalda was amused. "Whatever happened to the plutocrats' network?"

"*Networks*, plural. They're not all joined together."

"Why do you want to meet Paolo?"

"Money," Eusebio replied bluntly. "My father's set a ceiling on my investment in the rocket. If I'm going to have to build the whole structure myself—mining and transporting all the sunstone, incorporating it into an artificial shell… if I tried to match the scale of Mount Peerless the costs would be greater by a factor of several gross, but even the smallest viable alternative is far beyond what I can afford on my own."

"Have you thought of bribing all the people who are entitled to vote on the observatory?" Yalda suggested. "Not just with a shiny new telescope—with money they can put in their own pockets?"

Eusebio was insulted. "I'm not a fool; that was my very first plan. But Acilio has the Council scrutinizing the University's business very closely, and he has so many spies in the University himself that I doubt I could get away with that kind of thing."

Yalda joked, "I'm always willing to kill Ludovico, for a nominal fee."

Eusebio regarded her with a neutral expression for an uncomfortably long moment.

"Don't tempt me," he said.

As the train approached Red Towers, Yalda was surprised to discover that the city still lived up to its name. She'd read that the local calmstone deposit with the eponymous hue had been mined out long ago, but now she could see with her own eyes that the skyline still bore an unmistakable red tint. Perhaps the original buildings had been lovingly preserved. Either that, or they'd all been recycled as decorative veneer.

Nereo met her at the station—along with all four of his children, who fought with each other for the thrill of carrying her luggage. Seeing how young they were, Yalda guessed that his co must have lived almost as long as her own grandfather. Nereo was still healthy, though—and no doubt he'd made arrangements for the children to be cared for even if some tragedy struck him down.

"Your friend Eusebio's already at the house," Nereo said.

"He had some business in Shattered Hill," Yalda explained. "We've come in from opposite directions."

Nereo lived within his patron's walled compound. Yalda's skin crawled as they walked past the sentries with their knife belts, but the children took the sight for granted. "It's just a tradition," Nereo told her, noticing her discomfort. "Paolo has no enemies; those weapons have never been used."

"Don't the guards get bored, then?"

Nereo said, "There are worse jobs."

Eusebio was sitting on the floor in the guest room, reading a copy of *The Red Towers Report*. He greeted Yalda, then added in a tone of disbelief, "This man Giulio actually read and understood every word in the briefings I sent him. He raises some objections and concerns, but... they're all entirely *sensible*."

"Let's just strap the whole city to a rocket and get it over with," Yalda suggested. "Let Red Towers flourish in splendid isolation in the void for an age or two, then they can come back and teach the world how to live."

They only had a couple of bells before the show, so they went to the hall to familiarise themselves with the layout. Yalda hadn't been able to bring the equipment to produce the projected backdrops they'd used in Zeugma, but Giulio had organized printed sheets bearing the same material, which would be handed to the audience as they entered. That meant keeping the general lighting on during the performance.

"Seeing all those faces is going to make me anxious," she told Eusebio, standing on the stage at the front of the empty hall.

"Don't worry, you're a professional now." He squeezed her shoulder reassuringly.

The solution only came to her when she finally stepped out in front of the crowd: she delivered exactly the same message as in Zeugma, but she shifted her attention to her rear gaze and focused on the blank wall behind her, allowing herself to imagine that all the people in the hall were staring, not at her, but at the same soothing whiteness.

After Eusebio had done his part—with a few changes from the original version in which he'd boasted of a rocket the size of a mountain—it was time for questions. Everyone they'd spoken to in Red Towers had told them that they'd have to take questions from the floor; it was the custom here, and if they defied it they would not be forgiven. Giulio—whose employers had paid half the cost of renting the hall, in exchange for the right to display the paper's name prominently throughout the venue—joined Yalda and Eusebio on stage to moderate.

Yalda braced herself for the predictable "Why can't I walk to yesterday?" jokes, or perhaps even the perennial "Where's your co?"

The first questioner Giulio selected, an elderly man, called out, "How will you keep the machinery repaired?"

Eusebio said, "There'll be workshops within the rocket, equipped for every eventuality."

The man was unimpressed. "And factories? Mines? *Forests?*"

"There'll be stocks of minerals," Eusebio said, "and gardens for raw materials as well as for food."

"Stocks to last an age? Soil to last an age? All inside one tower? I don't think so."

Giulio chose another questioner.

"How will you control the population?" the woman asked.

"At the moment we have more of a shortage of travelers than an excess," Eusebio replied.

"Double that number a few dozen times," she suggested, "then tell me where you'll put them, and how you'll feed them."

Eusebio was beginning to look flustered. Yalda said, "There'll be the same mortality rates on the rocket as we experience anywhere else. No city's population actually *doubles* in a generation."

"So there'll be no progress in medicine, then? For era after era, the only thing these travelers will care about is dealing with the Hurtlers… which no longer even threaten them?"

Yalda said, "Progress in medicine could end up controlling population growth as much as it lowers mortality."

"*Could*—but what if it doesn't?"

The questions continued in this fashion: tough but undeniably pertinent. It felt like an eternity before Giulio called a halt; Yalda was so exhausted that it took her a moment to realize that the audience was now cheering enthusiastically.

"That went well," Giulio whispered to her.

"Really?"

"They took you seriously," he said. "What more did you want?"

In the foyer, they recruited more than three dozen ground crew volunteers, but no passengers. People here were far more willing than their cousins in Zeugma to accept Yalda's premise about the Hurtlers, and even the abstract principle behind Eusebio's solution—but no one was confident that he could build the kind of habitation in which they'd want their own grandchildren to spend their entire lives.

The servant ushered Yalda, Nereo and Eusebio into the dining room, then withdrew.

Paolo was standing at the far end of the room, flipping through a thick stack of papers. He looked younger than Yalda had expected, perhaps a bit more than two dozen years old. He put the papers down on a shelf and approached, gesturing at a wide circle of cushions on the floor. "Welcome to my home! Sit, please!"

Nereo introduced Yalda and Eusebio. Yalda tried not to be intimidated by the opulence of the room; the walls were decorated with an abstract mosaic, and there was a bewildering array of food spread out in front of them, almost none of it familiar to her. To her eye, there was enough to feed at least a dozen people—and when six young men entered the room, the quantity began to seem almost reasonable—but it turned out that Paolo's sons were just passing through to greet his guests, and would not be joining them.

Six sons! Had he adopted some of them, or taken two co-steads? Either way, if it was a family tradition the house would be overflowing with grandchildren.

The formalities over, Paolo sat with them and urged them to start eating. Yalda made a conscious decision not to hesitate—not to stare at the dishes and try to guess their origins. She was confident that nothing here would be too repellent, let alone dangerous, so it didn't really matter that she had no idea what she was putting in her mouth. The first few flavors were strange, but not unpleasant. She decided to adopt a fixed expression of mild enjoyment and maintain it throughout the meal, regardless.

Paolo addressed Eusebio. "I've heard about your rockets; an extraordinary venture."

"It's only just beginning," Eusebio replied. "To send people safely into the void will take many more years of work."

"I admire the audacity of your vision," Paolo said, "and I appreciate that the Hurtlers might well become dangerous. But what exactly do you think your travelers will bring back from a trip into empty space?"

"That's difficult to predict," Eusebio admitted. "Imagine, though, how wondrous our cities would appear to a visitor from the eleventh age. They had no engines, no trucks, no trains. Only the crudest lenses. No reliable clocks."

"But what comes next?" Paolo wondered. "An engine that runs a little more smoothly? A clock that loses no time in a year? Undoubtedly civilized refinements, but how would they safeguard us against the Hurtlers?"

Eusebio said, "Have you heard of the Eternal Flame?"

Yalda was glad she'd already committed to a policy of benign inexpressiveness.

Paolo buzzed amiably—not mocking his guest, but treating this invocation as if it could only have been meant as deliberate, flippant hyperbole.

Eusebio's tone remained scrupulously polite, but Yalda could see him struggling to keep his frustration in check. "The old stories of the Eternal Flame were misguided in their details," he said, "but modern ideas suggest that such a process might actually be possible." He turned to Nereo. "Am I wrong about that?"

Nereo said cautiously, "Rotational physics doesn't rule it out immediately, the way our earlier understanding of energy did."

Paolo was surprised. "Honestly?" He put down the loaf he'd been chewing. "So all those wild-eyed alchemists might simply have given up too soon? Ha!" He shot Nereo a reproving glance, as if his science adviser might have thought to mention such an interesting fact a few years earlier.

Eusebio said, "Sir, may I tell you one message we received very clearly from the people of Red Towers last night?"

"Certainly," Paolo replied.

"My venture, as it stands, is too modest," Eusebio confessed. "Nobody believes that a few dozen people in a vehicle perhaps the size of this compound could survive long enough to reap the benefits of their situation. The basic physics of the trajectory puts no limit on the length of their journey—no limit on the advantage they could have over us in years. But the practicalities of their situation will be the determining factor. A robust society requires a certain scale, in both people and resources. An isolated camp in the desert with well-chosen supplies might endure for a generation or two, but it takes a whole city to flourish for an age."

Paolo said, "I understand." He was silent for a while. "But how large a rocket would be large enough? No one knows. It's a very big risk to take, based on nothing but guesswork."

"If it stops the Hurtlers from destroying us," Eusebio replied, "how could it not be worth it?"

"But that judgment depends not only on the travelers succeeding," Paolo reasoned, "but also on an absence of other solutions. The same resources spent here on the ground might solve the problem more efficiently. I can't speak for others, but I do like having my own money doing its work somewhere nearby, where I can watch over it."

"Yes, sir." Eusebio lowered his gaze. The rejection could not have been clearer.

Paolo turned to Nereo. "So, perhaps the Eternal Flame could be made real?"

"Perhaps," Nereo conceded reluctantly. "But there are a number of subtleties to be considered, some of which we barely understand."

"What if I hired a gross of chemists to go out into the desert and start testing every possible combination of ingredients? Somewhere far from any people they could harm?" Nereo didn't reply immediately, but Paolo was already warming to his own vision. "We could require that each experiment take place at a location on the map that encoded the particular choice of reagents. That way, it would be apparent from the positions of the craters which reactions should never be attempted again."

"Ingenious, sir," Nereo declared. He was being sarcastic, but Paolo chose to take him at his word.

"The credit," Paolo replied, "should go to our guest, who delivered this inspiration to me." He bowed his head toward Eusebio.

Throughout their second, final show in Red Towers, Eusebio kept up an admirably professional veneer of optimism, but as soon as they were back in Nereo's guest room he slumped against the wall.

"It's too much," he said numbly. "I can't do this anymore."

"We can find someone else to take over the recruitment drive," Yalda suggested.

"I'm not talking about the recruitment drive! The whole project is impossible. I should give up this idiocy and go back to the railways; let someone else worry about the Hurtlers. I'll probably be dead before the worst of it, anyway. Why should I care?"

Yalda walked over to him and touched his shoulder reassuringly. "So Paolo won't invest in the rocket. He's not the only wealthy person on the planet."

"But Red Towers is as good as it gets," Eusebio said. "Journalists here understand the whole message. People listen to our plan and offer intelligent, constructive criticism. But no one here will volunteer to be a passenger, and the man who owns half the city would rather try to resurrect alchemy as his weapon against the Hurtlers than watch his money disappear into the void."

"It's a setback," Yalda admitted. "But don't make any decisions right now. Things might look different after a few days."

Eusebio was unconvinced, but he tried to receive her advice graciously. "Don't worry," he said. "I couldn't throw this all away in an instant if I wanted to. It's not as if someone's going to walk up to me tomorrow and offer to buy the mining licenses."

Yalda woke in the night, unsure for a moment where she was. She raised herself up on her elbows to look around the room. Soft-edged shadows tinged with spectral colors stretched across the floor from beneath the window, framing Eusebio's sleeping form.

He was beautiful, she realized: tall and strong, perfectly shaped even in slumber. How had she never seen that before?

But it was the thought of him that had woken her. If they brought their bodies together now, she was sure she could extract the promise from him. Her flesh wouldn't die; she'd let her mind and its anxieties fade away, leaving her children with a devoted protector. He was the closest thing to a co she could hope for, and she did not believe he would refuse her. Not here, alone with her; not if she insisted.

She rose to her feet and stood watching him, imagining his skin pressed against her own, rehearsing the words that would convince him. If Paolo could have six sons, why should Eusebio limit himself to two? She would not say a word against his co; she wasn't asking him to betray his lifelong partner, only to enlarge his prospective family.

Eusebio opened his eyes. She saw him register her presence, her gaze. She expected to be questioned, but he remained silent, as if everything between them was clear to him already. If she lay beside him now, it would not take much persuasion. They both wanted the comfort of this, and the promise of life for their children.

But as she took a step toward him, Yalda felt a chilling clarity spread across her mind. She wanted comfort—not oblivion. And whatever Eusebio wanted, it was not the encumbrance of her children. Nothing in this beguiling vision had any connection to their real plans, their real needs, their real wishes. The oldest part of her believed it could survive this way—as her mother had survived in her—but even that blind hope was misplaced. Eons of persistence would count for nothing when the sky lit up with orthogonal stars.

She said, "The Hurtlers woke me. I'm sorry I disturbed you."

Eusebio said, "That's all right, Yalda. Just try to sleep." He closed his eyes.

Yalda returned to her bed, but she was still awake at dawn.

After breakfast, Amando came in his truck to take Eusebio to another test launch. Eusebio didn't demur; the sheer momentum of the project still counted for something. At least until the money ran out.

Nereo walked Yalda to the station. "I'm sorry we didn't have a chance to talk optics," he said. "I've been tinkering with your light equation recently, trying to find the right way of adding a source."

"Really?" Yalda was intrigued. The equation she'd come up with five years before described the passage of light through empty space, but said nothing about its creation. "How far did you get?"

"I took some inspiration from gravity," Nereo said. "Think about the potential energy of a massive body, such as a planet. Outside the body, the potential obeys a three-dimensional equation very similar to the one for light: the sum of the second rates of change along the three directions of space is zero. Inside the body, instead of zero that sum is proportional to the density of matter."

"So you think I should add a similar term to the light equation, to represent the light source?" Yalda thought about this. "But a light wave involves a vector with four components; the source would have to be the same kind of thing."

Nereo said, "What about a vector that's aligned with the history of the light source—pointing into its future—with the length of the vector proportional to the density of the source?"

"That's the right kind of vector," Yalda conceded, "but what would this 'density' actually be describing?" He didn't mean mass; this was something else entirely.

"Whatever property matter needs in order to produce light," Nereo replied. "We don't have a word for it yet; maybe 'source strength'? But assuming we can put a number on it, we can talk about how tightly it's packed: the 'source density.'"

"Hmm." Yalda worked through the implications as they entered the station. "So if we're looking at the simplest case, where everything is motionless, only the time component of the equation would be non-zero, and it would have solutions a bit like gravitational potentials."

"But not quite the same," Nereo stressed. "These solutions *oscillate* as you move across space."

Yalda's train was boarding; they didn't have time to take the discussion further. Nereo said, "I'll send you a copy of my paper when I've written it."

On the journey back to Zeugma, Yalda managed to find one solution to Nereo's equation herself: the equivalent of the potential energy around a motionless, point-like mass.

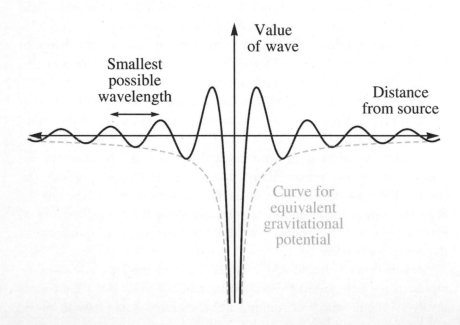

For gravity, it had been known since the work of Vittorio an era and a half ago that the potential was inversely proportional to the distance from the mass. For light, the overall strength of the wave diminished with distance in exactly the same fashion, but it also underwent an oscillation with the smallest possible wavelength—that of a wave traveling at infinite speed. All of this was just an idealization—the need to wrap around the cosmos smoothly would impose additional constraints and complications—but it was a start.

Yalda pondered the curve. Perhaps there was something like this present in everything from sunstone to a flower's petals. Light at the minimum wavelength would be invisible, so when the source was motionless the petals would be dark. But a system of oscillating sources, suitably arranged, might well be able to twist the original pattern into a set of tilted wavefronts, corresponding to light slow enough to lie in the visible realm.

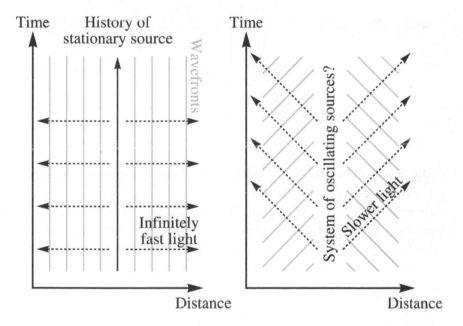

Exact solutions when the source was in motion wouldn't be easy to find, but the general idea made sense; to generate a wave that moved energy around, *something* had to feed in the energy in the first place, whether that meant jiggling the end of a string or vibrating your tympanum in air. That the creation of light would draw true energy out of an oscillating source—increasing its kinetic energy, rather than draining it—was a peculiar twist, but that was rotational physics for you.

There was, Yalda realized, another strange twist, arising from Nereo's choice of a vector *aligned with the particle's history* as the term to add to the equation. If you accelerated a light source long enough to curve its history around a half-circle and send it backward in time... then once it was settled on its new, straight trajectory it would be surrounded by a wave that was the opposite of the original. Compared with its earlier self, the pattern of light the source generated would now appear upside-down.

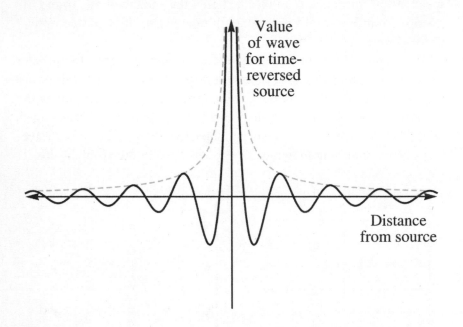

But how could a featureless speck of matter tell which way it was traveling through time? The arrow of time was meant to come solely from entropy's rise; a lone particle couldn't grow *disordered*. A wave changing sign wasn't as dramatic as the difference between a stone being smashed and the shards spontaneously reassembling, but it did imply that there might be two distinguishable kinds of source, at least when they weren't moving too rapidly: one "positive", one "negative".

It was evening when the train pulled into Zeugma. Yalda didn't have the energy to face the four squabbling brats at bedtime, so she wandered around the city center for a while, killing time until she was sure they'd be asleep.

When she finally braved the apartment, she was surprised to find Lidia sitting in the front room, in the dark.

"I thought you'd be at work," Yalda said. "Did they change your shift—or was there some problem with the helper?" The whole point of asking Eusebio to pay her had been to hire someone to watch the children in her place.

"The helper was fine," Lidia said, "but we didn't need her tonight."

"So you're working mornings again?"

"No, I've lost my job."

"Oh." Yalda sat beside her. "What happened?"

"Did I tell you about my new supervisor?"

"The idiot who kept asking you to become his deserted brother's co-stead?" Yalda didn't believe the rumor that Lidia had murdered her own co, but there were times when it might have been helpful if more people had taken it seriously.

Lidia said, "Two days ago he came up with a new offer: either I hand the children over to his brother, or he tells the factory owner that I've been stealing dye."

"But you only ever took from the spoiled batches. I thought everyone did that!"

"They do," Lidia replied. "But he told the owner I was taking good jars as well. He had some kind of paperwork prepared, inventory records that made it look plausible. So the owner believed him."

"What a piece of shit." Yalda put an arm across her shoulders. "Don't worry, you'll find a better job."

"I'm just tired," Lidia said, shivering. "I used to think everything would be different by now—by the time I was this old. But what's changed? There aren't even women on the Council."

"No."

"Why doesn't your friend Eusebio do something about that?" Lidia demanded.

"Don't blame him," Yalda pleaded. "He's already fighting the Council on a dozen different fronts."

Lidia was unimpressed. "The whole point of being a new member of the Council is to fight the old guard and get something useful done. But *sharing power* never seems to be a priority with anyone."

"Shocking, isn't it?"

"Will he have free holin on his rocket?" Lidia wondered. "I might join up for that alone."

Yalda said, "Of course there'll be free holin. In fact, it looks as if the entire crew will consist of solos and runaways: one of each, in a rocket the size of this room."

"That's beginning to sound less tempting."

Yalda rose. "I'm sorry about your job. I'll ask around, see if anyone knows of a position…"

"Yeah, thanks." Lidia put her head in her arms.

As Yalda crossed the room, a slab of sharp-edged brightness on the floor beside the window caught her eye. The diffuse light from the Hurtlers didn't look like this; it was as if one of their neighbors had stolen a spot-light from the Variety Hall and mounted it on their balcony.

She walked over to the window and looked out. The neighbors weren't to blame; the light was coming from high above the adjacent tower. A single bluish point was fixed in the sky, displaying no discernible color trail.

Lidia had noticed the light too; she joined Yalda by the window.

"What is it?"

Yalda suddenly realized that she'd seen the same object high in the east when she'd walked out of the railway station—but it had been a great deal paler then, so she hadn't given it a second thought. "Gemma," she said. "Or Gemmo." The naked eye couldn't separate them, so there was no point guessing which of the two had suffered the change.

Lidia hummed with exasperation; she was in no mood to be mocked. "I might not be an astronomer," she said, "but I'm not a fool. I know what the planets look like, and none of them are that bright."

"This one is, now." A dark, lifeless world that had once shone by nothing but reflected sunlight was turning into a star before their eyes.

Lidia steadied herself against the window frame; she'd grasped Yalda's meaning. "A Hurtler struck it? *And this is the result?*"

"It looks that way." Yalda was surprised at how calm she felt. Tullia had always believed that a large enough Hurtler could set the world on fire. Dark world, living world, star; they were all made of the same kinds of rock, the distinction was just a matter of luck and history.

Lidia said, "Now tell me the good news."

Good news? Gemma and Gemmo were far away, and much smaller than the sun, so at least the world wouldn't suffer intolerable heating from the new star.

In fact, the two planets were so far from the sun that the density of the solar wind in their vicinity was believed to be a tiny fraction of its value around the nearer worlds—and no Hurtlers had ever been seen at such a distance, in accord with the idea that it was friction with that gas that made the pebbles burn up. But the lack of the usual pyrotechnics hadn't prevented this unheralded impact.

The Hurtlers were everywhere, visible or not—and Ludovico's absurd explanation for them that blamed the solar wind alone was now com-pletely untenable. Yalda didn't expect him to recant, but the people who'd voted with him against Eusebio's offer didn't have the same degree of pride invested in the matter.

Perhaps the new star was no more exotic than the Hurtlers themselves, but its meaning was far easier to read: the only thing that had spared their own planet so far was luck. Any day, any night, the world could go the same way.

"The good news," Yalda said, "is that we might just get our flying mountain after all."

12

"Stay close to me!" Yalda called out to the group as they approached a bend in the tunnel. "Anyone suffering from nausea? Weakness? Dizziness?"

A chorus of weary denials came back at her; they were tired of being asked. She'd been pacing the tour carefully—and the mountain's interior was maintained at higher pressure than the air outside—but everyone's metabolism was different, and Yalda had decided that it was better to nag than face a crisis. She certainly didn't want any of these potential recruits associating the place with sickness.

"All right, we're now coming to one of the top engine feeds." For the last few saunters the tunnel had been lit solely by the red moss clinging to its walls, but the illumination from a more variegated garden could already be seen spilling around the bend.

As they took the turn, a vast, vaulted chamber appeared in front of them, a disk almost half a stroll wide and a couple of stretches high. It had been hollowed out of the rock three years before, using jackhammers powered by compressed air; no engines or lamps were employed in the presence of naked sunstone. The usual drab moss and some hardy yellow-blossomed vines covered the arched ceiling, but between the supports the floor was a maze of flower beds luminescing in every hue. Many of the plants were arranged haphazardly, or in small, localized designs, but long strands of cerulean and jade could be seen weaving from garden to garden around the gaping black mouths of the boreholes.

"It wasn't always so colorful here," Yalda recalled, "but the construction workers brought in different plants over the years."

"Will you keep the gardens when the engine's in use?" Nino asked.

"No—that would interfere with the machinery, and in the long term their roots could even damage the cladding. But these plants won't be destroyed; they'll be shifted to the permanent gardens higher up."

Yalda led her dozen charges to the edge of the nearest borehole and invited them to peer down into the gloom. Far below the chamber, the darkness was relieved by four splotches of green and yellow light; clinging to rope ladders that ran the full height of the shaft, workers wreathed in vines were inspecting the hardstone cladding that lined the surrounding sunstone.

"When the engine is operating," Yalda explained, "these holes will have been filled-in again, but liberator will be pouring down around the edges. If there are gaps in the cladding, the fuel could start burning in the wrong place."

"This is the top layer of the rocket, isn't it?" Doroteo asked.

"Yes."

"So it won't be in use for a very long time," he pointed out.

"That's true, and I'm sure it will be inspected again before it's fired," Yalda said. "But that's no reason for us to neglect the job now." Her ideal would have been to prepare every piece of machinery in the *Peerless* in such a way that the travelers would be able to turn around and come home safely whenever they wished—without requiring any new construction work, let alone any radical innovations. But given the current yield from the sunstone, this top layer of fuel would actually be burned away sometime during the decelerate-and-reverse phase, halfway through the journey. Relying on the status quo would not be an option.

Yalda led the group to a stairwell at the rim of the chamber, and they gazed up into its moss-lit heights. Four taut rope ladders ran down the center—installed early in the construction phase and retained in anticipation of weightlessness—but for now a more convenient mode of ascent involved the helical groove three strides deep that had been carved into the wall, its bottom surface tiered to form a spiral staircase.

"We'll be climbing up four saunters here," Yalda warned the group, "so please, take it carefully, and rest whenever you need to."

Fatima said, "I don't feel weak, but I'm getting hungry."

"We'll have lunch soon," Yalda promised. Fatima was a solo, barely nine years old; Yalda felt anxious every time she looked at the girl. What kind of father would have let her travel alone across the wilderness, to enlist in a one-way trip into the void? But perhaps she'd lied to him in order to come here; perhaps he thought she was hunting for a co-stead in Zeugma.

The group was evenly split between couples and singles; the singles were all women, except for Nino. Yalda hadn't interrogated Nino about his background, but she'd formed a hunch that he was that rare and shameful thing, a male runaway.

They began trudging slowly up the stairs; the pitch appeared to have been set to discourage running, should anyone have felt tempted. Their footsteps, and the whispered jokes of Assunta and Assunto up ahead, came back at them in multiple echoes from the underside of the stairs above. Beyond their own presence, Yalda could hear an assortment of odd percussive sounds, creaks and murmurs drifting down from higher levels. The workforce inside the mountain had fallen far below its peak, but it still numbered about a dozen gross, and most of the activity now was in the habitation high above the engines.

"Will the travelers be able to see the stars?" Fatima asked Yalda, trailing her by a couple of steps.

"Of course!" Yalda assured her, trying to dispel any notion that the *Peerless* would end up feeling like a flying dungeon. "There are observation chambers, with clearstone windows—and it will even be possible to go outside for short periods."

"To stand in the void?" Fatima sounded skeptical, as if this were as fanciful as walking on the sun.

Yalda said, "I've been in a hypobaric chamber, as close to zero pressure as the pumps could produce. It feels a bit… tingly, but it's not painful, and it's not harmful if you don't do it for too long."

"Hmm." Fatima was begrudgingly impressed. "And in the sky—will they be our stars, or the other stars?"

"That depends on the stage of the journey. Sometimes both will be visible. But I'll talk about that with everyone later." A moss-lit staircase wasn't the place to start displaying four-space diagrams.

They emerged from the stairwell into a wide horizontal tunnel; this one ran all the way around the mountain, but the nearest junction was just a short walk ahead. Yalda offered no warning as to what lay around the corner; the light gave some clues, but the thing itself always took the uninitiated by surprise.

The chamber was no wider than the one below, but it was six times taller—and the broad stone columns supporting the arched ceiling were all but lost among the trees. High above their heads, but far below the treetops, giant violet flowers draped across a network of vines formed a fragmented canopy that divided the forest vertically. With no sunlight to guide their activity, these flowers had organized themselves into two populations with staggered diurnal rhythms, one group opening while the others were closed. Through the gaps left by the sagging, dormant blossoms, shafts of muted violet reflected back by the stone above revealed swirling dust and swooping insect throngs. Even the air moved differently here, driven by complex temperature gradients arising within the vegetation.

Yalda strode forward through the bushes that had been planted around the chamber's edge, where the ceiling was too low for trees. "This might look like a strange indulgence," she admitted. "When we have farms, plantations and medicinal gardens, what need is there for wilderness? But if our survival depends on the handful of plants we've learned to harvest routinely, this place still encodes more knowledge about light and chemistry than all the books ever written. Every living organism has solved problems concerning the stability of matter and the manipulation of energy that we're only just beginning to grasp. So I believe it's prudent to bring as many different kinds of plant and animal life with us as we can."

"What kind of animals?" Leonia asked; she didn't sound too happy about the prospect of sharing the *Peerless* with a teeming menagerie.

"In here right now, there are insects, lizards, voles and shrews. Soon we'll be adding a few arborines." Yalda watched the group's reaction with her rear gaze; eventually it was Ernesto who said, "Aren't arborines dangerous?"

"Only when threatened," Yalda declared confidently. "Most of the stories about them are exaggerated. In any case, they're our closest cousins; if there are medical treatments we need to test, there's only so much you can learn from a vole." It was Daria who'd sold her on most of these assertions—the same Daria who'd made half her wealth from impresarios' claims about the creature's ferocity.

Fatima said, "What happens when there's no gravity? Won't everything... come loose?"

Yalda squatted down and cleared a small patch of soil, exposing the layer of netting that sat over it. "This is attached to the rock with spurs at regular intervals. The root systems bind the soil together, too—and the soil itself is actually quite sticky. A handful of soil will trickle through your fingers easily enough, but an absence of gravity is not the same as turning everything upside down. What I'm expecting is that the air here and in the farms will grow hazy with dust, but there'll be an equilibrium where that dust is re-adhering to the bulk of the soil as often as it's breaking free."

They took the stairs up to one of the farms, and ate a lunch prepared from the local crops. Wheat adapted well to sunlessness; it grew faster in here than on the farms outside, now that Gemma had all but banished night again. The disruption caused by the second sun varied with the season and the year—and there were periods when it rose and set close to the original, almost restoring normality—but the last Yalda had heard from Lucio was that he and her cousins had given up trying to adjust to the complicated cycle and were simply building canopies over all their fields.

Then it was on to the storerooms, workshops and factories, the school, the meeting hall, the apartments. They ended the day in an observation chamber close to the peak, where they watched the sun setting over the plain below, revealing the mountain's stark shadow in the rival light from the east.

There was a food hall beside the chamber. Yalda found a free patch of floor among the crowd of construction workers and sat everyone down. Up here they were far enough from the sunstone to use lamps; it might have been any busy establishment in Zeugma or Red Towers.

Yalda dropped her recruiting spiel and let the group eat, with no accompaniment but the sputter of firestone and the chatter of their fellow diners. By now they'd seen not the whole of the *Peerless*, but at least one example of everything it contained. They'd reached the point of being able to imagine what it would be like to spend their lives inside this mountain.

Leonia, who'd been tense throughout the tour, now appeared almost tranquil; Yalda's guess was that she'd made up her mind to find an easier way of avoiding her co than fleeing into the void in the company of wild animals. Nino looked haunted, but equally resolved to make the opposite choice. Looking back, Yalda realized that every question he'd asked her had concerned something innocuous or trivial; it was as if he'd wanted to appear engaged as a matter of courtesy, but he'd been so committed to his plan from the start that he'd preferred not to delve into anything that might risk swaying him.

With the others, she was unsure. It was as easy to undersell the problems the travelers would face as to oversell them. Anyone who reached the end of the tour believing that the project was hopelessly ill-conceived would walk away—but equally, anyone who was convinced that the triumphant return of the *Peerless* was inevitable would have scant motivation to join the crew. Rather than sentencing your descendants to indefinite exile, why not choose the version of events that lasted a mere four years, in which your death far from home was replaced by the imminent arrival of the most powerful allies you could hope for? Of course a Hurtler might incinerate the world before then, but it had been five years since Gemma's ignition, so it wasn't hard to imagine the same luck holding out for another five.

In between those two extremes was a sweet spot, where the mission's potential was beyond doubt but its success remained far from guaranteed—allowing a wavering recruit to imagine their own contribution tipping the balance. Yalda aimed squarely for that result, and she no longer felt guilty or manipulative for doing so. The truth was, though she and Eusebio had filled all the jobs that they knew beyond doubt to be essential, there was nothing gratuitous about raising the numbers still higher—increasing the range of skills, temperaments and backgrounds among the travelers. It was like bringing the forest as well as the farms: the *Peerless* was sure to find a use for everyone, even if they could not yet say what it would be.

"One came back!" Benedetta shouted ecstatically, running across the sandy ground between the main office and the truck compound. There was a rolled-up sheet of paper in her hand. "Yalda! *One came back!*"

Yalda gestured to the group to wait for her. She'd been about to take them over to the test site to watch a demonstration launch, but if she understood Benedetta's cryptic exclamation then this was worth a delay.

Yalda jogged over to meet her. "One of the probes returned?"

"Yes!"

"You're serious?"

"Of course I'm serious! This is the image it took!"

Benedetta unrolled the crumpled sheet.

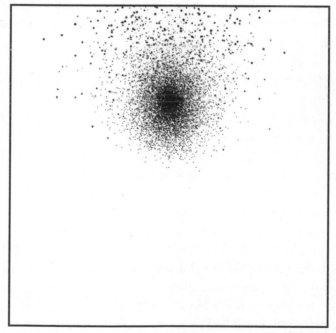

Yalda had barely taken in the spatter of black specks when Benedetta turned the paper over to show her the opposite side. It had been marked with three signatures in red dye: Benedetta's, Amando's and Yalda's, along with a serial number, an arrow in one corner to fix its orientation in the imaging device... and instructions to anyone finding it upon its return.

Apart from the image on the sensitized side, Yalda certainly recognized the sheet. It was one of a gross that she'd signed at Benedetta's request, two and a half years earlier, to guarantee their authenticity.

"Who sent this to you?"

"A man in a little village near Mount Respite," Benedetta said. "I'll need your authorization to pay him the reward."

"Do you know what state the probe itself is in?"

"In his letter he said there wasn't much left of it apart from a few cogs hanging off the frame, but it was still so heavy that he couldn't afford to send it to us."

"Add something to the reward to cover the freight, and get us the whole thing." Yalda took the sheet from her. "Octofurcate me sideways," she muttered. "You and Amando really did it." She looked up. "Have you told him yet?"

"He's in Zeugma helping Eusebio with something."

"I never thought this would work," Yalda admitted.

Benedetta chirped gleefully. "I know! That makes it so much better!"

Yalda was still having trouble believing it. She was holding in her hands a sheet of paper that had left the world behind, crossed the void faster than anything but a Hurtler, turned around and come back... and then traveled here by post from Mount Respite.

"Which stage was it taken in?" she asked.

Benedetta pointed to the serial number.

"Meaning...?" Yalda had forgotten what the numbers signified.

"Odd numbers were for the first stage of the journey, when the probe was traveling away from us."

"Good," Yalda managed numbly. She thought for a while. "I think you should come and tell my recruits what you've found."

"Of course."

Yalda introduced Benedetta to the group, then recounted some of the background to the problem. Years before, she had managed to identify a slight asymmetry in the Hurtlers' light trails, demonstrating that their histories were not precisely orthogonal to the world's. This had finally made it possible to say which direction they were coming from; until then, their trails might have marked a burning pebble crossing the sky in either direction. But it had revealed nothing about the Hurtlers' own arrow of time.

Doroteo was confused. "Why doesn't their arrow of time just point from their origin to their destination?"

Yalda said, "Suppose you drive toward a railway crossing, and you notice that the track doesn't make a perfect right angle with the road you're on; it comes in from the left as you approach the crossing. You might think of the 'origin' of the track as being a station that lies behind you, to the left—but assuming that this track is only used in one direction, you still have no reason to believe that *the trains* will actually be traveling from your left to your right."

Doroteo grappled with the analogy. "So… we can map the geometry of a Hurtler's history through four-space as a featureless line, but we can't put an arrow on it. We can't assume that the tilt you discovered means the Hurtler's arrow is pointing slightly toward our future; it might as easily be pointing slightly toward our past."

"Exactly," Yalda said. "Or at least, that was how things stood until now."

Benedetta was shy before the strangers, but with Yalda's encouragement she took over the story.

The probes had been launched two and a half years earlier: six dozen rockets fuelled by sunstone from the mountain's excavations, fitted with identical instruments and sent out like a swarm of migrating gnats in the hope that one of them would complete its task and find its way home. Their flight plan had been a less ambitious variation on that of the *Peerless*, reaching just four-fifths the speed of blue light before decelerating and reversing, with literally just a couple of bells spent in free fall along the way. Compressed air, clockwork and cams controlled the timing of the engines, with opposing pairs of thrusters built into the design to avoid the need to rotate the craft. The aim of the project had been to get an imaging device moving as rapidly as possible, parallel to the Hurtlers' path, first in one direction and then the opposite.

"This paper was made sensitive to ultraviolet light, about one and a half times as fast as blue light," Benedetta explained, holding up the travel-worn sheet. "The orthogonal stars all lie in our future, so we can't expect to see them, or image them under ordinary conditions. But the whole meaning of 'past' and 'future' depends on your state of motion."

She sketched the relevant histories on her chest.

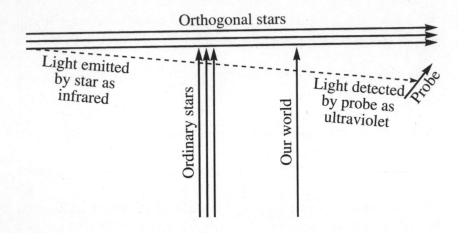

"With the probe traveling at four-fifths the speed of blue light, infrared light from the orthogonal stars would have reached it at an angle in four-space corresponding to ultraviolet light from the past." Benedetta held up the evidence again. "So we've managed to record an image of these stars—which to us still lie entirely in the future—by giving the probe a velocity that placed part of their history in its past."

Fatima said, "How do you know those are images of orthogonal stars, not ordinary ones?"

Benedetta gestured at her chest. "Look at the angle between the light and the histories of the ordinary stars. To them, the light's traveling backward in time! Only the orthogonal stars could have emitted it."

Yalda added, "And if the orthogonal stars' future had pointed the other way, then the probe could only have imaged them once it had reversed and was coming back toward us. So we know the direction of the arrow now—not from the Hurtlers themselves, but from the light of these stars whose origin the Hurtlers share." This finally put to rest Benedetta's old fear: that the *Peerless* might be headed straight toward the orthogonal cluster's past, requiring the rocket to function while opposing the entropic arrow of its surroundings. Now it was clear that it would not face that challenge until the return leg of the journey.

"And how far away are they?" Fatima asked. "These orthogonal stars?"

Benedetta looked down at the images. "We can't be sure, because we don't know how bright they are. But if they're about as luminous as our own stars, the nearest could be no more than a dozen years away."

The group absorbed this revelation in silence. Five Hurtlers were spreading lazily across the morning sky, and while Gemma itself was below the horizon, here was a promise of interlopers vastly larger than the baubles that had set that world on fire.

Just when Yalda was beginning to think that the stark new threat might push some of the waverers into making a commitment, Leonia broke the mood. "Six dozen probes went up," she said, "and this is the only one that's been recovered? What happened? Did all the others end up as craters in the ground?"

"That's possible," Benedetta conceded. "Landings are difficult to automate. But the real problem was returning the probes to this tiny speck of rock from such a distance. The world is a very small target; the tolerances required for attitude and thrust control were close to the limits of what any of us believed was feasible. We were lucky to get even one back."

"But the *Peerless* will be traveling much farther," Serafina noted anxiously.

"With people inside it to navigate," Yalda replied. "It won't be down to clockwork to get them home."

Leonia was unswayed. "Be that as it may, when you rehearsed your great project—on a much smaller scale—you only had one success in six dozen. And you were hoping to impress us by *juggling voles!*"

The demonstration launch Yalda had arranged would carry six of the animals above the atmosphere, then bring them back down again—hopefully still alive. While clearly no surrogate for the flight of the *Peerless*, this was not a trivial achievement—and some people did find it reassuring to see that Eusebio's rockets no longer exploded on launch, or cooked their passengers with the engine's heat.

"What would persuade you, then?" Yalda demanded irritably. "A full-scale rehearsal, where we send up Mount Magnificent with a crew of arborines?"

Leonia responded to this sarcastically grandiose proposal with a much more modest alternative. "It might mean something if you went up yourself, instead of the voles."

Before Yalda could reply, Benedetta said, "I'll do it."

Fatima emitted an anxious hum. "Are you serious?"

Benedetta turned to her. "Absolutely! Just give me a few days to check the rocket and re-arrange things for the new weight."

Yalda said, "We need to discuss this—"

"That would be a lot more convincing than voles!" Assunto enthused.

His co agreed. "What can an animal the size of my hand tell us about the risks of flight?" she complained. "Our bodies are completely different."

Yalda looked on helplessly as the group debated Benedetta's offer; the majority soon reached the view that nothing less would be of interest to them. Only Fatima was reluctant to witness such a risky stunt, while Nino struggled to summon up the appearance of caring one way or the other.

Yalda wasn't going to argue this out with Benedetta in front of everyone; she sent the recruits off to kill some time at the Basetown markets.

Benedetta was already contrite. "That was poorly judged," she admitted. "I shouldn't have sprung it on you out of nowhere."

Yalda said, "Forget about the timing." Being made to look foolish in front of the recruits was the least of it. "Why do you think you need to do this at all?"

"We've talked about it for years," Benedetta replied. "You, Eusebio, Amando… everyone agrees it would be a good idea to send someone up—but always later. How long is it until the *Peerless* is launched now?"

"Less than a year, I hope."

"And we still haven't put a single person on a rocket!"

"Flesh is flesh," Yalda said firmly. "What are voles made of—stone? When it comes to the *Peerless*, the things we have to worry about will be attitude control and cooling—and we've got both of them down to a fine art: in the last four dozen test launches, they've worked flawlessly. It's only the landings that have failed."

"And only three times," Benedetta pointed out. "So those aren't bad odds that I'd be facing."

Yalda said, "No… but if you did this, what would it actually tell us? Whether you survived or not, how would it make the *Peerless* safer?"

Benedetta had no ready reply for that. "I can't point to any one thing," she said finally. "But it still feels wrong to me to try to launch a whole town's worth of people into the void, without at least one of us going there first. Even if it's only a gesture, it's a gesture that will calm some people's fears, win us a few more recruits and quieten some of our enemies."

Yalda searched her face. "Why now, though? You see an image of the future—proof that it's fixed—and suddenly you're offering to surrender your life to fate?"

Benedetta buzzed, amused by the implication. She held up the paper from the probe. "If I stare at this long enough, do you think I might spot myself living happily among the orthogonal stars?"

Yalda said, "What if I tell you that I've seen the future, and it's voles all the way?"

Benedetta gestured toward the markets. "Then I can confidently predict that most of those recruits will be gone in a couple of days."

Silvio stood in the doorway of Yalda's office. "You need to see this new camp," he said. "Way out of town."

She looked down at the calculations Benedetta had submitted on the modified test launch. She'd checked them over and over again, but she still hadn't made a final decision on whether or not to approve the flight.

"Are you sure there's a problem?" she asked him. Traders sometimes arrived and set up camp in inconvenient places, but it usually only took them a few days to realize that they were better off in Basetown.

Silvio didn't reply; he'd given his advice, he wasn't going to repeat it. It was Eusebio who paid his wages, and if Eusebio put Yalda in charge of the project in his absence then that won her a certain amount of courtesy—but not much.

She said, "All right, I'm coming."

Silvio drove her a few strolls north along the dirt track that ran from Basetown to one of the disused entrances to the mountain. Yalda didn't know exactly what he'd been doing there himself; maybe Eusebio had him patrolling the whole area.

There were five trucks at the abandoned construction camp, most of them loaded with soil and farming supplies. A couple of dozen people were visible, digging in the dusty ground. In some respects it wasn't a bad place to farm, Yalda realized; the shadow of the mountain might well block Gemma's light enough of the time to allow the crops to retain their usual rhythm, without the need for unwieldy awnings. Having to truck in soil wasn't promising, but once a crop became established the roots of the plants, and the worms that lived among them, could start breaking down the underlying rock.

Yalda climbed down from the cab and approached the farmers.

"Hello," she called out cheerfully. "Can anyone spare a lapse or two to talk?"

She caught a few people looking away, embarrassed at the realization that they were being addressed by a solo, but one man put down his shovel and walked over to her.

"I'm Vittorio," he said. "Welcome."

"I'm Yalda." She resisted the urge to make a joke about his famous namesake; either he'd be sick of people doing it, or he'd have no idea what she was talking about. "I work with Eusebio from Zeugma—the man who owns the mines here." That had become the standard euphemism for the rocket project; everyone knew precisely what was going on inside the mountain, and why, but some people who took a dim view of Eusebio's whole endeavor were less hostile if they weren't confronted with explicit reminders of it.

"I don't believe he owns this land," Vittorio replied defensively.

"No, he doesn't." Yalda tried to keep her tone as friendly as possible. "But if you were hoping to trade with his workers, we have a whole town just south of here where you'd be welcome to set up." If they signed an agreement with some very reasonable conditions, they could farm just as much land as they were using here, sell their produce in the markets and have access to Basetown's facilities for no cost at all.

"We chose this location with care," Vittorio assured her.

"Really? It's a long way from everything but Basetown, and not as close to there as it could be."

Vittorio made a gesture of indifference. Other members of his community were watching them discreetly, but Yalda didn't sense any physical threat, just a mood of resentment at her interference.

"I need to be honest with you," she said. "In less than a year, this land won't be suitable for farming anymore." She was trying to work from the most innocent assumptions she could think of: that the chaos in the sky had driven them off their land in search of some reliable diurnal darkness, and they were unaware of quite how soon it would be before Mount Peerless ceased casting its convenient shadow.

"Are you threatening us?" Vittorio sounded genuinely affronted.

She said, "Not at all, but I think you know what I'm talking about. That you won't have shade for your crops will be the least of it."

"Ah, so your master Eusebio will consign us all to flames?" Vittorio made no effort now to hide his contempt. "He'd knowingly slaughter this entire community?"

"Let's not get melodramatic," Yalda pleaded. "You've barely begun to dig your fields, and now you've been informed of the danger so you won't waste your time putting down roots here. Nobody is going to be *consigned to flames*."

"So you pay no heed to the fate of Gemma?"

Yalda was confused. "Gemma is why half the planet has given its blessing to Eusebio's efforts."

"*Gemma*," Vittorio countered, "taught those of us with eyes that an entire world can be lost to flames. But your master has learned nothing, and in his ignorance he'd blindly set this one alight as well."

Yalda was growing irritated with the whole "master" thing, but it made a change from being told he was her co-stead. She glanced back toward the truck; Silvio was pretending to be taking a nap.

"You think the rocket would set the world on fire?" If that was his honest belief, Yalda could only admire him for deciding to become a living shield against the threatened conflagration, but he might have dropped by the office and asked a few questions first. "It was a Hurtler that ignited Gemma, and it would take a Hurtler to do the same to us," she declared.

"A Hurtler, and nothing else?" Vittorio buzzed, amused by her rhetoric. "How can you possibly know that?"

Yalda said, "I don't know that *nothing else* could do it—but I know what this rocket will and won't do. Under the mountain, beneath the sunstone, there's a seam of calmstone; I've been there, I've touched it with my own hands. We've tested the combination, burning one on top of the other, for far, far longer than they'll stay together at the launch. The calmstone is ablated by the flame, but there's no sustained reaction that spreads beyond the site. And before you start protesting that the calmstone is unlikely to be pure, we've tested dozens of other rocks as well."

"And how large was your flame?" Vittorio enquired. "The size of a mountain?"

"No, but that's not the issue," Yalda explained. "By holding the flame in place longer in the tests, we can achieve identical conditions in a slab a few strides wide."

Vittorio simply didn't accept this. "You've played around with some childish fireworks, and you think that proves something. The proof is in the sky."

"If you're so impressed by the example of Gemma, how do you propose fending off the Hurtlers that would re-enact the whole thing here?" Yalda demanded. "Thwarting Eusebio won't spare you from that."

Vittorio was unfazed. "Do you think there were people on Gemma?"

"No." This was becoming surreal. "What difference does that make?"

"*People* can douse small fires," Vittorio replied. "If one kind of stone is burning, the sand of another kind can be fetched to put it out. If there had been people on Gemma, that's what they would have done, and that world would not have been lost to the flames."

Yalda didn't know how to answer this. To hope that quick thinking and a bucketful of sand could defeat the Hurtlers was absurd… but if you scaled it up to something systematic with teams of rostered observers in every village and whole truckloads of inert minerals at the ready, that *might* actually contain the effects of a small impact.

"How large is a Hurtler?" Vittorio asked her. He held up two fingers, about a scant apart. "This big? Larger? Smaller?"

"About that size," Yalda conceded.

"So my choice is between a fire that starts from a pebble, and one that starts from *this*." Vittorio turned and gestured at the mountain. "Only a fool would choose the greater risk."

From the top of the rocket, Yalda could see the wind lifting brown dust from the plain to trace out its eddies and flows. "You can still change your mind," she said.

"But I've already completed the trip," Benedetta replied placidly. "Time is a circle. It's happened, it's over; there's nothing left to choose."

Yalda hoped that this fatalist blather was just Benedetta teasing her, but there was no point arguing about it now. The last three of the recruits she'd brought up to ogle the tiny cabin were on the ladder heading back to the ground. Benedetta was strapped onto a bench that had been installed in place of the rack of voles' cages in the original design; the same cool gases would blow over her body as those that had kept the animals safe from hyperthermia in previous launches. The elaborate clockwork around her that would control the timing of the engines and the parachute's release had been inspected thrice: by Frido, by Yalda, then finally by Benedetta herself. The voles had only merited two inspections.

"I won't say good luck then; you won't need it," Yalda told her.

"Exactly."

Yalda couldn't leave it at that; she squatted down beside the bench. "You know, if you're made famous by this your co might come looking for you."

"Whose co?" Benedetta retorted. "Nobody here knows my birth name."

"No, but how many people as crazy as you could have been born in Jade City?"

Benedetta was amused. "You think I'm from Jade City?"

"Aren't you?" Yalda had always believed that part of her story. "Your accent sounds authentic."

"You should hear the other six regions I can do."

Yalda squeezed her shoulder. "See you soon." She straightened up then climbed out of the cabin; perched on the ledge above the ladder, she slid the hatch firmly into place. Through the window, she saw Benedetta gesture toward the enabling lever, then make a four-fingered hand: on the fourth chime from the clock beside the bench, she'd launch the rocket. This was the normal protocol, but unlike the voles she'd have to initiate the process herself.

Yalda usually had no trouble with heights, but as she descended the ladder she felt a kind of sympathetic vertigo at the thought of the altitude the cabin would soon reach.

On the ground, she pulled the ladder away and let it fall to one side. The recruits were quiet now; even Leonia was subdued as they started back toward the bunker.

When a gust of wind rose up and sprayed stinging dust into their faces, Fatima said, "Someone should make a truck that runs on compressed air."

"They should," Yalda agreed. It had probably been discussed at some point, but then slipped off the agenda; that had happened with a lot of good ideas. Compounding the problem of the project's sheer complexity, some of Eusebio's fellow investors had insisted that their funds could only be spent directly on the rocket itself, lest they be viewed as mere secondary players when the descendants of the travelers returned. Yalda found it hilarious that anyone believed that such choices could guarantee them access to the project's ultimate harvest. If the *Peerless* really did come back after an age in the void—with the kind of technology that could defeat the Hurtlers and everything that threatened to follow them—they'd trade with whomever they liked, on whatever terms they wished. A certain amount of compassion for their distant cousins was the most she was hoping for; any prospect of scrupulous adherence to contracts signed by their long-dead ancestors was just a fantasy Eusebio had encouraged so the plutocrats could part with vast sums of money without having to confront the horrifying reality that it was actually being spent for the common good.

Frido was waiting by the bunker. "How was she?" he asked anxiously.

"Calm," Yalda said. "She was joking with me."

Frido stared back across the plain. Yalda decided that they were the ones who were getting the real taste of cosmic determinism; Benedetta could still decide either to launch the rocket or back out, but nothing her two friends did now could influence her choice.

Everyone clambered down into the bunker. It had been years now since a rocket had exploded at launch, but these precautions weren't arduous, and though the dust was even thicker down here it was good to get out of the wind.

Yalda lay between Frido and Fatima, watching the mirrored horizon. The rocket was almost lost in the brown haze. She glanced over at the clock; there were three lapses still to go.

Leonia said, "What if she loses her resolve, then regains it? If we come out of the bunker and that thing goes off—"

"That's not going to happen," Yalda replied. "She'll launch at the agreed time, or not at all."

"What if something jams inside the engine feed?" Ernesta asked. "How can you walk away from that safely, if it might unjam at any time and fire the engines?"

Yalda said, "There's a backup system to close off the liberator tanks. And if that doesn't work, Benedetta knows how to take the whole engine feed apart." *Can't you all be quiet, and just let this happen?* She closed her eyes; her head was throbbing.

Time passed in silence. Fatima touched her arm warily. Yalda opened her eyes and looked at the clock. Frido counted softly, "Three. Two. One."

The radiance of burning sunstone burst through the haze and lit up the plain. Benedetta hadn't flinched; she hadn't waited one flicker past the chime. As the rocket rose smoothly into the sky the walls of the bunker shook, but it was no more than a gentle nudge. Yalda felt a rush of empathetic delight. This courageous woman had pushed the lever, and the rocket had done her bidding. Cool breezes would be flowing over her skin, her weight would be no more than half above normal, and with her tympanum held rigid the noise of the engine wouldn't trouble her too much. Yalda, braced the same way, barely registered the sound of the launch as it reached her.

When the rocket went off the edge of the mirror, Yalda scrambled out of the bunker and stood watching it ascend. Frido followed her, and though she gave no instructions to the recruits everyone soon joined them.

In less than a chime Benedetta would be four slogs above the ground— almost nine times the height of Mount Peerless. From her bench, she would be peering through the window and watching the horizon growing ever wider. Yalda's skin tingled vicariously at the thought of this foretaste of the greater journey: to ascend and return, without the bitterness of parting from the world forever.

Frido had a theodolite on a tripod set up beside the bunker, but Yalda was content to use her naked eyes, merely checking the time on the clock that sat behind them both. Distance soon dimmed the rocket to a faint white speck, but it was not so pale that there was any ambiguity when the engines shut off and it vanished entirely. Now Benedetta would be weightless, as if she'd stepped into the skin of one of her descendants from the generations who would know nothing else.

The rocket would rise another two slogs before gravity brought it to a halt. As five lapses passed, Yalda pictured it slowing, approaching its peak. Would Benedetta have any way of knowing that she'd reached the midpoint of her journey, apart from the reading on her own clock? How well could you judge your speed, when the landscape that offered the only cues was at such a great remove? Yalda tried to imagine the view from this pinnacle, but the task defeated her. She would have to wait to hear it in the traveler's own words.

For five more lapses the rocket would fall freely, then the engines would start up again, burning more fiercely than during the ascent, slowing the vehicle sufficiently for the parachute to take over and ease its fall. Yalda kept her rear eyes on the clock and her forward gaze raised to the zenith, trying not to be distracted by the Hurtlers.

Where was the speck of light? She glanced at Frido, but he hadn't spotted it either. She forced herself to remain calm; the wind was whipping up dust all around them, and it was always easier to track the rockets to burn-out than to catch sight of them as they lit up again.

There! Lower and westwards from where she'd been looking, faint but unmistakable. The cross-winds would have given the rocket an unpredictable horizontal push, keeping it from retracing its trajectory precisely—and Yalda suspected that she'd lost her bearings a little, telling herself that she'd kept her gaze fixed when she'd really been following some slowly drifting streak of color in her peripheral vision.

Frido spoke quietly, his words for her alone. "Something's wrong," he said. "It's coming down too fast."

Yalda couldn't agree. He had watched more launches then she had, but he was more anxious too; his perceptions were skewed.

The flame grew closer, its intensity becoming painful; in her mind's eye Yalda followed it down to a point just a few strolls from the launch site. Benedetta would meet them halfway across the plain, waving and shouting triumphantly.

She waited for the flame to cut out, watching the clock as the moment approached. But when it had passed, the engines were still blazing.

"Something's wrong," Frido repeated softly. "The burn must have started late."

As he spoke, the flame went out. Yalda fixed the clock's reading in her mind: six pauses after the scheduled time. If the entire burn had been delayed for six pauses, the rocket would have been moving more than ten dozen strides per pause faster than intended when the engines cut out and the parachute was unfurled. Falling faster, from a lower altitude.

"What can you see?" Yalda asked him. The recruits were starting to notice their whispering, but Yalda ignored them and watched Frido searching the sky with the theodolite's small telescope. The unlit rocket itself would be impossible to make out from this distance, but if the parachute was open the white fabric would catch the sun.

Yalda saw it first—her view was wider, and no telescope was needed. Not a flutter of sunlight on cloth, but the full glare of burning sunstone again. She touched Frido's shoulder; he looked up and cursed in amazement.

"What's she doing?" he asked numbly.

"Taking control," Yalda said. The engines had no provision for manual operation, but Benedetta must have dragged the useless timing mechanism out of the way and re-opened the liberator feed herself.

Fatima approached. "I don't understand," she complained.

Yalda addressed the recruits, explaining what she believed was happening. The timer must have jammed for a few pauses while the rocket was in free fall, delaying everything that followed. The parachute must have been torn away when it unfurled at too high a speed. The only way to slow the rocket's descent now was with the engines. Benedetta would try to execute a series of burns that would bring her to the ground safely.

She said no more; all they could do now was watch and hope. But even with perfect knowledge and perfect control, a powered landing could only be a compromise. You needed to be as low as possible before you finally cut the engines, to spare yourself from the fall—but the lower you descended, the more the ground below you would trap heat from the rocket's exhaust.

And Benedetta did not have perfect knowledge, just a sense of her own weight to gauge the engine's thrust and an oblique view of the landscape from which to judge her height and velocity. As Yalda watched, the burn intended to slow the rocket's fall went on too long; the piercing light hung high above the plain for a moment then rose back into the sky.

The flame went out, leaving the rocket invisible again. Yalda tried to think her way back into the cabin, to regain the sense of empathy she'd felt at the moment of launch. Benedetta had already shown quick thinking and resolve, but what she needed most was information.

The engines burst into life once more, showing the rocket far lower than before. Yalda watched it approaching the horizon, afraid it was not slowing quickly enough, but as it entered the dust haze, sending rippling shafts of light and shade across the plain, her spirits soared. It was easier now to judge its trajectory, and it looked as near to perfect as she could have wished. If Benedetta cut the engines at the lowest point, the fall might be survivable.

The flame dimmed slightly, but it did not go out. Yalda peered into the dust and glare, struggling to discern any sign of motion. Frido reached over and touched her arm; he was looking through the theodolite. "She's trying to get lower," he said. "She knows she's close, but she doesn't think it's good enough."

"Is it good enough?"

Frido said, "I think so."

Then cut the engines, Yalda begged her. *Cut the engines and fall.*

The light grew brighter, but it remained in place. Yalda was confused, but then she understood: Benedetta hadn't increased the thrust, but the rocket was now so low that it was heating the ground below it to the point of incandescence.

Frido let out a hum of dismay. "Go up!" he pleaded. "You've lost your chance; give it time to cool."

The glow flared and diffused. The wind shifted, clearing the haze, and Yalda could see exactly what was happening. The ground was ablaze, while the rocket crept toward it, feeding the flames.

Yalda called out "Down!" and managed to push Fatima toward the bunker before the light became blinding and she stumbled. She lay where she'd fallen, her face in the dirt, covering her rear eyes with one arm.

The ground shuddered, but it was not a big explosion; most of the sunstone and liberator had already been used up. She waited for debris, but whatever there was fell short. When she relaxed her tympanum, all she heard was the wind.

Yalda rose to her feet and looked around. Frido was crouched beside her, his head in his hands. Nino was standing, apparently unharmed; the other recruits were still picking themselves up. Fatima peered out from the bunker, humming softly in distress.

In the distance, a patch of blue-white flame jittered over the ground. Yalda couldn't tell if it was spilt fuel burning or the dust and rock of the plain itself. She watched in silence until the fire had died away.

"When Benedetta wanted to launch her imaging probes," Eusebio recalled, "she just wore me down. Six dozen was what she wanted; six dozen was what she got. And if I'd been here for the test flight, it would have been the same. Whatever my misgivings, she would have talked me around them."

Yalda said, "I wish we'd had a way of contacting her family. Or at least a friend somewhere. There must have been someone she would have wanted to be told."

Eusebio made a gesture of helplessness. "She was a runaway. Whatever farewells she was able to say would have been said long ago."

Yalda felt a surge of anger at that, though she wasn't even sure why. Was he exploiting people, by helping them escape their cos? There was no crime in offering a way out, so long as you were honest about what it entailed.

The hut was lit by a single lamp on the floor. Eusebio looked around the bare room appraisingly but resisted making any comment. Yalda had spent the last ten days here, struggling to find a way to salvage something from Benedetta's pointless death.

She said, "We need to be more careful with everything we do. We should always be thinking of the worst possibilities."

Eusebio buzzed curtly. "There are so many of those; can you be more specific?"

"Igniting the planet."

"Ah, the Gemma syndrome," he said wearily. "Do you think the farmers rushing to plant crops in the blast zone came up with that themselves? Acilio has people out spreading the idea, and organizing paid relocations."

"That's an awful lot of effort just to spite you," Yalda suggested. "Maybe he honestly believes there's a risk."

"A risk *compared with what?*" Eusebio retorted. "Compared with doing nothing while we wait to slam into a cluster of orthogonal stars? I've seen the image from the probe; that's not a wild guess anymore, it's a certainty."

"The worst case," Yalda persisted, "is that the engines on the *Peerless* malfunction in such a way that they deliver less thrust than they need to raise the mountain. And they sit there doing it for chime after chime—maybe bell after bell or day after day, if everyone who could shut them down is dead. There must be *some* point where whatever the Hurtlers did to Gemma would happen here. We've done tests to rule that out if all goes well—but we can't test the most extreme case; there's no scale model that will tell us what happens when a whole mountain of sunstone sits and burns from below, for days."

Eusebio rubbed his eyes. "All right, if I grant you all of that… what do you propose?"

"An air gap, all around the mountain."

"An air gap?"

"A trench," Yalda explained. "As deep as the lowest engines, and maybe a stroll wide. Then we dig channels under the engines so that all the exhaust gas can escape freely. That would make a big difference to the heat build-up in the rock, if the engines end up running in place."

"*A stroll wide?*" Eusebio closed his eyes and swayed backward, fighting not to use indecorous language.

Yalda said, "Look at it this way: a trench that wide would be enough to displace all those irritating farmers—for a reason they can't really argue against. You could even ask Acilio to help pay for it, seeing as he's so keen on fire safety."

Eusebio opened his eyes and regarded her pityingly. "Yes, the need to take a reasonable, consistent position will win him right over."

"No?"

"Everyone has their own form of vanity," he said. "You and I enjoy *being right*: we want to understand how the world itself works, and then humiliate our enemies by proving that their guesses were wrong. Like... you and Ludovico."

"Hmm." Ludovico had been dead for a couple of years now, but Yalda couldn't deny that she'd taken great pleasure in his defeat over the nature of the Hurtlers.

"That's not Acilio's nature," Eusebio continued. "And it's certainly not how he was raised. In his family's eyes, the most important event in history was my grandfather cheating them out of a business opportunity that they believed they were entitled to enjoy. And now the family's honor depends on my humiliation. For that, Acilio doesn't have to be *right* about anything; all he has to do is see me fail."

Yalda was sick of the whole stupid feud, but if Acilio was committed to creating obstacles then they'd just have to find ways around them. She said, "Maybe Paolo will pay for the trench."

Eusebio stood. "Let me think about it."

"There's something more we need to do," Yalda warned him.

"Of course there is." He sat again.

She said, "We need a plan, to give people a chance of surviving a Hurtler impact while the *Peerless* is away. We need lookouts in every village, equipment they can use to try to douse the fire..."

Yalda stopped; Eusebio was shivering. She walked over and squatted beside him, then put an arm across his shoulders.

"What is it?" Not merely the threat of more costs and more work; he had long grown inured to that.

"My co gave birth," Eusebio said, struggling to get the words out. "That's why I was in Zeugma; to see the children."

"She—?"

"Without me," he said. "Not willingly. If she'd wanted it, we would have done it together. But we waited, and I wasn't around, so her body just... made its own decision."

"I'm sorry." Yalda didn't know how to console him. She wanted to tell him that she'd been through the same kind of shock herself, but any comparison she made to Tullia would just offend him.

"My father told me it was because I was away so much," Eusebio said. "If I'd remained close to her, her body would have understood that we were waiting for the right time. But without a co, it gave up hope that the children would ever have a father."

Yalda wasn't sure if any of this was real biology, or just a mixture of old folk beliefs and an attempt not to talk about holin. Making the drug available to the crew was one thing, but Eusebio could never admit its use in his own family.

"They do have a father," she said.

"No, they don't," Eusebio replied bluntly. "I still love them, of course, but I'm not promised to them. When I see them, it doesn't…" He struck his chest with his fist.

Yalda understood. She'd cared for Tullia's children as well as she could, but for all the genuine moments of joy she'd felt in their presence, she knew it was not the same as the love her father had felt for her.

When Eusebio left, Yalda put out the lamp and sat in the dark. The only certainty lay with the waves that wrapped the cosmos like the wrinkles in her prison sleeve: they would come full circle in agreement with themselves, along with everything they'd built. Nothing else could be relied upon. No one truly controlled their own body; no one ruled over the smallest part of the world.

And yet… it was still in the nature of every person that their will, their actions, and the outcome *could* be in harmony. That could never be guaranteed, but nor was it so rare that it could be dismissed as a meaningless farce. The will, the body and the world could never be brought into perfect alignment, but knowledge could bind the three strands together more tightly. The right knowledge could have granted Tullia and Eusebia more power over their bodies; the right knowledge could have brought Benedetta safely to the ground.

Yalda was tired of mourning; nothing more could be done for the dead and the divided. The only way to do justice to their memory would be to find the knowledge that would allow the generations that followed them to live without the same risks and fears.

13

Giorgio threw a farewell party for Yalda in his home, a few saunters west of the university. Though she'd been working full-time on the *Peerless* for six years he had never officially relieved her of her post with the physics department, so it was also a kind of retirement celebration. Zosimo, the only one of her fellow students who had remained in academic life, gave an amusing speech about her early discoveries. "It used to be the case that if you came across someone reading a scientific journal and they kept turning the pages sideways or upside-down, it was a sure sign that they had no idea what they were looking at. Now, thanks to Yalda, it's proof that you're in the presence of an expert in rotational physics."

As Yalda wandered among the guests, she struggled to keep her feelings from turning into grief or self-pity. It might have been better to have vanished without ceremony, but if it was too late for that she could still try to make the break as painless as possible. The day before, she had bid farewell to Lucio, Claudio and Aurelio in a final letter—short and simple, as Lucio had never learned to read as well as his co—but even without this parting note they would not have been expecting to see her again. When Giusto died and she did not visit the family to join them in mourning, they would have understood that she was never coming back. She still wished her brother and her cousins well, but she could not be part of their lives. Now she had to start thinking of her friends in Zeugma the same way.

Daria found her in the courtyard, and instead of offering distracting small talk chose to tackle the subject head-on. "In the old days," she said, "every dozen generations, families would split up and the travelers would move a whole severance away. With no mechanised transport, that was it: no hope of visits, no hope of returning."

"Why?" Yalda had heard of the custom, but she'd never understood its

205

purpose.

"They thought it was healthy, to bring new influences to the children."

"A separation wasn't enough?" The new farm her father had bought had been that far from the one where she'd grown up.

Daria said, "There was less travel then, less mixing of people for other reasons. This was a way of forcing it."

Yalda buzzed skeptically. "Was it worth the effort? Were the children any healthier?"

"I don't know," Daria admitted. "It's difficult to study that kind of thing. But every biologist accepts that influences spread from person to person; some make us sick, some make us stronger. I'm glad your travelers will be coming from every city; at least they'll be starting with a good mixture."

"So what do we do if the mixture grows stale?" Yalda wondered.

"Learn enough about the things themselves to make new ones of your own," Daria replied smoothly.

"Ah, as simple as that." Was an influence a kind of... gas? A kind of dust? How did it leave and enter the body? What exactly did it do when it encountered your flesh? Nobody had the faintest idea.

Daria said, "If the *Peerless* comes back without that trick, I'll just have to hang on long enough to work it out for myself."

"What are you waiting for?" Yalda scolded her. "The *Peerless* isn't an excuse for everyone else to take a four-year holiday. You should think of it as a contest; you should be trying to beat the travelers to as many discoveries as possible. We might have the advantage of time, but you'll always have the advantage in numbers."

Daria was amused by this idea, but not dismissive. "It would be a matter of some pride," she conceded, "if we could greet them with at least one triumph of our own."

Lidia entered the courtyard, accompanied by Valeria and Valerio.

"You missed the speeches," Daria informed them.

"I'm glad to hear it," Lidia replied. She embraced Yalda. "Is it true that you're going to be a Councilor on the flying mountain?"

"Dictator, I think," Daria corrected her.

Yalda said, "More like a factory supervisor: as far as I'm concerned, my main job will be to ensure that all the machinery is being operated safely. For the first year or two that's likely to take precedence over everything else, but once the technical issues are under control we'll have to make arrangements for... ongoing governance."

"That sounds promising," Lidia enthused. "In a city of runaways, no one is going to settle for anything less than a fair division of power."

"Do you want to come and organize that for me?" Yalda pleaded. "Right now, I'm just hoping that any heated disputes can wait until after I'm dead."

Lidia pretended to be taking the invitation seriously, but it was clear what her answer would be.

The children had been hanging back, waiting for Lidia to finish her greeting. Valerio embraced Yalda awkwardly then went looking for food, but Valeria didn't flee.

"Are you enjoying your studies?" Yalda asked her.

"I like lens design," Valeria replied.

"It's an important subject." Eusebio had promised to hire Valeria to work on the fire watch project—and cheap, light, wide-field telescopes would be part of the equipment every village would need.

"I brought a gift for you," Valeria said. She handed Yalda a wooden tube.

"Thank you." Yalda removed the cap and pulled out a sheet of paper.

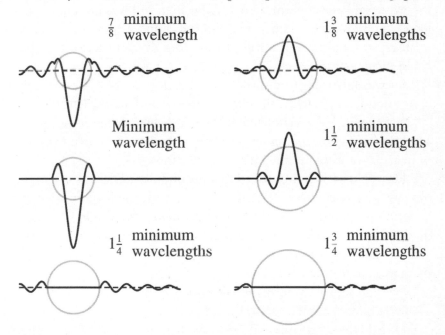

"It's beautiful," she said, touched and intrigued. "What is it?"

"Do you remember Nereo's equation?" Valeria asked her.

"Of course." Yalda had not had the time to do any original work in optics for years—and Nereo himself had died soon after she'd visited him in Red Towers—but she'd been longing to pursue his ideas about the interactions between light and matter.

"You explained it to me," Valeria said, "three years ago, when I'd just started at the university. And you showed me the solution for a source consisting of a single point—a 'luxagen.'"

"I remember." Yalda had been trying to convey to her just how little was still known about the subject, while offering a glimpse of one crack in their ignorance that might yet be widened.

"Not long after that," Valeria continued, "we were studying gravity. And I learned that the first thing Vittorio did after guessing the potential energy for a mass concentrated in a single point was to calculate what that meant for a mass arranged as a spherical shell."

"Ah." Yalda examined the sheet again, overcome with pride and delight. "And this is the equivalent, for the light field?"

"Yes."

Yalda studied the results. "These sizes you've written, they're the radius of each shell?"

Valeria said, "Yes. Vittorio showed that, outside the shell, the gravitational potential energy was exactly the same as it would have been if all the mass were just concentrated at the center, so I was hoping the light field would follow the same rule. When it didn't, I thought I'd made a mistake, so I had to wait until I'd learned a different technique that I could use as a cross-check."

Yalda was still trying to absorb the implications of what she was seeing. "For some sizes of shell... the external field *vanishes completely*?"

"That's right," Valeria confirmed. "That happens whenever the radius is a multiple of half the minimum wavelength. And when it's an odd number of quarter-wavelengths, the interior field vanishes."

Yalda would never have guessed that the undulating field from a myriad of point sources could cancel exactly over any extended region—let alone an infinite one, and from such a simple geometry. No wonder Valeria had doubted her first calculations; it was as if someone had claimed that a gross of clanging bells could be rendered inaudible merely by arranging them in a circle of just the right size.

"Have you shown Zosimo and Giorgio?"

Valeria said, "I wanted you to see it first."

Yalda held the sheet aside and embraced her. "It's a beautiful gift. Thank you." *Your mother should have been here to see this*, she thought, but the words were too strange to speak aloud.

Lidia said, "I don't want to risk annoying you both... but are these pictures of anything real?"

Yalda started to explain about the light field around the hypothetical particle Nereo had dubbed a luxagen, and how Valeria had added up that field for a multitude of luxagens arranged in a shell, but Lidia hushed her. "I meant something we can all see and touch."

Yalda thought for a while. What did it mean that luxagens were normally surrounded by furrows in the light field, but in the right configuration the landscape around them could become perfectly flat?

She said, "How about something you can feel, but never see?"

"What, thin air?" Lidia joked.

"Exactly." Yalda exchanged a glance with Valeria; she looked baffled for a moment, but then she understood.

"Nereo hoped that the light field might account for all the properties of matter," Yalda explained. "Not just burning fuel and glowing petals, but how a rock holds together instead of crumbling, and how it resists being crushed down to a speck. Why dust is sticky, and fine dust even stickier… but an inert gas like air, which everyone thinks of as the finest dust of all, doesn't stick to anything, not even itself."

"And these pictures are the answer?" Lidia was bemused.

"Not to everything," Yalda said, "but perhaps they're a clue to the last puzzle. It's not hard to see how *solids* could be built from luxagens: the particles would sit in the troughs of each others' serrated fields, which would hold them a certain distance apart from each other in a kind of array. Two stones you pick up off the ground won't stick to each other—even if you polish them flat—because with such vast numbers of particles you wouldn't expect them to form a single, perfect array. But a speck of dust is lighter, and small enough for the internal geometry to be less of a mishmash; there's more chance for everything to line up and make two specks adhere. So if gases are built from luxagens too—and are so fine as to be invisible—why don't they stick together even more strongly?"

Lidia still didn't see it; Yalda looked to Valeria for support.

"Suppose you arrange the luxagens in a spherical shell of just the right size," Valeria said. "Then the force that makes most regular arrangements of luxagens sticky will vanish outside the shell. A shell like that won't stick to anything—so maybe that's what gases are made of." She hesitated, then turned to Yalda. "I don't think that quite works, though. If you look at the potential energy curves at the edge of the shells with no external field, they always slope in such a way as to produce an outward force—so wouldn't that tear the shell itself apart?"

Yalda checked the diagrams. "Ah, you're right," she said. "So there must be something subtler going on."

"See, we don't have the answers here," Daria joked. "We need the *Peerless* to go out and fetch them for us."

"But this is close," Yalda insisted. "If it's not the whole story, it's still a powerful hint."

Yalda could have talked optics with Valeria all night, but that would only have made parting more difficult. "Have you seen your brother recently?" she asked.

"Two days ago," Valeria replied. "I looked after the children while he went to the factory."

"But you need to study!" Yalda hadn't meant to blurt out a rebuke, but she couldn't bear the thought of Valeria jeopardizing her own chances. "You can't afford to do that all the time," she added.

"I don't; Valerio helps too. And Amelio has other friends as well." Valeria was beginning to look uncomfortable; Yalda let it drop. Lidia and Daria would have helped with the children if Amelio had allowed it, but he was still angry with them for trying to persuade him and Amelia to wait. Yalda would never see Tullia's grandchildren, but she suspected Amelio would relent in the end and heal the rift with his other honorary Aunts.

Lidia said, "I'm glad I missed the speeches, but I hope I haven't missed all the food." Yalda led them indoors, where Giorgio's children were still running back and forth from the pantry, keeping everyone fed.

Yalda tried to keep the conversation from growing too solemn; she had no intention of making some kind of earnest declaration to each one of her friends, summing up and attempting to put right everything that had passed between them—as if they were business partners settling accounts. She had apologized often enough to Lidia for the unequal share she'd taken in the burden of raising the children, thanked Giorgio and Daria for their help at the times she'd received it, and offered encouragement to Valeria and Valerio whenever it had seemed likely to be well received. There was nothing more she could achieve with a few rushed words, and the last thing she wanted to do was sound like someone making death-bed reparations.

Around midnight, guests began making their excuses. Dozens of people from the university and the Solo Club—acquaintances with whom Yalda had played dice or argued some point of philosophy or physics—bid her good luck with the flight then departed without any fuss.

With the house almost empty, Giorgio approached her.

"Can we see you off at the station?" he asked.

"Of course."

Yalda had no luggage; everything she owned was in Basetown already, and everything she'd need was in the mountain itself. The six of them walked together down the quiet streets, with Gemma high above them lighting the way.

On the platform, with just a lapse to departure, Valerio started humming and wailing. Yalda was bemused; they hadn't been close since he was three. She bent down and embraced him, trying to quieten him before anyone else joined in.

"I'm not dying yet!" she joked. "Wait a year and a day, then you can mourn me. But don't forget that I'll have had a long life by then."

Valerio couldn't really make sense of this, but he recovered his composure. "I'm sorry, Aunty. Good luck with your journey."

"Look after your brother," she said. *And try not to imitate him.*

With her rear gaze, Yalda saw the guard scowling at her; the engine was already running and sparks were rising into the air. She released Valerio, raised a hand to the others, then leaped into an empty carriage as the train began to move.

She sat on the floor, eyes closed, braced against the shock of amputation.

From a distance, Mount Peerless appeared almost unchanged from its pristine state. As the train brought her closer, Yalda struggled to identify anything more than a slight thinning of the vegetation since the first time she'd set eyes on the peak. The mountain roads that had been widened and extended were still invisible from the ground, and even the mounds of excavated rubble from the new trench were lost in the haze.

Basetown was the end of the line. When Yalda walked out of the station the main square was deserted; where the markets had stood just two stints before there was bare, dusty ground. All the construction workers and traders had departed, and though there were probably dozens of Eusebio's people still around for the final cleanup, on her way to the office she encountered only fellow travelers. As well as inducing an eerie sense that she'd already parted company with the rest of the world, this raised the problem that, out of the six gross or so on the final list of recruits, she'd only managed to memorize a tiny fraction of their names.

"Hello Yalda!" a woman called from across the street.

"Hello!" That she knew the woman's face only made it more embarrassing.

"Not long now," the woman said cheerfully.

"No." Yalda resisted the temptation to take a bet on, "Time to tell your co to buy a telescope!" However good the odds were that this would be apt and welcome, it wasn't worth the risk of alienating someone who was actually bringing her co along for the ride.

Eusebio was in the office, poring over reports with Amando and Silvio; Yalda didn't disturb them. Her own desk was almost empty; before she'd left she'd been double-checking calculations for the navigational maneuvers the *Peerless* would need to perform if it encountered an unexpected obstacle. It looked as if they'd found the perfect route for the voyage—an empty corridor through the void, oriented in the right direction and long enough to take an age to traverse without coming close to a single star—but once they were above the atmosphere it was possible that fresh observations would reveal a hazard that needed to be side-stepped.

She worked through the details one more time. If the obstacle wasn't too large, they'd be able to swerve around it and still reach infinite velocity—albeit with even less fuel remaining for the rest of the journey than originally planned. There was no way of guaranteeing the *Peerless*'s triumphant return, but if the travelers failed to attain an orthogonal trajectory—with the Hurtlers tamed and time back home brought to a halt—they would have no advantage left at all.

When his assistants had left, Eusebio approached Yalda. "How did it go with your friends in Zeugma?" he asked.

"It was fine." Yalda didn't want him struggling to empathize, telling her that he understood how she must feel. She said, "I think we need name tags."

"Name tags?"

"For the travelers. Something we can all wear on necklaces, so we know who's who."

Eusebio looked harried; Yalda said, "I'll organize it myself, don't worry about it."

"All the workshops are empty," he said, spreading his arms to take in the whole ghost town. "Not just of people, of tools and materials."

"Not inside the *Peerless*, I hope."

The suggestion appeared to take Eusebio by surprise, but then he found himself with no grounds to object to it. "I suppose that makes sense." He checked a wall chart. "Workshop seven?"

"Yes."

Yalda found a spare copy of the recruits list. When she and Eusebio had first set out to sign up volunteers she could never have imagined filling a dozen sheets of paper with their names, but even this final census amounted to less than the population of her home village.

There were still trucks shuttling between Basetown and the *Peerless* every bell, but they were no longer in high demand; she ended up alone save for a driver she didn't really know, so she sat in the back by herself and watched the town receding into the haze. She wondered what would happen if she went to Eusebio and said: *I've changed my mind, I'm staying.* There were other people with the skills to take her place in everything she was expected to do; the project would not fall apart on the spot. But she knew she was caught in the trap she'd used herself on so many others: she was vain enough to believe that her presence might make the difference between success and failure. And if the thought of deserting the *Peerless* to while away four years on the ground waiting for the world's problems to be solved elsewhere made a thrillingly delinquent fantasy, the one thing she found more terrifying than the prospect of a journey through the void was the possibility of those four years of anticipation ending in silence.

The truck dropped her off at the nearest footbridge. The trench around the mountain was wider than the crevasse that split Zeugma, but this makeshift structure of rope and wood was no Great Bridge. Yalda gripped the hand-rope tightly as she began shuffling over the swaying planks.

The wind from the north was carrying dust from one of the excavation mounds directly toward her, stinging her eyes and skin. Halfway across she stopped, paralyzed. She'd crossed the bridge in stronger winds than this, but recalling those past ordeals didn't help.

The launch was five days away. It would take her a day to ascend to the workshop, and at least two to make all the tags. By that time, all the travelers would have joined her and the final evacuation of Basetown would have begun. If she entered the mountain now, she would not emerge again.

She hummed softly and tried to picture Tullia beside her, reassuring her. *What was she afraid of?* Death could claim her anywhere; there was no safe place left in the world. She could keep on dwelling on the dangers of the journey and the bitterness of exile—or she could treat this as a calculated gamble that might lead her to an almost perfect sanctuary: a place where generations could think and study, plan and experiment, test their ideas and refine their methods, for as long as it took to find a way to banish the threat and return home.

If the *Peerless* had simply been a city in the desert—a city of scholars, a city with free holin, a city with no knife-wielding thugs who could meld her arms together and throw her in a cell—might she not have wandered inside its walls and never come out? Might she not have happily declared: *this is the place where I will die?*

She steadied herself and walked across the bridge.

The meeting hall had been designed with room for twice the current population of the *Peerless*, though Yalda wasn't sure how well the elegantly tiered floor would function later, in the absence of gravity. She stood at the entrance, greeting people as they filed in, handing out name tags from the twelve buckets into which she'd sorted them, along with necklaces from a separate container. The travelers seemed remarkably calm; there was no time to talk with anyone at length, but she'd seen more anxiety on display at some of the recruitment drives in Zeugma.

At the appointed time there were less than two dozen tags unclaimed, and still a chance that some stragglers had merely been delayed. Yalda was astonished; only one volunteer in three dozen had changed their mind and backed out. If she'd been asked a year ago to bet on the chance of her own desertion, she would have put the odds at one in three.

Eusebio was waiting by the stage. He checked the clock and walked over to Yalda.

"Should I start?" he wondered.

"Give it another chime for latecomers," she suggested. "It's not as if any-one here will be worrying about baby-sitters charging them overtime."

Eusebio winced; a man who'd attended one of their free talks in Zeugma had cornered them and demanded payment on precisely those grounds. "Don't remind me," he said. "In a couple of stints I'll be back on the Variety Hall circuit, recruiting for the fire watch."

"Recruiting?" Yalda was surprised. "Does that have to fall to you? I thought the project had plenty of other backers."

"There are lots of people spreading the word," Eusebio agreed, "but we still need to build up support much further, or the whole thing will be too patchy to have any real chance of working."

Yalda wondered if she should wish him luck with his new endeavor and leave it at that, but then she decided that she had nothing to lose.

"You're not tempted to join us?" she asked. "No one can see this through to the end, but you could watch over the *Peerless* for a little longer."

A flicker of discomfort crossed Eusebio's face, hardening into defensive-ness. "I always made it clear what my role would be. I never promised to do more than build the rocket."

"I know," Yalda said mildly.

"I could leave my children if I had to," he admitted. "It's my father who's raising them, more than me. And it's true that other people would champion the fire watch." He trailed off.

Yalda fought against an urge to fill the silence, to tell him that she understood his choice and that she had no reason to reproach him for it. She didn't want to hurt him or embarrass him. But she wanted to hear his whole answer.

"If I joined you," Eusebio said, "and the *Peerless* failed… then I doubt that anyone else would have the resolve to try the same thing again. It would still be our only real chance to protect ourselves, but most people would see the whole idea as discredited. That's why I'm staying. I need to be able to fight for this"—he gestured at the mountain that surrounded them—"all over again, if it comes to that."

Yalda couldn't fault his reasoning, but the prospect he was painting chilled her. She should have been happy to imagine a second chance for the people she was leaving behind, but the thought of even the *Peerless* being dispensable in the end didn't do much to bolster her justification for her own choice.

She was spared the need to respond; an elderly man was approaching with an apologetic countenance. "I took a wrong turn," he explained. "This place is a labyrinth."

"Could you tell me your name, sir?"

"Macario."

As Yalda fetched Macario's tag, Eusebio left her and took to the stage. By the time the latecomer had his necklace in place, the hall had fallen silent.

"Welcome back to the *Peerless*," Eusebio began. "It's almost seven years now since I approached my friend and teacher, Yalda, to discuss what could be done about the Hurtlers. At that time, there didn't seem to be much chance of defending ourselves. We barely understood what we were confronting—and most of what we did know only made us feel more powerless. But now we have the start of an answer. Across the world, the *Peerless* and its travelers are reason for hope."

There were lamps throughout the hall, and no lighting technicians here to extinguish them and throw a spotlight on the stage. Yalda watched the audience with her rear gaze as Eusebio thanked them for their courage and commitment. She could see signs of apprehension here and there—bodies hunched anxiously, gazes lowered—but most people appeared steadfast, reconciled to their decision.

"My colleagues and I have worked as hard as we could to ensure that your journey will begin in safety and comfort. But I have never lied to you in the past and I won't lie to you now: we don't have the power to promise you anything. In spite of our best efforts, seven people have already died: six construction workers, and a volunteer undertaking a test flight. I can't guarantee that in two days' time, this whole mountain won't be turned into rubble and flames. If anyone in this hall believes that can't happen, then you should leave and return to your homes, because you are here under false premises.

"My colleagues and I have also tried to anticipate what you and your children will need in order to survive and flourish as the *Peerless* travels through the void. But nobody has made this journey before. There is no compendium of knowledge on these matters; there are no experts on the territory that lies ahead. If anyone has misunderstood this—if anyone thought that they'd been guaranteed the necessities of life for a dozen generations— then you, as well, should leave and look for those certainties elsewhere, because they are not present on the *Peerless*."

Yalda understood Eusebio's need to speak plainly, but she wondered if he wasn't going too far. Many people were clearly uncomfortable now, and a few were visibly agitated. It was not that they were learning anything new, but everyone had their own way of dealing with the same difficult truths.

"In two days' time, if all goes well, you will leave the world behind," Eusebio continued. "Your fate will be in your hands then, not mine. But the *Peerless* is a complex machine, and though you have all been trained as thoroughly as possible for your particular duties, only a few of you understand that machine in its entirety. The process of education will continue—and I hope that within a generation or two every adult living in the *Peerless* will grasp its intricacies more fully than I do myself. For now, though, it is Yalda's role to determine how best to operate this machine, how to ameliorate any crisis, how to resolve any dispute among you, and how to deal with any other difficulty or controversy that arises. Yalda, her deputy Frido, and whoever else she appoints to assist and advise her, are responsible for keeping you safe, and their decisions must be final. It's not for me to tell you how the *Peerless* will rule itself in the eras to come, but as of this moment—and for as long as she sees fit—Yalda must be your sole authority. If you can't promise her your absolute loyalty and obedience, then leave now, because you are a danger to everyone here."

Only a few people were discourteous enough to respond to this proclamation by turning to stare appraisingly at Yalda, and she suspected that she was, by far, the traveler least satisfied with these arrangements. But since her omnipotence included the power of delegation, it was probably Frido who should have felt most put upon.

"To those of you I have persuaded to walk away tonight," Eusebio said, "be assured that you've already earned my gratitude and respect, and you will not lose it by reappraising your position. But now I'm done with warnings and discouragement. To all of you who choose to remain—with your eyes open to the dangers and rigors ahead—my message is one of promise. Together, we've built this beautiful, intricate seed, and as we prepare to cast it into the void I believe that it has not only the resilience to survive, but also the capacity to grow into an extraordinary new civilization. I am already humbled by your courage and tenacity, but I leave you now with the hope that the achievements of your descendants will be the marvel of all ages. Good luck—and welcome to your home."

As the audience began cheering, Yalda decided that Eusebio's judgment had been right after all. If he'd said nothing to remind them of the risks they faced, all his praise would have sounded like empty flattery. Now, even if a handful of people backed out, those remaining could take some strength from the fact that they'd passed one more test of their resolve.

Eusebio called Frido to the stage. "I'm sure that everyone knows their stations for the launch," Frido said, "but I need to ask you to wait here and confirm them with me, or Rina or Lavinia—they'll be standing over to my right, shortly. And first of all, anyone leaving us, please come forward and return your name tags."

A few people began moving tentatively toward the stage. Eusebio spoke briefly with Frido, then embraced him. Frido had told Yalda that it was the sight of his grandchildren that had swayed him into joining her; he'd been paid well enough for his work on the project to ensure that they'd want for nothing, but whatever the prospects for dousing a Hurtler's fire, only the *Peerless* offered any hope of dealing with the coming orthogonal stars.

When they parted, Eusebio approached Yalda. "I need to get moving," he said. "The evacuation's on a tight schedule. Do you want to walk down with me?"

Yalda's launch station was three strolls below the hall, almost at ground level. They could spend a day traveling together, reminiscing, exchanging their final thoughts.

"I need to stay here and see how many people we've lost," she said.

"Frido and his staff can reallocate their duties," Eusebio replied. "You have to trust them to handle things like that."

"I do trust them," Yalda said. "But I should be here with them, until everything is sorted out."

"All right." Eusebio seemed confused by her decision, but he wasn't going to argue with her in front of so many onlookers. "Have a safe journey, then," he said.

"You too." She buzzed softly. "It's going to be a long four years for both of us. Just don't let my descendants find three suns when they get back."

"I'll do my best." Eusebio met her gaze, trying to judge where things stood between them. Yalda let nothing show on her face but simple friendship and a contained sorrow at their parting. There was no untangling the rest of it, no point even acknowledging it now. After a moment, Eusebio stopped searching for anything more.

"Good luck," he said. He lowered his eyes and walked past her, out of the hall.

Yalda stood watching her new neighbors jostling for access to Frido and his assistants. Out of nowhere, she felt a sudden surge of anger for

Daria. With no responsibilities, and so close to retirement, why couldn't she have come and taught here?

A young solo was standing at the edge of the crowd, one of the recruits who'd witnessed Benedetta's death. Only two people from that group had chosen to stay with the project.

Yalda walked up to her. "Fatima?"

"Hello," the girl replied shyly. Though they'd met before, Eusebio's proclamation of Yalda's powers had probably rendered her as unapproachable now as the most self-important Councilor.

"What's your job?" Yalda asked her. "I ought to know, but I've forgotten where we assigned you."

"The medicinal garden. Weeding." Fatima sounded disappointed, but resigned to her fate.

"But you'll still have classes. I'll teach you, if you're interested."

"You'll teach me about light?"

"Yes."

Fatima hesitated, then added, emboldened, "Everything you know?"

"Of course," Yalda promised. "How else are you going to end up knowing twice as much as I do? But right now, let's see if we can find some other people working in the garden with you, then we can all walk down together."

14

Yalda sat on her bench in the navigators' post, glancing across the moss-lit room past Frido and Babila to the clock on the wall, waiting for its counterparts to open the feeds and set the depths of the mountain on fire.

The engines that would lift the *Peerless* off the ground were controlled from three dozen feed chambers that were spread out across the width of the mountain. Within each chamber was a system of clockwork and gyroscopes that regulated the flow of liberator into the sunstone below, taking account of both the overall launch plan and the need to fine-tune the distribution of forces to keep the rocket from tipping or swerving as it ascended. Two machinists watched over each engine feed, ready to perform any simple interventions or repairs, while a network of signaling ropes made it possible to summon assistance from a circle of neighbors, or if necessary from farther afield.

Over the past year, the machinists and the navigators had rehearsed their responses to dozens of possible emergencies. Eusebio and Frido had written the first scripts, and then Yalda and Babila, an engineer from Red Towers, had joined in, until every survivable disaster they could imagine had been prepared for, and the whole team had agreed on the protocols. Well-made clockwork figurines, Yalda had joked, could have done the job in their stead, but then they would have needed a new set of protocols dictating what to do if those figurines jammed.

"Two lapses to ignition," Frido announced, as if no one else were watching. Basetown would be empty now, and the last train well on its way to Zeugma—though it would not have arrived at its destination before flames began consuming the far end of the track. If someone put their ear to the calmstone rails, they might hear the launch before the vibrations reached them through the looser, heterogeneous rocks below. The *Peerless* would rise silently above Zeugma's horizon, bright as Gemma in the eastern sky;

the rumble of the ground, the hiss in the air would come later. Standing on the balcony with Lidia and Daria, perhaps Valeria and Valerio would wave to their departing Aunt. Eusebio would still be on the train heading west; Yalda suspected that he would have secured the rear carriage for himself, for the sake of the view.

"One lapse."

Yalda experienced a sudden, visceral urge to flee—or commit whatever act of violence or supplication it would take to extract herself from danger. But there were no choices now that led back to solid ground, not even for the omnipotent ruler of the *Peerless*. Frido had let an earlier landmark pass in silence: three lapses before ignition had been the last chance to cancel the launch. Propagating the decree by rope relay all the way to the edge of the mountain might have taken as little as a lapse and a half—if everyone had responded swiftly, without mishap or delay—but in setting the cut-off time they'd erred on the side of safety. For the message to have reached some, but not all, of the feed chambers, leaving the rest to fire on schedule, would have been the worst outcome imaginable.

"Six pauses."

On this cue Yalda lay back on her bench and strapped herself in place, just as she'd done in the drills. Since Benedetta's death no one had attempted to reprise and perfect her feat, but two heavily sedated arborines had survived equivalent trips, disgruntled once the drugs wore off but physically intact. Traveling through the void had been shown not to be fatal, in and of itself. And with the riskiest part of the journey—the landing—indefinitely deferred, the odds for the *Peerless* were not so bad. The only real difference from all the test flights was a matter of scale.

Frido counted, "Three. Two. One."

Across the mountain, the feeds would be opening now, sending liberator trickling down crevices in the hardstone cladding that protected the fuel. Yalda turned to glance at the clock; only two pauses had passed, and the gray powder had a long way to fall before it reached exposed sunstone. Babila took on the duty of counting the descent: "Five. Six. Seven."

Yalda braced her tympanum.

"*Eight.*"

In less than a flicker the wave of compression came hurtling back up through the rock. Through the bench she felt the first insistent tremor from the nearest ignition points, then the pounding of ever more engines reached her until even the most distant were hammering at her body. For one terrified moment she could discern no change in her weight—her skin reported nothing but the bench's vibrations—then she tried to raise an arm and was rewarded with unambiguous resistance, easily overcome but enough to banish her fears. If the engines had been too weak to lift the mountain, she would not have felt this. No amount of ineffectual flame and fury, no mere buffeting and shaking, could have mimicked the glorious signature of acceleration.

Belatedly, she checked the balance beside her, isolated in a vibration-deadening frame from the jittering floor. The polished hardstone scrood-weight was stretching the spring by close to twice the original amount, putting the thrust within a notch of its intended value. There could be no doubt that the *Peerless* was rising, climbing ever faster into the sky.

Chilled air flowed through the room; the cooling system was working. Not only had the mountain failed to collapse into smouldering rubble, or squat on the ground building up heat until it set the world on fire, it wasn't even going to cook its passengers alive.

Yalda's relief turned to exhilaration. She tried to picture the events below: flame spilling out from the hole the severed mountain had left in the ground, hot gas and burning dust swirling across the plain to engulf the empty buildings of Basetown. If she envied Eusebio anything now, it was the sight of a dazzling white streak of fire splitting the eastern sky, when all she had before her was this trembling red-lit cave. But no matter; she'd write him a note and have it carved in stone to be passed down the ages: *You witnessed the launch in all its splendor, but when I looked down on your world it was small as a pebble.*

The room shuddered; Yalda was thrown sideways in her restraint, her euphoria banished. She looked to the gyroscopes at the center of the room, struggling to interpret their quivering. She'd sat with Frido and Eusebio, calculating the motion of these devices under all manner of calamities, but now her mind was blank and she couldn't match what she was seeing to any of those predictions.

Babila caught her eye with a series of symbols on an outstretched palm: **One engine failed, but we've recovered.** That made sense; if the rocket had remained unbalanced and the mountain had started tumbling, the axes of the gyroscopes would have ended up far from their starting markers. The machines feeding the other engines had detected the incipient swerve, and those positioned to compensate were doing so.

One feed had malfunctioned, out of three dozen. That was no worse than the proportion of recruits who'd pulled out. The machinists responsible for it wouldn't even leave their benches to attempt repairs while the engines were still producing extra thrust, laboring to overcome the world's gravity. This was failure at a level they'd anticipated, not an emergency. It could wait the six chimes until their weight became normal.

Yalda checked the clock; a single chime had passed. The *Peerless* would be about a separation above the ground now. She longed for a window—and some magic that would make it worthwhile by granting her a view through the flames—but even the lucky people in the highest observation chambers would only be able to see the distant horizon, gradually shrinking until it was obscured by the glare of the exhaust. By the time their path had curved sufficiently to allow them to look back on their starting point, the world really would appear as small as a pebble.

The room lurched again, a sickening swing abruptly curtailed. Yalda steadied herself and peered anxiously at the gyroscopes; the rocket remained level. Had a second engine cut out, or had the first recovered spontaneously? Even two dead engines didn't threaten their stability, but ongoing failures at this rate certainly would. Whatever had happened, the machinists on site would leave their benches now, make inspections and report.

Yalda looked across at Frido; he signaled tersely: **Patience**. Until they had more information there was nothing the navigators could do. The *Peerless* was still under control, and still ascending at close to the target rate. If that much of their luck continued, in two more chimes they'd reach the point where they could shut down all the engines without fear of plummeting back to the ground. In a wide, slow orbit around the sun, they could assess the situation and make repairs. Dispiriting as such a setback would be, better a delay and some damage to morale than have the *Peerless* turn into a spiraling firework.

For a third time, the rocket staggered and then caught itself. Yalda felt as if she were back on the footbridge over the trench, paralyzed by the sight of the abyss beneath her—and watching the ropes that supported her snapping one by one. *Where were the reports from the machinists?* She stared at the bank of paper tape writers connected to the signaling ropes. Though the devices had never been used outside the *Peerless*, they'd proved invaluable during the construction phase. Only adjacent chambers were connected directly, but messages that needed to go farther could be relayed from chamber to chamber. These particular units had been tested thoroughly—most recently when the machinists had first reached their stations prior to the launch.

Finally, one writer began disgorging a message. Babila could reach it without leaving her bench; she grabbed the end of the strip and peered at it, frowning, before the message was complete. Having the thing print actual symbols would have made it too complicated, so they'd devised and memorized a simple code that could be transmitted by tugging on either of two ropes.

From chamber four, Babila wrote on her palm, stretching her hand to fit more words. **Feed stopped. Waiting**. Chamber four was out at the rim; the message had reached them via two intermediaries.

That would have been the first failure, with the machinist following the protocol and delaying inspection until the thrust was reduced and movement became easier. But then almost immediately, another message arrived: **From chamber three. Feed stopped. Investigating.**

Chamber three was also at the rim, right next to chamber four. What source of failure, Yalda wondered, could depend on proximity? Dust from construction rubble—somehow missed in all the inspections—shaken out of its hiding place and rendered airborne by the vibrations?

That made no sense, though. Coarse enough debris might jam the clockwork—delaying the feed's opening in the first place—but Yalda was sure there was no part of the machinery where grit in the cogs could cause the feed to close once it was already open.

Chamber four, then chamber three… she wasn't going to wait to learn where the third failure had been. She held up her hand to Babila. **Message to chamber two, and all its neighbors: Make a full inspection.**

Babila started working the ropes. Frido caught Yalda's eye.

Sabotage? he asked. His face bore an expression of disbelief. This was not a scenario they'd anticipated.

Just being cautious, she replied. Whatever the cause of the first two failures, it could do no harm to test the assumption that their proximity was more than a coincidence.

Yalda turned to the clock; in a couple of lapses they would reach planetary escape velocity. The protocols dictated that three failures was the limit; one more and she'd have no choice but to shut down all the engines as soon as it was safe and let the *Peerless* drift around the sun until they'd diagnosed and remedied the problem.

Another of the tape writers started up. This one was out of Babila's reach; she unstrapped herself and lumbered across the floor, pausing to strengthen her legs with extra flesh from her torso. As she read the message her tympanum twitched, as if she couldn't stop herself silently cursing. Then she turned away from the machine and wrote across her chest: **From chamber two. Intruder sighted. Pursuing.**

Yalda and Frido joined her in spreading the news—first to those chambers that were close to number two but where the message would not have been seen already. The rope system was faster than any messenger on foot, but it was beginning to seem hopelessly slow and unwieldy.

When they'd finished Yalda stood beside the tape writers, disoriented and frustrated. *An intruder?* Accepting the notion was difficult enough, but her role made it even harder to bear. She should have been running through the feed chambers trying to catch the saboteur, not hanging around here playing message clerk.

Six chimes from ignition—precisely on schedule—the other feeds proved that they were operating flawlessly by cutting back the rocket's thrust from two gravities to one, all the while smoothly maintaining the balancing act compensating for the dead engines. The *Peerless* was four times as far from the center of the world now than it had been at launch—and moving almost five times faster than it needed to be to continue its ascent indefinitely. To the astronomers tracking their flight from the ground, the journey would appear to be proceeding uneventfully. One more jammed feed, though, and the whole world would have known that they were in trouble.

Yalda tentatively relaxed her tympanum; the hammering of the engines was still unpleasant, but it wasn't intolerable.

"I think speech is viable again," she shouted at her companions.

What? Babila wrote on her chest.

Yalda turned to Frido. "So who's the number one candidate to send in a saboteur?"

Frido's expression made it clear that he knew who she had in mind, but he still balked at the idea. "*Six gross* casualties, all innocent people...?"

"If it was Acilio, he wasn't trying to murder us," Yalda replied. "If that had been the aim he would have sent someone after the gyroscopes; he could have crashed the *Peerless* when it was barely off the ground, and made a big display of it for everyone watching from Zeugma."

"So he wanted us drifting?" Frido suggested. "Demoralised by the engine failures, hanging around in orbit until we'd taken every feed apart and inspected every component a dozen times. Nobody dead, but enough of a setback to humiliate Eusebio."

"Who's this Acilio?" Babila asked.

"A Councilor in Zeugma," Yalda explained wearily. "His grandfather and Eusebio's grandfather had a business dispute—"

Babila held up a hand to stop her. "I don't care about anyone's squabbling ancestors. His name and position should be enough for the people who return to find him and kill him."

Yalda said, "Yeah, we're not interested in those barbaric generations-long feuds."

One of the tape writers sprung to life; Yalda stepped forward and began decoding the message. "From chamber one," she read. "Intruder captured. Claims he's alone. Bringing him to you."

Half a bell later, four machinists entered the navigator's post. Pia, Delfina and Onesta were walking in single file, carrying their captive on their shoulders; they'd extruded extra arms to hold him in place, but he did not appear to be struggling. The fourth machinist, Severo, was too short to join in the formation, so he walked ahead of the women as a lookout.

The machinists dropped their burden in front of the navigators; the saboteur crouched on the stone, his face turned to the floor. He wasn't wearing a name tag, but Yalda was almost certain that she recognized him.

"Nino?"

He didn't reply. She squatted for a better look; it was him. She still remembered handing him his tag before Eusebio's big speech.

"Why?" she demanded, angry and perplexed. Nino had witnessed Benedetta's crash, but he had still chosen to stay with them; she'd thought that was a sign of his commitment. "What did Acilio offer you?"

At the mention of the name Nino's rear eyes flickered toward her, all but confirming her guess. "Is there anyone else here working for him?" she asked.

Nino's reply was inaudible beneath the noise of the engines. "Speak louder," Yalda yelled. "Who else did he recruit?"

"I only know about myself," Nino insisted. "If there are others, I was never told."

Yalda addressed the machinists. "You did a good job. You should go back to your posts now; I don't want any feeds left unguarded."

"Are you sure you can control him?" Delfina asked. "He's a fast runner. You should fetch some melding resin."

Melding resin? Yalda said, "We won't let him out of this room. Please, protect your feeds."

When they'd gone, Yalda sat on the floor in front of Nino. "Tell me the truth," she pleaded. "Is there anyone else? If the *Peerless* ends up damaged, it's your life too."

"There are tools in the next chamber," Babila announced darkly. "Frido could fetch them for us."

"Tools?"

"Screwdrivers, chisels, awls," Babila explained.

Yalda said, "Just… let me talk to him."

She turned back to Nino. "Start at the beginning. If you want us to believe you, you have to tell us everything."

Nino kept his eyes cast down. "I lied to you," he admitted. "I have children."

Yalda recalled him claiming that his co had died when he was young, but she'd never believed that; she'd thought he was fleeing from pressure to raise a family. "So why be apart from them?"

"Gemma destroyed my farm," he said. "I was already in debt. The Councilor said he'd pay what I owed—and pay my brother enough to look after all the children."

"In return for what?"

"First, just to join you and… spy for him." Nino's voice faltered, though Yalda wasn't sure if he was ashamed of his actions or merely embarrassed. "I was hoping that might be enough—that I might not have to go into the void myself. But then he gave me instructions for jamming the feeds, and said he'd double the payment to my family if the *Peerless* went dark within one bell of the launch."

"How did he know any details about the feeds?" Yalda had forgotten where Nino was meant to be working, but he certainly hadn't been in training for a machinist's job.

"I don't know," Nino replied. "The Councilor knew more about this rocket than I did. He must have had other spies."

"Other spies *where*?" Yalda pressed him. "In the construction crew, or among the travelers?"

"I don't know," Nino repeated flatly.

"What did you use to stop the feeds?" she asked.

"These." He opened two pockets and took out some small rocks. "I jammed them under the emergency shutoff levers for the liberator tanks. I was told to do that for as many feeds as I could, until the machinists got word to shut down all the engines."

There were several such levers in each feed chamber—some of them far from the machinists' posts. The chambers were so crowded with equipment that it would have been no great feat to enter and leave them unseen, especially while everyone was confined to their benches.

Yalda took one of the rocks from him. It was a kind of soft powderstone, shedding a fine sand even as she handled it. Jammed under a lever, before long it would have simply crumbled and fallen away. If Nino hadn't been caught in the act they might never have known what had really happened, and ended up convinced that the feeds themselves were at fault.

"And then what?" she asked.

"Nothing else," Nino said. "If I didn't get caught, I was meant to blend in again: just go back to my station and do my job."

"So after the sabotage was over, you'd be ready to pull your weight?" Yalda asked sarcastically. "Ready to be part of the team again?"

"I never wanted to harm anyone!" Nino protested vehemently. "The *Peerless* was meant to drift in the void for a while—that's all. Once the Councilor got what he wanted, why would I bear any ill will toward you?"

"Whatever your background really is," Yalda replied, "you've seen more than enough since we recruited you to know how dangerous this was. Don't pretend that it never crossed your mind that you could have killed us all."

Nino tensed angrily at the accusation, but his silence stretched on too long to end in an indignant denial. "I asked the Councilor about that," he admitted finally. "He said if the mountain crashed into the ground, it would be a mercy."

"*A mercy?*"

Nino looked up and met Yalda's gaze. "He said the whole idea of a city in the void was insane. One by one, things would go wrong—things that couldn't be fixed without help from outside. Within a generation you'd all be starving. Eating the soil. Begging for death."

Yalda sent a message up to the nearest construction workshop, summoning people with the skills to create a secure prison cell, but she expected it would take a couple of days for them to arrive, lugging supplies. As a stopgap she shifted the food out of the pantry that served the navigators' post and improvised a latch for the door, using tools and spare parts from the adjacent feed chamber. The navigators would be sleeping in shifts, so there would always be at least two of them awake—and by moving the bed right next to the pantry door, it provided a barricade and allowed even the sleeper to act as a third guard.

Babila had offered to escort Nino up through the mountain and organize his incarceration in a distant storeroom—for the sake of getting him as far away as possible from anything vulnerable to further sabotage—but Yalda preferred to have him nearby, in case she thought of something important that she'd failed to ask him about Acilio's scheme. According to the recruitment records Nino was unschooled, but as an experienced farmer he'd been destined for the same job on the *Peerless*. Yalda had no reason to trust him to tell the truth about anything, but his account of his own actions struck her as plausible, even if he was probably embellishing the story or omitting details in order to portray himself in the best possible light.

As her sense of shock and anger faded, Yalda found herself feeling a kind of battered exhilaration at the way things had actually unfolded. The *Peerless* had been tripped, three times, but it had kept its balance—and if the test had been unwelcome, the outcome was still worth celebrating. They had proved that the machinery on which their lives depended was every bit as resilient as they'd hoped—and they had humiliated an enemy in the bargain.

Perhaps she and Eusebio had been foolish not to anticipate how far Acilio would go. But what more could they have done to protect themselves? Hired people to travel the world and check every crew member's story? That would have done wonders for the recruitment rate—and told them nothing of value, since every runaway lied, with good reason.

If Nino's actions really were the end of it—the old world's last feeble swat at the new—that was cause for celebration, too. As Daria had said, separation was painful, but it was time to break away from the old influences.

We can't spare his life, Frido told Yalda, raising the words across his chest. Perhaps his silence was out of concern for the prisoner's feelings—but then, Babila was sleeping, and they all grew tired at times of shouting over the sound of the engines.

Why not? Yalda wasn't surprised by his advice, but she'd been dreading its eventual arrival from some quarter or another.

Once we have all the information we can get from him, Frido replied, **the most important thing is deterring anyone else in Acilio's pay. If we can't find the other agents, the next best thing is to make them too afraid to act.**

Yalda did not find this persuasive. **Once we're no longer visible from the ground, Acilio has no stake in doing anything more to us. Whatever setbacks we suffer, they can't embarrass Eusebio if they go unseen. And even if Acilio did want to harass us further, how could any agent be rewarded for carrying out his wishes when the payoff couldn't possibly depend on it?** She could understand Acilio's deal with Nino: even if Nino had no way of seeing it honored, his brother could have gone to Acilio and said "Everyone knows the rocket went dark, so where's the money you promised us?" But given that Acilio had made no effort to annihilate the *Peerless* at launch, she couldn't see him offering a second saboteur money for his family conditional on the *Peerless* failing to return at all.

You may be right about that, Frido conceded, **but even if Nino wasn't trying to kill us, he certainly betrayed us. He has no place among us anymore. People won't accept anything less than his death.**

"So are you planning on staging an uprising if I don't agree?" Yalda hadn't trusted her intended sarcasm to come across in symbols alone, but after shouting the words over the engine noise she wasn't sure that the shift in modes had been particularly helpful.

"All I'm saying is that it will weaken your authority," Frido shouted back.

So I should kill a man for the sake of my authority?

Frido considered the question seriously. **I suppose that depends on how many people you think will die, if you lose control here.**

Yalda said, "I don't flatter myself that I'm the one pillar of sanity that can keep the *Peerless* on course."

"I'm not suggesting that either," Frido assured her. **But whenever power changes hands, there's a risk of violence—unless you just resign at the first hint of dissatisfaction.**

Yalda didn't know how to reply to that. Did Frido covet her position? It had been less than two days since the launch, less than four since Eusebio had given her this role. She found the burden so unwelcome that the thought of anyone aspiring to take it from her had never crossed her mind before. But if it was so unwelcome, perhaps she should relinquish it? If Eusebio had appointed Frido ruler of the *Peerless* she would never have objected; why not correct his decision before anyone grew too attached to the status quo?

And then instead of Nino dying to keep her in power, he could die to give her an easy life.

The observation chamber was a shallow cave cut into the side of the mountain, sealed against the void by a tilted dome of clearstone panes. Standing at the edge of the cave, Yalda gazed down the slope and confirmed that the plains from which the mountain had once risen truly were gone. A haze of scattered light from the engines spilt past the rim of the mountain's base, like the harbinger of some spectacular dawn, yet it was above that glow—though still unprecedentedly *downhill*—that the blazing sun was now fixed. Yalda stretched out her arm, and with her rear eyes saw the shadow it cast on the roof of the cave.

The polygons of clearstone around her had become pitted by debris during the launch; the flaws caught the sunlight, creating distracting specks of brightness that competed for her gaze with the true sky beyond. She would have struggled to locate her target, had she not known in advance where to search for it: about halfway between the sun and the "horizon" implicitly defined by the chamber's floor.

To her naked eye the slender crescent cradled a disk of featureless gray, but through the theodolite's small telescope the planet's night side was revealed as an elaborate patchwork of hues. She recognized a few tiny splotches of pure wheatlight, but mostly the colors of the forests and fields were woven together too tightly to separate. She thought of Tullia—on the peak of this very mountain, not so long ago—hunting for the spectral signature of plant life on other worlds.

No cities were visible at this remove. No wildfires, either; even if the crater the *Peerless* had left behind was still smouldering, here was proof that the launch had not created another Gemma. Yalda shuddered, imagining for a moment how it would have felt to look back and discover that everything they'd been fighting to protect had been consigned to flames.

She recorded the bearing from the theodolite's dials, then took sightings of Gemma, the inner planet Pio, and a dozen bright stars. Four Hurtlers were visible, long gleaming barbs skewering the scene like the tools of a blind but indefatigable assassin. Clockwork and gyroscopes wouldn't be enough to guide the *Peerless* safely to its destination, the empty corridor where it could drift for an age without fear of being stabbed from any angle. Only a routine of meticulous observations, calculations and adjustments could lift the odds of a successful journey above those of Benedetta's automated probes.

The calculations took more than a bell, but the results were encouraging: the *Peerless*'s position and orientation were very close to the values specified in the flight plan, and the small adjustments she'd pass on to the feed chambers would easily nudge the vehicle back toward that ideal path.

Yalda was reluctant to leave. She aimed the telescope at her old home again, trying to commit its unfamiliar face to memory. On the ground, there'd been farewell after farewell, but this was the final parting.

As a pang of loneliness grew in her, she tried to assuage it by confronting the subject directly. If she'd had the chance to bring anyone she wished along with her, who would she have chosen? Eusebio and Daria would have been enough to keep her company, she decided; better that Lidia and the children, Giorgio and his family, Lucio and the others all stayed put. If everyone she cared about had come along for the ride, she might have felt tempted to abandon the idea of the *Peerless* ever returning, content to imagine this fortunate few, safe and self-sufficient, drifting on through the void with their rear eyes firmly shut.

Satisfied that the emergency had passed and no more saboteurs were likely to emerge in her absence, Yalda decided to take a short trip up through the mountain. She'd received news of some minor damage via the rope network, and though the repairs were reportedly proceeding smoothly she wanted to see how things stood for herself.

One of the feed chambers for the second tier of engines had suffered a partial ceiling collapse during the launch; it had been empty at the time, so no one had been harmed. When Yalda arrived a work team was still shifting rubble, and Palladia, a former mining engineer who'd been involved in the construction phase, was on site assessing the damage and making plans to insert a new supporting column.

"Can you fix this in five stints?" Yalda asked her. The second tier wouldn't be firing quite that soon, but as well as having its damaged parts replaced the feed mechanism would need to be cleaned, inspected and tested—none of which would be possible while there was building work going on.

"Three stints," Palladia promised her. Yalda looked around the chamber at the women and men with wheelbarrows, shovels and brooms, collecting up everything from fist-sized chunks of hardstone cladding to innocuous-looking streaks of powdered sunstone that had fallen through the broken ceiling from the surrounding lode. If the liberator tanks had ruptured, innocuous would not have been the word for it.

"I think it's good for morale that there's something to be fixed," Palladia mused. "Once you've repaired a building with your own hands, you really have a stake in it."

"You could be right," Yalda said. Nobody wanted to feel like a caged vole that Eusebio had tossed into the void, a breeding animal who was only here for the sake of their remote descendants' accomplishments. "Still, I wouldn't hope for too much more of the same."

"The kind of compressive forces that the launch produced here won't ever be repeated," Palladia replied, "but when the weight of the mountain vanishes entirely, that will be an experiment we've never really carried out before."

When the workers took a meal break, Yalda sat and ate with them, joining one group in a quick game of six-dice. The pantries on every level had been stocked with loaves—and holin, which the women passed around unselfconsciously, as if it were some kind of condiment. The few men in the team, most of them accompanied by their cos, appeared comfortable enough in this strange new milieu, and if anyone was suffering regrets over the ties they'd severed, the camaraderie here surely dulled the pain.

After the meal the cleanup resumed, but Yalda was out of synch with her hosts and in desperate need of sleep. When she woke she bid Palladia and the crew farewell, and continued her long trudge upward.

The moss-lit staircase stretched above her interminably, the view barely changing as she ascended. The higher engine tiers were undamaged—or at least, they'd passed a superficial inspection, and any further attention could wait until the second tier was in perfect shape—so she'd have no cause to linger in those deserted chambers. She could still hear the sound of the engines below, but distance took the annoying edge off it, leaving an almost reassuring buzz.

With no company, she passed the time sorting through a long list of anxieties. *Would these runaways do a better job of raising their friends' children than she'd done with Tullia's?* At least the fatherless wouldn't be a derided minority here—but if that were the deciding factor, what would be the fate of the fathered few? Then there was the transition that would inevitably follow: the rebalancing of the sexes in the next generation, bringing problems of its own. The *Peerless* had been a gift to runaways, but from here there was nowhere to flee. The only hope for their children would come from instilling the principle of autonomy so deeply that no one had reason to fear their own co.

When she reached the first level above the highest engines, Yalda unbarred the safety doors and stepped out of the stairwell; a short tunnel with three more sets of doors took her to the edge of the cavern. The arborines would have no reason to leave the most comfortable place in the *Peerless* for them, but she wouldn't have wanted a confused animal rampaging through the feed chambers below.

She stood among the bushes watching a nearby tree, one branch trembling as two lizards ran along it chasing mites. It had taken so much work to construct this buried forest that when it had first shown signs of flourishing—long before the launch—she'd felt as if they'd already succeeded in bringing the whole world with them into the void. But if that sentiment had been premature, at least the launch appeared to have done no harm here; the trees had proved resilient enough, and the lizards looked as vigorous as ever. She wouldn't seek out the arborines to inquire about their health, having seen the kind of mood they were in after the test flights—but those flights had included greater accelerations than the *Peerless* had experienced, and still caused the creatures no injuries.

The faintly rotting smell of the place was not quite the same as any odor Yalda recalled from childhood, and the violet light reflecting back from the ceiling was more eerie than nostalgic. Still, it might be good for people to come here now and then to remember—or in later generations, to imagine—the world from which this small, imperfect sample of life's richness had been plucked.

Yalda had received no reports of damage to the farms, but she stopped at one of the caverns of wheat to inspect the crop with her own eyes. Like the forest below, this field had been established for years, so if it had survived the briefly elevated gravity there was no reason to think it couldn't go on thriving. Half the red flowers were open and shining healthily, while the other half slept. As she walked between the rows, alone, she noticed an occasional broken stalk or disheveled flower, but none of the plants had been uprooted. She'd seen worse than this back home after a few stiff gusts of wind.

There'd been a ceiling collapse in one of the medicinal gardens, so Yalda made that her next stop. As she walked down the tunnel from the stairwell, the drab glow of the moss gave way to a richer light than even the forest had offered, and her first glimpse revealed a lush, vibrantly colored mosaic of plants spread out across the cavern. It was only when she reached the entrance that she saw the pile of rubble to her left, and the dozen or so people trying to clear it without trampling any of the precious shrubs.

Yalda approached the group, calling out a greeting. Everyone acknowledged her politely, but only one of the workers offered more than a deferential nod.

"Yalda! Hello!"

"Fatima?"

Fatima walked over to her, picking her way carefully through the debris and crushed plants.

"Was anyone hurt?" Yalda asked.

"No, we were all in the dormitory when it happened."

"That's something." Yalda looked up at the ceiling, which had lost a chunk the size of a small house; they were above the sunstone lode here, so the walls had no need for protective cladding, but the natural mineral formation exposed by the original excavation must have been less stable than the engineers had thought. "What about the plants?"

Fatima gestured at the rubble. "All of that used to be soldier's ease." Yalda knew the blue-flowered shrub, which had grown wild near the farm; its resin helped with wound-healing, though some less-than-helpful chemist had found a way to modify it to produce the melding formulation so beloved of the police.

"Don't take it too badly," Yalda said. "There's plenty more in the other gardens, and you'll get it started here again in a stint or two."

Fatima didn't actually appear grief-stricken by the loss. "We've really left the world behind?" she asked.

"Absolutely," Yalda assured her.

"You've looked back and seen it?"

"Yes." Yalda was sure that Fatima understood perfectly that if they had not reached the void they'd simply be dead—but with the weight of everything restored to normal, nothing in this cave conveyed the truth to her senses. "You should see it for yourself. All of you. Who's the supervisor here?"

"Gioconda." Fatima pointed her out.

Yalda approached the woman and asked her how the work was proceeding, then negotiated a break in a bell's time when anyone who wished could come with her to the nearest observation chamber.

"I'd like to see the world, myself," Gioconda said. "Before it's too faint."

While they waited, Yalda helped shift the rubble. Gioconda was planning to use it to build a series of paths through the garden—covering the bare soil between the plots that currently provided a sanctuary for weeds—but the larger pieces of stone would need to be broken up, and all of the paving would need to be bound to the netting so it would remain in place when the *Peerless* ceased accelerating.

The work was relaxing, and the team seemed to be in good spirits. Once the schools started up, Yalda decided, it would not take much more to make this flying mountain as good a place to live as any small town. It would never match Zeugma's range of cuisines—or be visited by touring entertainers—but there was nothing to stop people inventing their own new dishes, or devising their own variety shows.

The observation chamber wasn't far; the edge of the mountain was less than a stroll away, and then a short descent took them to a clear-domed cave much like the one on the navigators' level. Yalda hadn't come prepared with coordinates, but she managed to locate the world's tiny crescent without too embarrassing a delay.

The gardeners lined up to take turns looking through the theodolite, and Yalda watched their faces as they stepped away, silent and reflective. The ultimate purpose of the *Peerless* was more remote than ever now, with the site of its hoped-for return promising only to fade and vanish, never to be seen again in their lifetimes. But Yalda detected no signs of despair. They were not of the world anymore, but they had their own home to advance and protect. Best of all, even in parting they had not become rivals or deserters: if the *Peerless* flourished, the old world would share the rewards.

When everyone had seen what they'd come here to see, Yalda showed them Pio's stark terrain, then Sitha's glorious color trail.

"When will we be able to see the orthogonal stars?" Fatima asked impatiently.

"Not for a while yet," Yalda replied. "So far we've barely changed the angle we make with starlight." She looked around the chamber at the others. "Is there anything else someone would like to see?"

One of the gardeners, Calogera, gestured toward the barren slope beyond the dome. "I'd like to see the traitor Nino falling past: thrown off the peak of the mountain, on his way down into the engine's flames."

Yalda didn't speak until the cheering stopped, which gave her time to decide that it would be best not to respond at all. "I'll need to get moving now," she said. "I have more inspections to perform. I wish you well with your repairs."

Yalda returned to the navigators' post. A cell had been constructed in a corner of the room, but the builders had rendered it inconspicuous, the wall blending seamlessly with the original, the triple-bolted door almost invisible. Frido and Babila had been opening the small hatch and tossing in loaves without exchanging a word with the occupant, and with a floor of soil packed with worms to eat the prisoner's faeces, there really was no reason the door would ever need to be opened.

It took Yalda two days to work up the courage to pull the bolts and step into the cell. They weren't torturing their prisoner with darkness; the walls here emitted the same mossy red glow as they did outside. Nino sat, unrestrained, in a corner; he did not look up as she closed the door behind her and approached.

Yalda sat on the floor in front of him. "Is there anything you want to say to me?" she asked.

"I've told you everything," Nino replied dully. "If there are other saboteurs, the Councilor never mentioned them to me."

"All right. I believe you." Why would Acilio have told this man anything, beyond the instructions he needed to complete his own task? "Your confession is complete. So what now?"

Nino kept his eyes on the floor. "I'm at your mercy."

"Maybe," Yalda said. "But you must have your own wishes."

"Wishes?" Nino made it sound like an infant's nonsense-word.

"If you had a choice," Yalda persisted, "what would your fate be?"

Nino took a while to respond. "Never to have listened to the Councilor. Never to have got into debt. Never to have seen a second sun in the sky."

"That's not what I meant." Yalda had imagined the conversation proceeding very differently. "You're here, you've done what you've done, we can't change that. So what now? Do you want an end to it?"

Nino looked up at her, shocked. "Nobody wants to die," he said. "It's what I expect, but I'm not going to beg you for it. I'm ashamed of what I did, but I haven't lost all dignity."

"No?" Yalda spread her arms to take in the cell. "What dignity remains for you here?"

Nino glared at her, then touched his forehead. "I still have my mind! I still have my children!"

"You mean, you have your memories?"

"I have my past," Nino said, "and their future. My brother will struggle without the Councilor's second payment, but I know he'll do his best."

"So… you'll just sit here and imagine their lives?"

"With pleasure, for as long as I'm able," Nino replied defiantly.

Yalda was ashamed. She had tried to convince herself that she'd be offering him mercy, but in truth that logic was as odious as Acilio's. She had once believed that she faced a lifetime in chains herself, convinced that no one with the power to help her would ever give a thought to her plight. In the darkness of her cell, with Tullia's encouragement still fresh in her mind, she'd guessed the shape of the cosmos, no less—but robbed of any further companionship she doubted that her mental discipline would have persisted for long. Nino, too, had the life of the mind to sustain him for now, but it wouldn't last forever.

Yalda left him. She stood at her desk, pretending to pore over a star chart, ignoring Frido's enquiring glances.

What did she owe the crew of the *Peerless*? Safety, above all else, but Nino's death wasn't necessary for that. The satisfaction of revenge? It would please most of them to see him die, but did she owe them that pleasure?

And what did she owe Nino? He had been weak and foolish, but had he forfeited his right to live? When Acilio had dragged *her* into his stupid feud, her own pride had lost Antonia her freedom. Who was she to declare that Nino's crime was so great that he deserved no mercy whatsoever?

But if she did spare his life, that would not be the end of it. If she kept him locked up, she couldn't banish him from her thoughts and pretend that his welfare and sanity were not her responsibility.

She stared down at the chart, at the few crosses marked near the beginning of a course that stretched past the edge of the map. *What did she owe the generations to come, who'd follow the path set by her bearings?* The hope of a notion of justice less crude than their ancestors', where a few well-placed bribes and a sergeant's whims could bury anyone in a dungeon for life. She owed it to them to set her sights higher.

Yalda looked over at Frido. "There isn't going to be an execution," she said.

Frido wasn't happy, but he understood from her demeanor that there was no point arguing. "It's your decision to make," he replied. "Do you want him sent up the mountain?"

Yalda said, "Not while I'm down here."

"You still need to question him?"

"No. He has nothing left to tell us about Acilio."

Frido was confused. "So why keep him here?"

Yalda noticed that they'd woken Babila with their shouting, but she needed to hear this too.

"If I'm going to take his freedom away," she said, "then it's up to me to deal with the consequences. I'm going to need to find a way to keep him busy."

"Busy how?" Frido protested. "He's a farmer, not an artisan; you can't turn his cell into a workshop."

Yalda said, "I wasn't thinking of anything so ambitious."

Babila rose from her bed. "Then what?"

Yalda said, "Where do we start with anyone? If our records are correct, he's never been to school. So the first thing is to teach him how to read and write."

15

When the world disappeared into the glare of the sun, Yalda was relieved; the long farewell was finally over. A stint later, when she returned to the observation chamber, even Gemma had vanished to the naked eye. Through the theodolite's telescope, sun and erstwhile planet were just another double star, a bright primary and its fainter companion, with fringes of violet and red destined to spread into a full-blown color trail. If any Hurtlers were lighting up the skies of her old home, sheer distance had rendered those threads of color too faint to discern at all.

Yalda made her measurements and calculated the adjustments needed to keep the *Peerless* on course. As far as she could see they were heading for a region of unblemished darkness, but that was not a judgment to be made from her vantage, handy for directing the feed chambers but compromised by the haze that spread up from the engines' exhaust. Near the top of the mountain, in the pristine void, a team of astronomers were using the original telescope that Eusebio had bought from the university to scrutinize the corridor as they approached it. Whatever improvements in optics the future might bring, *now* was the time to confirm that the path they'd chosen for their long, straight run would be empty of ordinary gas and dust; once they were traveling at full speed any such obstacles would be like Hurtlers, with histories—by the travelers' reckoning—stretched momentarily across an expanse of space, impossible to detect in advance.

To Yalda, this encroaching blindness was both perfectly explicable and utterly strange. The line of sight between the *Peerless* and the region they planned to traverse would remain unobstructed—but as their history curved toward the corridor, their gaze would be forced away from it. Nature had granted everyone both front eyes and rear, but that symmetry only held in three dimensions; in four-space, you could only look back.

Right now, light scattered long enough ago from any dust that lay ahead could reach them at an angle in four-space that made it, on their terms, light from the past. But all too soon, light from such a source would be arriving from their future—so if it did fall upon their eyes, rather than absorbing it they would be emitting it.

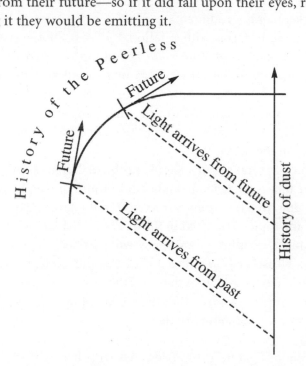

There was no fundamental reason Yalda could see why a living creature could not have possessed the ability to perceive the emission of light from its body—but the ordinary conditions of motion and entropy under which life had arisen would have rendered such a talent useless. The kind of sense organs that might have granted her arborine ancestors a view of the orthogonal stars eons in advance would not have helped them see which way a lizard was going to jump five flickers into the future.

The things worth knowing, the skills worth possessing, were changing. The *Peerless* had bought time for the world they'd left behind, but that was a trick that only paid out once; they couldn't subcontract their own problems to a second group of travelers. Whatever talents they needed in order to survive in a state orthogonal to the history that had shaped them, they would need to master in just a year and half.

Yalda traveled up through the mountain again. The second-tier feed repairs were almost finished, the medicinal garden had been tidied and the damaged plot replanted. She met the chief agronomist, Lavinio, and they walked through the thriving wheat crop together. Having long ago grown accustomed to sunlessness, the plants appeared oblivious to their new state of endless flight.

Classes were being held throughout the *Peerless* now, within half a bell's journey of everyone attending. Yalda sat in on one of Fatima's, aimed at giving workers with a rudimentary education the kind of background needed to come to terms with rotational physics. Not everyone could end up as a researcher, but if the level of common knowledge throughout the community could be raised from mere arithmetic to four-space geometry, that higher base could only bring any future advances into easier reach—and if it brought them to the point where every gardener pulling weeds was also musing about the problems with Nereo's theory of luxagens, all the better.

The teacher, Severa, posed a simple problem. "In an evenly ploughed field, a rope that is stretched from north to south crosses three furrows. The same rope stretched from east to west in the same field crosses four furrows. If the rope is stretched in the direction that allows it to cross as many furrows as possible… how many will that be?"

Diagrams blossomed on a dozen chests as the students sketched the scenario she'd described. Once they had the answer to this—and understood the reason it was true—half the secrets of light, time and motion would become second nature to them.

Back at the navigators' post, Yalda met with her own student. She'd explained her plans to Nino when she'd informed him of his reprieve, but since then she'd been too busy to make good on her promise.

She sat on the floor, facing him. "Can you read the first dozen symbols?" she asked.

"Yes." Nino's tone made it clear that he took the question as an insult, but Yalda didn't know how she could teach him if they weren't clear about such things from the start.

"Can you form them? On your skin?"

Nino gazed back at her sullenly, offering her no clue as to whether she'd simply compounded her offense, or whether the answer this time was too humiliating to utter.

Yalda said, "This isn't meant as some kind of punishment. I thought it might help you to pass the time, but if you want me to leave, I'll leave."

"As you wish," he replied coldly.

Yalda was tempted. "Why treat me as if I'm your enemy?" she asked. "If I can accept that you had no malice toward us, can't you return the favor?"

"You're my jailer," Nino said. "I make no complaint about my loss of freedom, but a jailer is not a friend."

Yalda resisted the urge to launch into a tirade on his ingratitude. "I'd send you another teacher in my place if that would help, but I might find it hard to fill that position, and I'm not sure what the rest of the crew would think of it."

"And what do they think of you coming here?" he asked.

"I haven't made it widely known," Yalda admitted. "But if I sent someone else, there'd be no end of talk about it."

Nino shifted one leg across the floor. "What difference does it make to you, if I can read and write?"

Yalda said, "No one can survive with nothing but their own thoughts. If there were people willing to visit you, I'd be happy for them to come and lift your spirits as often as they wished. But whoever in the mountain once counted themselves as your friends, they've either changed their minds or they're afraid to be seen to support you."

"So you'll teach me to read, then keep me quiet with your books?" He made it sound like a scheme for his subjugation, a conquest of his mind far more terrible than his physical confinement.

Yalda rubbed her face with her hands in frustration. "What would you prefer, then? I can't just set you free."

"So why are you trying to salve your conscience?" Nino demanded. "You have nothing to be ashamed of, for keeping me here."

"No," Yalda agreed, "but I will have if you lose your mind."

"Why?" Nino wasn't being sarcastic; he was genuinely puzzled. "Why wouldn't the shame be mine alone?"

Was this a matter of pride for him? Of self-reliance? The last thing she wanted to do was undermine the resilience he already possessed.

Yalda said, "You did something foolish that could have killed us all—but while you're alive on this rock, we still have the same duties to each other that apply to everyone else. Once I've ensured that the *Peerless* is safe from the risk that you might repeat your actions, everything else remains unchanged. Inasmuch as it's practical, I still owe you meaningful work and the chance of an education—and you still owe me your participation. It gives me no pleasure that this obligation is so much harder to fulfill now, but that's not enough for me to pretend that it has ceased to exist."

Nino fell silent, but he looked less sure of his stance now. There was nothing degrading in being asked to pull his weight.

Yalda struggled to understand his position. He did not despise his captors; he would not have joined the crew without Acilio's bribe, but he hadn't come here poisoned with contempt for their ambitions. Acilio had rationalized away the risk of mass murder by implying that the same deaths were just a matter of time, but even if Nino was skeptical about the mission's prospects, surely he gave the travelers some credit for good intentions.

"Where will it lead?" he asked. "If I learn what you want me to learn, what job could I end up doing?"

"That's hard to say," Yalda confessed. "But you can't be a farmer anymore. You need to start with a simple education, and then find out what other aptitudes you have."

Nino considered this, at length. Perhaps he was wary of raising his hopes too high. Yalda didn't want to set him up for a fall, but a few modest steps that might eventually open up new possibilities for him had to be better than letting him rot here until he died.

"What you say makes sense," he conceded. "If you're willing to try to teach me, I'll do my best to make it work."

As the layer of burning sunstone came closer, the noise and heat from the engines became oppressive and the machinists and navigators prepared to move up to the second tier feeds. The *Peerless* had acquired so much momentum that a few days without manual corrections would make little difference to the course it was following, and any slight drift that occurred could easily be dealt with once the second tier fired up.

This would be a perfect opportunity to dispose of rubbish, Babila noted, looking around the bare cavern of the navigators' post, now stripped of its benches and instruments. **Anything we don't want cluttering up the mountain, just leave it here to be blown into the void.** Her gaze lingered on the door to the prison.

Clutter is just another word for wealth, Yalda replied. **We're not so rich that we can afford to throw anything away.**

Frido had long ago stopped taking sides, at least openly. **Help me check the release charges?** he asked Babila; she followed him out of the room. Before igniting the second tier, they were going to set off explosions in the first-tier feed chambers to weaken the whole stub of rock that needed to be cast off.

Yalda opened the cell and led Nino out. For the first few steps he was disoriented, blinking and cowering at the strangeness of the vastly larger space, but he recovered his composure rapidly. Yalda knew better than to offer him solicitous words; they walked together in silence, through the empty feed chambers, out to the stairs.

"How much time has passed?" he shouted, as they began ascending. "Since we left?"

"Nearly half a year for us," Yalda replied. The teacher in her wanted to conduct the conversation in writing, but Nino was walking ahead of her and he hadn't yet mastered drawing anything on his back.

"And at home?"

"Almost as much. Let me think." Yalda had not been keeping track of the old calendar; she had to calculate the answer on the spot. The only practical approach was to use the home world's idea of simultaneity to link the two histories; the date obtained that way would cease advancing while the *Peerless* was traveling orthogonally, but was otherwise well-behaved. Attaching the definition of "now" to the *Peerless*'s own meandering history would have made the date back home race into the infinite future as they accelerated, swing back all the way to the infinite past as they reversed, and then return to sanity just in time for the reunion.

"About ten days less," she said.

"I see." Nino looked away across the stairwell, pondering something. "Why?"

"Maybe I'll have grandchildren soon," he said.

"Oh." Yalda wasn't sure if he expected congratulations.

"I forbade it until my children had two years more than a dozen," he explained. "I'm hoping that they'll wait a few years longer, but it's hard to know what they'll choose."

"I'm sure they'll be sensible," Yalda offered, without much conviction. "So what did you tell them, about joining the *Peerless*?"

"I said Eusebio was in such desperate need of farmers that he was willing to pay my family to have use of my skills."

"How did they take that?"

Nino paused on the stairs. "They wanted to come too. I told them it was too dangerous for all of us."

The noise of the engines gradually receded. However disturbing it was to contemplate the prospect of weightlessness, Yalda had decided that it would be worth almost anything to be rid of the endless hammering of flame on rock.

"Are your brother's children older or younger?" she asked Nino.

"Younger."

"So do you think he'll put pressure on his nieces and nephews?"

"No," Nino replied. "That's not his way. I'm more worried that they might have trouble controlling themselves."

At the top of the second tier they left the stairs. The only way to reach the new navigators' post was through the feed chambers, and these ones would not be empty.

"Put your hands behind your back," Yalda insisted. "For appearances' sake."

Nino complied; she pressed them together, then wrapped one of her own, larger hands around them. She would never have actually used melding resin, but it couldn't hurt that anyone who saw them would be unable to tell at a glance that her prisoner was in fact topologically free.

They crossed the outermost chamber unseen, but in the next, Delfina was at her post inspecting the tape writer. "You're letting that murderer walk through here?" she shouted at Yalda, incredulous.

"There's no other route to his cell," Yalda replied. The machinists had just spent days cleaning and testing their shiny new feeds; in the circumstances she could understand why anyone would feel affronted by Nino's presence. But she'd had no choice.

Delfina approached them. "I can't accept this!" she told Yalda angrily. "When Eusebio appointed you leader, do you think he intended you to put the life of one traitor above all of our own?"

Yalda had learned not to waste time taking issue with hyperbole like this. "I'm glad you're here," she said. "I wanted another guard to help watch over the prisoner as I escorted him to the new cell, but Babila and Frido were busy with the release charges."

Delfina hesitated, but refusing the request would have been tantamount to conceding that Nino already posed no risk.

"If you could walk ahead of us," Yalda suggested, "ready to block him if he tries to break free…?"

They threaded their way in silence through the banks of pristine clockwork, then into the next chamber. Onesta was inspecting the valves at the base of the liberator tank, but when she saw Delfina leading the procession she simply nodded in greeting.

In the navigators' post, Delfina stood and waited until Nino was locked in his cell.

"I appreciate your help," Yalda said.

"It shouldn't have been necessary," Delfina replied. "There shouldn't have been a prisoner to move."

"Nonetheless, I'm grateful," Yalda insisted.

"That's not the point."

"Don't forget the transition drill," Yalda reminded her. "That's the day after tomorrow."

Delfina gave up. When she'd left, Yalda checked in on Nino. "Are you going to be—"

"Comfortable?" he suggested. "It's identical to the last one."

Yalda said, "If there's anything in particular that you want, now might be the chance for me to sneak it in."

"In the sagas," Nino mused, "the rulers who survived were the ones who identified their enemies in time, and disposed of them swiftly."

"I'll be sure to keep that in mind." Yalda began to leave, but then she stopped and turned back to him. "You learned the sagas?"

"Of course."

"You've memorized them?"

"My father taught them to me," Nino replied. "I can recite them all, word for word."

Yalda said, "How would you feel about putting them on paper?"

Nino was bemused. "Why?"

"It would be good to have them, for the library." In fact, she suspected that the library had a copy already. But every family passed down its own version, and perhaps in the future someone would want to ponder the nature of that variation. "If I bring you dye and paper, would you be willing to make a start on it? See how it goes?" Nino's written vocabulary might not yet be up to the task, but any problems he struck would give them something to address in their lessons.

Nino considered it. They both knew this would be a kind of make-work compared to tending the wheat fields, but if he wasn't yet sick of the uninspired calligraphic exercises Yalda had been setting for him, she was sick of thinking them up.

"All right," he agreed.

Yalda was relieved. "I'll get the supplies for you, before Frido and Babila arrive."

"I taught the sagas to my sons, a few years ago," Nino said. "After I'd done that, I thought I wouldn't need them—I thought I'd just forget them."

"But you didn't forget them?"

"No."

Yalda said, "I'll bring you everything you'll need."

The new engines started up without mishap, blasting the stub of rock remaining at the top of the first tier away into the void. As Frido and Babila cheered, Yalda imagined herself congratulating Eusebio on the success of his design. Lately she'd found herself thinking about the return of the *Peerless* as if she'd be there in person—but then, she'd pictured Tullia walking beside her in Zeugma often enough; was it any more absurd to have the same kind of thoughts when she played the ghost herself?

Nino filled page after page with his transcripts. Yalda visited him to read these first drafts and suggest corrections—but only when one of her fellow navigators was sleeping and the other was out at the rim making observations. No one was being deceived, but she could still avoid provoking them with reminders of her contentious decision. The astronomers at the summit had found no obstacles ahead, but ensuring that the *Peerless* remained on course was still more than enough to keep everyone around her, machinists and navigators alike, far too busy to want to organize an insurrection if there was nothing forcing their hand.

When the *Peerless* reached the halfway mark of its acceleration phase, matching the speed of blue light, Yalda traveled up the mountain to speak to Severa's class.

They met in one of the observation chambers. The students fell silent as they entered; they'd been told what to expect, but Yalda could understand how daunting it must be to see every star they'd grown up with—every subtle, distinctive smudge of light, every Sitha, Tharak, Zento or Juhla—raked into streaks of color more like a barrage of Hurtlers than anything else.

That was the view that first confronted them: looking straight out from the side of the mountain, where the small, haphazard motions of the stars were overwhelmed by the velocity of the *Peerless*. The speed of the mountain's ascent was enough to align every color trail vertically, making a field of parallel furrows in the sky. The trails began and ended at disparate points, but all of them spanned about half a right angle, with red at the top and violet at the bottom. In this history made visible, the most recent report in violet always showed the star lower in the sky than the tardy red version.

Looking up toward the zenith, though, shattered any expectation that this pattern would merely repeat itself into the distance. Here, the stars' own sideways motion could compete with the rocket's forward rush, complicating the geometry enough to keep the trails from converging on any perfect vanishing point. More surprisingly, many of the trails here were completely inverted compared to the norm, their red ends poking down—and both kinds of trail faded out before traversing the full spectrum, the red-tailed never getting past green, the violet-tailed barely reaching indigo. On top of all this, the upper part of the sky was simply more *crowded* than the lower, giving the bizarre impression that the stars the *Peerless* was approaching had somehow receded into the distance, clumping together like the buildings of a town you were leaving behind.

Yalda addressed the students. "I know this looks strange to you, but we're here to make sense of it. Everything you're seeing here can be explained with some simple geometry."

Severa had earlier had the class construct two props for the occasion. Yalda took them from her and set them down on the floor of the chamber.

"To start with, I'd like you to examine these objects, please, and draw them as they appear side-on."

The props were octagonal pyramids made of paper, one with a fairly shallow pitch and the other much steeper, mounted on simple wooden stands. The students gathered around them and squatted down to obtain views square with the base.

"The *stem* of each stand represents a short stretch of the history of the *Peerless*," Yalda explained, "before it was launched. Time is measured vertically, straight up from the floor; space is horizontal. Back then, the stars were only moving slowly in relation to us, so we can think of them as being spread out evenly across the floor, with their histories rising up almost vertically." She glanced across at Fatima's neat, stylized rendering.

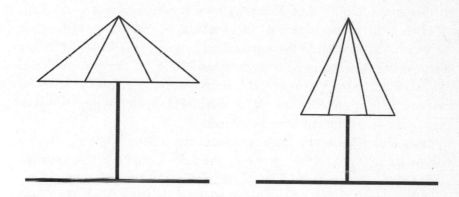

"And the pyramids are light?" Ausilio asked.

"Exactly," Yalda confirmed. "Incoming light, emitted long ago by the surrounding stars and finally reaching us at the apex of the pyramid. The two pyramids represent violet light and red light, as seen by us. The steepest one is…?"

"Red," Prospera volunteered. "The edges cross less space in a given time—a slower velocity."

Yalda said, "Right. A cone would provide a more detailed model, showing *all* the rays of a given color, but the eight edges of each of these pyramids are enough to give us a good idea of how the light behaves—and the fact that they mark off equal angles around the *Peerless* is going to be helpful to us."

Everyone had finished the first view. "Could you look down from above now, please," Yalda instructed them, "and draw what you see."

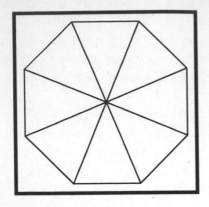 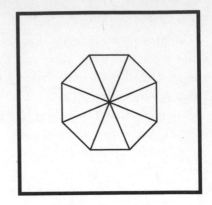

She waited until most of the students had new sketches on their chests before continuing. "Think about the light rays that reach us," she said, "between the edges of each of these triangles. When the *Peerless* was motionless compared to the stars, each of these equal segments in our view of the sky took in light from an equal slice of our surroundings. The stars were arranged uniformly around us in space, more or less—so we saw them scattered uniformly across the sky, with no one direction appearing very different from another."

Yalda looked around and chose one of the quieter students: Ausilia, whose co did most of the talking for the pair. "Could you tip the stems over for me, please? Try to make them both as close as you can to a one-eighth turn down from the vertical. Halfway to orthogonal. The speed of blue light."

The stems were connected to the base with a swiveling joint; Ausilia approached the task diligently, stepping back several times to check the angles.

"Could everyone draw the new configuration, please," Yalda said. "From the side first."

Severa approached her and whispered, jokingly, "You know you're robbing them of the big payoff when we learn to do all of this algebraically."

"Ha! How far away is that?"

"A couple of years, I expect."

"And how many of this class will stick with it that long?"

Severa thought for a while. "More than half."

Yalda was encouraged; for the first generation that would be a good result. But right now, she was going to ensure that every one of these people could make sense of the view around them using nothing but their eyes and their intuition.

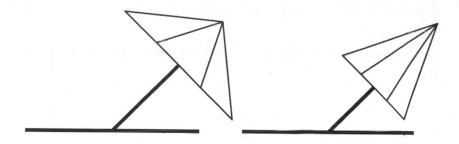

She addressed the class again. "This drawing tells us something straight away, about the view we can expect from the *Peerless*. Any suggestions?"

Prospera said, "The violet light coming in from behind us has been tilted so far that it's... gone past horizontal." Her tone made it clear that she knew the change had to be significant, but she couldn't quite see what it implied.

"So if you follow the light in toward us," Yalda suggested, "what happens to its height?"

"It gets less, as you move in," Prospera replied.

"*Its height gets less.* And what does height stand for, in this picture?"

"Time." Prospera pondered this for a moment. "So the light would have to come from the future?"

"Exactly. It would have to be *traveling back in time*. Not for us—it's still coming from our past—but for the star that emitted it. So what you've found tells us that no ordinary star that lies directly behind us—in the rear one-eighth of our view, or a bit beyond that—can appear to us in violet, because that would require the star to have emitted light into its own past."

"But it would be different for an orthogonal star, wouldn't it?" Fatima asked eagerly.

Yalda said, "Well, their time is horizontal in this picture, and their future is aligned with the direction in which we're traveling, but—"

Fatima ran forward to the edge of the cave and peered down the slope of the mountain.

"—but unfortunately, the rock below us hides that part of the view." Between the mountain and the haze from the engines, there was no chance at all of observing the orthogonal stars yet.

Yalda asked the students to draw the tilted pyramids from above. A few people became confused, or drew some preconception rather than the actual view, but after noticing the emerging consensus of their peers they looked again and refined their own versions.

She waited until everyone had the essential features correct.

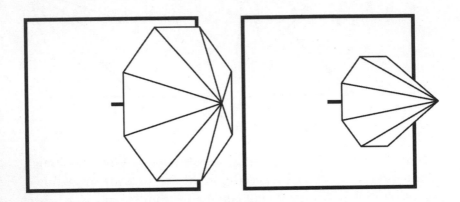

"Each of the eight segments still represents *an equal portion of our view*," she reminded them. "But their relationship with the surroundings has changed. Let's start with the violet, the broader pyramid. Can someone tell me what's going on?"

Ausilia spoke up. "At the front," she said, pointing out the triangle on her chest, "the angle between the edges is much bigger than one-eighth now, seen from above."

"Which means…?" Yalda pressed her.

Ausilia hesitated, but then followed through. "*Our* one-eighth of the view is taking in light from more than one-eighth of the stars?"

"Exactly!" Yalda approached her and had her turn so the whole class could see her sketch. "In the direction in which the *Peerless* is traveling, this slice of the view has a wider reach, so light from more stars gets crammed into it. We still see it as an equal eighth, but as far as our surroundings are concerned it's much more." She stepped away from Ausilia and gestured toward the zenith. "Focus on the violet ends of the trails. They started out scattered uniformly around us, before the launch; now they're crowded together around the direction in which we're traveling. And the reason is simple: when you take two lines that are a fixed angle apart—like the edges of that front triangle—the more you tilt them, the greater the angle between them will seem to be."

She waited for the simple logic of it to mesh with the evidence before their eyes, then added, "In the opposite direction there's an opposite effect. The mountain makes that harder to see—and we've already shown that there's a region behind us where we won't be getting violet light from the ordinary stars anyway—but in general, looking back the view is sparser."

Fatima was standing closer to her than Ausilia now, so Yalda moved beside her and pointed to her drawing of the red pyramid.

"What about red light? If you compare the rear triangles in the two pyramids, it's clear that the angle for the red light is even smaller than it is for violet—so we should see the red images behind us spread out across the sky *more* than the violet, *pushed forward* compared to the violet. And that difference persists as you move away from the rear. For any given star, *the red light* ends up further from the nadir. Does that sound familiar?" Yalda pointed to the vertical trails behind her, the red ends all higher than the violet.

"But what happens with the red light," she continued, "when we look in the direction in which we're traveling? There are only five triangles from the pyramid visible here. What's going on with the three triangles that point to the front for us?"

Fatima helpfully added three lines that made the hidden triangles visible:

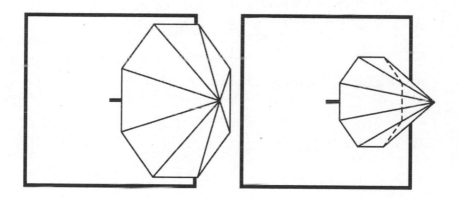

"They've ended up pointing backward," Ausilia said.

"Yes!" Yalda raised her eyes to the zenith. "See those strange *red ends of trails* poking out the wrong way? They're stars that are actually behind us! The pyramid shows us that in red light, we can't see *anything* that's in front of us—in the sense that an onlooker fixed to the stars would judge something to be 'in front'. But our view isn't empty of red in that direction; instead of seeing what's in front of us, we're seeing some of what's behind us."

"And all of it twice," Fatima said, running a fingertip across the diagram toward the apex of the pyramid. "Every star we see behind us in red... we also see in front of us in red."

"That's right," Yalda said. "But though it's light from the same star—and it looks the same color to us—it's not the same light."

Fatima thought for a moment. "The red light we see, looking back, left the star at a greater angle than the angle it makes with us. So it left the star as faster-than-red light… but because we're fleeing from it, it's not gaining on us as quickly as it would if we were still. Our motion has changed the color from violet or ultraviolet to red."

"Yes." Yalda pushed her, "And the other light? The red light we see looking forward that came from the very same star?"

Fatima gazed down at the diagram, struggling. "From the angles, I think it must have left the star moving quite slowly. But if it's moving so slowly, how could it ever catch up with us?"

Yalda said, "If you're getting confused, just draw… whatever it is you need to draw."

Fatima made a new sketch, paused, then added some annotations.

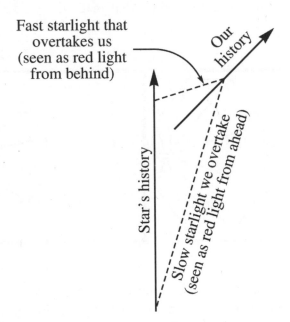

"The red light we see as coming from ahead," she said, "must have left the star behind us long ago… but now we've caught up with it, we're overtaking it. That's why it strikes us from the front. The star is behind us, but the light *was* ahead of us."

Fatima looked up at the zenith, then a fresh revelation struck her. "That's why those upside-down star trails sputter out at green! However long ago the light left the star, the angle it made with our history could never end up greater than the angle for blue light. But blue would be the absolute limit—light from infinitely long ago. In real life we can't expect to see that far back."

She modified her diagram to show what she meant.

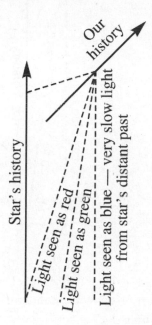

Yalda said, "That's all true—though the reason we don't see any blue in those trails is also a matter of how much power the star emits in different parts of the spectrum. The light we'd see as blue would have to leave the star as far-infrared, traveling incredibly slowly. So it can't be carrying energy out of the star at a very high rate… which means the star itself simply won't be shining very brightly in that color."

Ausilia had been following the discussion closely, though Yalda wasn't sure how much she'd understood. But then she pointed to Fatima's chest and said, "If that star happened to be in front of us instead, its slowest light would still end up looking blue, wouldn't it? It would just approach it from the other end of the spectrum. So its trail would start out violet, but never quite get as far as blue."

She hesitated, then produced a diagram, echoing Fatima's, to illustrate her point.

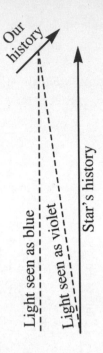

Yalda chirped with delight. She gestured to Ausilia to turn so that everyone else could see the picture. "That's the last puzzle solved: why some trails above us are just violet and indigo. And that's it: between you, you've unwoven the whole sky."

In fact, not everyone had caught up with Fatima and Ausilia, but Yalda stood back and let the students help each other past their lingering puzzlement. As they looked to the stars and back, connecting the details of the color trails to the figures before them, the thrill of understanding spread.

This alien sky belonged to them, now. Its transformation would become even more extreme as the *Peerless* moved faster, but the new ways of seeing it that they had acquired would handle those changes with ease.

Yalda knew that only a few of these people would end up as researchers, only a few as teachers. But even if they did no more than pass their understanding on to the children of their friends, it would all be a part of strengthening the culture, ensuring that their descendants were at ease in this strange new state.

And the most beautiful thing of all, she realized—struck by it anew, because she'd almost begun taking it for granted—was that every one of these solos and runaways, every one of these partnered women and their cos, would have the chance to live out their lives without coercion, making use of their talents, untrammeled by the customs of the old world.

Forget the Hurtlers, forget the orthogonal stars. For that alone, the struggle had been worth it.

16

Strapped to her bench in the navigators' post, Yalda counted down the pauses. It had always been Frido or Babila doing the honors before, but she'd taken the role for herself this time, knowing it would be her last chance.

"Three. Two. One."

The anticlimax that followed was welcome; any sudden, perceptible change would have meant that something had gone horribly wrong. The clock advanced another two lapses before Yalda noticed anything at all—and even then she had her doubts; the hint of dizziness, of balance gone awry, could as easily have been nothing but anticipation. The machinists were tapering off the flow of liberator in an excruciatingly protracted manner; it would take a full chime for the engines to shut down completely.

"Can you hear that?" Frido asked.

"Hear what?" Babila raised her head to listen.

Yalda said, "The rock." Over the hammering of the engines, she could make out a low creaking sound coming through the ceiling. The mountain had lost only a fraction of its weight, but it was already beginning to rearrange itself, stretching out beneath the diminishing load. That was not a bad sign; better that it start adjusting now than save up the changes for a sharp transition later that released all its energy at once.

Four lapses into the shutdown, Yalda could have sworn that the skin on her back was growing numb—and knowing the true reason that she was starting to register less pressure did nothing to make the illusion less compelling. At seven lapses her dwindling weight began triggering flashes of panic, in which she was convinced—for a moment or two—that the legs of the bench had given way beneath her. The engines were producing a strange, soft patter now; the rock above had fallen silent. For the first time since the launch, she could hear the ticking of the clock from across

255

the room.

Babila turned and vomited up her last meal, thoughtfully depositing it out of sight of her companions—though the floor itself might not hold the mess down much longer. With no hope of reconciling the room's apparent steadiness with the alarming sense that everything was slipping, Yalda closed her eyes. She found herself visualizing the *Peerless* from a distance, a dark cone against the color trails. But in this fanciful vision the middle third of the mountain had turned as soft as resin, and she watched in horrified fascination as it stretched out into a narrow tube, then snapped—

She braced for the impact that must have followed the same plummeting sensation for every one of her ancestors who'd had the misfortune to experience it. That the crash never came was no surprise, but nor was it a relief; the threat of impending damage refused to be dispelled.

Yalda lay on her bench humming softly, waiting for something to change. Finally, she grew sufficiently inured to the sense of dread to open her eyes and look around. Frido had removed most of his straps and was sitting up; Yalda did the same, and felt no worse for it. In fact, the actions were reassuring, proving that she still had control over her body.

Half a dozen ropes had been strung across the room at shoulder height. Frido finished unstrapping himself and reached up to take hold of the nearest of them. At first he tried to walk across the floor, using the rope as an aid, but his feet kept slipping on the stone. Then he changed his approach, curling his body up and gripping the rope with his feet as well, forming them into a second pair of hands. After a few unsteady moments, he mastered the technique and scurried along the rope, hand over hand, as far as the wall. Then he swung onto a second rope that was fastened to the stone beside him, and set off in a new direction.

Babila watched him, stupefied. "I'm not doing *that* for the rest of my life," she moaned. "You can send me home right now."

Yalda removed the strap from around her waist and took hold of the nearest rope. Following Frido's example, she re-formed her feet and tried to raise them, but then she found herself tumbling slowly in mid-air, still clinging to the rope with a single hand but unable to seize it with any other appendage.

"Hunch up, you fool!" Babila suggested irritably; in her state of nausea even Yalda's clumsiness was a personal affront. But it was good advice; Yalda had no control over her body's orientation, but she could still bring all four hands together at the point where she held the rope. From there, she slid them along it, spacing them out more comfortably. She looked across the room to study Frido's technique—he was never taking more than one hand off the rope at a time—then she began tentatively pulling herself along.

She was fine at first, until her sense of the vertical flipped and the cozy illusion that she was hanging down from a horizontal rope was replaced by the equally false conviction that she was perched above it, precariously balanced, certain to tumble over at any moment. She closed her eyes and pictured herself *ascending* instead: climbing up a vertical rope. When she opened her eyes and started moving again, her chosen illusion persisted; the small forces on her body as she dragged it along the rope were oriented in the right direction to reinforce the idea.

After practicing for a while she became reasonably proficient, but it was disconcerting to be so dependent on the ropes. If one of them snapped, installing a replacement would not be easy; it was clear now that they'd underestimated the number of handles needed on the walls to ensure that a chamber like this remained navigable, come what may. And if threading a new rope into place was a major task, any kind of construction work would be impossible.

Frido left the navigators' post, dragging himself through the doorway to see how the neighboring machinists were faring. Babila was still sitting on her bench looking miserable. Yalda approached her.

"Try the ropes," she said. "I'll stay close to you."

"I can't do it," Babila declared.

"You can't hurt yourself. You can't fall."

"What if I get stranded?" Babila retorted. "Drifting in mid-air?"

It wasn't an entirely ridiculous objection; the chamber was high enough that someone really could end up out of reach of anything solid—let alone anything they could actually grasp.

"Even if you let go of the rope accidentally," Yalda pointed out, "you won't drift away from it very quickly. You'll always have time to grab hold of it again. And I'll stay in front of you, I'll make sure you're all right."

Babila wasn't happy, but she reached up with one hand and grabbed the rope beside her, released the strap around her waist, then refashioned her obsolete feet and curled her body up so she could grip the rope in four places.

"We're all animals now," she declared forlornly. "I feel like an arborine."

"Is that so bad?" Yalda wondered. "We're going to have to re-learn everything we do, but if we've done something similar before, in the forests, that can only help."

"And which zero-gravity forests were they?" Babila began pulling herself along the rope with surprising speed.

Yalda backed away from her hastily. "None in the past," she said, "though it might be interesting to see how they deal with it now. We might learn something from all of the animals."

"They won't know what hit them," Babila predicted gloomily. "They'll cope much worse than we do."

"Maybe."

For all her reticence, Babila proved to be quite agile. Yalda suspected that most of her pessimism was just the nausea talking, and that both would wear off soon enough.

"A part of me keeps thinking that this is temporary," Yalda admitted, clinging to the rope near the center of the room; the chamber now seemed to her like a disk-shaped space standing up on one edge. "As if it's a trick that's all down to some clever new way of using the engines, and if we get bored with it we can always just stop."

"I know what you mean," Babila said. "How can a condition that came without effort back home require a whole burning mountain to sustain it… while one that was impossible for more than a pause or two becomes the natural state?" She shivered. "Think of all the people who'll live and die like this: feeling as if they're endlessly falling."

Yalda listened to the silence of the dead engines. She'd always expected that she'd welcome it ecstatically when it finally came, but it was going to take a while to grow accustomed to the absence.

"They won't feel as if they're falling," she said. "They'll feel the way they always feel. Only the old books will tell them that there was once a thing called 'falling' that felt the same."

A day after the shutdown, Frido, Babila and a group of the machinists set off up the mountain. New jobs were waiting for them, close to the summit. Yalda lingered in the navigators' post, promising to follow them later; nobody pressed her to explain why.

When she opened the door to the cell a thick haze of dust spilled out, red in the moss-light. The soil on the floor here was covered with the same netting as they'd used in the gardens, but without plant roots to help bind it, it was scarcely contained.

Nino was at the back of the cell, clinging to the netting; bundles of paper tied with string drifted around him, along with several clumps of faeces and half a dozen dead worms.

"Come out of there." Yalda heard the anger in her voice, as if it were Nino's fault that he'd been living in this squalor. She should have checked on him much sooner.

"Is there anyone around?" he asked.

"No."

Nino used the netting to crawl across the floor. He hesitated at the doorway, confused for a moment, then Yalda backed away and made room for him on the rope that was anchored to the wall beside the entrance. He took hold of the rope and drew himself toward it, then reached back and swung the door closed, stopping any more of the dust escaping.

He looked over at the navigators' bed, fully enclosed beneath a tarpaulin. "I was thinking you must have done something like that. Is it easy to use, without everything spilling out?"

"Not really," Yalda confessed. "I think we're going to have to start adding some kind of resin to the sand."

Nino said, "My only problem is that it's been hard to read, through the dust. If you could spare a couple of those tarpaulins—"

"Forget about that mess." Yalda gestured dismissively toward his cell. "I'll make sure you have a proper bed, upstairs."

Nino hesitated; she recognized the way he held the muscles around his tympanum when he was struggling to find the most tactful way to phrase something. "That's kind of you," he said, "but it would be better if I could fix what I have already."

"Nobody's staying down here," she said. "Now that we're orthogonal, barring an emergency the engines won't be fired again in our lifetimes."

"I understand," Nino replied. "There'll be no full-time navigators, and you'll have work to do elsewhere. But it's better if I stay."

"Are you worried about the trip?" Yalda asked him. She hadn't handled the last move as well as she might have. "I'll get some of the machinists to play guard on the way up. No one will be able to accuse you of running wild, if you have a whole escort."

"No one will accept me being up there at all," he said. "Let alone accept the sight of you coming to my cell—"

Yalda cut him off irritably. "If you think that's a problem, I'll put your cell inside my apartment. Then no one need know how often I visit you."

Nino buzzed with bleak amusement. "Do that, and we'd both be dead in a stint."

"I don't believe that."

"No? Then you don't know what people are capable of."

Yalda was angry now. "Don't patronize me. I was in prison myself, remember."

Nino said, "You suffered for a while at the hands of a spoilt brat who was more interested in hurting someone else. That's not the same as trying to live in a world where everyone is your enemy."

"And the stunt you pulled for the same spoilt brat," Yalda retorted, "is not the be-all and end-all of life on the *Peerless*. People have more important things to think about." She took her hands off the rope and drifted free for a moment. "Do you know how to make a loaf, like this? How to fix a lamp? How to sow a crop?"

"So everyone will be preoccupied with weightlessness for a while," Nino conceded. "That's no reason for us to push our luck. Leave me here, let people forget about me. Or if they think of me at all, let them be satisfied that I've been banished as far from them as possible. Banished and abandoned."

Yalda could not accept this. "Abandoned to starve? Abandoned to go crazy?"

Nino said, "The moss is edible; have you really never tried it? But if you want to help me… choose someone you trust—someone whose movements will attract no attention—and send them down here with a few loaves and books every couple of stints. If I can read something new every now and then, I won't lose my mind. And I still have another draft of the sagas I can work on."

"If I leave you here alone," Yalda said, "what's to stop someone from coming down and killing you? You're afraid that if I take you to the summit and make it clear that you have my protection, people will be so outraged that they'll turn against me… but how long do you think you'll last with no protection at all?"

Nino thought about this, seriously. "If you put enough locked doors in the way, that might help. You can justify it as a way of keeping me down here, even if I manage to break free from my cell. Some people will be happy enough with the thought of me buried in an impenetrable dungeon—and I'll be a little safer from the others, who won't be happy until I'm dead."

Yalda said, "If I call a meeting and explain to everyone why you did what you did, they should accept that your imprisonment is punishment enough. And they should respect me more, not less, for refusing to bow to tradition. The *Peerless* exists to bring change. Every last runaway here should be ready to shout: *octofurcate the old ways!* If they really wanted to live by those rules, they should have stayed in a world where they still held sway."

Nino took his time replying, striving for tact again. "That's a brave speech, Yalda," he said, "and I can't fault it, myself. But before you try it on the whole crew… can you name one person who started out opposing your decision, who you've managed to bring around with the same fine words?"

"Yalda! Are you busy? Please, you have to see this!"

Isidora was calling from outside Yalda's office, too excited to waste time dragging herself into the room. Yalda was in the middle of a long calculation on the energetics of oscillating luxagens, but after a moment she slipped her notes into a hold and latched it. Isidora's bursts of enthusiasm were annoying at times, but it was thanks to her efforts that the optics workshop was functioning again so soon. If she wanted to share her excitement at having rendered one more piece of apparatus usable without gravity, it would be churlish to refuse her.

Yalda dragged herself across the room and through the doorway, four hands shuttling her along the two parallel ropes. She retained the extra pair of hands she'd been using on her papers, in anticipation of having to twiddle a focusing wheel or adjust the angle of a prism.

Before Yalda had come within half a stretch of her, Isidora was already backing away down the corridor toward the workshop.

"What's the great achievement?" Yalda called after her.

"You have to see this for yourself!" Isidora replied.

The walls of the optics workshop were kept free of the ubiquitous luminous moss, so the room's deep shadows and controlled lamplight made it eerily reminiscent of its counterpart in Zeugma University—with the surreal placement of people and equipment only heightening Yalda's sense of wandering into a nostalgic hallucination. Isidora was waiting in a corner where Sabino, a young researcher, was operating one of the microscopes, while clinging to two wooden bars that ran between the erstwhile floor and ceiling.

The microscopes had been back in action for days. Yalda approached, intrigued.

"What's the new development?" she asked. Two closely spaced clearstone slides were positioned at the focus of the instrument; whatever they enclosed was—unsurprisingly—too small to discern with the naked eye, but they were attached to an elaborate mechanism of levers and wheels that Yalda hadn't seen before, with a slender rod reaching into the space between them. In front of the small sunstone lamp that was illuminating the specimen was a thin slab of material that she recognized as a polarizing filter.

Sabino said, "Please, take a look for yourself." He was shy with Yalda, but she could see that he was at least as excited as Isidora.

He moved aside and let Yalda take the bars in front of the microscope. Even the solid wood trembled a little from the shifting forces as they changed places; Yalda waited for the vibrations to die down, then peered into the eyepiece.

The field was full of translucent gray specks, most of them roughly spherical, albeit with jagged outlines. Shape aside, they possessed no visible features, no apparent parts or fine structure. Not all of the specks were in focus; the slides hadn't been pressed together tightly enough to touch the material, to hold it in place. But the focal plane of the microscope had been adjusted to take in one particular speck; this one *was* fixed, gripped by a tiny pair of callipers that appeared solid black in their opacity. The other specks, though unconstrained, were barely quivering, demonstrating that the air between the slides was almost motionless.

"What am I looking at?" Yalda asked.

"Powdered calmstone," Sabino replied.

"Under polarized light?"

"Yes."

A pinch of fine sand—ground from calmstone or anything else—would not normally look like this. The grains would generally appear variegated in polarized light, made up of half a dozen regions of very different shades of gray. These were uniform, homogeneous.

"So you sorted them?" Yalda asked Sabino. "You picked out the purest grains you could find?"

"Yes. Maybe one in ten gross were like this."

"One in *ten gross*? You've been busy."

Yalda hadn't had time to learn about Sabino's project since coming up from the navigators' post, but she could guess the rationale for his painstaking efforts. If solids such as calmstone were composed of regular arrays of indivisible particles—such as Nereo's putative luxagens—then the best way to study their properties would be to obtain pieces of the material in question in which the array was as close to geometrically flawless as possible. An array of particles that maintained a regular pattern should have the same optical properties throughout; the usual mottled appearance of sand under polarized light ruled that out, but by chance there could always be exceptions. Sabino had found those exceptions, and discarded everything else.

"Try moving the wheel," he suggested. "The top one on your right."

Without looking away from the eyepiece, Yalda reached up with the right hand of the pair that sprouted from her chest, and found the wheel. She drew her fingertip along the rim, nudging it very slightly. In response, the callipers between the slides shifted, dragging their tiny cargo some fraction of a scant.

"What am I missing?" she asked. She didn't think anyone expected her to be impressed by the fact that they could move single grains of sand around.

"Don't just look at the callipers," Isidora urged her. "Watch what's happening around them."

Yalda turned the wheel gently again; something caught her eye, but as soon as she stopped to try to scrutinize it, it ceased attracting her attention.

She moved the wheel a little more, then when the unexpected thing she hadn't quite seen began to happen again, she started jiggling the wheel back and forth: jiggling the callipers, jiggling the tiny piece of calmstone it held.

As she did so, a second piece beside it moved in lockstep. Light was visible between the two; they were not touching. But whatever she did to the captive grain, its mimic followed as if they were two parts of a single, rigid body.

"Nereo's force," she said softly. "This is it? We can actually see it?"

Isidora chirped with glee, treating the question as rhetorical. Sabino was more cautious. "I hope that's what it is," he said. "I can't think of any better explanation."

According to Nereo's equation, every luxagen should be surrounded by furrows of lower potential energy, within which any other luxagen nearby would prefer to reside. For a single luxagen, the furrows would simply be a series of concentric spherical shells, but the same effect acting on a multitude of particles could bind them together in a regular array—and in that case, the pattern of indentations in the energy landscape would extend beyond the array itself, offering the chance for another fragment of a similarly composed material to become ensnared in it. In effect, a sufficiently pure speck of rock could "stick" to another such speck, without the two actually touching.

"You tried this before, when the engines were running?" Yalda asked Sabino.

"Stint after stint," he replied. "But gravity and friction must have overwhelmed the effect, because I never saw anything like this."

Which meant that nobody back home could have seen it, either; it was only the condition of weightlessness that had made the experiment viable.

Yalda had been watching Sabino with her rear gaze; now she leaned back from the microscope and turned to face him. "This is excellent work!" she declared. "I'll want you to give a talk on it to all the researchers, sometime in the next few days. Have you done anything on the theoretical side?"

Sabino produced a sheet of paper from a hold beside the microscope. "So far, only this," he said.

"These are the energy troughs around a hexagonal array of luxagens," he explained. "I drew it when I was first thinking about this project, back on the ground. It took about four stints to calculate."

"I can believe that," Yalda replied. It was a nice example of the kind of pattern that could persist beyond the edge of a solid—and she could easily picture a second array getting caught in those energy pits, like a truck sinking into another's wheel ruts. She said, "We're going to need to find ways to estimate the forces arising from much larger arrays, and to take account of the whole three-dimensional geometry. But don't worry about that for now; you should concentrate on refining this setup."

"All right." Sabino was still a bit dazed, and though Yalda was trying to keep him as grounded as possible, he could not have failed to realize the importance of his discovery. If this experiment could be repeated and elaborated upon, it promised to make *the nature of matter* the subject of systematic inquiry—ending the days when the differences between a stone and a puff of smoke had no better explanation than the empty incantation that "solid objects occupy space". Nereo had paved the way, but until now all his beautiful mathematics had remained untested guesswork. It was possible that Sabino and Nereo would be spoken of alongside Vittorio, who had made sense of the orbits of the planets—but Yalda thought it best not to overwhelm the young researcher with florid praise and promises of immortality. What he needed to do now was pursue the work itself.

The three of them talked through some possibilities for the next step;

simply measuring the force that had to be applied to pull one grain of calmstone free of another was one obvious goal, but the torques required to *twist them* out of their preferred alignment might also yield information about the underlying geometry.

They took the discussion to the food hall, where it turned to the question of other minerals: were they all made of the same kind of luxagens, differently arranged? Could geometry alone account for all the differences between hardstone and clearstone, calmstone and firestone? The experiments they'd envisaged so far would only be the start; Yalda could see the chase that Sabino had begun lasting a generation.

But as she finally dragged herself off to her apartment to sleep, she thought: *That's the beauty of it—there is no rush.* Time back home had come to a standstill, and any Hurtler that struck the *Peerless* now would barely leave a mark. The mountain's resources would not last forever—and they certainly didn't have enough sunstone to get themselves home by burning it the old way—but at last a tiny crack had opened up in their ignorance as to what a slab of sunstone might actually *be*.

Yalda climbed into her bed, shrugging at the resin-sticky sand until it covered her body beneath the tarpaulin, more hopeful now than ever that they were following the right course.

Fatima appeared outside Yalda's office, back from her latest errand. Yalda ushered her in, then asked quietly, "How was Nino?"

"He didn't look too bad," Fatima replied. "He said to thank you for the books."

Yalda was embarrassed. "You're the one who should be thanked."

"I don't mind taking things to him," Fatima said. "Climbing all those stairs would have been hard work, but now it's not much different than going anywhere else."

Yalda did not believe that she was endangering her with these trips—Fatima wouldn't be blamed merely for following instructions—but she was worried about the effect on the girl of being Nino's only visitor.

"It doesn't upset you, having to see him like that?"

"I'd rather he was free," Fatima said candidly. "He's been punished enough. But I know you can't let him out yet. He was kind to me, back when we were both still recruits, so I'm happy to go there and try to cheer him up."

"All right." This was the arrangement Nino had wanted, and for now Yalda had no better ideas. "Just promise that you'll tell me if you start finding it difficult."

"I will." Fatima swung back on the ropes as if to depart, but then she stopped herself. "Oh, I checked in on the forest too, on my way back."

Yalda had almost forgotten that she'd asked her to do that. No one had been officially assigned to monitor the *Peerless*'s tiny patch of wilderness, and she'd been loath to divert any of the farmers to the task while they were still coming to terms with the onset of weightlessness. "How's it looking?"

"It's less dusty there than in the fields and the gardens," Fatima said. "There were a lot of twigs and petals and dead worms in the air, but nothing larger—the trees haven't become uprooted, and I didn't see any arborines flailing around on the ceiling."

"That's a relief."

"I don't think the wheat's doing too well there, though," Fatima added.

"Wheat?"

"There's a plot of wheat in one of the clearings," Fatima explained. "It looks as if the stalks were moved there whole—dug up from a field and replanted, not grown there in the plot. But none of their flowers were open when I was there."

"I see." Yalda was perplexed; whoever was conducting the experiment hadn't mentioned it to her.

She sent Fatima to rejoin her physics class, and went looking for Lavinio, the chief agronomist. A note at the entrance to his office said he'd be down in the fields for another two stints. Yalda tried counseling herself to be patient; she didn't expect to be kept informed about every last scientific activity on the *Peerless*, and it might attract Lavinio's resentment if she showed up far from her usual haunts for no other reason than to question him about some trivial experiment.

But how trivial was it? The farmers were far too busy addressing the logistics of weightless harvesting to go and plant wheat in the forest just to test an idle conjecture about the effects of companion species on growth rates. No one would have done this unless it was important.

She couldn't wait two stints.

Weightlessness had transformed the stairwells from sites of interminable drudgery to the mountain's smoothest thoroughfares. With a pair of ropes all to herself and no one else in sight, Yalda switched to her high-speed gait: propelling herself forward with all four limbs at once, then releasing the ropes and moving ballistically for as long as possible before brushing them again with whichever hands were necessary to correct any sideways drift and replenish her speed. The moss-lit walls flew by, while the threatening edges of the helical groove that wrapped around her, its jagged steps proclaiming a vertiginous descent guaranteed to end with her head split open, only added to her triumphant sense of control. Once you could survive throwing yourself down a staircase as tall as a mountain, anything seemed possible.

Yalda reached the level of the forest in what felt like less than a bell. When she moved from the stairwell to the access tunnels, her mind insisted on treating all the arborine-proof doors along the way as hatches, and she emerged into the chamber with a strong sense of ascending through a floor. The trees stretched out "above" her did their best to persuade her to realign her sense of the vertical, but all the loose detritus suspended around them rather undermined their case.

The refitting of this chamber had been perfunctory, with just a few unpaired guide ropes suspended between hooks on the wall, so Yalda had to push off from the rock and drift freely through the air to enter the forest itself. Once she was among the trees, though, the branches offered plenty of hand-holds. Tiny dark mites darted past her with exuberant energy, coming and going in a flicker. A green-flecked lizard scampered out of her way, its claws still finding easy purchase in the bark. However ancient and unvarying their instincts, these animals had not been defeated by the change.

She found the clearing Fatima had described—and Lavinio with it. He'd crisscrossed the small treeless space with ropes, the better to access the dying wheat plants. Only now did Yalda feel that the netted soil was *below* her: she was an aerial spy, sneaking through the canopy like the arborine in her grandfather's story. She descended with as much creaking of branches as possible, to dispel any appearance of furtiveness.

Lavinio watched her in silence as she approached. He looked grimly unsurprised by her presence, as if he'd already faced such a run of bad luck that an unwelcome visitor right in the middle of it was just what he'd expected.

"Can you tell me what this is for?" she asked him, clambering down a trunk then taking hold of one of his ropes.

"I was hoping the wheat might learn from the trees," he said.

"Learn what?"

"Up."

Yalda dragged herself nearer. Disconcertingly, the floor of the forest had become vertical to her again, a cave wall from which the trunks around them sprouted like giant, bristling outgrowths. The wheat stalks *were* aligned with the trees—but presumably they'd been planted that way, so what was there to learn?

"I don't understand," she said. "Is something going wrong in the fields?" She gestured at the limp gray wheat-flowers.

"Not like that," Lavinio replied. "Here, the flowers don't know when to open; something in the light confuses them. But up in the fields the mature plants are still healthy."

"That's good to hear. And the seeds?"

Lavinio reached down into the soil between the stalks and scrabbled around for a while, then pulled out a seed. It must have been put there by hand, in a separate experiment; none of the sickly plants around it could have produced it, let alone possessed the means to embed it in the ground.

Yalda took the seed from Lavinio and examined it carefully. It was covered with dozens of fine white rootlets that had broken through the skin in all directions, favoring no particular side. There was no shoot, though, no beginning of a stalk. The seed did not know which way to grow.

"I thought light and air were the cues for stalk formation," she said.

"That's what I was taught. That was the dogma; I never questioned it." Lavinio took the seed back and turned it between his fingers. "But however shallow the placement... they still don't seem to find *up*. Even if half of the seed is uncovered—exposed directly to the light and the air—they don't get the message."

Yalda said, "So when the test seeds you sowed in the fields wouldn't grow, you came down here to see if the forest had a stronger message?"

"That was the idea," Lavinio said. "With all of this plant material oriented the same way, I was hoping some kind of influence could pass from the trees to the wheat. But the mature wheat just dies here, and the seeds do exactly what they do in the fields."

Yalda forced herself to remain calm. The mature plants in the fields were still healthy, so the coming harvest wouldn't be affected; they weren't facing imminent starvation. But they did not have long to solve this, or there would be no harvest after that.

"What's happening in the medicinal gardens?" she asked.

"All those shrubs grow from runners, not seeds," Lavinio replied. "Some of them are sprouting at odd angles, but once the gardeners correct them by hand they're fine."

"That's something."

Lavinio made a sound of begrudging assent; the disaster was not all-encompassing. But they couldn't live on holin and analgesics.

Yalda said, "I wish you'd brought this to me sooner." She could understand him wanting to prove his expertise by dealing with the problem himself, but there was too much at stake for that.

"Frido thought it would be best to find the solution first," Lavinio explained. "Instead of spreading panic when there was no need."

Yalda pondered this revelation. *Frido knew about the wheat, and he'd kept it from her?* Lavinio might have felt that the responsibility for the crops was his alone, but what was Frido's excuse?

"I'm not interested in spreading panic," she said. "But we're going to need as many people thinking about this as possible."

"I've already set up every experiment you could wish for," Lavinio insisted. "I'm looking at every combination of factors: light, soil, air, neighboring plants… what is there left to test?"

"And nothing appears to be working?"

"Not so far," Lavinio admitted.

"Then we both know what's needed," Yalda said. "The wheat's been fine until now—and only one thing has changed."

Lavinio buzzed humorlessly. "So what are we going to do? Fire the engines again, until the next crop is established? And the next one, and the next?"

"Hardly. We'd run out of sunstone in a generation, and then just starve to death a few years later."

"Then what?" Lavinio demanded. "If only gravity will make the wheat grow—?"

Yalda held up a hand and twirled a finger around. "*Spinning* creates gravity too. We could put the seeds in a rotating machine—a centrifuge—until they germinate."

Lavinio considered this. "It's an idea," he said. "But what if germination's not enough? What if it takes half a season under gravity to establish the plant's growth axis?"

Yalda was reluctant to answer that. The crew was still struggling to adapt to the last change: refitting every apartment, every workshop, every corridor; relearning every daily routine. How much discontent would it foster, to announce that all their efforts had been misdirected, and that everything they'd achieved was about to become obsolete?

Without wheat, though, they couldn't survive. And it was no use wishing that the cure would be painless; they needed to be prepared for the worst.

She said, "If germination isn't enough, we'll have to set the whole mountain spinning."

The meeting hall continued to fill slowly long after the scheduled time had passed, but Yalda had no intention of starting until everyone had arrived. People were coming from every corner of the mountain, many of them making a journey they had never attempted before under weightlessness.

Yalda stayed close to the entrance, greeting people and marking off their names on a list. Frido had offered to do the job for her, but she'd insisted on making the most of this chance to come face-to-face with every member of the crew again, however briefly.

Now Frido waited in the front tier, clinging to the ropes beside Babila and half a dozen of the old feed chamber machinists. Yalda hadn't been able to bring herself to confront him, to accuse him of acting in bad faith. She suspected that he'd been keeping the problem with the wheat to himself as a way to strengthen his position, hoping to make himself a hero to the crew by announcing a simple, biological remedy that would save them all from starvation—courtesy of Lavinio, but still created under his patronage and Yalda's neglect. No doubt he'd also been prepared to claim the rotational cure as his own, if it had come to that. In fact, Yalda remembered Frido as being part of a group who'd discussed the possibility of spinning the *Peerless*, when the first real plans were being made for the mountain. The consensus they'd reached was that it would have made navigation and course corrections far too complex, for the sake of some very uneven gains in comfort. It had never crossed their minds that gravity could be a matter of life and death.

Half a bell later, the list of non-arrivals was down to one unavoidable entry. Yalda gave a few quick words of thanks then introduced Lavinio, who explained what he'd seen, and the experiments he'd tried.

"There must be something within a wheat seed that's sensitive to gravity," he concluded reluctantly. "Three days in a centrifuge will make the seed sprout, but then it stops growing when the signal is taken away. The established crop didn't die in the fields when the engines were switched off, so we're going to keep trying longer periods in the centrifuge in the hope that we'll find a point where the seedlings can be taken out and planted. But there is no guarantee that such a point exists, short of maturity."

He moved aside, and Yalda dragged herself back on stage. She clung with four hands to the ropes behind her, surveying the anxious crowd, wondering what would happen if someone took this opportunity to lambast her over her leniency toward the saboteur. But these people had just learned that they risked starvation; Nino was a long-vanquished enemy, rotting away out of sight.

"Sometime in the next dozen stints," she began, "we *might* discover that a few more centrifuges and a bigger workforce in the farms are all we're going to need to fix this problem. But if that turns out to be a false hope, the only alternative will be to spin the *Peerless* itself, which is not going to be quick and easy. So we need to begin work to prepare for that immediately, doing all we can to make it possible in time for the next harvest—even as we hope that we won't need to do it at all.

"It might seem tempting to try to spin the *Peerless* around a horizontal axis, in the hope of making the gravity in the fields as close as possible to the old direction—but I'm afraid the mountain's center of mass is so low that it wouldn't work out that way. There's also a question of stability: if you try to spin a cone around anything other than its axis of symmetry, the slightest disturbance can set it wobbling. So we really have no choice: the mountain needs to spin around a vertical axis, running from the summit to the base."

She glanced down at Frido. Should she have had him stand beside her, backing her up, confirming these technical claims? Everyone understood centrifugal force, but half the crew would still have to take the finer points on faith.

Frido gazed back at her with a neutral expression. They both knew that he'd been preparing to move against her. It was too late to try to bring him on side.

"We'll need to install two dozen small engines," Yalda continued, "spread out down the slope of the mountain, along two lines on opposite sides of the axis. These will be very gentle devices compared to the ones we've used to accelerate, but we'll still need to put them in deep pits so their thrust doesn't merely tear them loose—or peel away parts of the surface of the mountain.

"That means digging into the rock out there, with no gravity to hold us down. It also means working in an air-filled cooling bag, to avoid hyperthermia. No one has ever done anything like this before. And however optimistic we are about it, it's more work than the usual construction crews could hope to complete in time for us to sow the crops. Everyone who isn't working in the farms will have to help. Once the construction crews have worked out the protocols, they'll start training other people to join in. I'll be among the first of their students, myself—because nothing could be more important than this."

"Stints of dangerous work in the void, possibly for nothing?" Delfina interjected. She was in the front tier, a few strides left of Frido. "That's your solution to an agricultural problem?"

"What do you suggest instead?" Yalda asked her.

"Find another food source that isn't so dependent on gravity," Delfina replied. "What are the arborines living on, in their forest?"

"Lizards, mostly. Which are living on mites—which in turn feed on bark and petals."

"We could get used to lizard meat," Delfina declared. "If it's good enough for our cousins, why not eat it ourselves?"

"I'm sure we could," Yalda conceded, "but the whole forest only supports about six arborines."

"We can't farm the lizards more intensively?"

"That's... worth considering," Yalda said. "But it would be another gamble, and even if we could make it work the payoff would come too late. The only thing we know for sure is that we *can* raise a wheat crop under gravity. Once we spin the *Peerless*, all we'll have to do is prepare new fields and plant the seeds."

"Where, exactly?" Delfina pressed her. "Which chambers were built with their floors pointing away from the mountain's axis?"

"We'll have to improvise for the first crop," Yalda admitted. "We'll have to lay down fields on surfaces that used to be walls—we won't have time to carve out new chambers with the ideal geometry."

"And what happens if we need to fire the engines? To avoid some unanticipated obstacle?" Delfina was enjoying this; someone had prepared her well.

Yalda did her best not to grow flustered. "As things stand, we'd need to get rid of the spin first. But there's no reason in principle why we couldn't redesign the attitude controls and the engine feeds to work while the *Peerless* was rotating."

Delfina hesitated, as if she'd finally reached the end of a list of objections that she'd committed to memory. But her contribution wasn't over.

"I'm sorry," she said, "but I'm not convinced. On balance, I don't think your plan is worth the risk. I won't be joining any work team for this purpose."

Yalda said, "There is no coercion here. You're free to make your own decision on this."

"And free to persuade my friends to make the same decision, I hope," Delfina added cheerfully.

"Of course." Yalda was angry now, but she was not going to change her stance and start making threats. *Help spin the mountain, or you can go without food next harvest.*

Far better, she decided, to call the spoilers' bluff.

"But we'll need to start drawing up the rosters," she said, "so I'd like to get the numbers clear right now. How many people are prepared to work to make this happen—either in the farms, or out on the slopes? Please raise a hand if you're willing to do that."

About a third of the crew responded immediately. For a long, painful moment it looked to Yalda as if that burst of enthusiastic support was all she would get, but then the numbers began to grow.

In the end, only about two dozen people chose to side with Delfina.

Most were from the feed chambers, sending her a message about Nino. No doubt there were many more who wanted the saboteur dead, but they weren't going to risk the crops—or even risk being seen as risking the crops—just to express their anger over something else entirely.

Frido was not among the dissenters. At some point he had counted the numbers around him and decided to raise his hand.

17

As they waited to use the airlock, Yalda helped Fatima into her helmet and cooling bag. No one's flesh was flexible enough to conform to the shape of the fabric perfectly—and the whole point was to ensure that there was air moving freely over your skin—but if you let the bag hang too loosely anywhere it just blew out into a rigid tent, leaving you fighting it with every move. The trick was to come close to filling the bag but to wrinkle your skin as much as possible, creating a series of small air channels between skin and fabric.

Yalda finished checking the fit. "I think you're right now," she said.

"Thanks." Fatima reached into the hold beside them and took out two canisters of compressed air, passing one to Yalda. Yalda attached it to the inlet at the side of her own bag.

"Someone should find a better way to keep cool," Fatima suggested.

"In time for the next shift?" Yalda joked.

Ausilio had finished pumping down the airlock pressure; he slid the external door open, took hold of the guide rail just outside the exit, then pulled himself through. As soon as he'd reached back to slam the door closed, Fatima opened the equaliser and air hissed slowly back into the lock.

Yalda was growing tired of these laborious preparations, shift after shift, but she kept her frustration to herself. Three more stints, and she'd never have to go through this rigamarole again.

Fatima entered the airlock and began working the pump energetically, bracing herself with three hands against the clearstone walls.

By the time Yalda was through onto the slope, Fatima and the rest of the team were already out of sight. Yalda swung herself between the guide rails and set off down the mountain, moving briskly but always keeping at least two hands on the rails. In the absence of gravity she ought to have been oblivious to the gradient of the slope, but the rim of the inverted bowl of garish color trails above her matched the old horizon perfectly, making it impossible to think of the ground as level.

The new horizon was a dazzling, multicolored circle where the fastest ultraviolet light from the old stars was shifted to visible frequencies before giving way abruptly to blackness. Straight ahead of her—"downhill"—the more modest trails of the orthogonal cluster shone sedately. Away from the guide rails, silhouetted in the starlight, dead trees sprawled at odd angles. Notwithstanding the high altitudes to which they'd been accustomed, their roots had not been enough to keep them cool in the complete absence of air. Patches of red moss had colonized the deadwood, but its faint light suggested that it was struggling.

A few saunters from the airlock, Yalda reached the pit. Lamplight from deep within the tunnel shimmered off the dust emerging from its mouth. At first glance it was easy for a planet-trained eye to see these motes as being borne on some kind of breeze, but then the thumb-sized fragments of rock scattered among the specks—moving more slowly, but just as freely—put an end to that illusion. Nothing was propelling the dust; it was flowing out of the tunnel for no other reason than its own chance collisions, inexorably driving it to occupy more space.

The guide rails, dating from before the launch, ran right past the tunnel's entrance but couldn't take her in. Yalda shifted her grip to a pair of ropes anchored to a series of wooden posts that veered off into the light. The floor of the tunnel sloped gently down into the rock; it was another half saunter before the roof was above her.

The haze of dust and grit thickened. When Yalda gripped the rope close to the posts, she could feel the vibration of the jackhammers. When she raised her hand, backlit motes of rock swirled away from it, driven by the air slowly escaping through the fabric. Fatima was right to be dissatisfied; it was a crude business when the only way they could cool themselves was to throw warm air away.

Gradually the rock face came into view, ringed by blazing sunstone lamps. Seven members of the team were working it with jackhammers, braced against the rock within their cages. Three taut guy ropes ran from the top of each cage to the tunnel wall, holding worker and cage in place against the tool's relentless kick. Yalda had done that bone-shaking job for two stints, and then finally conceded that she was past it.

Four other workers were moving between the cages, clinging to the guy ropes and dragging the open mouths of their rubble sacks over the fragments of broken rock that were bouncing away from the hammers. It was impossible to scoop up all the debris, but their efforts kept the workspace more or less navigable.

Fatima spotted Yalda and waved to her, then turned her attention back to the rubble she was chasing. With the cooling bags covering everyone's skin, communication was reduced to glances and hand gestures. If you brushed against someone you could exchange a few muffled words, but mostly the shifts were spent in a kind of tacit camaraderie, where the rhythms of the work itself—shifting the hammer cages, re-pinning the guy ropes—had to take the place of friendly banter.

There were already two full sacks waiting to be removed, the drawstrings at the top pulled closed and used to tie them to hooks on a pulley line that ran the full height of the tunnel. Yalda dragged the line around to bring the sacks within reach, slipped their drawstrings over her shoulders, then set off back to the mouth of the tunnel.

The catapult sat on the other side of the guide rails. Yalda put the rubble sacks on holding hooks at the side of the machine, grasped a nearby support post with her two left hands, then started turning the crank that ratcheted the catapult's launching plate back along its rails, stretching a set of springs below. As the crank began stiffening its resistance, she could feel the support post working itself loose from the ground. Cursing, she shifted her lower hands to the catapult, dug a mallet out of the tool hold, and bashed the support post half a dozen times.

Yalda checked the post; it felt secure now. But as she bent to put the mallet back in the hold, she could feel a tiny rocking motion in the catapult itself: she'd managed to loosen some of the tapered wooden pegs that held its base against the ground.

Never mind; she'd deal with that later. She swung the first sack onto the launching plate, checked that it was properly closed and sitting squarely on the plate, then reached down and released the catch. The plate shot up a full stride before the springs stopped it, leaving the whole machine reverberating. The sack continued on, gliding away smoothly into the void. Yalda had had her qualms about disposing of the rock this way; who knew what demands their descendants might have for even the most mundane materials? But the effort that would have been needed to secure the rubble on the slopes—let alone cycle it all through the airlocks and stash it somewhere inside the mountain—was more than they could spare.

She launched the second sack into oblivion, then headed back down the tunnel.

The haze was growing thicker. Two of the hammers had hit a lode of powderstone, which left no solid pieces to collect and just wafted out like smoke, coating everyone's faceplates with gray dust.

Four more sacks were waiting on the pulley line. Yalda brought down two of them, then paused to wipe her helmet clean and squint up at the rock face. The crumbling powderstone was a nuisance, but it would speed progress. Once the main excavation was completed, half a dozen small feed chambers would be constructed behind the rock face, accessible through a separate tunnel leading straight up to the surface. Apart from Benedetta's probes, this would be their first real test of an engine that wasn't gravity-fed, with the liberator pushed through the fuel by compressed air. Yalda was already feeling anxious about that, but in some ways the test would be forgiving. The geometry of the engine placement would be the most important thing; small variations in the thrust wouldn't be critical.

She slogged her way back out to the catapult. As she cranked it, the support post she was holding came loose again. She fumbled for the mallet—the simple task of retrieving it made harder by the streaks of gray powder still stubbornly clinging to her faceplate—then she realized that one of the sacks was actually blocking the front of the tool hold, so she shifted it onto the launching plate. Then she gripped the base of the catapult with her lower pair of hands to brace herself, and started bashing the support post.

Yalda was upside-down and two strides above the ground before she felt the tightness around her lower wrist; she dropped the mallet and reached down frantically toward the catapult, but it was already too late to grab any part of it. With her rear gaze she stared up at the sack's drawstring, twisted around her hand. She must have left the drawstring protruding from the side of the launching plate, and then slipped her arm through its loop.

Her first, idiotic, impulse was simply to disentangle herself from the sack—as if it alone were the cause of all her problems, and if only she were free of it she'd drift gently back to the ground. Her next thought was to pull it closer to her body, which she did. Then she freed her wrist from the string and clutched the coarse fabric of the sack against her chest, but she managed to stop herself from completing the plan: tossing the sack upward in order to propel herself back toward the mountain. Her instinctive sense that this tactic ought to work was almost overpowering; had she been stranded in the middle of a chamber inside the *Peerless*, it would certainly have done the trick. But even if she'd pushed the sack away with all the strength in her four arms—even if she'd burst the seams of her cooling bag and extruded two more—*it would not have been enough*. She knew how long she'd labored to turn the crank on the catapult, how much energy she'd put into the springs. A single burst of effort couldn't match that. And a partial victory that merely slowed her ascent would be completely useless, if in the process she lost the means to do anything more.

Yalda glanced back at the receding light from the tunnel mouth. If she panicked and acted without thinking, she was dead. Her rapidly increasing distance from the ground was terrifying, but it was not her real enemy. It didn't matter how long it took her to reverse direction; once she was headed back to safety, the length of her trip would be irrelevant. Or very nearly so: the sole criterion was that she needed to return before her air canister ran out—and it held enough for an entire six-bell shift.

Could the canister itself help? She ran a hand over its cool surface, imagining a swift burst of air that would send her hurtling down to safety. But without any tools, she doubted she could break open the valve that limited the outflow—and even if she could, the momentum of the entire contents might not be sufficient for the task. What's more, a marginal success would make a lie of her indifference to distance; if she ended up drifting slowly back toward the ground, without cooling she could easily die of hyperthermia on the way. There were a dozen replacement canisters in the catapult's tool hold, but did she really want to smash this one open and gamble on reaching the others in time?

No air rocket, then. All she had for exhaust was the rubble in the sack, and all she had to propel it was her own strength. But the catapult had put her in this plight using nothing but stored muscle power; if she parceled out the rubble in a manner that allowed her to expend more energy on this task than she had on turning the crank, she should be able to reverse the consequences.

Her body's slow spin had her facing back down toward the light from the tunnel again. Her fellow workers would certainly miss her as the rubble sacks began filling up the pulley line, but they would not be in a rush to come looking for her; she could easily have spent all this time on minor repairs to the catapult. The rock face was where serious accidents happened; what kind of fool managed to shoot herself into the void? But whenever they did start to worry about her absence, she could forget about anyone throwing her a rope; she was already too far away for that.

No matter; if she stayed calm, she could fix this. She identified the point on the star-trail horizon that, as near as she could tell, marked the direction in which she was traveling: precisely opposite the shrinking patch of light on the ground. She loosened the drawstring and opened the sack a little, fearful of spilling the contents with her jostling, then reached in and took out a handful of rubble. She waited for her rotation to bring the target in front of her again; she wasn't going to try to reconfigure her flesh to give equal strength to a backward throw. Then she brought back her arm and flung the handful of rock away with all her strength.

The effort felt puny and ineffectual—and she suddenly realized that in her haste and agitation she'd been laboring under yet another delusion. If she threw a heavy object, like the whole sack of rubble, the energy she put into it would be limited by the maximum force her muscles could apply. If she divided the sack in two and threw each half separately, the same force would let her throw a half-sack faster than a whole one, transferring as much energy to each half as she would have used on the whole.

Two throws, twice as much energy—hooray! But two throws would still not be enough, so why not four throws, a dozen, a gross, taking her time but increasing the total energy as much as she needed? That was what she'd been thinking: matching the energy she'd put into the catapult would simply be a matter of cking out the rubble with sufficient care.

But the pattern of throwing ever smaller weights *ever faster* only held true up to a point—for a half-sack, yes, but not for a handful of pebbles. By that point, the limiting factor would be the speed at which her muscles could contract, not the force they could apply. And when the speed was fixed, the energy she could put into a given quantity of rubble became proportional to its mass—which meant that it would add up to the same total, regardless of how many separate throws she made.

It didn't matter how much strength she still had in her body; it didn't matter that she could have cranked that catapult ten dozen more times without tiring. Her fate was completely determined by the total mass of rock in the sack, and the speed at which she could throw, not the greatest load, but the smallest.

Yalda looked back at the mountain. She could see three other worksites now, the bright mouths of tunnels further down the slope. But her trajectory was carrying her off to the side, and an expanse of dark rock was now spread out below her. There was an entire second line of worksites a half-turn around the mountain; the full set of engines would consist of a dozen diametrically opposite pairs. But if any of those sites came into view she'd know that something was wrong—that she'd been misdirecting her throws and inadvertently bending her trajectory.

She took another handful of rubble from the sack, waited for the target, then threw it. Her spin provided a rhythm for the process, giving her a chance to rest her arm without delaying the next throw too long. After a dozen cycles, she switched arms. She couldn't extrude any new limbs without damaging her cooling bag, but although she felt some jarring at the end of each throw it didn't build up to enough pain or damage to slow her down.

What she could have done with, though, was a good slingshot.

Yalda could see ten of the worksites now, with the remaining two from her side of the mountain probably just hidden behind small outcrops. All these engines would be completed, with or without her. The *Peerless* would get its spin, the crops would thrive once more. The real purpose of their journey would soon come to the fore again. Sabino had opened up a path that the brightest young students—Fatima, Ausilia and Prospera—would follow. Her death would not mean the end of anything.

And Nino? She cut off the morbid train of thought. The rubble sack was still more than half-full, her situation had not yet been proved unsalvageable.

As she threw another handful of rubble, she saw a flash of light in her rear gaze. She tried to place it exactly, to backtrack from the afterimage, but her spin confused her. Had she glimpsed one of the other worksites, the lights from its tunnel peeking briefly over the edge of the mountain? It had been too bright for that, hadn't it? The tunnel mouths all faced the same way around the mountain—so those at the other worksites would be pointing away from her. The most she could have seen was the spill of light from the ground near the pit, and the scatter in the dust haze. How could *that* have outshone the sites where she was facing straight into the tunnels?

A few turns later, she was facing the mountain when she saw a second flash: far from any of the worksites, surrounded by blackness. She wondered if someone might have lit a sunstone lamp inside one of the observation chambers—but why would they do such a thing, let alone light it only for an instant?

The third flash was at a different location, still nowhere near any worksite—and too brief and too bright, Yalda concluded, to be an artificial source at all. Something must have collided with the *Peerless*—something small that nevertheless carried enough energy to turn the rock white-hot.

The telescopes had shown a corridor devoid of matter, but there'd been a limit to the sensitivity of those observations. Any speck of dust here, drifting along at a leisurely rate relative to the ordinary stars, would now be like a Hurtler to the *Peerless*. That was the price of taming the Hurtlers by matching their pace: ordinary dust could now do as much damage to the mountain as a Hurtler could do to an ordinary world.

So much for the city of carefree scholars, working in safety and tranquility until the secrets of the cosmos were laid bare to them. Just like the people they'd left behind, they would be living with the constant threat of conflagration. And not for four years: for generations.

Worst of all, Yalda realized, she was probably the sole witness to these events. The dust could have been striking the mountain for days, but most of the surface was invisible from the worksites and observation chambers.

She had to get back and organize a fire watch for the *Peerless*; they had to prepare themselves to reach and douse a wildfire anywhere on the slopes, or risk going the way of Gemma.

Yalda cast another few stones—imagining them heavier in the hope of tricking her body into dispensing a little more force. The sack was a quarter full. She believed she was still heading away from the mountain, but judging tiny changes in the view at this distance was almost impossible.

How could they keep a lookout for fires? From a cage tethered on a rope, high above the surface, stabilized… somehow. Once the mountain was spinning, though, the problem wouldn't be stability, but the strength of the rope.

And once the mountain was spinning, it would be far harder to move around on the surface. Weightlessness had made it difficult enough, but every part of the slope would be transformed into a ceiling. How did you douse a raging fire on a ceiling?

The sack was empty. Yalda clutched it to her chest, unwilling to presume that she'd have no further use for it. *Was she moving toward the mountain, or away from it?* For some time now, she hadn't discerned any change in the angle it occupied in the sky, but she'd been too distracted to give the task much thought. She needed to pick a few distinctive stars close to the edge of the mountain, then wait to see if they crept away from it, or whether its silhouette slowly grew and hid them.

Yet another flash of light came from the mountain, this one very close to one of the worksites. Perhaps someone there, outside the tunnel on catapult duty, would have seen it? Yalda counted the pit lights down from the summit, and realized that the site was her own.

The light winked again, from exactly the same direction. Not an impact, then. By now, she realized, her team would be out scouring the area for her, their sunstone lamps occasionally turning up into the sky. Yalda pictured them inspecting the catapult, feeling how loose it was, wondering if anyone could possibly have been careless enough—

The same light appeared, brighter than before, crossing her line of sight so slowly that it dazzled her. When she completed a half-turn it struck her rear gaze and stayed—wandering a little, but never fading out completely.

The lamp wasn't on the surface of the mountain; it was moving straight toward her through the void. And it couldn't be aiming itself, searching her out itself.

Yalda spread the empty sack out in front of her, hoping to make a larger, more reflective target. The approaching light began wavering oddly, as if seen through a heat haze. *Through a burst of air, spreading out through the void.* Some beautiful idiot had come after her—launched along the same trajectory by the catapult—and now they were using compressed air to brake. Not from a tiny canister like her own, but from one of the giant cylinders that powered the jackhammers.

The dazzling light overshot her, passing to one side. It rebounded, then overshot in the other direction. It was excruciating, but Yalda could do nothing to meet her rescuer halfway. By trial and error, by eye and airburst alone, the distance and difference in speed that separated them was whittled down to the point where the lamp became superfluous and its owner shut it down. No longer blinded by its glare, by starlight alone Yalda could see the figure before her, clutching an air tank and a coil of rope, wrapped in a familiar cooling bag.

Fatima took hold of a portion of the coiled rope and tossed it toward Yalda. This sent her gliding backward, but she didn't bother trying to compensate, she just let the rope uncoil. Yalda reached out and grabbed the end, then brought it around her waist twice and held on tight.

There was a jolt as the rope went taut, then they were bound together, moving in a broad circle around a common point. Yalda dragged herself along the rope a short way, then gestured to Fatima to use an airburst to get rid of some of their angular momentum. By the time they were within arms' reach of each other, their spin was almost gone.

Fatima took hold of Yalda's helmet and pressed it against her own. "Help me get down. Please."

She sounded terrified, and for a moment Yalda couldn't reply. *How could she have come after her at all, if she was so afraid?*

"Let me take the canister from you," Yalda suggested gently. "Don't release it until I'm holding it."

Fatima had two arms wrapped around the cylinder. Yalda embraced it herself the same way, then eased it out of Fatima's grip.

With her other hands, she rearranged the rope, forming two coils and bringing them around their bodies, then securing the connection with a series of knots. Fatima was shivering; she'd already done more than Yalda could have asked of anyone. It was her own job now to get them safely down.

"I keep thinking about Benedetta," Fatima said. "Landing is the hardest thing."

"This won't be like that," Yalda promised. "No fire, no heat, no danger—" She noticed the sunstone lamp still strapped to Fatima's shoulder. "We won't need that anymore." She pulled it loose and swatted it gently away into the void; with all the jarring it had suffered already, it was a miracle it hadn't exploded.

Yalda found her target on the horizon and opened the valve on the air cylinder a notch; the effortless kick against her arms was the most beautiful sensation she'd ever felt. She'd never know if she'd already been heading back toward the ground before Fatima reached her; she didn't want to know.

A pinprick of light appeared on the dark rock below them. "Did you see that?" Yalda asked Fatima. She'd been hoping that she might have been delirious before—or that Fatima's ascent might have included enough unlikely swerves for her search lamp to account for everything.

"Yes. What was it?"

"I have no idea," Yalda lied. "Don't worry; we'll work it out later."

As the mountain loomed closer, the line of worksites spread out beneath them, the most distant fading to black. Yalda made a sideways correction, steering them toward the mouth of their own tunnel. When that patch of bright rock began to grow alarmingly, she squirted air down, slowing their descent. For a pause or two she thought she might have overdone it and launched them away from the mountain again, but they were close enough now that the cues did not remain ambiguous for long. She used another quick burst to slow their horizontal motion, lest they scrape all their skin off on the rock.

As the guide rails running past the tunnel mouth rushed into view, Yalda discerned a new feature: the team had tied dozens of lengths of rope to the rails, spread out along a couple of stretches, pointing away from the rock with their free ends high above the ground. If she could steer into this soft, forgiving fence—

"Try and grab the ropes!" she urged Fatima, as they swooped toward them. "The more arms to share the jolt, the better."

A flicker before the glorious fool-catcher came within reach, Yalda used a tiny kick from the cylinder to give them a slight upward velocity. Then she dropped the cylinder and flailed around, managing to seize one of the ropes. Fatima had gripped another one, in two places. Yalda brought all her own hands onto her rope before it went taut; the shock to her joints made her cry out in pain, but she didn't lose hold of it.

They were a few strides above the guide rails. Yalda had been expecting to have to drag herself hand-over-hand down to the ground, but the ropes' elastic tug had delivered a little more force than was needed to stop them, and they were actually drifting slowly toward the surface.

Fatima began humming from the shock. Yalda almost joined her, but she was afraid that if she started she'd never stop.

She said, "We're safe. You did it, my friend, and now we're both safe."

18

Lavinio said, "Without gravity, I think this is the best we can do."

Yalda bent down from the ropes that crossed the test field and examined the plants. The wheat stalks were barely two spans high.

"They're... mature? They're making seeds?" The tiny structures protruding from the stalks certainly resembled seed cases, but they were so small that it was hard to be sure.

"Yes, they're mature," Lavinio confirmed.

"But they're a twelfth the size of normal wheat!"

"However long we keep the seedlings in the centrifuge," Lavinio explained, "they always stop growing when we take them out—but if we raise them to this height first, they don't die when we replant them in the fields. They don't get any bigger, but they do form seeds of their own."

"Wonderful."

It was not the outcome they'd been hoping for, but Lavinio couldn't hide his fascination. "It's as if the maturation process is triggered directly by the cessation of growth, so long as the plants are larger than some critical size. If we really understood the mechanism, perhaps we could intervene further. But for now—"

"For now, we have the option of growing six crops a year—each with extremely low yields." Yalda prodded one of the seed cases with a fingertip. "And these actually germinate?"

Lavinio said, "Yes—if we put them in a centrifuge, like their parents. The seedlings start out extremely stunted, but they catch up in size by about the fourth stint."

Yalda had been expecting a clear-cut verdict, one way or the other, to force her hand. The utter failure of the centrifuged seedlings would have left her with no choice but to spin the *Peerless*, while a perfect fix that let them grow the old-style crops would have allowed her to declare that building the engines had been a worthwhile precaution, but actually firing them had mercifully proved to be unnecessary. "So where does this leave us?" she asked.

"It would be much more labor-intensive than ordinary farming," Lavinio said. "And we'd need at least ten dozen centrifuges to yield the same total volume of grain as we were harvesting in a year, when we had gravity."

Ten dozen centrifuges, running around the clock. Burning fuel, demanding maintenance. Spinning the whole mountain would eat into their sunstone reserves—but they would only need to do it once.

"It would be survivable," Lavinio added. "Not ideal, but not completely impractical."

Yalda thanked him, and promised a decision within the next few days.

She headed back to the summit, skimming along the stairwell's ropes. With ordinary wheat in ordinary fields, it would be a simple matter to increase the size of the crop to feed a larger population. Having to build and run a dozen more centrifuges just to increase the yield by one tenth would change everything.

But if they went ahead and spun the *Peerless*, and then some wayward pebble set the slopes on fire, how much harder would it be to douse the flames when the mountain was flinging everything off into the void?

Yalda left the stairwell in the academic precinct and dragged herself down the corridor toward her office, trying not to betray her anxiety as she returned the warm greetings of passersby. Now that the tunnels were finished, the completion of the spin engines was in the hands of skilled machinists—but everyone here had been out on the slopes in the dust and danger, everyone had earned the right to think of the project as their own.

Some people flashed her looks of excitement and anticipation; some called out "Three stints to go!" If she turned around and announced that all of their work had been for nothing—and that they would now have to live on meager supplies of machine-raised, stunted wheat—she was going to need a spectacularly compelling argument to back up her decision.

Marzia was waiting outside her office. "The test rig's ready," she said. "Just give the word, and we'll launch it."

"Are you sure this is safe?"

"It will be five strolls from us when it ignites, and still moving away," Marzia reminded her. "I don't see how we could make it any safer without giving up the chance to observe it at all."

Yalda accepted this, but it was hard to be relaxed about the experiment. The engines of the *Peerless* had failed to set the world on fire, but that had never been their purpose. Marzia's rig was designed to ignite a mineral that had never been seen burning, except perhaps on the surface of a star.

"What if a spark comes back and hits the mountain?"

"Any debris that would be hot enough to harm us will be hot enough to burn up long before it reaches us."

"Unless you ignite the Eternal Flame," Yalda joked weakly.

Marzia gave an exasperated buzz. "If you're going to start invoking those kinds of fantasies, why not throw in another twist and let us survive anyway? Then we can all head home to see our families."

Yalda said, "Go ahead and launch the rig. Just make sure that the fire lookouts know what to expect."

Three bells later, Yalda met Marzia in the precinct's observation chamber. Marzia had set up two small telescopes and trained them on the rig, which from their point of view appeared almost fixed now as it drifted away from the mountain. By starlight the device was just a slender silhouette, but after Yalda had taken a peek to confirm that the instrument was aimed correctly, Marzia handed her a filter to slip into the optics. The image was about to brighten considerably.

As Yalda checked the wall clock with her rear gaze, a globe of light erupted at one end of the rig's calmstone beam, spraying luminous shards into the void. The beam had been slotted straight through the middle of a spherical charge of pure sunstone, encased in a solid hardstone shell; on the timer's cue, the fuel had been saturated with liberator and the heat and pressure had risen until the casing was blown apart. A slight equatorial thinning of the shell had directed the explosion outward from the beam, sparing the other equipment attached to it and leaving almost no net force or torque; the beam had acquired a barely perceptible rotation, and had remained squarely in view.

And it was burning. The sunstone had scattered, and the calmstone itself was ablaze.

Marzia let out a chirp of triumph at this unprecedented feat. Yalda would have been far happier to learn that calmstone was impossible to ignite—and that the stars, and Gemma, must have simply lacked the mineral that covered most of the surface of the world. Calmstone sand could douse burning fuel. Calmstone had contained the Great Fire of Zeugma. Calmstone had borne the launch of the *Peerless* without succumbing to the flames. But now—

"Air does make a difference," Marzia muttered happily. Similar experiments had been attempted back home, but with air always present to carry away some of the heat, the calmstone had never reached its flashpoint.

They'd soon know if the same effect was enough to put out the flame once it was already burning. A few strides along the beam from the ignition trigger, four tanks of compressed air were fitted with clockwork ready to discharge their contents onto the flame. There was no missing this when it happened: as the air rushed down the beam the whole rig accelerated sideways, and Yalda had to start turning the scope to keep the apparatus in view. Once she managed to track it closely enough to steady the image she could see the artificial wind distorting the incandescent halo around the beam—but the calmstone itself grew no dimmer. The fire remained self-sustaining: the creation of light by each tiny patch of the disintegrating mineral was accompanied by enough heat to guarantee the same fate for its neighbors, with enough to spare to make up for whatever the surrounding gases were carrying away.

Yalda was dismayed, but there was one more stage to the rig, one more trick to test. A pause or two after the first four tanks emptied, a second set opened up—but now the air, though much gentler, was being routed through pipes half-filled with powdered hardstone. This was the ultimate bucketful of sand: a dose of the most inert mineral of all to draw the heat into itself and try to disrupt the cascade of energy.

The hardstone sand was poured radially, with four symmetrical flows directed straight down onto the beam to cancel out any rocket effects and allow the material to accumulate as much as possible in the absence of gravity. It was a model for the best-case scenario: the equivalent of dousing the mountain's slopes in the absence of any confounding spin.

The timing of the release had been guesswork, chosen on the basis that earlier was better, and the portion of the beam subject to this treatment had not yet caught alight. Some sand was drifting away, but there was more than enough being added to make up for that; Yalda could see the mound growing by the light of the encroaching flames.

As the fire hit the mound, the view faded to black; with the filter in place even the stars were invisible. Yalda restrained herself; anything could still be happening beneath the sand. But if this worked, she thought, one more experiment would be enough. If they tried the same thing with a spinning rig and found that the centrifugal force ruined the dousing effect, then stunted wheat would be a small price to pay to retain the ability to protect themselves.

A light flickered and brightened, illuminating the remains of the rig. The fire had continued to consume the beam; it had merely been hidden. There was no "dousing effect" to be saved.

Yalda turned to Marzia. "What now?" she asked numbly.

"We could vary some parameters," Marzia suggested. "Tweak the flow rate, or the quantity of the hardstone powder."

"I thought this was already the best setup you could think of."

"It was," Marzia said. "But my guesses aren't infallible; some small change might still improve it."

"Enough to make a difference?" Yalda pressed her.

"It's not impossible."

Yalda said, "Then it's worth trying."

There had to be a solution. She could not accept a life for the travelers as hazardous as the life they'd left behind. The flashes of light on the surface had been harmless enough so far—but they wouldn't get a second Gemma moment out here. The proof that the worst could happen would only come when the *Peerless* itself burst into flames.

Marzia said, "You know I studied chemistry in Zeugma?"

"Of course. I think we met once, after I visited Cornelio."

"We always worked with a knife beside us," Marzia said. "We protected our bodies as much as we could… but when something went wrong, you couldn't really hope to find an effective extinguisher in time."

Yalda was horrified. "And you think that's the best we can do? *Prepare ourselves for an amputation?*"

"I had to cut off my own hand twice," Marzia replied. "It was either that, or lose everything."

"I admire your resolve," Yalda said, "but hands can be reformed. Flesh can be replenished. Any rock we discard is gone forever."

Marzia thought for a while. "Our 'empty corridor' has turned out not to be as empty of ordinary matter as we hoped," she said. "Could we have missed some orthogonal matter as well?"

"That's possible." The orthogonal star cluster was more than a dozen blue light-years away, but the dust and pebbles of the Hurtlers themselves were all around them, and there could be larger non-luminous bodies as well.

"Whittling the mountain down to nothing over the generations is an alarming prospect," Marzia said, "but if tossing the occasional fire-afflicted portion off into the void is the only way to protect ourselves… maybe we can take comfort in the possibility that what we're losing isn't really irreplaceable."

Yalda said, "Comfort isn't quite the word I'd use."

Marzia persisted. "The idea of crossing the void to try to mine another body of rock might seem daunting to us now, but who knows what our descendants will be capable of?"

"How much more are we going to load onto them?" Yalda asked wearily. "It's bad enough that we expect them to invent their way home with whatever fuel they have left. Now they're meant to find *mines in the void* in time to patch up the mountain before fire damage shrinks it to an uninhabitable core."

"What choice do we have?" Marzia replied. She gestured toward the dying embers of the rig. "I'm happy to try more experiments, but I can't see our luck changing there. Whatever the solution is, we have to trust the people who come after us to play a part in finding it. If we'd had all the answers ourselves, we would never have needed to make this journey at all."

Three times a day, the fire lookouts climbed down their rope ladders for the change of shift. The number of impact flashes they reported rose and fell, but no more than Yalda would have expected for random collisions.

If the dust had comprised some kind of well-defined obstacle with known borders, they could have planned a route around it, or at least done the calculations and decided whether it was worth the cost in fuel. But they had not seen any hint of this in advance, before their velocity blinded them to all the ordinary matter ahead, and now any maneuver that sought to escape the problem would amount to no more than trying out random detours one by one and then seeing if they'd made things better or worse. They did not have that much sunstone to burn.

Marzia's follow-up experiments came to nothing. If burning calmstone could be extinguished at all, they were as far as ever from discovering how to do it.

Yalda sought out Palladia, the most experienced of the construction engineers, and asked her to consider the possibilities for *discarding parts of the mountain*. After a couple of days pondering the matter, she returned to Yalda's office to sketch out her preliminary ideas.

"The two simplest options," Palladia said, "would be to install a kind of sacrificial cladding—expendable tiles covering the surface that could be detached easily if they caught alight—or leaving the exterior as it is, and being prepared to blast an outer wall away, if necessary."

"Blast an outer wall away?" Yalda was no longer prepared to rule out anything. "So we lose pressure, then spend a couple of years with everyone in cooling bags trying to make repairs?"

"Hardly," Palladia replied, amused. "We'd divide the outer precincts into individual sections. We'd put pressure doors in all the access corridors, and pre-install a set of charges in each section. Once the lookouts identified the precise location of the fire, there'd be a procedure to follow: start the timers on the charges, evacuate everyone, seal the section... then the wall is blown into the void, taking the fire with it."

"Tell me about the first option." Yalda resisted adding: *the sane one.* "The tiles, the cladding."

"There are two issues there," Palladia said. "Can we mine enough material from the interior to put an effective layer of cladding on the surface, without causing structural problems? We need to be able to guarantee the integrity of every chamber under the loads arising from centrifugal force, not to mention the eventual re-use of the main engines. But even if we have enough raw material, the next question is whether we'd have time to clad the whole exterior before our luck runs out and the surface catches fire. That would be a massive task under any conditions—but with the mountain spinning it would be the hardest thing we've ever attempted."

"We could delay the spin-up, if it was worth it," Yalda suggested reluctantly. They could live off stunted wheat while they completed this shield, if it was actually going to be capable of protecting them.

Palladia said, "Let's try to get some solid numbers."

They worked together for ten days. Thanks to Marzia's experiments they knew the rate at which calmstone burned, and though no one had yet been able to find one of the tiny impact sites on the surface, Yalda could estimate the depth to which dust particles of various masses would penetrate the cladding when they struck with infinite velocity. Palladia had surveyed the whole mountain during the construction phase, compiling the first detailed records of its composition, and she'd witnessed firsthand how various chambers had stood up to the stresses of the launch.

The numbers were not in their favor. To cover the mountain with a worthwhile protective layer would leave it gutted and weakened inside, to the point where its spin alone could start breaking it apart. But giving up on spin wouldn't save them; the next time they fired the engines, to decelerate, the *Peerless* would turn to rubble.

"I want you to draw up plans for… our other option," Yalda said.

Palladia regarded her with something close to panic.

"I'm not asking you to rush anything," Yalda assured her. "You should take as long as you need to get this right. But you should make all your choices on the basis of structural considerations alone. We'll address the other practicalities separately—if we have to move some pieces of equipment to safer locations, or duplicate some facilities, so be it."

Palladia was still not happy. "When are you going to speak to Frido about this?"

Yalda said, "I'm speaking to you, because I know you can do the job. You can have as many assistants as you need—just pick whoever you want. You might have to wait until the spin engines are finished for some people to become available, but once that's done this will be our highest priority."

Palladia replied carefully, "I'm honored to be given this responsibility—but with respect, I think Frido and Babila should be involved. *Assistants* can follow instructions and check my calculations, but they won't have the confidence to argue with me if I head down a wrong path. This is too important to be left to one person."

Yalda could see the logic in that. "Why Frido and Babila?"

"They're the most experienced engineers we have," Palladia said. "Who else should I consult?"

She was afraid, Yalda realized. If something went wrong with the scheme and the *Peerless* ended up crippled and airless, the architects of the plan would be held accountable. Though Yalda would take most of the blame, anyone who had been too close to her on this would share the opprobrium. But if the most powerful members of the only other viable faction were equally enmeshed in the project, Palladia would have some protection in the aftermath.

Was that so unreasonable? And regardless of the politics, Yalda didn't doubt that Frido and Babila would scrutinize the plans diligently. Whatever their disagreements, they were not going to jeopardize the *Peerless* itself just to undermine her.

"All right," she said. "Let's talk to Frido."

They found Frido in his office. He listened patiently to their summary of the problem and the results of their calculations.

"Of course I'm happy to help," he said. "But before we go any further, I think we should put this to a crew meeting—just as we did with the spin engines."

Yalda said, "Why? The construction crews can handle this; we won't be taking anyone away from their ordinary jobs."

"No," Frido agreed, "but it will still affect everyone. Having explosives set up all around the mountain is not the kind of change we should be making lightly."

Yalda glanced at Palladia, but she remained silent. "It should be clear that we haven't come to this *lightly*," Yalda said. "Are you in favor of the plan, or not?"

"Of course I'm in favor of it," Frido replied calmly. "And I want to do everything I can to see it carried out, safely and successfully. The question is, how can we bring the crew along? Can we convince them that, in protecting the *Peerless* from external threats, this won't increase the risk to their lives from the enemies within—from saboteurs?"

Yalda traveled down from the summit to check the preparations before the spin engines were fired. In the fields, the last of the crops to grow up from the old cavern floors were being harvested. In the gardens, workers shifted plants and netted soil onto walls that would soon be horizontal. A haze of dust and organic detritus filled these chambers, leaking out into the corridors and stairwells to dim the moss-light and coat every surface with black grime.

After consulting with Lavinio and the other agronomists, Yalda had decided to leave the forest untouched. It was near enough to the axis of the mountain to remain unaffected by centrifugal force, and the effort required to shift the whole tangled maze of full-grown trees—as well as capturing and moving the arborines—seemed disproportionate to any benefit, when all the plants and animals it contained were doing well enough without gravity.

Boards were being fitted over the helical grooves in the outer stairwells, to bridge the gaps in the floors of the tunnels they'd become. The ring corridors could be left as they were, their walls already traversable, but crews were busy fitting rope ladders to their radial offshoots.

Every factory, every workshop, every office needed to be *rethought*, if not literally reconstructed. But as Yalda traversed the length of the *Peerless* from field to mill to kitchen, from plantation to carpenter's workshop, from the medicinal gardens to the holin store, everyone she spoke with accepted the upheaval without complaint.

This was not the time to tear people away from their work to confront them with the news of Palladia's plan, and she doubted that Frido would be foolish enough to do that himself. While they were as busy as this, united by the common cause of rescuing the crops, no one would be interested in hearing about anything else.

When the work was done, though? Frido could undermine her whisper by whisper, spreading his own message about the new project, leaving people wondering why she hadn't explained it to them herself. However she handled this, she would not be able to put off the confrontation for long.

Yalda waited in the observatory for the fireworks to begin. She'd invited her old work team to join her, but not everyone had accepted; there were observation chambers lower down offering much better views of the pyrotechnics. But she had something different in mind: she'd locked the big telescope on a point just above the horizon, so her companions could take a look and commit what they'd seen to memory. The flames pouring from the tunnels they'd helped carve into the slopes would be spectacular enough, but the actual proof of the engines' efficacy would first appear as a tiny shift in the view through the telescope.

Fatima let go of the ropes she'd been holding and curled up in midair. "This is where you discovered rotational physics, isn't it?"

"It must be," Yalda replied, "but I don't really recognize anything. The ground, the buildings… everything's changed." Even the telescope itself had been rebuilt, with the original lens inserted into a new frame.

"Someone should put a sign here," Fatima suggested. "To commemorate it."

"I'm sure that can wait until I'm dead."

Yalda glanced at the clock beside the telescope; there were still three lapses left to ignition. Ausilia and her co were clinging to the lowest of the cleaners' handles at the edge of the dome, peering down the mountain expectantly. Prospera and her friends were over near the entrance, daring each other to attempt ever more intricate ricochets off the clearstone panes. It would be hard to end up stranded in midair, and Yalda had no fear that they'd break the dome, but if anyone collided with the telescope she'd be annoyed.

"I saw Nino yesterday," Fatima said.

"How was he?" Yalda asked, wishing she didn't have to hear the answer.

"Not so good."

"Did you take him some books?"

"He's not reading anymore," Fatima said. "He told me he's lost the power to concentrate; the words just make him dizzy."

Yalda said, "I'm sorry. But I'm sure you cheered him up."

Fatima's expression hardened. "If he knew when he was getting out, it might be easier for him. If you could set a date—"

"Set a date? Do you think it's that easy?"

"You're the leader, aren't you?" Fatima replied bluntly. "And everyone respects you even more, since you decided to build the spin engines. You're going to save the crops, save us all from starving! Do you really think people will throw you out, after that?"

"It depends on what else I do," Yalda said.

Fatima was drifting disconcertingly far from the support ropes; she reached down in time to pull herself back.

"If it's getting too hard for you, maybe someone else could join you in the visits," Yalda suggested.

Fatima turned to face her squarely. "I'll tell you exactly what it's like," she said. "I go and see him every two stints. I bring him some loaves, tell him some gossip, try to make a few jokes. But that's it, that's all I can do. When I turn around and leave, nothing's changed for him. He's my friend, I'll never abandon him… but it's like holding someone's hand while they're being tortured."

Yalda's skin crawled. "I'm sorry."

"Stop apologizing," Fatima said angrily. "Just do something for him."

Ausilio let out a chirp of delight, and Prospera's group quickly scrambled to the edge of the dome to catch sight of the flames from the engines. Yalda motioned to Fatima. "Let's take a look; it will be a while before anything shows through the telescope."

They pulled themselves along the ropes to the nearest pane. Looking down the slope, they could see three pale cylinders of blue-white fire emerging sideways from the starlit rock. Yalda waited anxiously for something to go wrong; she'd had visions of one of the engines tearing itself out of the ground and cartwheeling off into the void, spraying the mountain with fire as it went. But the pale flames remained motionless and steady, and she could barely feel the vibration of the engines.

She should have been ecstatic. Their ignorance about the wheat might have killed them, but now they were close to guaranteeing the success of the next crop. She remembered when Nino had told her of Acilio's sneering prediction of their fate: *Eating the soil. Begging for death.* The fact that it had almost happened only made it infinitely sweeter to imagine Acilio's face when the *Peerless* next lit up the sky over Zeugma.

But what could she do for Nino? Stand up in front of the crew and declare that he deserved to roam freely now—right after informing them that she wanted to fit explosive charges in every wall that separated them from the void? Or simply wait for Frido to explain to them that Palladia's plan required a new leader who would send the right message to all the would-be saboteurs lurking among them, by finally disposing of the last one who'd been caught in the act?

Yalda dragged herself back to the telescope, and called the team to gather around. The red end of one star trail that she'd centered in the view had now shifted, just detectably, out of the cross-hairs.

"How do we know the telescope didn't get bumped by the engines' vibrations?" Prospera asked, only half-joking. "How do we know that the mountain's really turned at all?"

All that hard, dangerous work, all that beautiful fire pouring out across the slopes, for an incremental change that could as easily be an illusion.

Yalda said, "How do we know? Be patient, wait a while, then look again."

Two days into the spin-up, one of the lookout posts—wisely left unoccupied for the duration of the process—snapped free of its ropes and was lost to the void. Isidora, whom Yalda had put in charge of the lookouts, had the other three reeled back in to be strengthened and tested before anyone tried to use them again.

By the time the engines were shut down there'd been no other reports of serious damage. In the academic precinct there was a series of small annoyances to deal with—most of them involving the realization that the centrifugal force here, though too strong to be ignored, was also too weak to produce enough friction to hold things in place in the conventional way. Equipment and furniture that would have stayed put under old-style gravity now had to be re-secured just as firmly as when it had been weightless, in order to resist the pushes and tugs of ordinary use.

Yalda quite liked the slight weight she'd acquired in her own office and apartment; she could still use the old system of ropes to get around, but she no longer found herself flailing in panic if she ended up out of reach of all the walls, ropes and handles around her. Slow as she was to fall toward the walls that had turned into floors, her body now accepted that she couldn't end up stranded.

After helping to get the optics workshop functioning again—with Sabino moved to a perfectly weightless room of his own, dead on the axis—Yalda headed for the fields. As she soared down the central staircase it was as if nothing had changed, but when she took hold of the rope ladder at the mouth of the radial exit, she dutifully reformed her lower hands and descended feet-first.

The tunnel led into the top of the nearest chamber; the flat disk of the interior was now standing on edge. The rope ladder continued down one of the rock faces, and as Yalda moved between the sheer walls, even in the moss-light she found it hard to think of the place as an underground cavern anymore. It was more like descending by night into a secret valley.

The gravity was still weak here, but it had cleared all the dust out of the air. The floor of the valley was deserted, but when Yalda stepped carefully between the furrows she could see that the newly planted seeds had already sent up shoots. The sight sent a shudder of relief through her body.

A flimsy guardrail surrounded the mouth of the radial tunnel leading down into the next chamber; nothing about this exit now looked remotely sensible. "Ah, Eusebio," Yalda whispered. "Everything's turned sideways in your beautiful design." She slipped between the rails and reached across to the rope ladder, which followed what had once been the corridor's floor. As she gripped the ladder's side and the structure swayed toward her, her old, dormant sense that a fall could injure her was abruptly reawakened.

The second field had been sown later than the first; no shoots were visible, but Yalda found a buried seed and checked that it was sprouting. Lavinio would have told her if there'd been any problems—but to touch the promise of the next harvest with her own hands reassured her, made her feel strong.

In the third field, the closest to the mountain's surface, farmers were still at work. Half a dozen firestone lamps had been strung on a pulley line that stretched from the entrance at the top of the chamber to a corner of the field. As Yalda descended, she could see the giant shadows she cast sideways across the rock face.

When she reached the ground, one of the farmers, Erminia, approached and greeted her.

"Thank you for your work here," Yalda said. "How long until you finish sowing?"

"One more day, but then there's another field…" Erminia gestured in the direction of the summit, unsure how to refer to it now that "up" had two different meanings. "Two days there, then the whole crop is planted."

"As soon as there's a chance, we'll join the two chambers," Yalda promised.

"Really?" Erminia didn't sound enthusiastic.

Yalda was puzzled. "One large field here would make things easier, wouldn't it?" They needed the extra space for the crops that they'd gain by cutting through the intervening rock, but in any case she'd have thought it would be more convenient to work a single expanse of soil.

"I heard you were going to put explosives here," Erminia said, "to blow out any fire that starts below us. If that's what it comes to, I'd rather we lost as little of the crop as possible."

It was a fair point, but Yalda didn't reply; she didn't want to confirm the plan in a casual conversation, let alone start debating the pros and cons of individual section boundaries.

The rumors were already spreading, though. The longer she delayed dealing with them, the weaker her position would be.

She said, "Can you spread the word to all your friends and colleagues: there'll be a meeting at the summit, five days from now, on the third bell."

"A meeting about what?" Erminia asked.

Good question, Yalda thought. *Why you should be perfectly relaxed about the prospect of your wheat fields exploding beneath your feet?*

"We've fixed the crops," she said. "Now we need to talk about what we're going to do to avoid going the way of Gemma."

Yalda waited outside the meeting hall, counting the people as they entered while she rehearsed two speeches in her head.

One speech was about the time the crew had spent working together on the slopes, with their lives in each other's hands and the fate of the *Peerless* in the hands of everyone. She'd been rescued from a near-fatal accident herself, but they all had their own stories of their friends' courage and ingenuity. After that, why would they imagine that they needed a rule of fear to keep them safe? One weak-willed farmer with starving children had been persuaded to commit one dangerous act. But Nino had repented and been punished, and he had no reason to try to harm anyone again. He did not need to die, either for the sake of his own crimes or for the sake of the *Peerless*'s future. Letting him live would not be an act of weakness; it would be an affirmation of everyone's mutual trust.

The other speech she had ready, in case her first one went badly, concerned the equipment and protocols that could be developed to limit access to the charges, without rendering the fire response so slow as to be useless. And if she grew desperate enough, she was prepared to start talking up the prospects of contingency plans to rescue anyone who ended up outside the mountain in the event of an unplanned breach of the walls.

Palladia emerged from the hall. "Who are we waiting for?" she asked Yalda.

Yalda checked the roll. "Isidora and three others; I think they were all on lookout shifts." The shifts ended precisely on the bell, but even if they'd forgotten about the meeting and worked through to the usual time, they were later than she would have expected. "I'll wait until four chimes past, then we'll have to start without them."

"You don't think someone…?" Palladia asked anxiously.

"Snapped a rope?" Yalda had been too distracted to even think of such a thing, but the pang of horror at the thought passed quickly. "The others would have sent for help by now." The lookouts had already completed one shift safely with the newly-strengthened designs, but in any case the protocols were clear: if someone had ended up adrift in the void, the other lookouts did *not* try to retrieve their colleague themselves, they returned to the mountain immediately to raise the alarm.

"What's the mood in there?" Yalda asked. She'd greeted everyone as they'd arrived, but they'd all been equally polite to her. When even Babila and Delfina congratulated her on the success of the spin-up, she could hardly trust anyone's words or demeanor to reveal their true plans.

"You should take a look for yourself," Palladia suggested.

Yalda dragged herself over to the entrance. There was plenty of room in the hall for people to spread out comfortably, and many had done just that, but about a third of the crew were clustered together toward the front, clinging to the support ropes that held them up against the weak gravity, jostling each other excitedly, buzzing and chirping.

In the center of this pack was Frido, dispensing his wisdom. She couldn't hear what he was saying, but the enthusiastic responses were deafening.

She'd heard all this noise from out in the corridor, but she'd imagined it was down to boisterous groups of friends rejoicing in their achievements, not one man charming the crowd.

Who was she fooling? She was not a politician or an orator; no one would listen to her words about *building the future on trust*. If she'd wanted to defeat Frido, she should have started poisoning people against him long ago—making up some story about him having forced his runaway daughter back to her co. Either that, or listened to Nino's advice from the sagas and just had him killed.

She returned to Palladia. "If you went to him and offered a deal from me, do you think he'd listen?"

"What kind of deal?"

Yalda said, "I'll stand aside, I won't oppose him at all, if he promises to let Nino live. Let him threaten hypothetical future saboteurs with any octofurcating thing he likes—just let him respect the decisions I made in my own time, and leave Nino be."

"What if he says no?" Palladia asked. "You'll have weakened your position for nothing."

Yalda could hear the mirth surging in the hall again. "What else can I do? Ask him. Please."

Reluctantly, Palladia pulled herself back along the rope toward the entrance.

"Yalda! Good news!"

Yalda turned. It was Isidora who'd called out; she and the other three lookouts were approaching in the distance.

Palladia hesitated. "So everyone's safe?"

"Well, there they all are," Yalda said.

"And that's the good news?" Palladia was confused. "Of course it's good, but…"

Yalda was about to reply that she couldn't think of any other possibility, but something in Isidora's tone gave her pause.

Palladia made a move toward the entrance again. Yalda said, "Wait." She turned and called down the corridor to Isidora, "What good news?"

The expression of joyous bafflement on the woman's face started Yalda's skin tingling before she said a word.

"No impacts!" Isidora shouted back. "Two shifts, nooooo impacts!"

Yalda waited in silence until they were close enough to speak properly.

"*Two* shifts?" she asked Isidora.

"I was going to tell you after the first shift," Isidora explained, "but you were so busy, and I thought the observers might just be confused by the new setup. We reconfigured the lookout posts… I know it makes no sense, that couldn't explain a null count, but I had to be sure. I had to see it for myself before I made a fuss about it."

Palladia said, "No impacts since the spin-up? You're serious?"

Prospera, who was one of the other lookouts, said, "Staring at dark rock for four bells, the miracle is I didn't start hallucinating flashes. Zero means zero."

Palladia turned to Yalda. "How? You think we've just passed out of the dust?"

"Do you believe in that kind of coincidence?" Yalda replied.

"What else could explain it?" Palladia countered.

Yalda exchanged glances with Isidora, and let her speak. "The spin-up," Isidora replied. "Whatever's been making the flashes, whatever's been striking the surface, the centrifugal force must be enough to cast it off before it can heat the rock."

Palladia was incredulous. "To a dust particle with *infinite velocity*, that force is nothing, it's completely irrelevant!" She addressed Yalda imploringly. "You agree with me, don't you? Or is everyone going mad?"

Isidora nodded to Yalda: *your turn.*

Yalda said, "I agree with you completely—which means the flashes can't be coming from anything moving so fast. They must be coming from orthogonal dust… I mean dust that was orthogonal to us before the launch, not now."

Palladia blinked. "Hurtlers? *Original* Hurtlers?"

"How else could it make sense?" Yalda replied. "Whatever it is that's been causing the flashes must be moving so slowly relative to the *Peerless* that our spin is enough to brush them away. Well, we always knew that our trajectory would tame the Hurtlers."

Palladia grimaced. "But if we've tamed them, what caused the flashes? How could something striking us so slowly turn the rock white-hot?"

"I have absolutely no idea," Yalda confessed, "but if it wasn't kinetic energy that was heating the rock, all I can think of is some chemical process—and the dust must have needed to stay on the rock long enough to react with it in some fashion. Now that the slopes are unable to hold on to debris… no more flashes."

Palladia was angry now. "You're telling me that Hurtlers are made of… what? *A liberator for calmstone?* The dust from the orthogonal worlds that fills the void here isn't actual rock, it's a refined substance people extract from plants with the express purpose of causing fuel to burn?"

Yalda said, "Not the sarcastic bit at the end, but whatever's been hitting us must act as a liberator for calmstone. Don't ask me how—but if you don't believe that, tell us how else you can explain the sudden cessation of the flashes."

Palladia glared back at her in silence, then she said, "I have no idea. But you're right, it can't be a coincidence. The spin is protecting us. So whatever's been striking us, it's *not* high-velocity material."

"Which means there's no reason, now, to believe that even a piece dozens of times larger than those that caused the flashes could set the slopes on fire," Yalda suggested.

"No reason at all," Palladia agreed.

"So our plan for exploding walls is superfluous?"

Palladia hesitated. "Absolutely. We just need some sacrificial cladding near the axis—at the summit and the base, where the centrifugal force offers no protection…" She stopped speaking; she was trembling with relief.

Yalda put a hand on Palladia's shoulder then turned to Isidora. "I think we should all go in there and share the good news with Frido and his friends."

19

"Be warned," Yalda said, "that I'm going to be spending most of my time telling you about things I don't understand. Along the way I'll offer you a few facts and a few guesses—but then I'll explain why those facts aren't quite enough and why those guesses can't quite be right."

She looked out across the room. Many of the faces were familiar to her, young women and men whose education she'd been following from the start. But there were half a dozen students she barely recognized, too, which was even more encouraging. Once they put the old barbarities behind them, everyone on the *Peerless* could live the life of the mind. One day they'd all be doing rotational physics with their eyes closed, thinking about the symmetries of four-space as naturally as they moved their limbs.

"What don't I understand?" she continued. "I don't understand why solids are stable. I don't understand why gases aren't sticky. And I don't understand why the gentlest contact with the dust that surrounds us can turn rock white-hot."

"I thought we proved that solids were stable," Ausilia interjected. "In our last class with Severa."

Yalda said, "What you did, I think, was show that there are several geometries that an array of luxagens can assume in which Nereo's force, acting between them, would hold them in place. Is that right?"

"That's how I understood it," Ausilia replied.

"So how does that work?"

"Every luxagen is surrounded by hills and valleys of potential energy," Ausilia said. "If you have a number of them, you can drop them all into their neighbors' valleys, making a nice, neat pattern in which they should all prefer to stay put."

"That's perfectly true," Yalda said. "But there are a couple of problems

Severa wouldn't have raised, to avoid confusing you while you were still learning the fundamentals."

She sketched a basic one-dimensional example.

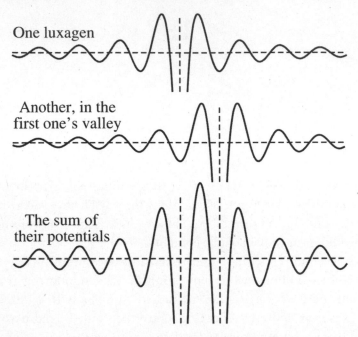

One luxagen

Another, in the first one's valley

The sum of their potentials

"A luxagen can sit in its neighbor's energy valley," she said. "And I've put it in the first valley, rather than any of the more distant ones, which are shallower than the first. But is that really the deepest place there is?"

There was silence for a few pauses, then Prospera offered, "The pit would be deeper."

"Of course," Yalda replied. "The pit centered on the luxagen itself is bottomless, though I've only drawn it going down a short way. Once they're close enough, two positive luxagens just keep attracting each other ever more strongly, until they collide. So why don't all the luxagens in a piece of rock simply end up falling into each other's energy pits, until the whole rock has shrunk down to a speck?"

"Isn't that like asking why the world doesn't crash into the sun?" Fatima suggested. "If there's any sideways motion, the two luxagens wouldn't actually collide. If they started outside the pit, they'd just skim around it and end up outside again. And even if they had the right amount of energy to stay in the pit, wouldn't they just orbit each other, like Gemma and Gemmo?"

"You're right," Yalda said. "But if two luxagens end up orbiting each other, there's something more to think about: a luxagen moving back and forth *makes light*. If the luxagens create light, they need to provide true energy to do that. But to *provide* true energy—to lose it themselves and turn it into light—they need to *gain* kinetic or potential energy. So why don't they end up moving faster and faster, and breaking the whole solid apart?"

Silence again. Then Giocondo—a young man Yalda could only name from his tag—said, "What if the luxagens are moving too fast to make light?"

Yalda waited a pause to let the other students ponder that. "Go on," she said.

"There's a maximum frequency of light," Giocondo began tentatively. "In the equation for light, the sum of the squares of the frequencies in the four directions must equal a fixed number—so none of the individual frequencies can have squares that are bigger than that number. If a luxagen is moving back and forth with a greater frequency than that... It *can't* create light in step with its motion, because there's no such thing."

Yalda said, "That's correct. And eventually we'll work through the calculations for the amount of true energy that an oscillating luxagen passes to the light field, and we'll show that when the frequency crosses the threshold Giocondo's just described, the energy flow drops to zero."

"Then why is there still a problem?" Ausilia asked. "Oh... why don't all the luxagens end up orbiting in one single energy pit?"

Prospera said, "Because the peaks around the pit keep getting higher. Maybe a few luxagens *are* orbiting in the same pits, but the more of them you throw in together, the higher the energy barrier around them becomes."

"Right," Yalda said. "The more luxagens you have, as long they're sitting in each other's pits or valleys, the potential just keeps adding up: all the valleys become deeper and all the peaks get higher. So eventually the pit would become inaccessible, because it's surrounded by insurmountable peaks."

Fatima said, "So that keeps all the luxagens from falling together completely, and the rest just end up in each other's valleys rather than each other's pits?"

"Go on," Yalda pressed her.

"I suppose they'd roll around in the valleys too, just like they orbit around the pits," Fatima mused.

"And if they roll fast enough in the valleys," Giocondo added, "they'd be stable there too. They wouldn't emit light and end up tearing the solid apart."

Yalda was delighted. "Bravo, everyone! A few lapses into the class, and we have solids rendered almost solid again."

Ausilia said, "Almost? What's the catch?"

"The idea that Giocondo raised is very appealing," Yalda said, "and as far as our measurements can guide us, it seems to be true. The energy pits and valleys in real solids seem to be shaped in such a way that the natural frequencies of motion for the luxagens are greater than the maximum frequency of light.

"The only trouble is: if a luxagen isn't going to make *any light at all*, there can't be any wobbles to its orbit in the pit, or its rolling around in the valley. If there was even the tiniest imperfection in its motion that progressed at a sufficiently low frequency, then *that* would start to generate light."

"Which would make the imperfection stronger," Ausilia realized. "So it would lose true energy faster, grow stronger even faster… and the whole thing would get out of control."

Yalda said, "Exactly. And the thing is, the shape of the potential energy that we get from Nereo's equation doesn't allow for perfect orbits, or perfect rolling in the valleys. The main cycle can have a high enough frequency to avoid creating light, but the potential has built-in flaws that guarantee that there'll be lower-frequency motion as well. It seems to be unavoidable."

"But solids *don't* blow themselves apart," Fatima proclaimed irritably. "Not without a liberator."

"Of course," Yalda said. "So although we seem to have most of the story, although it *almost* adds up… there must be something we're missing, something that nobody yet understands."

She let them ponder that for a moment, but then moved on swiftly. Being told that you'd reached the point where you could only make progress by breaking new ground was a daunting thing to hear for the first time.

"The second mystery," Yalda continued, "is the structure of particles of gas. There are plenty of symmetrical polyhedrons where putting a luxagen at every vertex gives you a mechanically stable configuration—which seems to make them good candidates for the little balls of matter of which we expect a gas to be comprised. But those polyhedrons share the problem solids have: the luxagens rolling in their energy valleys will always have some low frequency components to their motion, so they ought to give off light and blow the whole structure apart.

"There's another problem as well, though: tiny, pure fragments of solids are sticky, as Sabino's experiments have shown. But the gases that make up air don't seem to be sticky at all; it's as if the field around them has somehow canceled out, almost completely.

"A young friend of mine back home, Valeria, showed that a spherical shell of luxagens of the right size would have no external field, so you might think that a polyhedron of a similar size could get close to that perfect cancellation. The trouble is, the need for mechanical stability gives you one size for the polyhedron, and the need to cancel the external field gives you a different size. It seems to be impossible to meet both criteria at once."

Some of the students were beginning to look dismayed. Proving the mechanical stability of an icosahedron built out of luxagens had not been an easy exercise, and now they had to accept that all that hard work had been nothing but the first step into a larger, unknown territory.

"The third mystery," Yalda said, "is the strangest, and the most dangerous. The *Peerless* is surrounded by fine dust that we believe is the same kind of material that we saw back home as Hurtlers, when it burned up in the solar wind at close to infinite velocity. But we've more or less matched its velocity now… so why should it behave any differently toward us than any other dust?"

Tamara, another near-stranger to Yalda, had heard the theory that had begun circulating a few days after the news that the spin of the *Peerless* had stopped the impact flashes. "The luxagens are swapped," she said. "Any that would be positive in our own materials will be negative for that dust, and vice versa."

"Can you say why?" Yalda pressed her.

"It's come to us… around the cosmos," Tamara struggled, tracing out a loop with one hand.

"And why does that matter?" Yalda persisted. "How does that swap the luxagens?"

"I don't know," Tamara confessed.

Yalda sketched out the general idea.

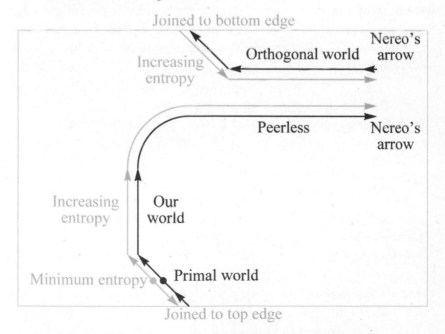

She said, "Suppose the orthogonal stars, the orthogonal worlds, are fragments that broke off the primal world *backward*. They've come full circle around the cosmos, and we're moving alongside them with our arrows of increasing entropy in agreement. We know that *those* arrows agree, because otherwise the orthogonal stars would be invisible to us.

"But Nereo's equation ties the field around a luxagen to a vector that points along its history—and there's no reason for *that* arrow to have anything to do with entropy; it should simply stay the same along the luxagen's entire history. That vector determines whether the luxagen is positive or negative: if we meet a luxagen with the vector pointing into our future, we call it positive; if the vector's pointing into our past, we call it negative."

"So who drew the arrows on the luxagens?" Fatima joked.

"Well, exactly," Yalda conceded. "No one really knows what this vector means. Still, we ought to be able to tell when two luxagens have different signs. Close up, a negative luxagen will *repel* a positive one, and the whole pattern of potential energy seen by a positive luxagen around a negative one will be upside down: all the usual peaks will become valleys, all the usual valleys will become peaks."

"Which would cause havoc if you mixed the two," Prospera suggested.

"Not necessarily," Yalda replied. "You can't replace a positive luxagen with a negative one in exactly the same location in a solid, but the negative one wouldn't want to be there anyway—it sees the potential energy curve upside down, so it would prefer to be at a peak rather than in a valley. And if it's located at a peak, it won't disrupt the original pattern, it will reinforce it."

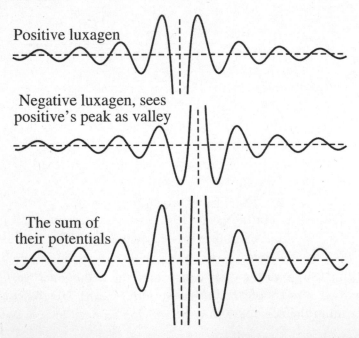

Positive luxagen

Negative luxagen, sees positive's peak as valley

The sum of their potentials

"So it's not really clear why a speck of dust with its luxagens swapped should cause any more damage when it collides with ordinary rock than an ordinary speck of dust traveling at the same speed. But then... we don't really know how plant-derived liberators work, nor do we understand why rocks don't simply burst into flames all by themselves. So we're a very long way from determining what will or won't set any given solid on fire."

Yalda paused to take in the students' expressions, to see who was beginning to look burdened by the uncertainty they were facing, and who was exhilarated by the prospect of searching for something entirely new.

"I don't have the answers," she said. "All I can do is give you some tools that will help you probe these mysteries, then stand back and see what you discover."

"Yalda, can I speak with you?"

Yalda looked up from her notes to see Lavinio on the ropes at the entrance to her office. "Of course."

As he approached, the solemnity of his demeanor became apparent. "Don't tell me it's the wheat," Yalda begged him.

"The wheat's fine," Lavinio assured her. "But there's blight in some of the goldenrod."

"Some of it?"

"Not every plant is showing signs of infection," he said, "but there are infected plants in all four gardens."

"How could that happen?" The gardens were worked by different staff, and even Lavinio refrained from visiting all of them. An infection in one should not have spread easily to the others.

"We can't know for sure."

"Can't we make a guess, to try to stop it happening again?" If the protocols for disease limitation were flawed, they needed to be corrected urgently.

Lavinio said, "It was probably all the re-planting work, just before the spin-up. All that dust in the air was impossible to contain; it would have spread throughout the mountain."

That did make sense—and if the hazard had not been avoidable, at least there was a chance it would never be repeated.

Yalda braced herself. "So, how do things stand?"

"We've taken three cuttings of goldenrod from each garden and started growing them in a dozen new locations," Lavinio said. "The transfer was done with all possible care; two separate couriers who'd never been in any of the gardens took each cutting part of the way, and I've recruited new people to look after the plants. But realistically, we can't expect them all to stay free of the blight."

"No."

"We can't risk harvesting petals from the cuttings at all, until they're established," Lavinio continued. "And it might be unwise to take too many from the original plants either, right now; we don't want to weaken them unduly before we know that at least some of the new ones have ended up in good condition."

"I understand." For the next few stints there would not be much holin produced; that was unavoidable.

But Lavinio had done everything possible to safeguard their future supplies. With a bit of luck, the shortage need not be severe or long-lasting.

Yalda said, "Let me know if anything changes."

In the pharmacy, Sefora checked the stock of holin tablets. "We have enough for about seven stints at our current usage," she said. "There are some petals still being processed, but that will only add a day or two to the supply."

Since the launch, every woman on the *Peerless* had been taking a regular dose of holin that depended on her age, using tables Daria had drawn up that erred on the side of caution. Until now, the gardens had been providing more than enough goldenrod petals to keep the stores replenished; the real limit on building up a larger stockpile had been the shelf life of the drug.

"Can you draw up new dosage tables?" Yalda asked.

"On what basis?"

"We need to stretch out the stockpile—but there's no point letting the holin sit and go bad."

"So… stretch it out how long?" Sefora pressed her.

"It's hard to say," Yalda admitted. "It's not clear when the gardens will be producing again."

"How much are you willing to cut the dosages?"

"How much can I, without putting people at risk?"

"No one has those numbers," Sefora replied. "Holin's efficacy has never been properly studied, never quantified. All we've ever had are anecdotal reports: if you heard of a woman of a given age who wasn't protected by the dose you heard she'd been taking, you assumed it would be wise to take more."

On the *Peerless*, that uncertainty was meant to have been subsumed by a constant surplus of the drug—and with four bountiful gardens, that should have been possible.

"I suppose it's too late to start testing it on arborines," Yalda lamented.

"That would take years," Sefora agreed.

"Not to mention some actual holin we could spare."

Sefora said, "I'll draw up dosage tables that will let the stockpile last ten stints. Any longer than that, and I wouldn't trust the quality. Do you want me to make any exceptions?"

"Exceptions?"

"If we cut the older women's doses in strict proportion to everyone else's," Sefora explained, "I can't promise that they won't face a greater increase in risk."

Yalda said, "You mean a drop of three parts in ten could be enough...?" She pictured Tullia, lying motionless on the floor of her apartment. No one had the numbers, but they all had their fears.

"I could always leave the dosage for the senior women unchanged," Sefora said "If we made an exception for everyone older than a dozen years and ten, that's less than a sixth of the female population. Spread out between all the younger cohorts, the difference would scarcely be noticeable." She was not quite as old as Yalda, but she would fall into the same category.

Yalda considered the suggestion. Wouldn't it be fairer, to protect the most vulnerable members of the crew? It would certainly be prudent: they couldn't risk having the most experienced women taken without warning, leaving the *Peerless* drifting aimlessly through the void.

She said, "I think you should do that."

"If a particle is moving in an energy valley that takes the form of a parabola," Yalda told the class, "it will repeat the same harmonic motion over and over, with a frequency that depends only on a single number describing the parabola's shape."

"Like a weight oscillating on the end of a spring?" Prospera suggested.

"Or a pendulum under gravity?" Fatima added.

"In idealized versions, yes," Yalda agreed, "though in reality both those systems experience friction, and both have small deviations from a parabolic potential.

"Still, in the absence of friction—or light generation—the particle's energy will be conserved, and if it's moving back and forth in just one dimension, even if the valley isn't shaped like a parabola the particle will always return to its starting point. So its motion will be perfectly cyclical, and it won't have any harmonics with a lower frequency than that cycle.

"But in two or more dimensions, things start to get more complicated. Even when energy is conserved, a particle need not retrace its path exactly. If the shape of the valley is a perfect paraboloid it will do so—" Yalda sketched an example:

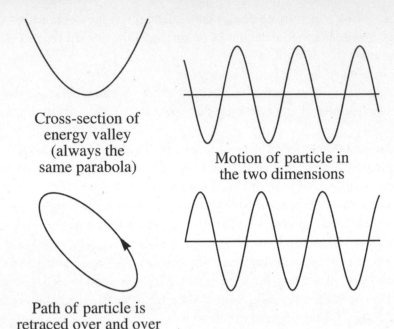

Cross-section of
energy valley
(always the
same parabola)

Motion of particle in
the two dimensions

Path of particle is
retraced over and over

"But that's not the case for the energy valley in a solid, due to Nereo's potential. There, the cross-section isn't exactly parabolic, and it will be shaped a bit differently when you slice it in different directions."

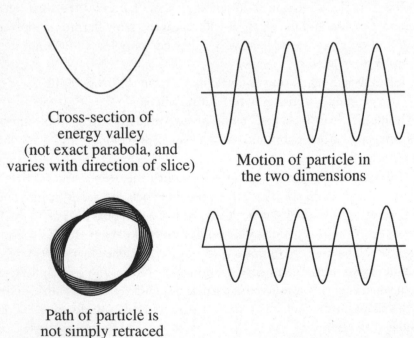

Cross-section of
energy valley
(not exact parabola, and
varies with direction of slice)

Motion of particle in
the two dimensions

Path of particle is
not simply retraced

"So instead of moving back and forth with a single, pure frequency, a luxagen in this energy valley will follow a path that we need to describe with a multitude of different frequencies, all present in different amounts."

"Like describing the strengths of all the colors in a flame?" Ausilia asked.

"Very much like that," Yalda said. "What we're going to be doing, eventually, is trying to predict both the colors of solids in ambient light and the spectrum of the light that we'd expect them to emit. And then the question will be: *why are our predictions so wrong?* Why does it actually take some kind of disruption for solids to start emitting any light at all?"

After the lesson, half the class moved to the food hall, unwilling to end the discussion. Yalda watched the young women among them swallowing their two tablets of holin with their loaves; each cube was smaller on its side than the old ones by just one part in six, which made the rather greater reduction in its volume almost invisible. But she'd taken her own dozen full-strength cubes in the privacy of her apartment, ashamed of the discrepancy even though it was unlikely that anyone would have noticed it.

Yalda listened to the students' excited chatter and answered their questions with care. Who else could have taught them harmonic analysis of Nereo's potential, if not her? Who else could have set them on the path to a future where everything the *Peerless* would need in order to survive its exile and return in triumph was finally understood?

Isidora, Sabino, Severa. Perhaps a dozen people in all. She was not indispensable.

Fatima lingered after the others in the group had gone. "Have you thought any more about Nino?" she asked Yalda.

"You know I'd be happy to free him," Yalda replied. "But to do that, I need to be in a position of strength. I'm sure Nino understands that."

Fatima was unmoved. "You rescued the crops and swatted away the orthogonal dust with the same hand! Everyone knows that they owe their lives to you. How much stronger do you think you'll ever be?"

"This goldenrod problem—" Yalda protested.

"That's hardly your fault."

"Whether it is or it isn't, people won't be happy until it's resolved." Suddenly self-conscious, Yalda looked around the hall with her rear gaze, but no one was paying them any attention.

Fatima said, "There'll always be something. If you just saw Nino, if you spoke with him—"

"Anyone else would have gotten rid of him by now," Yalda declared irritably.

Fatima regarded her with disbelief, then lapsed into a reproachful silence.

Yalda said, "I didn't mean that. I'm sorry. When things have improved, I'll look at his situation again."

"You were in prison once, weren't you?" Fatima replied. It was a rhetorical question; she knew the answer. "Waiting for someone to set you free?"

"I won't abandon him," Yalda said. "I promise you that. Just let me find the right time."

"Ten of the goldenrod cuttings are infected with blight," Lavinio announced. "The other two appear to be healthy. But those two cuttings are all we have now; the plants in the four main gardens are lost."

Yalda absorbed the news, and tried to think through the consequences calmly. They would not be able to harvest any petals from the cuttings until they'd grown larger, or they'd risk killing the plants. It could be as long as half a year before any more holin was being produced—and after that, it could take another year or two for the rate of supply to return to normal.

"What if you split each cutting—after a few stints—and grew the halves separately?" she suggested.

"That would just delay the time until they were strong enough to survive harvesting," Lavinio explained. "The most important thing is keeping those two plants strong and uninfected."

"I understand."

"We're lucky we haven't lost the goldenrods completely," Lavinio said bluntly. "If we're not careful, it might yet end that way."

When he'd left, Yalda clung to the ropes beside her desk, fighting a growing sense of helplessness. Word of how serious the problem had become would not take long to spread; if she failed to deal with it swiftly there'd be chaos.

Rationing the stored holin more severely wouldn't help; there was no point eking it out so slowly that it began to lose its potency. The only way she could survive the wait until production started again was to commandeer enough of what remained to increase her dose as time went on, to compensate for the drug's deterioration.

But then even when the holin was fresh again, there would not be enough to go around.

She could ask Sefora to draw up a plan to save the oldest women, leaving the others to take their chances. No one on the *Peerless* was a child, though; no one would be immune to the risk. The shortage would take its toll across the mountain—while the drugs that kept each old woman alive could protect half a dozen of their younger crew-mates.

Yalda struggled to clear her mind. How was she meant to weigh up the choices and reach the right decision? Eusebio had given her Frido to share the burdens of leadership, but she'd destroyed any chance of trust between them, any hope of getting honest advice from him.

She dragged herself along the ropes to the front of the office and pulled the doors closed. She let her body relax completely, then she felt herself begin to shiver and hum.

How close had she come to snatching a few more years for herself, by risking the futures of all the young women who still had their lives ahead of them? How close had she come to stealing the hard-won promise of Prospera, Ausilia and Fatima—Fatima who'd never shown her anything but loyalty, who'd had the love and courage to pluck her from the void?

What had she imagined her own role would be? To see the journey through to the end? To return to Zeugma to share the triumph with Eusebio, and join in the celebrations with all her lost friends? She'd made her choice: she'd been vain enough to believe that the *Peerless* needed her. But it needed her only to set its course; everything else belonged to the generations to follow.

Yalda composed herself. Once her body was still again she felt calm and lucid.

She'd played her part, and it was almost over. But now she knew what needed to be done.

Isidora's co worked in the pharmacy, and he'd done the same job for eight years back home. Yalda met him to gauge his loyalties. While Sefora was in charge he would follow her instructions, but he accepted Yalda's right to replace her. And he did not want his own co to lose control over her body.

Yalda picked a dozen young women to accompany her. They made their move a bell before the main shift began; none of the junior pharmacists put up any serious resistance, and by the time Sefora came on duty Yalda's team had the holin store surrounded.

"Are you going to punish me for doing what you asked?" Sefora demanded angrily. She looked to her colleagues for support, but they wouldn't meet her gaze; they were backing the new guard.

"I'm not punishing you at all," Yalda replied. "You served the *Peerless* well, but now this job needs someone new. You can retire to a life of ease."

"Really?" Sefora emitted a mirthless buzz. "Is that what you intend doing yourself?"

Yalda said, "You can hear about my plans at the meeting, along with everyone else."

Yalda surveyed the faces of the assembled crew. "I wish we had holin for everyone in the mountain," she said, "but that's beyond our control now. So the time has come for the women like myself who would use the most of it to step aside, and leave what remains to those who have the most to lose."

She listed the replacements for a dozen senior positions. A trace of discontent rippled through the crowd, but she could see expressions of acceptance, too. There was no painless way through the shortage, but any other scheme would have ended in insurrection.

"On the question of who should take my place as leader," she said, "everyone knows there is an obvious choice." Yalda stretched out an arm toward Frido, who was clinging to a rope near the front of the hall. "But before I appoint my successor, I need to ask him if he's willing to meet some conditions."

Frido said, "Tell me what you want."

"When I step down," Yalda said, "I want the right to choose my own co-stead. And when I'm gone, I want my family to be left unharmed. I want my co-stead and my children to be given your respect and protection, and to suffer no revenge."

Frido regarded her with an expression of wounded horror. "What kind of monster do you take me for? Yalda, you have the love and respect of everyone here. No one will harm your family."

"You give me your word, before the whole crew?" she insisted.

"Of course. Everything you've asked for, I promise it will be done."

Yalda had no idea what was going through his mind, but what else could he have said? She'd just granted the young runaways the best prospects they could have hoped for to make it through the holin shortage. If Frido had so much as hinted that he expected to assert some bizarre, paternalistic right to veto her choice of co-stead, they would have torn him apart.

She said, "Then it's done. I resign the leadership in your favor. If the crew accepts you, the *Peerless* is in your hands."

Frido moved forward, toward the stage. Behind him, half the crew began chanting Yalda's name—affirming her decision, not rejecting her successor, but it still made Frido flinch.

Watch your back, Yalda thought. *Get used to it.* That's what your life is going to be like now.

20

Fatima moved ahead of Yalda down the center of the stairwell, pausing now and then to allow her to catch up. Yalda didn't mind being hurried along this way; if they'd been traveling side by side they would have had to pass the time discussing the reason for their journey.

When they came to the first radial tunnel, Fatima let herself free-fall most of the way, only snatching at the rope ladder when she began to veer away from it. Yalda declined to follow her example, and descended slowly, rung by rung. The locked doors they encountered along the way did not appear marked, let alone damaged. No one had been sufficiently motivated to try to assassinate the half-forgotten saboteur.

In the abandoned navigators' post above the second-tier engines, Yalda waited outside the cell. Nino trusted Fatima, so it was best that he hear most of this from her. But after a few lapses, she invited Yalda in.

"Hello, Yalda." Nino hung in the center of a sparse network of ropes. He was much thinner than she remembered him, and he kept his eyes averted as he spoke.

"Hello." The cell was crowded with books and papers. As in Yalda's own apartment their not-quite-weightless state would make them difficult to manage, but the place had been kept scrupulously tidy.

"Fatima explained your proposal. But she wasn't able to say what would happen if I refused you."

"Nothing is by force," Yalda said. "Whatever you choose, I'm willing to take you to the summit and do my best to protect you."

"I don't know if I could look after myself up there," he said. "Let alone... anyone else."

Fatima said quietly, "I'll help."

Nino seemed paralyzed, unable to reach a decision. How could any of them know what was or wasn't possible? Yalda surveyed the papers stacked against the rear wall. "We can come back for these later," she said. "Unless there's something you need?"

Nino buzzed softly. "I never want to be in the same room as the sagas again."

Outside the cell he faltered, gawping at the preposterous spaces around him. Had Fatima never broken the rules and let him out during a visit? Perhaps he'd refused, afraid that even a small taste of freedom would make his imprisonment too hard to bear.

On the journey back Fatima was patient, demonstrating to Nino how to negotiate the changing forces on his body. Yalda looked on, trying to be equally encouraging herself, but wondering if she'd made a terrible mistake. Nino might learn to be agile again, but what had she done to his spirit? When she'd been teaching him, she'd had no doubt that his memories of his children were keeping him sane. But he'd spent more than three years excluded from any kind of normal life—and she still didn't know if he'd be accepted back into the community of the *Peerless*.

When they left the central stairwell in the academic precinct, Nino blinked and squinted at the lamps around them as if he'd been thrust into the searing blaze of noon. When the first passerby looked their way he stopped moving and clutched the ropes tightly with four hands, his posture growing cowed and defensive. Yalda watched the woman's expression change from confusion to recognition, then from shock to comprehension. As she passed them on the opposite ladder she glanced at Yalda with what might have been an acknowledgment of her audacity, but exactly what fate she wished for the happy couple was impossible to discern.

Fatima took Nino with her everywhere, introducing him to friends, fellow students and acquaintances without a trace of self-consciousness, as if he were a long-lost uncle who'd just arrived in their company by some mysterious alternative route. At first Yalda took this as some kind of unspoken reproach for her own reticence at the task, but then she realized that it was nothing of the kind. People put up with a very different attitude from Fatima, as Nino's advocate, than they would have from the woman they blamed for the fact that he was still alive at all. Fatima was utterly partisan on her friend's behalf, but there was no reason for anyone to think of her as self-serving.

Every day, Yalda tagged along as Fatima showed Nino the food halls, the workshops, the classrooms. He was getting reacquainted with places he hadn't seen since before the launch, and roaming far enough from the axis to grow familiar with the changing centrifugal force. Some of the people they encountered were brusque, but no one started screaming threats or accusations. And even those who had no particular respect for Yalda, or Fatima, or for Frido's oath of protection, might have been given pause by the realization that Yalda's choice of co-stead was the bluntest possible assertion of a woman's right to decide when, and with whom, she had children. With holin scarce, with pharmacology failing them, any purely cultural force in favor of autonomy was all the more precious.

Isidora and Sabino took turns teaching Yalda's old class. Yalda sat in and listened, watching Nino struggling to extract some sense from all the arcane technicalities as Fatima whispered explanations to him. This was his world now, not the wheat fields, and whatever role he played in it he'd have to learn some of its language and customs.

Yalda made a bed for him in her apartment, and he accepted that intimacy without complaint or presumption. The first night he was with her she could barely sleep; she did not expect him to wake her and demand what she had offered him, but his presence made it impossible for her to forget the ending she had chosen for herself. Better that than to be taken by surprise, like Tullia. Her only other choice would have been to launch herself into the void again and wait for her cooling bag to run out of air, leaving her to cook in her own body heat. Because whatever she might have wished for in a moment of weakness, however strong the urge to renege might have become, the holin that could have bought her a year or two more was now irrevocably out of her hands.

Nino clutched the rope at the edge of the observation chamber and peered down at the countless tiny color trails fixed above the rocky slope.

"Those are the orthogonal stars?"

Yalda said, "Yes."

He grimaced. "They look just like the stars back home. But now you're saying that their worlds could kill us with a touch, if we so much as set foot on them?"

"That's how it seems," Yalda replied. "But then, who knows what will happen down the generations? We might even find a way to mine their rock, to render it harmless."

Nino looked skeptical. He still found it difficult to accept that the *Peerless* had a future at all.

"Look at what we've survived already," Yalda said. "Harder tests than any you gave us at the launch."

"If those stars lie in the future," he said, "why can't you just search among them with your telescopes and see if they strike the world, or not?"

"Light from that part of their history can't reach us here," Yalda explained. "When we looked out at the ordinary stars, back home, we saw them as they were many years ago. The same is true of these stars—but 'many years ago' by our measure, now, means far from the world, far from any collision that might happen."

"But if they continue as we see them—?"

"Then the world will end up in the thick of them," Yalda said. "That much is clear."

Nino was silent. Yalda said, "What we're doing has the chance to help your children, far more than Acilio's money ever could. Don't you want to be a part of that?"

"It's worth trying," he conceded. "Better than rotting in that cell. And if you really can trust me with your own flesh—"

"Why wouldn't I?" Yalda did her best to silence her doubts. "You've been a good father before. Just promise you won't force the sagas down their throats."

"I might tell them a couple of the old stories," Nino said. "But the rest would be about the flying mountain whose people learned to stop time."

He reached over and put his hand on Yalda's shoulder. Nature dulled her fears, lulling her into a sense of rightness at the thought of what lay ahead. If she waited, if she asked for time to say her farewells, that would only make it harder. This was her last chance at the closest thing to freedom: her will, her actions, and the outcome in the world could all be in harmony.

Yalda said, "I want you to name our children Tullia and Tullio, Vita and Vito." For all that she'd cared for Eusebio, if he was going to outlive her his name could look after itself. "If there's a solo, call her Clara."

Nino dipped his head in assent.

"Love them all, educate them all."

"Of course," Nino promised. "And you'll be no stranger to them, Yalda. What I don't know about you, your friends will tell them. Fatima will tell them a dozen stories of you a day."

He'd meant to reassure her, but Yalda shivered with grief. A mountain could fly through the void, but she could not see her own children.

She fought against her sadness; if she succumbed to it now and stopped what they'd begun it would only be twice as painful the next time.

Yalda took hold of the ropes with three of her hands; with the fourth she drew Nino's body closer. The color trails of the old stars were splayed out above them. His chest pressed against hers, innocently at first, but then their skin began to adhere. Yalda twitched, panic-stricken, picturing herself tearing free, but then she stifled her fear and let the process continue. When she looked down, a soft yellow glow could be seen passing through their conjoined flesh, its message older than writing.

Her eyelids grew heavy, and a sense of peace and reassurance suffused her thoughts. There was no need for words now. They were sharing light, and the light carried Nino's promise to protect what she would become.

APPENDIX 1:
UNITS AND MEASUREMENTS

Distance			In strides
1 scant			1/144
1 span	=	12 scants	1/12
1 stride	=	12 spans	1
1 stretch	=	12 strides	12
1 saunter	=	12 stretches	144
1 stroll	=	12 saunters	1,728
1 slog	=	12 strolls	20,736
1 separation	=	12 slogs	248,832
1 severance	=	12 separations	2,985,984
Mt. Peerless's height	=	5 strolls and 5 saunters	9,360
World's equator	=	7.42 severances	22,156,000
Distance to sun	=	16,323 severances	48,740,217,000

Time			In pauses
1 flicker			1/12
1 pause	=	12 flickers	1
1 lapse	=	12 pauses	12
1 chime	=	12 lapses	144
1 bell	=	12 chimes	1,728
1 day	=	12 bells	20,736
1 stint	=	12 days	248,832

			In years
1 year	=	43.1 stints	1
1 generation	=	12 years	12
1 era	=	12 generations	144
1 age	=	12 eras	1,728
1 epoch	=	12 ages	20,736
1 eon	=	12 epochs	248,832

Mass

			In hefts
1 scrag			1/144
1 scrood	=	12 scrags	1/12
1 heft	=	12 scroods	1
1 haul	=	12 hefts	12
1 burden	=	12 hauls	144

Prefixes for multiples

ampio-	=	12^3	=	1,728
lauto-	=	12^6	=	2,985,984
vasto-	=	12^9	=	5,159,780,352
generoso-	=	12^{12}	=	8,916,100,448,256
gravido-	=	12^{15}	=	15,407,021,574,586,368

Prefixes for fractions

scarso-	=	$1/12^3$	=	1/1,728
piccolo-	=	$1/12^6$	=	1/2,985,984
piccino-	=	$1/12^9$	=	1/5,159,780,352
minuto-	=	$1/12^{12}$	=	1/8,916,100,448,256
minuscolo-	=	$1/12^{15}$	=	1/15,407,021,574,586,368

APPENDIX 2:
LIGHT AND COLORS

The names of colors are translated so that the progression from "red" to "violet" implies shorter wavelengths. In the *Orthogonal* universe this progression is accompanied by a decrease in the light's frequency in time. In our own universe the opposite holds: shorter wavelengths correspond to higher frequencies.

Color	IR Limit	Red	Green	Blue	Violet	UV limit
Wavelength, λ (piccolo-scants)	∞	494	391	327	289	231
Spatial frequency, κ (gross cycles per scant)	0	42	53	63	72	90
Time frequency, ν (generoso-cycles per pause)	49	43	39	34	29	0
Period, τ (minuscolo-pauses)	36	40	44	50	59	∞
Velocity, v (severances per pause)	0	41	57	78	104	∞
(dimensionless)	0	0.53	0.73	1.0	1.33	∞

The smallest possible wavelength of light, λ_{min}, is about 231 piccolo-scants; this is for light with an infinite velocity, at the "ultraviolet limit". The highest possible time frequency of light, ν_{max}, is about 49 generoso-cycles per pause; this is for stationary light, at the "infrared limit".

All the colors of light arise from the same pattern of wavefronts, rotated into different orientations in four-space.

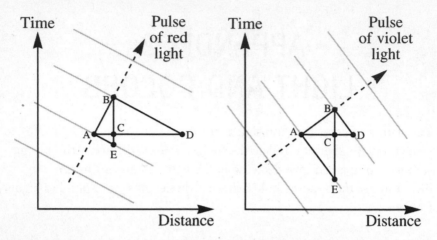

In the diagram above, AB is the separation between the wavefronts in four-space, which is fixed regardless of the light's color. AD is the light's wavelength (the distance between wavefronts at a given moment) and BE is the light's period (the time between wavefronts at a fixed location).

The right triangles ACB and ABD are *similar triangles*, because the angles at A are the same. It follows that AC/AB = AB/AD, and:

$$AC = (AB)^2/AD$$

Also, the right triangles ACB and EAB are similar, because the angles at B are the same. It follows that BC/AB = AB/BE, and:

$$BC = (AB)^2/BE$$

Pythagoras's Theorem, applied to the right triangle ACB, gives us:

$$(AC)^2 + (BC)^2 = (AB)^2$$

Combining these three results yields:

$$(AB)^4/(AD)^2 + (AB)^4/(BE)^2 = (AB)^2$$

If we divide through by $(AB)^4$ we have:

$$1/(AD)^2 + 1/(BE)^2 = 1/(AB)^2$$

Since AD is the light's wavelength, 1/AD is its spatial frequency, κ, the number of waves in a unit distance. Since BE is the light's period, 1/BE is its time frequency, ν, the number of cycles in a unit time. And since AB is the fixed separation between wavefronts, 1/AB is the *maximum* frequency of light, ν_{max}, the frequency we get in the infrared limit when the period is AB.

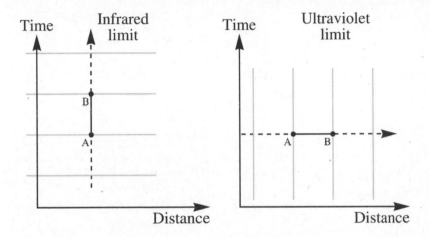

So what we've established is that the sum of the squares of the light's frequencies in space and in time is a constant:

$$\kappa^2 + \nu^2 = \nu_{max}^2$$

This result assumes that we're measuring time and space in identical units. But in the table above we're using traditional units that pre-date Yalda's rotational physics. The data Yalda gathered on Mount Peerless showed that if we treat intervals of time as being equivalent to the distance blue light would travel in that time, the relationship between the spatial and time frequencies takes the simple form derived above. So the appropriate conversion factor from traditional units to "geometrical units" is the speed of blue light, ν_{blue}, and we have:

$$(\nu_{blue} \times \kappa)^2 + \nu^2 = \nu_{max}^2$$

The values in the table are expressed in a variety of units that have been chosen so that the figures all have just two or three digits. When we include a factor to harmonise the units, the relationship becomes:

$$(78/144 \times \kappa)^2 + \nu^2 = \nu_{max}^2$$

Now, the velocity, v, of light of a particular color is simply the ratio between the distance the light travels and the time in which it does so. If we take the pulses of light in our first diagram, they travel a distance AC in a time BC, giving $v = AC/BC$. If we then use the relationships we've found between AC and AB and the spatial frequency κ, and between BC and BE and the time frequency ν, we have:

$$v = \kappa/\nu$$

Again, we can only use this formula with traditional units after applying the appropriate conversion factor:

$$v = (v_{blue} \times \kappa)/\nu$$

which, if we're taking frequencies from the table above, becomes:

$$v = (78/144 \times \kappa)/\nu$$

The velocity we've been describing so far is a dimensionless quantity, related to the slope of a line tracing out the history of the light pulse on a space-time diagram. (The way we draw our diagrams, with the time axis vertical and the space axis horizontal, it's actually the inverse of the slope.) Multiplying the dimensionless velocity by a further factor of 78, the speed of blue light in severances per pause, gives us the values in traditional units that appear in the table.

AFTERWORD

Much of what we know about the physics of our universe can be understood in terms of the fundamental symmetries of space-time. If you imagine any experiment that can be fully contained on a floating platform out in space, then orienting the platform in different directions or setting it in motion with different velocities will have no bearing on the outcome of the experiment. The particular directions in space and in time with which the platform is aligned make no difference.

However, in our universe the laws of physics distinguish very clearly *between* directions in space and directions in time. While you're free to travel through space precisely due north if you wish, as you do so you will also be moving forward in time (as measured, say, by GMT). Expecting to be able to depart from Accra at 1:00:00.000 GMT and arrive at Greenwich to see the clocks showing exactly the same time—because you'd arranged to move "purely northwards" without any of that annoying progress through other people's idea of time—is not just a tad optimistic, it's physically impossible. "North" is a "space-like" direction (whatever else might be merely conventional about it), while "the future" is a "time-like" direction (however much it might differ from person to person traveling at relativistic speeds). No amount of relative motion can transform *space-like* into *time-like* or vice versa.

The underlying physics of *Orthogonal* comes from erasing that distinction between time and space—giving rise to an even more symmetrical geometry—and then applying a similar kind of reasoning to that which links the abstract geometry of space-time to the tangible physics of our own universe.

Does every last phenomenon described in the novel follow with perfect mathematical rigor from this process? Of course not! Centuries of effort by people far more able than I am has still not put the physics of our own universe on such a rigorous footing, and to reconstruct everything under different axioms—with no access to experimental results—would be a massive undertaking. So while I've tried to be guided throughout the novel by some well-established general principles, at times the finer details are simply guesswork.

That said, the most striking aspects of the *Orthogonal* universe—the fact that light in a vacuum will travel at different speeds depending on its wavelength; the fact that the energy in a particle's mass will have the opposite sense to its kinetic energy; the fact that like charges will attract, close up, but then experience a force that oscillates with distance between attraction and repulsion; the existence of both positive and negative temperatures; and the fact that an interstellar journey will take longer for the travelers than for the people they left behind—are all straightforward consequences of the novel's premise.

My initial thoughts about the *Orthogonal* universe were clarified by the discussion of the consequences of different numbers of space and time dimensions in Max Tegmark's classic paper, "Is 'the Theory of Everything' Merely the Ultimate Ensemble Theory?" (*Annals of Physics* 270, pp 1-51, 1998; online at **arxiv.org/abs/gr-qc/9704009**). Tegmark classifies universes with no time dimension as "unpredictable" (p 34). However, he appears not to have considered cases where the underlying space-time is a *compact manifold*, making the universe finite. As discussed in the novel, finite universes with the right topologies can exhibit physical laws that support predictions—albeit imperfect ones if the data available spans less than the entire width of the universe. But this isn't all that different from the situation under Newtonian physics, which also allows the possibility that an object with an arbitrarily high velocity might unexpectedly enter the region whose future you're trying to predict.

Readers with a background in physics might be aware of a mathematical technique known as Wick rotation, in which equations that apply in our own universe are converted to a form with four spatial dimensions, as part of a strategy for solving the original equations. It's worth stressing, however, that these "Wick-rotated" equations are *not* the same as those governing the physics in *Orthogonal*; there are some additional changes of sign that lead to very different solutions.

Supplementary material for this novel can be found at **www.gregegan. net**.